ALSO BY VALERIE BLOCK

None of Your Business
Was It Something I Said?

DON'T MAKE
A SCENE

DON'T MAKE A SCENE

a Novel

VALERIE BLOCK

BALLANTINE BOOKS
NEW YORK

Don't Make a Scene is a work of fiction. Names, characters,
places, and incidents are the products of the author's imagination
or are used fictitiously. Any resemblance to actual events, locales,
or persons, living or dead, is entirely coincidental.

Published in the United States by Ballantine Books,
an imprint of The Random House Publishing Group,
a division of Random House, Inc., New York.

BALLANTINE and colophon are registered trademarks
of Random House, Inc.

ISBN 978-0-345-46185-8

Printed in the United States of America

www.ballantinebooks.com

2 4 6 8 9 7 5 3 1

First Edition

Book design by Katie Shaw

*This book is dedicated
to Vanessa Block and Jeremy Block.*

All but the most durable books serve us simply by opening a window on all we wanted to say and feel and think about. We may not even notice that they have not said it themselves till we go back to them years later and do not find what we loved in them. You cannot keep the view by taking the window with you.

—JAMES RICHARDSON, *Vectors*

The romance of movies is not just in those stories and those people on the screen but in the adolescent dream of meeting others who feel as you do about what you've seen. You do meet them, of course, and you know each other at once because you talk less about good movies than about what you love in bad movies.

—PAULINE KAEL, "Trash, Art, and the Movies"

DON'T MAKE
A SCENE

JULY

As DIANE KURASIK NEARED the rapids of her fortieth birthday, her world seemed to be taking on the bittersweet tones of a life-change comedy from the 1970s, something starring Glenda Jackson or Jill Clayburgh. Although nothing in her own sphere had changed in quite a while, she was surrounded by movement: family, friends and acquaintances were giving birth, obtaining patents, marrying, divorcing, dying, coming out of the closet, traveling to and from exotic Third World dictatorships and going into and out of business with astonishing speed. Her niece was entering the sixth grade; her father was retiring from his second career; her longtime guitar teacher was closing up shop and moving to Brazil.

And Diane was showing *Indiscreet* again at the Bedford Street Cinema.

On the bulletin board, Ingrid Bergman gazed at Cary Grant with offended longing in a publicity still. With five hundred cable channels, free videos at the library, and DVDs selling for $5.00 on the sidewalk, why would anyone go out in the rain to pay $9.50 to see *Indiscreet* (Stanley Donen, 1958)? But if it was part of a series called "Heels, Cads, Sadists and Heartbreakers," there would always be a few who would show up to see Ingrid Bergman explode on the big screen, "How *DARE* he make loff to me and not be a married man!"

This was the premise of the Bedford Street Cinema, and the place was holding its own, barely, in a time of rampant multiplexia. Ms. Kurasik had not been the first choice for the job, but she hadn't hesitated to take it three months after she'd originally been rejected. After all, fifteen other, bigger names had turned down *M*A*S*H* (1970) before Robert Altman agreed to direct it. In almost ten years, she'd perfected a repertory formula that attracted partisans who lined up around the block.

A second screen to present new, independent features would expand the crowd, but until then, Diane confined new releases to a three-week festival during the summer, when she judged the audience to be more adventurous. Under her stewardship, the theater had achieved nonprofit status, landmark status, "best place to see a movie" according to *New York* magazine status. She was pleased, she was proud, she was bored out of her mind.

The phone rang as Diane squeezed grapefruits in her kitchen on a muggy afternoon in late July. It was her old friend Lara Freed with a new man for her to meet: a newly divorced intellectual-property lawyer, no children, fascinating.

Diane hadn't heard from Lara in perhaps six months. Come to think of it, she hadn't heard from her old friend Claire Giancarlo, either.

"Does he like movies?"

"Who doesn't like movies?"

"You'd be surprised," Diane said, and because she had nothing going on, agreed to take his call, which came two minutes later, giving him points for decisiveness, and points off for desperation. She would meet him in a week and no doubt find something objectionable about him in person. Why had Lara and Claire stopped calling her? If Diane was noticing only now, did she really care?

She retrieved her mail and walked down Seventh Avenue South toward the theater, sucking grapefruit juice through a straw. The neighborhood had once had a Fellini feeling, and it was still possible to see someone walking down Barrow Street with his head wrapped in tinfoil. But over the past ten years the city had been tweezed, buffed, homogenized; the neighborhood now seemed entirely populated by bland white Banana Republicans driving silver SUVs, who were probably no less insane, but managed to conceal it in the collective uniform of the moment. The Bedford Street Cinema stood in a tiny, irregular curve of the West Village that was much photographed for its aura of old New York. The marquee projected its seedy glamour among the plate glass of a tobacconist's shop, a boarded-up wall plastered with peeling posters, and a totemic brownstone with fire escape and stoop. On that afternoon, *Indiscreet* was playing with *The Talk of the Town* (George Stevens, 1942).

Diane paid attention to the marquee: it served the public as a light source, a meeting point, a billboard and a shelter from the rain. It could comment on the passing scene, as in the Weegee photo of a crowd gawking at a newspaper-covered corpse beneath a marquee announcing "Irene Dunne in *The Joy of Living*." A crank regularly denounced Diane at Bedford Street Block Association meetings for poisoning the neighborhood with cynicism when, for example, the marquee advertised a double bill of *Contempt* and *Repulsion*. A marquee could define an era: one Saturday night in a previous decade, Diane had waited at the Loew's 84th Street beneath a marquee promoting *Husbands and Wives* and *Singles*. By the time she realized she'd been stood up, *Husbands and Wives* (Woody Allen, 1992) was sold out. So she saw *Singles* (Cameron Crowe, 1992).

Floyd was sweeping the carpet and Cindy was adding syrup to the soda machine when Diane got to the theater. The smell of popcorn, which had once excited her, now made Diane a little nauseated. Cindy gave her an update: The third toilet in the ladies' room was clogged again. There was a new tear in the carpet. A ticket buyer had reported something dripping on his head during the early show. One of the regular patrons had exposed himself during the second feature. There were three messages from Jack Lipsky, her boss. The beginnings of an average day.

Or so she thought, until she sat down at her desk and saw that the stack of mail she'd brought from home included an eviction notice.

All New York stories are ultimately about real estate. Even stories that appear to be about something else—lust, love, money, jealousy—ultimately turn on the matter of space. New York is so densely packed with vertical life, so overflowing with noise, opportunity and heartbreak, that in order to survive one needs a lair to crawl into at the end of the day, if only to recover enough strength to face another round. Those whose lairs are too small, too dirty, up too many flights, in the wrong neighborhood, or lacking air, light, a view, or all three, live primed to pounce on something better.

There was a time when Diane chatted up anyone hosing down a sidewalk in hope of finding a better place. Until one wet spring, when an affair with an Italian sound engineer beset by legal troubles resulted in the ultimate Manhattan windfall: her name on the lease of a one-bedroom with a roof deck on a tree-lined street in the West Village. The rent was exactly half of what she'd been paying for a studio with an intractable roach problem and a view of the approach to the Lincoln Tunnel. When Paolo went back to Cinecittà, the place was hers to keep. The constant scheming for a better apartment had taken up so much of her time, energy and thought over the years that when she finally moved into this haven, she had no idea what to do with herself.

That was twelve years ago. It had been a good run, and now it was over. The building had changed hands. The new owner had also bought the vacant lot next door. All tenants were required to find a new place to park themselves, in order to make way for a swanky new six-floor condominium with health club and concierge. It was all perfectly legal. The constant had become a variable.

Diane couldn't remember when she'd reached the Age of No— no smoking, no alcohol, no drugs, no fat, no thank you. No parties, no sex. No blind dates. No double dates with married couples and "the nicest guy you ever met." An occasional man passed through her life, usually not for long. Was it harder as she aged because there were so few men available, or because she herself was less receptive?

This she pondered as she walked over rutted, damaged sidewalks to make the acquaintance of the newly divorced intellectual-property lawyer at a place on Spring Street. There was a feeling of high summer in the air, she was on her way to meet someone new, but she didn't have an open outlook. She was tired and annoyed to be going through the motions of presentation, the tedium of decoding signifiers embedded in small talk. Thank God this was just a drink: she couldn't possibly do something as intimate and sustained as eating a whole meal with a male stranger.

A man's complete attention wasn't a realistic possibility at this late stage of the game. All the generalists—the easygoing, well-adjusted fellows such as her father, her brother-in-law, the husbands of most of her friends—who were capable of giving their complete attention to a woman, had married before the age of thirty.

The remainder tended to be specialists, obsessed with something—often their work, but not always. In twenty-five years of dating, fifteen of them dedicated exclusively to specialists, she'd met Lactose Intolerant Man, Open Up American Trade with Vietnam Man, Blues Man, Bluegrass Man, Second Amendment Man, and Windsurf Man. Some men had one issue they talked about, so that any conversation, no matter where it started, returned to the topic—the imperative of legalizing marijuana, for example—as if to magnetic north. None of these men, no matter how childish or arcane his fixation (seventeenth-century French mortuary instruments included), bothered to ascertain whether she was interested in his interest, or, if not, whether she had an interest of her own.

Being a specialist herself, Diane had a slight contempt for the generalists who, although clearly happier and more pleasant as people, were vague, somewhat passive and easy to push around. On the other hand, who wanted to be lectured incessantly about the Detroit Red Wings? Given the choice, wouldn't she rather stay at home and read the new Truffaut biography? Or stay at the theater and watch *Indiscreet* for the nth time? So few people shared her enthusiasm, and when she found one who did, there were problems of competition and scope: she'd had a brief fling with a screenwriter who admired her complete mastery of dialogue from *Double Indemnity* (Billy Wilder, 1944), but became impatient when she admitted she hadn't memorized lines from any of Fred MacMurray's other monumental pictures.

The fact was, she was bored with her specialty. She could remember seeing *Children of Paradise* (Marcel Carné, 1945) for the first time, at the age of fifteen, alone on a wet Thursday night at the old Regency on the Upper West Side. The trip into the city alone excited her, but the teeming energy of the film blew her head off. She was particularly intrigued by the way the mature yet ageless French actress Arletty received a compliment from a man in the street. The actress—playing an actress—didn't run, didn't put herself down, didn't appear vain by accepting the compliment. And it was clear when she smiled at her admirer that she wasn't inviting him home with her.

Increasingly, charming French movies put Diane to sleep. Every day, six or so new films seeking distribution arrived in the mail; making headway against this flood of DVDs was at the top of her to-do list every day. Watching anything on a small screen was not conducive to attention or respect. It was somehow less than a *séance*—the French word for screening, which Diane liked because it conveyed the otherworldly side of the movies, the irrational and perhaps "fixed" channel into the spirit world. She presented *Children of Paradise* at least once a year, and although she appreciated it, she didn't feel transported by it, even on the big screen, even in a private *séance*. Most movies barely aroused her interest now. Was she nostalgic for a time when she was susceptible to nostalgia?

THE BLIND DATE was waiting inside, reading *Outside*, as he'd specified. He was a less handsome, twenty-first-century version of Joel McCrae, in his late thirties, on the short side, muscular, with leathery skin and sun-bleached bangs. He was drinking sparkling water, and he began by quizzing her about her athletic pursuits.

"No sports," she said, signaling the bartender.

"Oh?" Clearly the wrong answer.

"No watching sports on TV," she declared, "no attending sporting events in person, and certainly no playing sports."

The blind date blinked disapproval and scanned her body with his eyes. Diane had made whatever kind of peace was possible with her proportions: like a long line of women on her mother's side of the family, she wore a size 4 top and a size 10 bottom. Her rear end had been the subject of much torment in her adolescence. But most people suffered in some way during adolescence, and no amount of stair climbing changed anything. Diane chose to put it all *behind* her.

She ordered rum on ice. He looked impatient. Clearly the wrong drink.

"I had a blind date last week with a woman in love with her cat," he said, violating Diane's Number One Rule: Never mention any other dates when on a date. No doubt she'd have to hear all about his failed marriage, too.

He must have noticed her face darken. "Oh, you're a cat person?"

"No cats," she said, taking a swig of rum. "No cats, no dogs, no ferrets. No rodents of any kind, no thank you."

He nodded; apparently that was the correct answer.

She asked polite questions about his professional life, which he answered politely.

Then, as if opening the curtain to reveal an exciting new spectacle, he leaned forward to say, "Every day, I wake up and wonder: What can I do today to become a better rock climber?"

The bar got very loud. A fanatic even as specialists go. Still, she was intrigued by the focus, the energy and the ambition. He showed her his hands, which were scabbed and scarred. His schedule involved climbing rock formations every weekend. She told him about "Heels, Cads, Sadists and Heartbreakers," and invited him to a movie. He declined—he was due at the gym at five a.m. for speed drills. He walked her back to the theater and she shook his calloused hand under the marquee, which proclaimed: *Carnal Knowledge* and *An Unmarried Woman*.

She took a seat near the back just as the lights were dimming. Two women behind her continued their chitchat. She shone her flashlight in their eyes, and when they didn't stop yakking, she beeped Floyd, who arrived instantly to escort them out.

This was the best part of her job.

She settled in to watch *An Unmarried Woman* (Paul Mazursky, 1978). She had seen it for the first time as a teenager and felt a profound kinship. All her life, she'd felt forty-two and divorced. Probably when she hit forty-two and got divorced, it would be like coming home. As she watched, she did some math: Jill Clayburgh couldn't have been forty-two in the film. She had to have been somewhere in her mid-thirties. This made Diane uncomfortable.

She dropped by the concession stand to get some popcorn and soda for dinner. She was thirteen weeks away from eviction. She had to do something. She went back to her seat to await *Carnal Knowledge* (Mike Nichols, 1971).

And she wondered: What, at this late date, was the burning issue around which she structured her life? What did she wake up every morning determined to become better at? Every once in a while she became excited about a film at a festival—most recently, a Venezuelan heist comedy—that she knew no one else would pick up, and then she felt that what she did had value. Of course, the night it played, it was pissing rain, war was being declared, and there were all of five people in the theater. If she reached five people with something wonderful, had she done something of value?

Was it possible that she had outgrown her specialty, and was now just an easygoing generalist, albeit a single one, without a mate and offspring? If *Children of Paradise* no longer had the power to move her, what did?

AUGUST

Uptown, in an old gray courtyard building on Riverside Drive, a woman was trying to do something with her hair and having little luck getting beyond the pain in her shoulder when she raised the brush to her head. Miss Dorothy Vail had a standing appointment once a week with Laurence, but her daily hair was up to her. She remembered going nearly every morning to the hairdressers' precincts on the Metro lot, and the conversations that one struck up with all and sundry while waiting for a wash and set. She'd taken it all for granted back then.

Her mail was piling up. Miss Payton came once a month, but that wasn't nearly enough. All attempts to flatter Miss Payton into coming more often were met with a tight smile: Miss Payton felt she was doing her a favor, out of loyalty to her late boss. How poor Norman had put up with this woman on a daily basis was a mystery, but there had been the office, and work, and she was naturally more deferential to him, a man. Last time, Miss Payton had said, "You know, Miss Vail, you really don't have to RSVP to every last piece of junk mail, especially if you're not going."

"Who says this is junk mail? This is an invitation," Dorothy Vail said, and moved on to the next one.

Diane Kurasik was due in twenty minutes, there was nothing to serve, no clean ashtrays, no guest towels, and Miss Vail's head still looked like a bird had flown through it, with a big gaping hole in the upsweep.

Not that Diane expected much ceremony: the last time Dorothy had gone all the way down to Bedford Street to pay her an impromptu visit, the woman barely stood up to greet her. Diane certainly did nothing about *her* hair, which was long enough for her to sit on—an absurd, unhealthy attachment, and not even such beautiful hair—which was clearly why she was still single, poor thing. Perhaps she could ask Diane to help her with her hair. Of course, after Diane, she didn't have to look good for anything. But she didn't want Diane to think this was how she greeted her guests.

Miss Vail called down on the house phone, announced herself, and asked the doorman to send the porter for cookies. "Not the nursery school cookies he got last time," she instructed. "Something elegant, like shortbread, or pecan sandies." She tipped all year round, not just at Christmas. Still, it was a problem. She needed a Girl Friday. Miss Payton once a month wasn't enough.

Her phone was ringing.

It was Estelle. Estelle had a personal assistant, a personal trainer, a full-time maid and a part-time driver. In all three of her homes. Naturally, she had more energy, and her hair was always perfect. Dorothy hung up and went to the mirror, pushing herself, bringing her head halfway down to meet the brush. That's right! She did have another appointment that afternoon—the Oral History fellow! If Estelle hadn't called, bringing the Goldwyn Girls into her mind, she would have forgotten the whole thing. So unprofessional.

Diane came in wearing torn jeans and smelling like a breeze in a citrus grove. She presented Dorothy with an envelope full of printed matter that Dorothy already had. Why was Diane always barraging her with paper? Dorothy told her to put it on the piano bench with the rest of the mail.

"You smell divine, Diane. You must tell me the name of your perfume."

"Trade secret," Diane said, inspecting photos on the mantel. "How can I help?"

"Sit down, dear. Would you like a sherry?"

"I'm being evicted: what I want is a bottle of vodka and a gun. But okay, I'll take a sherry."

Which was easier than boiling water for tea, and made fewer dishes. Dorothy poured two glasses. She settled down on her sofa and beckoned Diane to join her. "The reason I asked you here was that I have a potential candidate for the Board to consider, and I wanted to run her by you first."

"Who is she?"

"Her name is Estelle DeWinter, and I've known her forever. We met on the MGM lot, when I was in *Summer Swans,* and she was doing something forgettable with Donald O'Connor. She was a Goldwyn Girl. She did lots of stuff with Danny Kaye in the fifties. When she wasn't a chorus girl, she played cigarette girls, or hatcheck girls. *Not* a distinguished career in cinema. But that's not the point."

Diane sipped her sherry.

"I didn't know her first husband. When I met her, she was seeing that producer Milton Duff, and I was dating Hal Sterling, you remember, the director, and we got very friendly, going out on the town, the four of us, all the time. We married around the same time. I was her matron of honor. Her third wedding was written up in *all* the tabloids and magazines."

Diane put her glass of sherry on the coffee table. "Dorothy, are there any apartments available in this building?"

"What? I don't know."

"Are you friendly with your super?"

"What? Well, I give him money all year round, not just at Christmas. But listen, I know you're busy, so let me tell you about Estelle. Her current husband, her fourth, has a building."

"Where is it?"

"You'll never guess—it's the old carriage house right next to the cinema."

"That's too close. It would be like living at the office."

"What? No, listen. He hasn't done anything with the property since he bought it. Estelle thinks he may be persuaded to donate the building to our little revival house."

"Do you mean the wreck next door? That leaking pile of garbage between us and the smoke shop?"

"That's the one. He gets a tax deduction, we get a second screen, and a bigger lobby, and whatever else you think we need."

Diane leaned forward, her elbows on her knees, and her hands over her eyes.

"It's too early in the day to ruin your makeup," Dorothy advised. But of course, Diane didn't wear makeup. She was a good ten years too old to pull off the come-as-you-are look; Dorothy had tried to talk to her about this once, and Diane had given her a strange smile and hadn't taken the advice.

"We'd have to get an architect to take a look at it." Diane rubbed her eyes. "We'd probably need to tear it down and start from scratch."

"Which would be better anyhow. Right?"

"Probably. Wow, Dorothy," Diane smiled. She should smile more often, Dorothy thought, she wouldn't look so grim. "This isn't the real estate news I wanted to hear today, but what a nice surprise."

Dorothy Vail was pleased. "I thought I'd bring up the subject at the Board meeting next Tuesday."

"I can't imagine that there would be any objection to Estelle. I'd like to meet her. Shall we have lunch the three of us, sometime after the meeting?"

"I'll find out when she's free. I should tell you that she never really got the Bensonhurst out of her voice, and that her grammar is atrocious."

"Now, now, Miss Vail. Not every girl is classically trained for the stage."

"You didn't touch the cookies."

"See you at the meeting. Don't get up. Would you ask your super about an apartment? I have three months before a wrecking ball tears through my window."

Diane left and her perfume remained. Dorothy poured another glass of sherry and checked her hair, which seemed to be holding. She reapplied her lipstick and fiddled with her rings. The house phone would let her know when the next visitor arrived.

◆

Vladimir Hurtado Padrón emerged from the subway on Twenty-third Street and turned to walk west to his office. Two young women were planted in the middle of the sidewalk with clipboards, accosting passersby. As he passed, one of the women approached him.

"Do you have a minute for Greenpeace?"

"Do you have a minute for democracy in Cuba?" he responded.

She looked surprised, but she agreed to hear him. He motioned her to go first; she gave him her speech, then asked him to sign a petition. He signed the petition. He gave her his speech, then wrote down the address of a website that had a petition to sign. She said she'd visit it. They shook hands. He continued walking west, wondering what it would take, just how bad it would have to get, for an attractive young woman like this to commit her time and energy to the cause of ending repression in Cuba.

In the lobby, Vladimir greeted the janitor and the super, who treated him with a deference that made him uncomfortable. He waited with assorted models, hipsters and gallery hoppers for the most elegant freight elevator in Chelsea. Upstairs, on the terrazzo-paved sixth floor, he headed for the galvanized steel door that had his name on it, along with his new partner's. The sight aroused mixed emotions—pride, fear and a reflex that said, Don't stand out, you're just asking for trouble.

Chris Wiley was talking on the phone. He waved and pointed to a set of documents on Vladimir's chair. Vladimir nodded: his signature was needed. First he checked in at www.cubaencuentro.com for news of the demise of the dictator.

Like something out of a bad science fiction movie, the monster lived.

Vladimir Hurtado Padrón fell into and out of jobs, freelance assignments and business partnerships with ease. For an architect under the age of forty, he had an impressive portfolio. But sooner or later he would find himself in an argument that got out of hand, or would ask a question that showed him to be completely ignorant of basic business practices, or someone would take exception to his attitude, which was inflexible, because he was right. It was an irony of his American life that his clients and business partners were only too ready to divorce him, whereas his wife wouldn't even hear of it.

He had a very good feeling about his new partner. They shared a common approach to design, and Chris was only too happy to handle the clients, the billing and the running of the business, leaving Vladimir to deal with the materials, the construction documents, the details. It might be the perfect partnership: each thought he'd gotten the better end of the deal.

Another irony of his American life: His new partner was gay, and Vladimir liked him much better than any of the so-called normal men and women he'd partnered with previously. If his father had ever heard him say such a thing, he would have given him a fast swipe to the face. Vladimir had been changed by America. He'd been speechless when a woman he was seeing his first year in New York had confessed that she'd assumed that *he* was gay. She'd told him this jokingly after he'd spent the night in her apartment.

"Why would you assume that?"

"Because you're good-looking, and you're an architect."

"Architects are gay?"

"Design in general is predominantly gay, yes."

"It is?"

"You hadn't noticed?"

He was thunderstruck. At a trade show the next day, he scrutinized each person passing by, not knowing what he was looking for. This woman had pointed out men in the street who she said were gay—muscular men with shaved heads, mustaches, heavy key chains, leather jackets. "No, these men are very macho," he'd insisted, and she had laughed for a good long time. This kind of gay didn't exist in Cuba.

Vladimir had learned things in America that confounded him. The whole banking system, for example, was a constant source of anxiety and disbelief. He'd been a remedial case: he'd never written a check, he'd never seen a credit card. In Cuba—where there was nothing—if money existed, it was cash, and if you were lucky, it was in dollars. He had handed over his wages to his father. The equivalent of fourteen dollars a month: a good wage for a professional. His sister, a doctor, had made seventeen dollars a month. Americans always reacted strangely to these figures: some argued with him, refusing to believe him. One woman had burst into tears.

He now understood that if he had a question about consumer democracy, it was better to approach a woman. A simple question had ended his first American job. "What is the debit card?" he had asked his then-boss, a man.

"What do you mean, '*What is the debit card?*' "

"I've been using the credit card and the debit card, but I don't understand the difference."

"The company credit card?" the boss said.

"One is blue and one is silver, but tell me the real difference."

"You have got to be kidding."

"Please be patient: I come from the land that time forgot."

"Vladimir, the answer to everything can't be that you come from Cuba."

Why not?

Cuba was everywhere, if only because, by being Cuban, he started the dialogue. That evening, for example, Vladimir and Chris went to a new restaurant to talk about a possible job, renovating a suite of offices for Jan Mattias, whom Chris had called a "hot-shit young successful movie producer."

They waited at a table and watched the action at the bar. Such nonsense in New York: the crowd was young and single, the dance music was loud, but there was no dance floor, and the women were dancing in place with each other, while the men stood at the bar talking business. Talk about gay.

A woman with cropped white hair and unnaturally green eyes stopped at their table and introduced herself as Amanda Nash, Jan Mattias's business partner. She plunked down a pack of cigarettes and a lighter and leaned toward the bartender to order a drink. In Havana, this would mean nothing. Here, Chris gave him the *problem client* look.

Amanda Nash smiled and said in a smoker's voice, "Yeah, I smoke and I drink. Hell, I drink and drive." She added a key chain with a Mercedes-Benz logo to the collection on the table. "It's amazing I'm alive."

Chris laughed politely, and Vladimir took note: The women were macho, and the machos were gay.

The waitress arrived with the drink, which Amanda eagerly accepted. "Vladimir, where are you from?"

Always the first question. "I am from Cuba, the impossible island."

"Were you named after someone?"

"Many of my generation were burdened with Russian names."

"Your parents were communists?"

"Do you have ideas about the office suite?" he asked.

"So what's going to happen after Fidel dies?"

"Because we can open up the space, or we can leave the individual offices as they are."

"Fidel has to go at some point, right?"

Americans were ridiculous sometimes. "What will happen when he goes," he said. " '*What will happen when he goes?*' This is all anyone wants to know. What about what's happening now that he's still there? Any interest in that?"

"Okay," said Amanda, "what's happening now that he's still there?"

"Journalists are sent to prison if they don't report what he likes. Poets are sent to prison, some of them for twenty years."

"For poetry? That's pretty extreme." She laughed.

In many ways, Vladimir wished he were his interlocutor: he always had something interesting to say. He was always bringing people fresh news that opened their eyes. "Why do you call him Fidel?"

"Isn't that his name?"

"Are you two close? In Cuba, you could be arrested for calling him anything but Fidel. In the U.S., you can call him Castro. It is a great privilege to live in a country where you are free to call the president what you want."

She shook her head. "Oh, but are we really free in this country?"

"Please. Don't give me that bullshit. You can call the president a moron on television! You can join any group, write what you want, say what you want. In Cuba, you can't even *think* what you want, without someone coming to take you to prison."

"You're exaggerating."

This restaurant had terrible traffic flow.

"You have free health care, free education," she said, toying with her straw.

There was a certain kind of American, someone who had fallen in love with Fidel Castro and Bob Dylan at the same time, and who hadn't really thought about anything since. He felt it his duty to wake these people up, especially the ones driving Mercedes-Benzes.

"I had a friend when I was twelve," he told her. "He had a seizure. He had to get to a hospital, but his family didn't have a car. So they went around the neighborhood asking. One of the neighbors had a car, but he didn't have gas. So my friend's father took him in the back of his brother's bicycle. And by the time they arrived to the hospital, my friend was dead. But the health care is free, yes."

"Why didn't they call an ambulance?"

"Because they didn't have a phone. Which isn't unusual, even now. Even if they did, there are no ambulances."

"That could have happened in this country."

"Who in this country doesn't have a phone? Which capital city in this country does not have an ambulance?"

"True. Your English is amazing," Amanda Nash said. "Most people don't see the purpose of it."

"The purpose of it is communication," Vladimir said.

Chris cleared his throat.

"Of course *I* know that. But my maid, Yolanda, pretends not to speak English so she doesn't have to take my phone messages."

There was so much wrong with this, he couldn't even begin to address it. Chris put a hand on his arm, but at this point Jan Mattias arrived in casual but tight clothing. He was blond, slightly dirty, slightly effeminate; he sat next to Amanda and nodded at Chris, who leaned forward to shake hands.

"You are so used to having freedom, you don't even know a dictatorship when you see one. What do you want done with the space, I am asking you."

"Don't be offended, Vladimir."

"You Americans are full of shit, if you don't mind my saying."

She laughed. Jan Mattias ordered a beer.

"You say, 'Oh, we don't live in a free society; oh, you Cubans have such a lovely system.' If it's so lovely, you should go live there. Really. Go live there. Cut sugarcane for the Revolution. See how fabulous it is. I don't think you'd last three days."

"Vladimir, you're right," Chris said, hand on his arm. "You *can* say anything you want in this country. But not to a client."

"*Potential* client," Amanda said, laughing.

"What are we talking about?" Jan Mattias asked.

VLADIMIR WAS NEVER short of female company, as it appeared he was the only straight man in New York who wasn't afraid to approach a woman and talk to her. Sooner or later, these women found out that he was unavailable, being married to the one lunatic in Cuba who took the vows seriously. He hadn't seen her in twelve years, hadn't missed her, had no plans to go back, and she had no plans to come here. This stalemate excited a certain kind of woman, and sent the rest of them packing. He never lied about it, although he no longer told a woman about the situation immediately.

The weekend came, and with it the Sunday-evening phone call. These twice-monthly chats structured his life like studio review deadlines. The woman he was seeing now was one of the complication junkies; she wanted to stay.

"No, Ellen, you must go. I have to call Cuba."

"I'll sit quietly in the other room and read," she pleaded. "You won't know I'm here. I'll make you dinner afterwards."

He expressed regret, and she got herself together to leave. At the elevator, she kissed him and told him that friends of her parents were going to Havana—a group tour through some Canadian museum. Should they look anyone up for him, did he have anything he wanted to send? He said he'd let her know. The elevator arrived and he went back into his apartment with determination.

He geared up for the call the rest of the day, eating lightly, and organizing his thoughts as he vacuumed and straightened up. Each time he called Cuba, he was defeated anew. María's involvement with his family was absolute. His parents had picked up where he had left off; they were married to her now. In New York, he had briefly dated a therapist who had taught him words to describe the situation: "enmeshed," "triangulation," "emotional blackmail," "child abuse." He was now equipped with new techniques to handle the family. Not that these techniques changed the situation. The situation was the situation.

"Pucho got us an apartment on the beach in Varadero for a week," María said with excitement when she picked up the phone. "When can you come?"

"For the six-thousandth time: I'm not coming, María."

"You have an obligation to your family."

"And do I not send you the maximum amount of money I can send you as often as I'm legally allowed?"

"I'm not talking about money. All sorts of people come back to visit."

"If I went back, they'd take my passport and refuse to let me leave. Why don't you move on with your life? Why have you not remarried?"

"Remarried? I never divorced."

"And why is that?"

"You have no right to talk to me this way."

"I'm speaking to you honestly. Face reality, María. I'm not going back."

She let out a scream that seared through his head, shredding any hope that he might get away with a pleasant chat on this Sunday. There was a tumult. She was passing the phone to someone else. He felt a wave of relief.

"She's crying again," his mother said.

In spite of all his attempts to deal with each family member individually, it was a collective conversation. Privacy was an Anglo concept.

"That's her problem." He wondered why on earth he had thought it would be more pleasant to talk to his mother.

"Your father will not be there, in Varadero," she said, and she might have been talking about Valhalla. Varadero was restricted to foreigners. It was illegal for Cubans to be there without special dispensation, which Pucho was able to acquire on occasion. "He'll make sure that there's no passport issue."

"And why should I accept a gift from that swine?"

His mother's voice broke into clattering sobs.

"Mother. I refuse to talk to you if you cry. Mother. This is ridiculous."

Another tumult. His sister came on the phone. "So Vlade, how are you? You've made two women cry in less than three minutes."

"Nadia, what's new?"

"Vladimir, the passport won't be a problem."

He felt another surge of irritation.

"There are new rules," Nadia continued. "You submit your passport, they investigate you, and they habilitate it with a permanent stamp. So you can come back whenever you want. You don't need to get an Entry Permit."

"You're not listening to me. I'm not coming! Not now, not later. Not ever. Never."

"Well, you're very negative."

"I'll be glad to see *you* when you get *here*. So when are you coming?"

Nadia was a doctor married to a doctor. Doctors weren't allowed to leave the country (taking all their expensive education with them), not even for a vacation. Not alone and especially not with family members. Perhaps Pucho could work around that one, too, but hadn't.

"Shall we have two members of the family corrupted by greed?"

"*Cojones!*"

"Dad says you're a coward," she said.

"Tell Pucho to go fuck himself."

"Tell him yourself."

Vladimir hung up the phone.

It had been five years since he'd last spoken to his father, but of course he could feel him there in the room, like a malodorous animal. Listening to the conversation, coaching them all, telling them what to say. The only good part about calling Cuba was that they couldn't call back. Too difficult, too expensive. Even for Pucho.

He went into the kitchen and looked in his empty refrigerator. He wished he hadn't sent Ellen away. On the other hand, he didn't really want to talk to Ellen, and had almost called her Janet just that morning. All the women in his quasi-bachelor life put together weighed less than María. Literally and physically—his taste in American women ran to light and thin, and not a Latina among them. He supposed María had gotten heavier. Who knew, and who cared?

He walked out into the summer night, heading to the closest movie theater. He bought a ticket to a film he'd never heard of that had already started. It was a kung fu movie with explosions, car chases and lots of shooting. It hit the spots, as they said around here. Whatever else you could say about America, entertainment wasn't against the law. As he walked back home through the heat-stricken streets of SoHo, he made a mental note to ask Ellen about her parents' friends who were going to Cuba. They could take Band-Aids, aspirin and Tampax, which his mother could use herself, or sell or trade.

SEPTEMBER

LIKE A BAD JOKE, the Bedford Street Cinema had just begun a new series: "Apartments We Covet." Diane had planned this nearly a year earlier, believing that fall in New York, with its mass return from the watering holes and its back-to-school feeling, was just the right time for a real estate theme.

She had scheduled *A Perfect Murder* (Andrew Davis, 1998) for the cold, marble-paved sumptuosity of Michael Douglas's corporate-raider pad in Carnegie Hill, in a double feature with *Green Card* (Peter Weir, 1990), which centered on Andie MacDowell's West Side bohemian oasis, as an antidote. She chose *Hannah and Her Sisters* (Woody Allen, 1986) for the Old World charm of Mia Farrow's apartment on Central Park West, and *Unfaithful* (Adrian Lyne, 2002) for Olivier Martinez's book-and-curiosity-filled SoHo loft. Was it a coincidence that infidelity was an integral part of most movies featuring enviable real estate? *Indiscreet* would play again, for Ingrid

Bergman's vibrant London flat with sunken living room. The squads of brightly framed pictures around the fireplace and the vivid throw pillows on the couches seemed to say, Yes, she's single, but that doesn't mean she's sad. Not Bergman's best movie by a long shot. But surely an apartment to covet.

The actual real estate Diane had seen since receiving the eviction notice ranged from the squalid to the sordid. The prices were obscene.

"What on earth is going on here?" she asked in a grimy, chopped-up one-bedroom with less than five hundred square feet in a seedy building on a bad block with a scary elevator and a littered hallway. The rent was $3,100 a month.

The broker wore a red blazer and a permanent smile. "Where have you been?"

"In a rent-controlled cloud, apparently. This is awful. How much would it cost to find someplace that I'd *want* to live in?"

The broker's expression changed into a look of conspiracy. "Come with me," she said, and steered Diane west on Tenth Street, asking impertinent questions about her personal life and finances until they reached an old, lovely, well-maintained brownstone with thriving plants in front. The apartment was quiet, freshly painted, and had high ceilings, elegant moldings and built-in bookcases. It had one bedroom, one bathroom, one living room, a large, renovated kitchen and a garden in the back. The asking price was $6,000 a month.

This number hit Diane like a body blow. *"What?"*

"It came on the market this morning," the broker said, looking at her watch. "By tonight, it'll be gone. Get out your checkbook or forget about it. Are we done here?"

Diane's summer had passed in frustration; for much of it she'd found herself awaiting permission to enter places in which, it turned out, she didn't want to spend ten minutes. She didn't want much. She was looking for the minimalist glamour of Jean Gabin's Parisian pied-à-terre in *Touchez pas au grisbi* (Jacques Becker, 1953), which was outfitted with everything a gangster bachelor on the lam might need, including an impossibly chic late-night snack for two, with place mats, napkins, champagne flutes, table water crackers and a tin of pâté. Simple was hard to find.

"WHY DO YOU NEED twenty minutes between screenings?" Jack Lipsky put his bare feet up on the desk. These monthly meetings always seemed to stick on the issue of turnover. "We have ten minutes between shows at the two-dollar theater in West Simsbury. Nobody complains it's not clean."

"For a two-dollar admission, your audience should clean for you," Diane said.

The phone rang: it was Dorothy Vail: She had just spoken to her agent. "He gives me modeling opportunities for adult diapers and assisted living homes for the 'vibrantly mature'! Diane, I am at the end of my rope!"

"Oh dear, Dorothy," Diane said pointedly, taking the phone to her office.

Lipsky gave her a disgusted look. The Board of Directors had been a natural consequence of getting the nonprofit designation. The idea of putting anything to a vote went against Jack Lipsky's nature, and in recent years Diane had come to regret changing his mind, as management of Board personalities took up at least half of her time. Management of Miss Dorothy Vail often represented the lion's share of that.

On Diane's first day of work, Lipsky had followed her around the office like a puppy, bumping into her. Lipsky retained, at fifty-three, the smirking look of a teenage boy thinking about something dirty when he talked to you. At one point, in the projection room, he appeared to be smelling her. Then he took a phone call.

"You said we'd have it yesterday, and it's today already. Why should I do business with you, you lying bastard?"

He slammed the phone down and hiked up his pants. "Where were we?" he asked, undoing his belt and buckling it at a tighter notch.

Diane had wanted the job so badly she'd ignored the whiff of instability he'd given off during the interview. His desk abutted hers.

She would have to look at him and listen to him all day. He didn't wear shoes in the office. Her predecessor had lasted only a month and a half. It was just a matter of time before she was the recipient of this abuse.

The phone on Diane's desk rang. Lipsky gestured that she should pick it up. It was clear from the first word that the caller had been stewing in anger for at least ten years.

"Hello. This is Ronnie Lipsky," the caller announced. "I want to tell you, I know all about you and your hair, Diane Kurasik. You stay away from my husband."

Diane blinked. "Mrs. Lipsky, I assure you: wild horses couldn't drag me anywhere near your husband."

Lipsky knocked over her coffee in the process of grabbing the phone out of her hand. "How dare you call here? No, *you* shut up."

He was sweating. Diane blotted up the coffee.

"Bitch!" He slammed the phone down. "She hung up on me."

"What could she possibly know about me or my hair?"

"I think I may have mentioned you," he said with a needy look.

Unemployment couldn't be worse than this. Still, this boor had said that he'd be out of town most of the time and that she would run the show. The Bedford Street Cinema was a unique opportunity, perhaps worth the nonsense.

Her phone rang again. "Look, Mrs. Lipsky," she said, smiling sweetly at Lipsky and channeling the spirit of Carole Lombard. "I agreed to run your husband's shitty little theater, but fucking him was not part of the deal. I have no intention of getting involved with him, and if he comes anywhere near me, I'll call you so fast his head will spin. Are we clear?"

There was silence on the other end, as well as six feet away, where Diane's new boss lurked uncertainly. "Give me your phone number, Ronnie," she added, and wrote it down on the front page of her date book. "Okay, have a nice day, then."

Lipsky burst into a wheezy laugh. "You'll do fine here," he said, and spent the rest of the day with his bare feet on his desk, repeating the line to everyone who called.

She *had* done fine there, mainly because Lipsky spent most of his time in northern Connecticut attending first to the messy drama of his bitter marriage and then to the messy drama of his bitter divorce.

Lipsky also owned a small chain of seedy second-run cinemas that kept him in places like West Simsbury and Yelping Hill; "high-tone" cinema went against his better judgment. Diane had somehow convinced him that Bedford Street was a prestigious asset. He was soon mesmerized by the newspaper and magazine articles when they launched the new repertory format. He began to enjoy the gloss of Culture the Bedford Street Cinema gave his empire, even if he never watched the old, obscure and/or foreign films they featured.

Dorothy was still talking.

Diane could never be a therapist, she decided: she had no patience for this.

"Dorothy, I have a deadline at the printer," she said finally.

"I forgot to tell you why I called!" Dorothy screamed. "I've been thinking about how you said you spend at least thirty percent of your time on the bathrooms. And I have an idea for you: an attendant! You don't remember, you weren't old enough, but every restaurant, club and theater used to have ladies' room and men's room attendants."

"Would anyone want that job?"

"They have services now. The attendant would stay in the bathroom, replace soap and towels, and tell you when you needed to call the plumber."

"Perhaps the plumber could take the job, cutting out the middle man."

She went back into Lipsky's office, which she had moved into an enclosed space behind the projection room, out of her way. "I have to call the plumber. Dorothy just suggested we get a bathroom attendant."

"Maybe you'd like the job," Lipsky said.

As she did every month when her routine and tranquillity were disturbed by the omnipresence of Lipsky, Diane reminded herself of Frank Capra, who had noted that he had more independence as an employee on a contract at a studio than he ever did in a subsequent era as an independent director.

Demolition was six weeks away. Diane felt like a character Jack Lemmon might have played: cranky, harassed, powerless.

"So come home," said her mother each time she mentioned it. "Your room awaits you. We haven't changed a thing."

Diane squeezed her eyes shut. Single, almost forty, and living with her parents in New Jersey? She slipped into the theater to watch *Something's Gotta Give* (Nancy Meyers, 2003), a middle-aged fantasy of real estate pornography, in which two very different men in all-cotton sportswear court a professionally successful woman at the end of middle age. But mainly it was an East Hampton beach house to covet, a beach house so large, and in such a desirable location, that its cost was incalculable. Did movies satisfy yearnings, or merely fan the flames?

OF ALL THE marginal things Daniel Dubrovnik did in this life, such as teaching classic cinema to college students who slept through films as well as lectures, and writing "think pieces" for magazines that no one read, screenwriting had to be the most absurd. Even though Daniel had received an Academy Award nomination in the late sixties (for *Dodge*, an antiwar comedy), his name was familiar to most because of Ira Dubrovnik, his father, also a screenwriter, who had invoked the Fifth Amendment during the McCarthy era and fled to Europe, supporting his family during the blacklist period as a dishwasher and a clown.

It was a clear blue day in late September, and Daniel decided to walk downtown to his meeting at the Bedford Street Cinema. *Aretha Franklin—Queen of Soul: The Atlantic Recordings* streamed out of his headphones. He wondered why "Ain't No Way" had gone triple platinum, while "Never Let Me Go"—featuring the same personnel and arrangements, recorded on the same day, presumably in the same mood—barely made a dent. He passed through the cleaned-up yet still sleazy neon commercial hell of Times Square. Critically and commercially, he had done okay. Others had done much better. Others had certainly done worse.

Earlier that week, Daniel had sat in a sleek red-leather reception

room in Hollywood, waiting to make a pitch at ten a.m. Three people arrived after him and were ushered in right away. The only thing
on the coffee table was a copy of *Vanity Fair*, which he refused to
read on principle. He felt unclean when he picked up *Vanity Fair*.
And yet he'd ridiculed a colleague at Columbia for making an obscure reference recently, and hated himself for succumbing to the
know-nothing doctrine.

Daniel made his pitch at twelve-fifteen p.m. while the boy executive looked at his watch and his assistant poked her head in repeatedly to schedule appointments. Daniel's agent called the next day:
the son of a bitch wanted to buy the option for chicken feed and
have someone else write the script. In the last decade, Daniel had
had no trouble getting in to see a few top people like this, who op-
tioned his treatments and scripts preemptively, almost as if making a
small contribution to a liberal cause. By these people, many lesser
vehicles were produced and promoted relentlessly; by these people,
many lesser vehicles were produced and sent straight to video. Why
Daniel's movies remained on paper in a file cabinet was one of those
mysteries never explained or even questioned, like why Cain's offering to God was lesser than Abel's in the first place.

The Board of Directors of the Bedford Street Cinema met twice
a year on a Tuesday morning at a long table set up on the stage in
front of the screen. Daniel arrived early, but not early enough:
Dorothy Vail, queen of MGM's B movies in the fifties, had taken
the head of the table. Lipsky, that foul beast, had parked his fat ass
at the other end. News of the potential expansion and the largesse
of the former Goldwyn Girl went over the Board meeting like a
love bomb, and Dorothy Vail flashed triumphant smiles.

"Congratulations, Miss Vail," said Jan Mattias, Chairman of the
Board, ass-kissing political animal and absurdly youthful producer of
sweeping, big-budget historical epics featuring pulsating contemporary soundtracks. "What a coup!"

"Anyone know what's in there?" asked Don Gleason, a strug-
gling documentary filmmaker who made his living composing meandering New Age sounds for yoga videos. He still owed Daniel
twenty dollars from three years ago.

"I heard that it's a carriage house that was converted into a garage sometime in the thirties," said Rebecca Temple, a Midwestern film preservationist with a Deanna Durbin overbite. "We may have landmark issues with the building, or at least the façade." Rebecca had been brusque to him at the last Board meeting when he suggested lunch afterwards. She was no great shakes, and not a true intellectual, either: she'd thought "Jason and the Argonauts" was a Saturday-morning cartoon. He regretted the overture.

"There may be ghosts inside," said Dario Travisini, a stooped, elderly Italian neorealist film director with a gray, papery complexion. Daniel had included one of Travisini's movies in his illustrated history, *Narrative in Cinema,* which was still in use as a college textbook. Daniel used it in his own course, "The Screenplay: Innovators and Iconoclasts," at Columbia. Diane Kurasik had suggested that they sell the book at the popcorn stand.

Diane should lecture to his class—why hadn't he thought of this before?

"We've had lots of leaks on the side that abuts that building," said Diane. Such a smart, attractive woman wasting her time with plumbing and managing the egos of Jan Mattias, Dorothy Vail and Lipsky, that cretinous mound of bad taste.

"I know a wonderful architect," said Hamilton Ferris, an aging Southern actor who had played the weak son of rich, domineering men in films of the fifties and sixties.

"We should use someone who specializes in cinemas," said Gary Masters, a high-powered attorney from a white-shoe corporate law firm. His wife, a desiccated professional Park Avenue socialite, had snubbed Daniel on every possible occasion.

"I know a very up-and-coming team," Jan Mattias butted in. "They're not cinema specialists, but they're, like, masters of space."

"Where's the money to renovate coming from?" Daniel interrupted, to stop Jan Mattias from imprinting up-and-coming thoughts on the suggestible collective mind of the Board.

"That's a good question," Jack Lipsky shouted from the head of the table.

Strange that they should be on the same side of an issue.

"First things first," said the lovely Diane. "Let's see the building."

"If it's protected as a landmark, we could sell it," Lipsky said.

"Sell it!" Dorothy Vail shouted. "The second screen will make Bedford Street a real player in New York cinema. How could you even think of selling it?"

"Jack isn't saying we should sell it," Rebecca Temple said. "But if the building is a designated landmark, it may not be our choice."

"That's outrageous!" Miss Vail shouted.

That doddering old bat, Daniel thought. Someone should shut her up.

"Dorothy, keep your hat on," Diane said. "Let's not argue about a hypothetical situation. Let's invite Estelle DeWinter to a meeting, get this donation in writing. Then we'll see what's lurking in the building, and if it's landmarked. Next item!"

Daniel stood on line to have a word with Diane afterwards. As usual, everyone automatically organized themselves into a power hierarchy: Jan Mattias first, as the dominant male; Dorothy Vail second, up several rungs today as the source of the new acquisition; Gary Masters third, as the éminence grise. On and on, until finally Daniel Dubrovnik, has-been screenwriter, son of the blacklist, could speak to her.

Long ago, Richard Schickel had taken the "bitterly gossiping literary gentlemen" of Hollywood to task for failing to recognize and move toward directing as the creative center of filmmaking. Well, not everyone wanted to direct, or had a feeling for the visual. What was wrong with knowing your strengths? Daniel had met people who quoted lines from his movies verbatim. One of them was Diane Kurasik. And this was before she knew who he was—she hadn't done it to impress him. Sweet Diane—she might have been the last woman in New York who didn't have a cellphone or use the word "journal" as a verb.

When it was his turn, Daniel asked her to lunch to discuss coming to his class. She said she'd be delighted to lecture, but lunch was out of the question.

"Nothing personal, Daniel." She held her books and folders like a schoolgirl. "I'm being evicted. Every spare moment of my life now is spent on the search. Anything for rent in your building?"

"I can certainly find out," he said, and went home to do just that. If Diane moved into his building, he could see her every day. His mood improved just thinking about it.

◆

ESTELLE DEWINTER walked into the restaurant that Dorothy had chosen. They had been friends for more than fifty years, through two of Dorothy's marriages and three of her own. Dorothy was the godmother of Estelle's son, Seymour. And every time the woman left a message on Estelle's machine, she said "Hello, this is Miss Dorothy Vail."

Miss Dorothy Vail had always taken herself too seriously. She'd appeared in twenty-two also-ran costume dramas, where her angular looks, upright posture and breathy, cultured diction were suggestive of besieged royalty. Estelle and Dorothy had bonded in the ladies' room on a double date with two other contract players over what losers the fellows were. The friendship took off when they began dating two friends. Within a year both of them were married; it was the second marriage for each of the four parties.

When the marriages broke up, there was a cooling-off period. Then, in 1975, Estelle bumped into Dorothy in New York, and they began a weekly movie-and-burger ritual. Estelle realized that although she missed having a man in her life, she enjoyed dishing with Dorothy. These dates reminded Estelle of her early days in Hollywood and, since she was aging much better than Dorothy, she always went home feeling energized.

The maître d' led Estelle back to the table. Dorothy's face lit up when she saw her. Estelle smiled and waved. Old friends were important, especially lately. Not a week went by that she didn't hear that someone else had died. She was glad she'd decided to get involved with the Bedford Street Cinema, if only to see Dorothy more often.

◆

DIANE SPOTTED the ladies in a corner booth; they were engaged in animated conversation, although neither one was looking at the other. They were both in full makeup and costume. The dueling perfumes began to wash over her at the bar.

"We were just talking about you," Estelle said, with her hand out ready for a shake. She was pale, petite and quick to smile, with short gold curls and delicate features. Before Diane could sit down, Dorothy announced that she would have to leave early.

"It's a radio play on NPR," she crowed. "A real job!"

Dorothy received congratulations, the waiter took their order and the talk naturally turned to the Bedford Street Cinema, specifically the Board. Estelle knew Ham Ferris from her nutritionist's office in LA.

"I think he's a bit lost in New York, but he came here to shake up his life," she said. A tailored navy handbag with elegant white stitching sat parked on the table beside her. It matched her navy blue pantsuit.

"Poor boy, his tan has faded," Dorothy said, smiling at passing men. She wore enormous mollusk earrings in mother-of-pearl and had placed an exquisite burgundy leather handbag on top of the table. Her bag also matched her suit.

"He's a lost soul," said Estelle. "Any pretty actor over forty is completely vulnerable."

"Hardly," Dorothy said, gazing at herself in the mirror opposite, sitting up straight, turning her chin to catch her profile.

"We both separately came to the conclusion in the late forties that actors as men were a waste of time," Estelle told Diane as the food arrived. There was a shifting of water glasses, as neither woman took her handbag off the table. Diane suggested that the waiter take the flowers away.

The women tucked in to their salads.

Estelle leaned toward Diane. "I understand you're single," she said.

"I'd rather have needles stuck in my eyes than discuss my personal life."

Estelle smiled. "Let me know if that changes, I have a nephew."

"I'm so sorry, I don't do nephews."

Estelle let out a girlish cackle. "Well, I hear that Jan Mattias is quite a catch."

"Oh, please." Jan Mattias always came to Bedford Street events with a starlet from an upcoming film or a woman Diane was sure was paid by the hour.

"I heard he used to be a big druggie and party boy," Dorothy said.

"Nothing would surprise me about him," Diane said.

When the time came, Dorothy patted her lips, painted a new mouth with coral lipstick and bustled out of the booth stiffly, but with purpose.

"Break a leg!" Estelle said. There was kissing and wrist grabbing.

"I can't tell you how excited we all are about the new building," Diane said as they went to the ladies' room.

"I think the place is going to be a real mess," Estelle called from inside the stall. "Herb says nobody's been there since he bought it in 1982."

"Why did he buy it?"

"Who knows? My husband is impulsive." Estelle opened the door. She was smiling and buttoning up her pants.

Diane's impending eviction was a low-level anxiety that flared into an active fear event every three days. Tenants in the building had spent the summer scrambling to find new homes; some had been priced out of Manhattan and were moving to the outer boroughs or New Jersey. Diane had discovered a temporary solution to her housing crisis: a one-year sublet in a generic redbrick building on East Twenty-sixth Street. The apartment was an average studio with a pass-through kitchen that had been renovated in the 1980s. There was nothing special about it. But the rent was not too pricey, the view was not too obstructed, the single closet was not too tiny, the lobby was not too dingy, the street was not too noisy and the neighborhood was not too inconvenient. It was a single room for a single woman for a single year.

Diane heard rhythmic tapping. "Estelle, is that you?"

When Diane emerged from the stall, Estelle was tap-dancing in front of the sink.

Gotta Dance! she sang, and performed a little combination, ending with a kick, a pose, and a wink. She sailed through the restaurant and into the revolving door. A chauffeur emerged from a black car parked directly in front of the restaurant and opened a door. They were whisked to the theater, where a contractor that Gary Masters had recommended was waiting to help them get into the building.

"We went into a closed-up place like this not long ago in the Bronx," said Joe Franco, peering through a crack in the boards. "Remember?"

"Crack addicts had been holed up in there for years," said Roy, his second-in-command. "You wouldn't believe the smell."

"Yikes!" said Estelle. She produced a set of keys and a yellowed piece of paper. It was a property survey dated 1927, which identified the building as a carriage house and stables, two stories tall. Roy attacked one of the boards with a claw hammer, yanking nails out one by one. The board fell inward with a crash and a puff of dust. A smell of plaster and urine rose from the opening.

Joe handed Diane a flashlight.

Eleanor Roosevelt said that you must do the things you fear the most.

Joe turned the key and pushed on the door, but it didn't open. He tried again, throwing his shoulder into the door, and it opened with a bark.

Diane gripped the flashlight with both hands. In his autobiography *What's It All About?* Michael Caine advised that if you're required to do something dangerous on a movie set, you should make sure the stunt is scheduled at the very beginning of the production, when your life is at its most valuable to your director and producer. If you do it on the last day, with the film in the can, they literally don't care if you live or die.

Diane felt a pulse in her stomach; she couldn't remember the last time she'd dared herself to do anything. She reached for Estelle's hand as the men removed debris from the entrance.

"I was in a movie, *Haunted Hotel,*" Estelle said, squeezing back; she was wearing gloves. "It looked abandoned on the outside, but inside, ghosts of the family were running the hotel in secret. The chorus girls were chambermaids. I had a tap solo on top of the front desk."

As they entered the gloom, a dark object flew across the floor.

"Look at the size of that!" Roy exploded, and Diane dropped her flashlight. She and Estelle screamed in unison and bolted out to the street, tripping over each other on the steps. They stood panting on the sidewalk. Estelle bent over, hands on her knees. Diane leaned on the hood of a car and tried to catch her breath. Her heart was throbbing in her throat, and she was covered in sweat.

The chauffeur rushed into frame. "Mrs. Greenblatt! Are you all right?" He disappeared for a moment and returned with two bottles of cold water. Estelle sipped delicately; Diane sucked down half a bottle.

"It was a cat," Joe emerged to report. "A very well-fed cat, I must say."

"I think I'll sit out the rest of this safari," Estelle said. She followed her chauffeur to the car and got into the backseat. She rolled down the window and called, "I'll be here for the full story when you come back."

"If we come back," Diane said.

A damp odor saturated the space. There were four dark wooden stalls along the length of the space; apparently, horses—and later, cars—had lived here. Windows at the far end illuminated a large, dark pile, which Diane and the two men approached with caution. At one time the pile must have been a collection of tools, drop cloths, and a ladder; now it looked as if it were reverting to primeval forest.

"Somebody never got around to that paint job," Roy said.

In almost ten years Diane had had no curiosity about what lay behind the boards next door. Now she tried to imagine how the space connected to her theater, and where she would put the second screen. She had never been able to visualize things that weren't there. Architecture: another profession she had no aptitude for.

SHE RECOGNIZED a distressed-leather jacket in front of the box office: Bobby Wald was chatting up a woman, blocking the line to buy tickets for *The Prisoner of Second Avenue* (Melvin Frank, 1975), which she was showing as part of the "New York, NY" series. The Star of the Month was Robert De Niro, who had put antisocial behavior and Tribeca on the map. Tribeca was now too chic for Diane's budget.

Bobby Wald had been an eleventh-grade heartthrob with black curls and a wolfish smile when Diane was a freshman. He'd led her on with significant eye contact by the lockers and had once briefly fondled her knee in the bleachers at a Montclair High School hockey game. She'd never told her friend Claire Giancarlo, who had a crush on him. Now Bobby reminded Diane of the beefy, well-dressed thirty-year-old guys without occupations in Fellini's *I Vitelloni* (1953). She'd bumped into him occasionally over the years; each time, he was recovering from a girlfriend and a professional setback. He'd dropped out of architecture school, and he had tried selling things over the phone. He was currently making furniture with a master carpenter. He'd lost hair, developed a paunch. Since he'd moved to Carmine Street, he'd been coming to the Bedford Street Cinema three or four times a week, routinely chatting up Cindy at the box office and Storm at the concession stand. Storm, who was twenty-one, had patiently inserted ever-larger wooden circles into her earlobes so that the original pierced holes were now the size of quarters, and you could see through them. It was a disconcerting look, but most people didn't get past the lip ornament.

Bobby spotted Diane and came over to talk. "I saw this movie with Debbie in college. She couldn't believe Stallone played the mugger in the park! I loved that scene when Jack Lemmon rants on the terrace. My aunt lived in a building like that on Second Avenue."

Not everyone was a film critic. Bobby projected a loose, unstructured charm, but what worked on fourteen-year-old girls next to the lockers didn't do it for her anymore. After a few minutes she cut him off. "Glad you enjoyed it, Bobby. I have to get to work."

ON SUNDAY MORNING, Diane took the bus to Montclair from the Port Authority Bus Terminal and walked east in a light drizzle to the house she'd grown up in. There were grisly Halloween vignettes being played out on many lawns and porches. Ah, New Jersey, where people had time to decorate for Halloween.

"Margie has a man for you to meet," Connie Kurasik greeted her at the door.

"Thanks, I'm on strike," Diane told her mother, shaking the rain out of her hair.

"That's a stupid thing to do when you're almost forty," said Rachel, sliding off a stool to peck her hello.

"Thank you," Diane said, setting a bag of citrus fruit on the counter. "That's tactful."

She heard her sister's children shrieking somewhere in the house, her sister's husband sat in front of a Sunday-morning talk show on TV, a generalist in desperate search of meaning and focus.

"You meet the wrong men because you do the wrong things," Rachel said.

"Such as?"

"Such as talking to the creeps and weirdos who come to your theater! Such as dressing like a math teacher from 1978."

"And turning down blind dates," her mother said.

"Excuse me: The last four creeps and weirdos were all fix-ups."

"I think a strike is a good move," her father said.

All eyes turned toward him. Gene Kurasik was sitting with the Sunday crossword at the kitchen table. "You can use the extra time and energy to apply to graduate school, inherently a smart idea." Diane and her father had an ongoing argument about the movies, which he considered passive entertainment. Diane regarded the bloated celebrity memoirs of the stars that her father liked to read as passive entertainment. "And incidentally, you might meet someone there."

"I went to graduate school," Diane said.

But she hadn't finished; this hung in the air unsaid. They all looked at her.

"You know, until you get married, there is no other subject," her sister said.

Rachel was a competitive person without a sport.

"I think I found an apartment," Diane said, to change the subject.

Her uncle Mort arrived, with a big, elaborate fruitcake. "How's business?" he asked Diane.

"We had a great summer. Attendance is up in every category."

"But don't you have a script, Diane?" he asked. "I thought you wanted to direct, produce, right? Be higher up on the food chain?"

"In case the apartment I'm counting on falls through, I was wondering if I might stay at your place, Mort."

"I don't think that would be a good idea," Mort Kurasik said.

Her uncle spent the fall and winter in Santa Fe. His pied-à-terre in the NYU area was a ten-minute walk from the theater. Why couldn't she stay there, especially if he was going to be out of town?

"Try the cake," he said, and dumped an enormous piece in front of her. It plopped off her plate onto the table with a clatter. Diane left it there.

"You'll stay with us," her mother said. "The train is fabulous. Just forty-five minutes from Penn Station. Everybody takes it. All the young people."

Diane stayed seated as the table was cleared around her. She was being evicted. She was about to be homeless. Not without resources, of course—one of them being family. Her uncle was talking to her father in the kitchen. The swinging door opened as he said, "Well, I'm sorry," and closed. It opened again as he said, "no obligation."

What exactly did her uncle think she'd be doing in his apartment?

"You have so much going on, Diane." Her mother sat down next to her, squeezing her arm. "It would be great to have less to worry about. Stay here. I'll cook for you."

"Sometimes I leave work after midnight. I'd prefer not to take a forty-five-minute train ride at that hour. If there are trains at that hour."

"The bus is twenty minutes at that hour," her dad said, sitting on her other side.

"Stay with us," her sister said. "It's a cab ride."

"Maybe you'll meet somebody on the train," her mother said. "Remember Robert De Niro in *Falling in Love?*"

"Diane isn't waiting for the man on the train," Uncle Mort said. "She's waiting for the man who'll climb up her hair and rescue her from the tower."

What did that mean? Diane got up to make juice. From the kitchen, she heard muffled talk at the table. Everyone looked up at her when she returned. On the bus ride back, she decided to find a way to make her uncle regret his behavior.

THE PHONE awakened her at eight the following morning.

Nothing good comes of phone calls at that hour.

The apartment on East Twenty-sixth had been rented, her latest broker told her.

"That's right." Diane cleared her throat, trying to wake up. "I rented it."

"No, this is what I'm trying to tell you," the broker said. "The apartment was already under contract to be rented when we saw it."

"How is that possible?"

"I'm sorry, it happens. Let me round up some other places for you to see."

Connie and Gene were ready to let her stay on indefinitely; her friend Claire Giancarlo had offered her a room in Westchester without an end date; Rachel would put up with her for a few weeks, perhaps.

"A wrecking ball will crash through my window in a month."

"So let's go this afternoon, then," the broker said.

OCTOBER

Vladimir woke up breathless in a sweat. He'd dreamed he was back in Cuba. In the peeling blue bedroom with the open window overlooking the decrepit house opposite. His family was raging outside his door; soon they would storm in without knocking. He was trapped and sweating on his bed. He could hear neighbors fighting, diesel trucks shifting gears to get up the hill, the yowling of neighborhood cats. The Authorities were in possession of his passport. They would now begin the process of retaliation. He'd brought this on himself. Why had he gone back? How could he have been so stupid?

"Nice of you to show up," Chris called as Vladimir walked into the studio. Then he gave him the news: Jan Mattias's office renovation was on hold. A firm that had just been featured in *The New York Times Magazine* would get a crack at it. Jan Mattias apparently needed to be on the crest of the wave at all times. The good news: Jan Mattias had invited Chris and Vladimir to discuss a movie theater expansion.

"Well, I don't mind not doing another office," Vladimir said.

"Me neither. It'll be interesting."

Vladimir checked his e-mail. In his in-box was a letter from Migdalia Rosario, forwarding a speech by the Minister of Foreign Relations about the tight new U.S. restrictions on travel to Cuba, and the new, more lenient Cuban policy toward Cubans returning to the island. She wrote, "Perhaps the *gusanos* should read the following."

He let out a scream.

"What happened?" Chris asked.

"Every day, I am bombarded with BULLSHIT! I haven't seen this woman in twelve years, and now she sends me propaganda and calls me a worm."

Chris laughed out loud. "She called you a worm?"

"*Gusano* is Castro's word for everyone who went to Miami, or anyone who opposes him. And whatever he says, people repeat it. Some exiles call themselves *gusanos* now. They think it's a badge of honor to say they're worms. Such nonsense!"

Chris mentioned a meeting at the cinema later and left the office.

Vladimir poured himself a cup of coffee. Why waste time getting into a discussion with this robot? On the other hand, how dare she reveal his e-mail address to twenty strangers?

"Dear Migdalia," Vladimir wrote back rapidly.

"If I wanted to read the blood-drenched propaganda of the Regime, I'd go to the official website.

"Why are you proselytizing? It's one thing to be trapped in Havana, with no information, promoting the 'Revolution.' It is quite another to sit in Mexico, as you do, with access to a free press and the Internet, and extol the virtues of a totalitarian regime that has completely destroyed our country. You must be suffering from amnesia and blindness. I am sorry for you.

"Vladimir."

Vladimir pulled out a roll of vellum and began to sketch. He preferred the pencil and vellum for thinking through new ideas. He could work on the computer if he had to, although since Chris had hired Magnus, one of his old students, as an intern, Vladimir wasn't so motivated to keep up with the new programs, or the updates of the old ones. It was nice to be alone in the studio, without Chris on the phone.

But there was someplace he was supposed to be. The movie theater!

He raced outside. The sky opened up a block away from the subway. He didn't have an umbrella. He began to run. It was the end of hurricane season. Many of his childhood memories involved tropical storms that swept down, scattered everything, damaged buildings and made people do foolish things. A single storm can alter your whole life, all your plans.

A woman with a silver spike coming out of her face led him into the theater, where seven people were sitting at a large table directly in front of the screen.

Chris stepped down from the stage to greet him in the aisle. "You're half an hour late," he whispered. "How many times do we have to go through this?"

Vladimir climbed up the stairs to meet the people at the table.

"Okay! I am late, I am wet, please forgive me. You play wonderful movies, Bedford Street Cinema. I've seen many great films here. There's a scary building next door. Tell me about it."

He sat down across from a woman with long black hair and vivid blue eyes. She turned her pointy face to him and smiled.

◆

How could this man have attended many films at her theater? Wouldn't Diane have noticed him? He was distinctive, serious—and drenched. She sent Cindy back to her office to get a towel for him. His thick black hair, shot through with white threads, was done like Toshiro Mifune's in *Yojimbo* (Akira Kurosawa, 1961)—a messy samurai knot at the back of the head.

Sidney Lumet, in his unpretentious, process-oriented memoir *Making Movies,* wrote something interesting about *the mysterious alchemy between star and audience:* "Every star evokes a sense of danger, something unmanageable. Perhaps each person in the audience feels that he or she is the one who can manage, tame, satisfy the bigger-than-life quality that a star has." Vladimir Hurtado Padrón exuded something dangerous and unmanageable, like a film star. Was it just the foreign, unfamiliar aspect of him that made Diane feel that he was bigger than life?

"We should tell you up front that we've never designed a cinema or a theater," said Chris Wiley, "and we're very excited."

"We learn so much doing things we haven't done before," said Vladimir, with an accent she couldn't place. He seemed simultaneously sophisticated and naïve. Gary Masters caught her eye; he counted Clearview Cinemas as one of his clients, and had given her the name of the firm that handled all their New York construction work. *Go learn on someone else's dime,* Gary's face said.

Chris Wiley, a tall, elegant blond man in his late thirties with alert green eyes and a diplomatic demeanor, had kept the meeting moving before Vladimir arrived, peppering the renovation committee with questions about the space, the history of the theater, the connections each Board member had to the cinema. He worked the crowd like an old pro. Dorothy and Estelle were charmed by him; Jack Lipsky, Daniel Dubrovnik and Gary Masters were not. When fifteen minutes had passed, and it became clear that his partner might not show, Chris had begun to present their portfolio, which included photos, paintings, sketches and two small models. Diane was impressed with the thought that had gone into the design of the public spaces. She complimented Chris on one sketch, an analysis of the traffic flow in the lobby of an apartment building, which he had used to determine where to put floor joists.

"If I had to tell you how we differ from most firms, I'd say that this is it," Chris responded. "We don't come in with a design. We investigate the space, and the design really flows out of that. You have to put floor joists somewhere, so instead of putting them every two feet, why not add more where there's more traffic? The floor will last longer."

"But it's uneven," Daniel Dubrovnik had said.

"Underneath, which no one can see. But the tiles on top are regularly spaced."

Chris impressed her. Then this wet, beautiful, serious man showed up. She'd felt off-kilter ever since he bounded up the steps and sat down across from her and fixed her with a direct gaze.

"Tell us how you'd like to use the extra space," Vladimir said.

"We want as wide a screen as possible, and as many seats as possible," Diane told him. "But the lobby is cramped and we have ticket holders lining up around the block. So I'd want to add as much space to the lobby as we can."

Vladimir seemed to be listening actively. It took guts for a man to wear his hair like that. She felt out of breath, but she couldn't stop talking.

"Also, the bathrooms are a disaster. My ideal renovation would include ripping out both bathrooms and starting from scratch."

"What kind of feeling would you like the space to convey?" Chris asked.

She had been thinking that this was the perfect opportunity to really give the theater an identity. "We are about the glamour and mystery of classic movies in a comfortable, neighborhood place."

"The glamour of black-and-white movies themselves, or the glamour of the old movie palaces?" Vladimir asked.

That was a good question. "Yes, we don't want stars on the ceiling and Moorish décor. I think we'd like a clean, sleek, glamorous look."

"You like the art deco look?" he asked, passing a book to her.

"Very much." It was a book of photos of deco theaters all over America. "Wow. I've made pilgrimages to some of these places."

He smiled at her. She felt everyone around the table watching her. But it was probably just a professional smile. She smiled back at him, and then looked down at the book.

"Where are you from, Vladimir?" Dorothy asked.

He exhaled, as if he were tired of this question. "Cuba."

"Oh," everyone around the table said, as if this made everything clear.

"How long have you been here?" Estelle asked.

"Almost five years in the U.S. Before that, seven years in London."

"You grew up in Cuba," Dorothy said and sighed. "It's not the way it was."

"No, they ruined it," Estelle agreed.

"We used to go down there every year, to Havana, to Varadero. Have you ever been there?" Dorothy asked Vladimir.

"Cubans aren't allowed in Varadero. Only foreigners. And I should tell you, they didn't just ruin your vacation. They ruined the entire country."

"I don't think we want a retro look," Gary Masters said.

"No, you want something sleek and contemporary that evokes nostalgia without imitating the deco look," Chris said.

"Exactly," Diane said.

"I like black marble," Daniel said. Diane had forgotten he was there.

"Black marble! That would cost a fucking fortune," Lipsky said.

"I don't think we should be specific about the materials yet," Diane said. "Why don't we get a picture of what the whole thing is going to look like, and cost, and then we can fight over the materials."

The meeting broke up to make way for the first screening of the day. Diane stayed behind with Vladimir and Chris, who began to look around the space as the early crowd of partisans pushed in to grab good seats for *Royal Wedding* (Stanley Donen, 1951). The "Song and Dance" series had just started, and would sell out. Diane had a limited appetite for sticky-sweet musicals, but they paid the rent, so to speak. It irritated her, in the movies, when people just burst into song on public transportation, just as it irritated her, in the movies, when two people met and romance bloomed immediately, because he was a man and she was a woman, and this was how it worked. Her life was proof of how this didn't happen. But these movies had an eternal allure. During the Depression, people flocked to see men in top hats expensively courting fur-draped ladies and gliding over shiny white floors. Didn't their drab lives seem that much more depressing afterwards?

The two architects began to take rough measurements, and Diane became self-conscious; she felt superfluous. "I have nightmares about the place next door, so I'm going to let Floyd take you over there," she said, giving Floyd the keys. "Come see me when you're done and we can talk about the next step."

Diane walked back to her office, wondering what to do with herself.

Ten years of sitting across the table from men with tedious verbal tics and annoying personal behavior (on with the glasses, off with the glasses, into the case with the glasses, snapping shut the case with a *BANG!* And on again with the glasses when the waitress arrived). Ten years of trying to get interested in men with careless hygiene, disagreeable politics, questionable business practices, dreadful taste in music and/or lousy table manners. Many of these men seriously overestimated their importance in the world. Quite a few were sexually dysfunctional, when it got to that stage, which was rare. Often an ex-girlfriend hovered in the background, sometimes even in the foreground. Everybody had somebody, it seemed, for the purpose of ending the evening, whether or not the date with Diane worked out. These arrangements often didn't surface until Week Six, which was the step-up-or-cut-off point.

The films Vladimir remembered seeing at Bedford Street were martial arts movies and Italian comedies. Diane looked at the schedule to see if there was anything coming up: nothing till February. But if he and his partner were doing the renovation, she'd be seeing quite a bit of him. She wondered how she might make sure that they got the commission.

She heard a ruckus in the lobby and went out to investigate. Four busloads of senior citizens had showed up two hours early for *South Pacific* (Joshua Logan, 1958), mobbing the theater, singing "Some Enchanted Evening" on the ticket holders' line. A rival faction chanted "I'm in Love with a Wonderful Guy" from the concession stand. It was only noon, only Monday!

She stalked up Hudson Street in search of quiet and fresh air. A massive headache had lodged itself above her left eye. How many times had she tried to work herself up over an otherwise unattractive specialist because he was there, only to find herself ignored or dismissed? Nobody came close to what she was looking for, so it wasn't truly tragic. But the pattern was tedious. An entire decade of her life had drifted by in the mood of *Summertime* (David Lean, 1955), in which Katharine Hepburn plays a single American woman of a certain age, in Venice for the first time. She puts on a brave face, marching through the streets solo with her movie camera, perching at cafés as the sensual Italian street life swirls around her. She is exalted by the beauty of Venice and humiliated by the difficulty of experiencing it as a woman alone. She is flummoxed when an attractive Italian man of a certain age begins to follow her around, and receives his attentions with a clumsy rigidity that does not disguise her longing. Of course, her handsome Italian suitor is unsuitable—married, etc. Pauline Kael had written: "There is an element of embarrassment in this pining-spinster role, but Hepburn is so proficient at it that she almost—though not quite—kills the embarrassment."

Diane couldn't remember the last time she'd wanted something to happen.

AFTER VIEWING the carriage house, Chris Wiley and Vladimir Hurtado Padrón were cornered in a narrow area near the concession stand by the two older women present at the meeting. Chris noted that they addressed themselves to Vladimir.

"You know, Diane started the revival repertory here," said the one who carried herself like a theatrical actress.

"She's a very lovely girl," said the one who had been a chorine.

Vladimir gave them both the blankest of slight smiles.

"She seems like a wonderful person," Chris said, when the silence from Vladimir became rude. Vladimir could be so tactless.

"So, where do you live?" asked the chorus girl casually.

"I live in NoHo," Chris said.

"And you?"

"SoHo," Vladimir said.

"Oh, so you don't live together," said the theatrical actress, casting a look at the chorus girl, as if there had been a discussion, and a bet.

"Would you ladies excuse us?" Chris said. "We're on our way to another meeting, but we wanted to take a quick look at these bathrooms to see if they're as horrible as advertised."

"Oh, they're worse!"

The chorus girl was right: the bathroom was a horror show.

Chris and Vladimir bumped into Diane in the lobby, and she pointed out problems in traffic flow.

"So when do we get to see you again?" she asked, looking from one to the other, her gaze lingering on Vladimir. They made a date, there were handshakes and she gave them a cheery goodbye.

"Oh! Vladimir," she called after him.

They turned around.

Diane came running toward them. "May I borrow that book?"

"Certainly." He presented it to her with a slight bow of the head.

"Thank you," she said, suppressing a smile in a shy way.

THIS DIANE WAS quite charming, Chris thought, although in desperate need of fashion advice and a serious haircut. On their way up Seventh Avenue South to the subway, Chris said, "Don't be put off by those busybodies."

"What do you mean?"

"Don't be dense! Diane. She's nice, and I think she liked you."

"Most women like me," Vladimir said.

Vladimir could be so arrogant sometimes. It was almost endearing.

"I think she's interested," Chris said when they'd boarded the No. 1 train.

"I need another woman in my life like I need a heel in the head."

"A hole in the head."

"A *hole* in the head."

The subject was dropped. From what Chris had gathered, Vladimir was in trouble with women in three countries; it was kind of refreshing that none of this ever really came up in conversation, as if it were a business-only relationship—which, of course, it was. Still: it was unnatural not to talk about personal things *ever* in a day-to-day business partnership. Weirdly, politics came up every day with Vladimir, and he took politics very personally.

More interesting and less obvious to Chris: Why was Jan Mattias throwing him business? And why now? It had been over ten years ago and there had been no contact since. Jan often had his picture taken at premieres with starlets in tiny dresses. Chris didn't care if Jan needed to pretend that it had never happened.

So what did Jan want, and why now? Except in situations of very difficult personalities or a mismatch with a client taste-wise, Chris never turned down work, especially high-profile public work. But he didn't trust the Bedford Street Cinema situation; Mattias's absence from the meeting only added to the ambiguity. Others would be bidding. Just as the office renovation had been offered out of the blue and then withdrawn, so the cinema project might simply disappear—snatched away out of spite, perhaps, or for some reason knowable only in the unfathomable mind of Jan Mattias. Not that Jan Mattias knew his own mind. Clearly not.

But Chris wouldn't bring it up, as he and Vladimir didn't discuss their personal feelings or lives, current or historical. The topic of orientation had never come up, although it must have been clear to Vladimir from the moment Chris opened his portfolio, with the Queer Book Shop, the AIDS Crisis Center waiting room and all the restaurants on Eighth Avenue. No doubt he had the Latin male's homophobia and had moved on for reasons of practicality and respect. Chris was flattered that Vladimir respected his work.

Vladimir had of course met Paul Zazlow, who often dropped by the office. Vladimir always greeted Paul cordially and chatted with him, sometimes at great length. But he'd never had anything to say about him.

Paul, on the other hand, had choice words about Vladimir.

"Oh my GOD!" Paul said to Chris, the night he'd met Vladimir for the first time. *"The cross section can wait! I must address my energies to the Overthrow of the Regime!"*

Paul did a very good Vladimir imitation, with the intense eyes, forward-thrusting head and Latin drama. One day when Paul had stopped by for a studio lunch, Vladimir arrived late, coming from the doctor. Small talk about doctors and health insurance followed, and apropos of nothing, Vladimir said:

"If I were that doctor, I'd be grateful to have me for a patient."

Paul burst into cackles.

"I mean, I am funny, I am intelligent, I ask good questions. I liven up his day," Vladimir said without irony. "He's lucky to have me."

Now, when Chris got home from work, Paul would ask, "How was Vladimir's desk chair? Was it aware of how lucky it should feel, being sat upon by Vladimir? And what about the waitress? Was she grateful to have Vladimir at her table?"

Paul kept alive a running joke that Chris had a crush on Vladimir, because Chris had originally described Vladimir as being tall. "How tall is he?" was always Paul's first question: Paul was not tall at all.

"I think he's six feet. Six-one," Chris had said.

"He is *FIVE-SEVEN!*" Paul accused, after meeting Vladimir. "Five-eight, *tops!*"

"You think? Well, I don't know, he seemed very tall. He's so specific and says things with such authority, I guess he seems taller than he is."

As a matter of fact, Chris didn't have a crush on Vladimir. Vladimir was a talented architect, a great-looking guy, an angry, frustrated, amusing, somewhat lost person. As different as they were, their ideas meshed, and they worked well together. But no crush. Not everything had to turn into a *thing*. After spending a good ten years working and socializing exclusively with gay men where things often turned into *things,* Chris was glad to have a straight business partner, some straight clients and a few good straight friends. He felt his world was getting broader. Moreover, he'd had several romantic episodes with straight men who were on the fence. He had no need to live in that kind of frustration again. Not that Vladimir appeared on the fence in any way.

It was insensitive to assume that Vladimir didn't discuss his personal life just because he was straight and Chris was gay. Not everything was about straight and gay.

National origin, on the other hand, came up every day. Chris was constantly waiting for Vladimir and lecturing him about the importance of being on time. It would be bigoted to conclude that this was a Latin problem. However, Vladimir seemed to spend at least half his time in the office reading articles online about Cuba and organizing protests over the phone. Chris had to physically stand over Vladimir until he turned off his computer, in order to get to meetings on time. If he didn't, like today, Vladimir would be late—up to two hours late.

"Let me just check one thing," Vladimir would say each time Chris tried to get him to leave for a meeting.

"You checked ten minutes ago. He's still alive. What did you do before the Internet?" Still: Vladimir worked on weekends and stayed at the studio until midnight many nights, so what did it matter, if that was how he structured his time? Vladimir was an adult.

They emerged on Twenty-third Street and saw a ragged man defecating on the sidewalk in front of a doughnut shop. New York was like a collective insanity pact. New Yorkers ignored the psychotics, the homeless, the crowds, the piercing racket, the lousy public amenities, the nightmarish scaffolding, the ubiquitous garbage and decay, in order to pretend that they had the best of everything. The cynicism ("Knock yourself out," said the litterbug when Chris picked up his trash), the lazy mental habits ("Enjoy," said the dry-cleaning clerk when Chris dropped off his clothing), the pushiness ("Could we cross this street sometime *today*?" said the hopped-up pedestrian behind him), the incessant and inappropriate yakking on cellphones in public spaces, the savage honking that penetrated their sixth-floor studio from truck drivers on their way to the Holland Tunnel, and other evidence of the decline of all civilized behavior in New York City left Chris breathless, exhausted and angry at the end of every day. He no longer saw possibilities on every corner. All he saw was soot and sludge, the rudeness of corner-cutters and the arrogance of chiselers who knew that in a city of eight million strangers running late, they would never be called to account or have to apologize.

When they got back to the studio, Vladimir put the cinema measurements in the computer to come up with some general floor plans, and Chris began tracking down drawings of another theater he'd designed for a competition some time in the last decade (he hadn't gotten the job). He'd been doing this for twenty years. Historically, Chris had dreamed of big public works—airports, museums, stadiums, ferry terminals. Manhattan interiors were getting tedious: the smaller the job, the nastier the negotiations with the client and/or the co-op board. Suburban jobs tended to focus on how loudly the client could trumpet his financial health from the façade, and how cheaply it could be done. Vladimir had coined the phrase "*dinero*-driven design" one frigid morning in Westchester, when a client suggested that the front door be surfaced in gold leaf.

They didn't take jobs where taste was an issue anymore, although it went against his grain as an office manager. Between work they ultimately turned down and bids and competitions they didn't win, Chris estimated that he spent more than 65 percent of his time working on things that didn't get built. In any other city—which would no doubt be more livable—he would have a better shot at making a name for himself.

Chris's brother was an engineer with a huge firm in Atlanta. He lived a fine life. Granted, a heterosexual life with children in a humid climate, but the family had space, a front porch, a patio, a thriving garden and a fully funded, well-appointed community center with an Olympic-sized swimming pool around the corner. They had barbecues year round, friendliness, neighborliness, a porch culture—possibilities unavailable here in the confrontation capital of the world.

But now he had this new professional partnership, and it was working out so well.

"By the way, what time are you coming in tomorrow?" Chris asked.

"Ten o'clock."

"Would that be ten o'clock New York time, or ten o'clock Havana time?"

Vladimir blew him a kiss.

Now, that was a first.

WHEN CHRIS GOT HOME, Paul turned off the sound on New York One and came to greet him with a glass of scotch. Paul had thick, straight black hair and a magnificent, chiseled face; he was the sort of person everyone looked at on the street—male, female, straight, gay, young, old, everyone.

"As you know, half the buildings in New York don't take dogs," Paul said as they settled into the sofa. "The other half don't take lawyers. So today I had my nightmare client: a lawyer with a dog." Paul worked as a real estate broker for the largest firm in the city. He enjoyed everything about his job—the voyeurism, the office politics, the awful personalities, the entrée into his clients' personal and financial lives, crisscrossing town every day and holding all the keys. He lived and breathed favors, secrecy and drama. He would never, ever leave New York.

Scenes of local violence flashed on the TV. Chris took a sip of the drink and told Paul about the cinema project, omitting any reference to Jan Mattias.

"And what's new with *Vladimir?*" Paul asked. "How about that keyboard? Was it sufficiently impressed to be pushed by the fingers of *Vladimir?*"

Chris thought about Vladimir blowing the kiss. What did it mean to him?

"He had the chorus girls of MGM reminiscing about Havana in the good old days."

"More Cuba!" Paul said, crunching ice, eyes on the TV.

"We met a lovely person today," Chris said, unknotting his tie. "I think Vladimir had an immediate positive effect on her."

"How tall?"

He reminded himself how lucky he was to have found Paul. "There's a show at the Atlanta museum that I'd like to see," he said, removing his shoes.

"Don't even start," Paul said.

"It's a *weekend*."

"I know you. You want to plant tulips and start all over in Mayberry."

"Atlanta is not Mayberry."

"Even the idea of thinking about this idea gives me hives."

On the other hand, Paul could be so rigid. Chris tried to stand up.

"I missed you today," Paul accused, blocking him with his knees.

"Me too," Chris said, and untangled himself to go wash up. Paul was a positive force in his life, after years of celibacy, which had followed years of mindless roving, which had followed years of denial and despair. "If we don't have anything planned that second weekend in January, I think I'll go then."

"You don't believe it, but you do have roots here."

"I don't have trees here. I want something to survive me."

"You mean other than me?"

◆

THE LAST DAY of October, with a dreadful feeling, Diane packed two suitcases and three small tote bags with vital things. In the afternoon, she had a moving company put her furniture, summer clothing, books and videos into a storage locker in Queens. Three other tenants were moving out at the same time, and the halls were filled with boxes, furniture, vacuum cleaners and bicycles. Part of her was frightened that she might lose something, and another part wanted to be rid of all the broken and mismatched things she'd acquired.

Random memories surfaced as she packed. Behind, beneath and amid the furniture, she found buttons, coins, the missing remote control device, dust, paper clips and hair, hair, hair. Also, business cards: of a British film distributor (specialty: Orchids); a school administrator from Rockland, Illinois (specialty: Mission Furniture); a TV-commercial producer she'd had two dates with a decade earlier (specialty: *The Godfather*). She had a Rolodex full of cards from people she hadn't seen or spoken to in fifteen years. For some reason, she hadn't been able to throw them out, though surely these people had moved on, personally, professionally. Something about all the hair gave her a feeling of futility. She dumped the Rolodex down the incinerator shaft whole, gave her keys to the super, hailed a cab on Hudson Street, and rode uptown without looking back.

NOVEMBER

DIANE LET HERSELF into the dark house quietly, holding her breath as she passed the master bedroom at the top of the stairs. She was trying to spend as little time with her parents as possible without offending them. This was easy, as they were in bed by eight-thirty. They sat around in their bathrobes in the morning, drinking coffee from five till nine, reading the newspapers and discussing, no doubt, her irregular hours, her lack of a mate, a graduate degree and now even a place to live. When she opened her door, the sprawl she'd expected had been replaced by streamlined surfaces; everything on the bed and floor had been put away neatly. There was a note on the desk:

"Darling, let's talk in the morning. Love, Mom."

What was there to talk about? She had no leads. She couldn't give them an exit date. They couldn't be angry that she was a bad houseguest—all she did here was sleep. With the commuting and the apartment hunting, she didn't even have five minutes to squeeze juice in the morning.

She undressed, throwing clothes on the floor. After a shower, she spent some time deciphering the "Apartments for Rent" section of *The Village Voice*. Many sounded familiar from previous weeks. Queens and the Bronx were not options. Washington Heights was not realistic. Brooklyn, if she had to.

Vladimir had come to the cinema twice since the meeting to look at the space. He'd made quick work of preliminaries in her office, declined the movie, agreed in principle to drinks or dinner at some undefined other time, and had gone out to measure, draw or take photos. Once, Vladimir and Chris had spent a rainy evening measuring foot traffic in the lobby, and the three of them went around the corner for a quick coffee afterwards. The conversation had been friendly but limited; the goodbye had been inconclusive. No wedding ring. No personal details revealed, except that Vladimir rented an apartment in a building he'd helped renovate. He carried a black nylon bike messenger bag and often wore black jeans and sneakers. When he didn't shave, he had more of a mustache than a beard. The lack of information was maddening, but she expected a visit from him the following afternoon, and she couldn't stop herself from looking forward to it.

IN THE MORNING, Connie was seated at the kitchen table, fully caffeinated.

"Your father and I were thinking," she began, as Diane hit the bottom of the stairs.

"Sorry, Mom, I have to catch the 9:02," she said, running out the door.

"What about *buying* an apartment?" her mother shouted after her.

"I'm seeing three places for sale today—I'll call you!"

Diane ran three blocks, and propelled herself across the intersection just as barriers fell over the Boonton Line tracks. This was the third day in a row she'd done this; she looked at all the calm commuters lined up for the Midtown Direct, armed with newspapers, umbrellas and stainless steel travel mugs of coffee from home. These people had thought far enough ahead to realize that they should be married and commuting calmly by now.

She fell into a window position in a three-seat row and caught her breath. The last thing she wanted was to own property. But nobody was moving, and the rental market was absurd. And why not subscribe to a newspaper if you had a permanent home address? Christmas nonsense was everywhere. She had to get gifts for family and for everyone at the theater. When?

That morning, she saw six possibilities. Although the apartments for sale were in much better condition than the apartments for rent, all the apartments were still too small, too dark and in the wrong neighborhood. She hit the theater just as Floyd finished seating the first show, *An American in Paris* (Vincente Minnelli, 1951).

All afternoon, she hovered near her phone, but Vladimir didn't call. She was reminded of a prospect from at least five years earlier, an advertising executive (specialty: New Restaurants), who asked who her favorite leading men were and, not seeing himself in any of her choices, stopped calling her.

At six she called Vladimir. He said he'd been working on sight lines and columns, and had completely forgotten about stopping by. He'd call her another time.

Oh dear, said a voice in her head that sounded a lot like Connie.

Bobby Wald swung into her office to chat about Gene Kelly. Bobby liked to watch movies and talk about them. Granted, the level of discourse was not very high, but he absorbed what interested him. He was a regular guy. Still Bobby Wald should have found some kind of focus by the age of forty-two or forty-three.

"What are you up to these days?" she asked him.

"I'm making a coffee table in walnut," he said. "I love wood."

Diane inhaled, expecting the specialist's lecture to unfold.

But Bobby stopped there, with a goofy smile. Apparently, that was all there was to say about it. The gorgeous, exotic practicing architect was not calling, and the boy-next-door who dropped out of architecture school was popping by with regularity. Diane never saw her friends anymore, not even the cineastes. Why?

She lined up at Port Authority for the bus to New Jersey. Vladimir would age nicely, she thought—amusing that this was now part of the job description. She wondered what his situation was. His partner was probably gay, but that didn't mean anything. Vladimir shook her hand with both of his hands, but he had done the same with everyone at the meeting. The Renovation Committee was meeting the following week to look over the designs from three different architectural firms. If Vladimir and Chris didn't get the bid, there would be nothing standing in the way of romantic involvement. If they did, the professional association didn't automatically mean that a personal situation was out the question—they weren't in the military, after all. And almost anyone associated with the cinema would be happy for her, she hoped. She wouldn't have to persuade herself to be interested in this one. What did it take to rate a lousy phone call? She should stop thinking about him now, to avoid disappointment.

THE FOLLOWING AFTERNOON her parents knocked on her door at two.

"Your father and I have been talking," her mother began.

"And I was talking to my old friend Milt Ostrowsky," her father continued. "You remember him. And Milt thought it might be a great idea for you to take a cruise. There's a singles cruise that leaves the New York docks every week for the Caribbean."

"Why would I go on a cruise?"

"Okay, you don't like that idea," Connie said, looking at Gene.

"A *singles* cruise! I need that like I need a pet llama."

"Forget the cruise," her mother said quickly. "You take a plane . . . to Greece!" She smiled at Diane broadly. "There's an adult artists' camp that Ruth's daughter went to. She made ceramics. She had a wonderful time and met some very lovely people."

Diane leaned against the wall to stretch her calves. "I can't take vacation now."

"Well, nobody said right now," Connie told her.

"Who said right now? We were talking about next week!" her father said, and laughed.

She stared at them.

"Okay! You don't like that idea," Connie continued: "What about this idea: You come with us to synagogue next week."

"Since when do you go to synagogue?"

"We don't. But we thought since you're living here now, you might want to reconnect with old friends in town? No? She doesn't like any of my ideas, Gene."

"It's Saturday. I just wanted to hang out. That's *my* idea."

"Yes, it's Saturday," her father said. "Diane should be allowed to hang out in her own home. Come, Connie."

They left, simmering with unsaid business. She could hear them whispering in their bedroom with an urgency that she hardly felt was warranted. Gene had gone to Columbia, Connie had gone to Barnard. They'd been introduced by friends in 1964, and had been together ever since. Diane supposed she could meet anyone on a singles cruise. But she wasn't looking for *anyone*. How did Federico Fellini find Nino Rota? Rota's festive music was perfectly suited to Fellini's amused examinations of human activity; the soundtrack to *La Dolce Vita* (1960), for example, acted like carbonated coffee racing through the veins. On the other hand, Luis Buñuel avoided music; he thought it made for too easy an effect. Still what was wrong with an easy effect, now and then? How many people saw Buñuel's films again and again?

On Monday morning, the Renovation Committee approved the Wiley Hurtado Padrón design. Diane called the architects up to give them the good news. She got Chris, who sounded pleased and relieved. He suggested a meeting the week after Thanksgiving, and she wrote it down in her date book in turquoise ink.

The next morning, Diane pedaled a bike without interest at a swanky gym in Midtown, trying not to watch sixteen or seventeen TVs, all on different channels, each displaying overgroomed anchors discussing plastic surgery, diet, exercise and holiday food. She was using the guest pass that Jan Mattias had given her the previous year as a Christmas present; he would no doubt give her another one just like it this year.

As models, actresses and trophy wives in camera-ready shape wearing thong leotards passed by, Diane bore in mind Judy Garland, who never got over the fact that she didn't look like Lana Turner, and burst into tears day after day as stylists bound her in corsets to control her figure and stuck plugs in her nose to make it less pug-like. Most of the members of this gym had had some kind of face work done; Diane doubted that half the breasts on display were real. The atmosphere changed completely when a minor celebrity entered the room and was received with slavishly deferential behavior. Diane made a mental note to cancel her trip to the Sundance Film Festival.

Judy Garland took amphetamines to control her weight and sleeping pills because she was wired from the amphetamines and needed to rest for the next day's shooting. MGM repeatedly suspended her contract because she didn't show up for work, because she couldn't wake up from the sleeping pills. So then she took amphetamines to wake up, and became so dependent on them that her weight once fell to eighty-five pounds and she had to be fed intravenously. Diane didn't need the attitude of this kind of place, but she could definitely use a gym in the city. If she couldn't have an apartment, a shower and a locker would be helpful until she did. She made a mental note to check out the YMCA near the theater.

On her way to the subway, Diane stopped into a beauty salon that didn't look too flashy, and made an appointment with a hairdresser. She wasn't waiting for Vladimir. She wasn't even thinking about him.

That afternoon, Floyd pulled her out of a screening of *House Calls* (Howard Zieff, 1978) as per her instructions. Vladimir was on the phone, asking if he could make a date with her later that day, about five o'clock, to talk about specifics. He said "date," not "meeting." Of course, English wasn't his first language. Still, Vladimir had been in the United States for five years and in business for much longer. He knew the difference between a meeting and a date.

Diane hung up with him and immediately called the salon to cancel her appointment. When Ingrid Bergman was brought to Hollywood for screen tests, David O. Selznick had immediately sat her down with a stylist to discuss how they would tweeze her eye-brows, fix her teeth and put her on a diet. "If you don't like the way I look," Bergman asked him, "what am I doing here?" And that was the end of that. Interesting that Ingrid's beautiful daughter Isabella Rossellini, who famously said that she didn't have much use for makeup, turned around after her modeling contract with Lancôme had ended to open up her own cosmetics company.

Feeling confident, Diane called the latest broker to make an offer on a small, dark, poorly located L-shaped studio for sale that she'd seen the day before. She caught the end of *House Calls,* a film in which Glenda Jackson must compete with every widow, divorcée and single gal in greater Los Angeles for the ultimate swinging bachelor, Walter Matthau. This wasn't a great moment in cinema, but for some reason the film retained positive associations for Diane. Peter Bogdanovich had said, "There's no way around it: Even out-right trash can achieve a special glow for someone if the person as-sociates it with a happy time in his or her life." On the way out of the theater, she removed some old material from the bulletin board. Surely no one in Hollywood had ever told Walter Matthau what to do with his hair or his nose.

VLADIMIR ARRIVED in her office about a half an hour later than he'd specified, looking foreign and busy, his hair tied back in a ponytail with a rubber band. Diane offered him popcorn and soda, which he declined, and then she gestured to the sofa, where they both sat down. He looked at her intently as he questioned her about what kind of equipment she used to do her job and how often she used it, what storage needs she had, what kind of lighting she needed, what sort of changes she wanted made in her office. Although she appre-ciated his interest, it was clear that it was professional attention that was being paid. After a conclusive handshake in the lobby she drifted back to her office, angry with herself for having thought otherwise.

Not everyone stood up to the moguls. According to David Daniel Kaminsky, Samuel Goldwyn assessed his talents while he stood in front of him. "Now we have to be very careful with this kid, because he's not good-looking, he can't act, and he has no sex appeal." The actor submitted to the Goldwyn touch, dying his hair blond and changing his name to Danny Kaye.

She felt defeated looking at her to-do list, which she never reached the end of. When would she have time to shop for presents for "Season's Greetings," the corporate holiday, which involved her employees, her boss, the plumber and perhaps now Chris and Vladimir. When would she have time to shop for "Chranukah," the secular celebration of the retail aspects of both holidays, which involved her family and friends? And which friends? Her holiday plans this year included several stuffy cocktail parties sandwiched between obligatory family dinners (Uncle Mort would be present) and the annual big nothing of New Year's.

She went to the corner and brought back twenty dollars' worth of fruit. She had forgotten to tell Vladimir about her juicing needs. She set the machine on her desk and squeezed a large glass of grapefruit-orange-and-lime juice, and walked around the block, sipping and thinking. She would have to go to the Sundance Film Festival. A singles cruise was a ridiculous idea, though.

When she returned, there was a message from the broker. Her bid had been accepted.

She stood at her desk, which was littered with spent citrus halves, and felt relief surge through her body. Then a wave of panic hit her. She had bid on a one-room second-floor apartment facing an airshaft! Her lower back began to sizzle with flashes of pain. The bid was accepted—of course it was! Who else would want to live like that? *Dark, small, airshaft!* It was in the East Thirties. There was no subway service over there. The crosstown bus came once an hour! It would be an odyssey getting to work—it would almost be easier to commute from New Jersey! She called her parents in a panic.

"It's called buyer's remorse," her father said. "But you can get out of the deal. You haven't signed anything yet, have you?"

She sat at her desk with her hand over her eyes. "Not yet."

"So call the broker and tell him you had a change of heart. If he gives you a hard time, tell him that you don't have a mortgage letter yet. Be prepared to be yelled at, and be prepared to find a new broker."

Feeling like a naughty ten-year-old, she did as she was told, received a lecture from the broker, hung up exhausted and snuck into the theater to watch *The Goodbye Girl* (Herbert Ross, 1977). She remembered that she and her friend Claire had approached a likely adult in front of the box office on the film's opening day, and each had given her the price of a ticket. (Was it five dollars? Less?) *The Goodbye Girl* was rated PG, and her mother only took them to movies she'd read reviews of. The film was another real-estate-driven New York love story. The apartment in question, Marsha Mason's two-bedroom with high ceilings on the Upper West Side, was opulent by current New York standards.

When the lights came up she got to her feet and looked around and realized the upholstery was ripped on five seats in the row behind her. She felt too scattered to get anything further accomplished that day. She took the subway to Port Authority and lined up with all the married people who took the bus home to New Jersey. She wanted large doses of ibuprofen and a long, long shower.

HER PARENTS were waiting up for her in their bathrobes. The fact that they were still awake at eight-thirty, and that the talk was taking place in the living room and not the kitchen signified that it would be serious.

"Poor darling," her father said, patting the couch next to him for her to sit down. "You must have been so frightened."

"I knew it was a mistake. I just wanted to end the searching."

"Why didn't you at least discuss it with us?" Her mother paced in front of the fireplace. "Sometimes a person can use a sounding board. If you had come to us, we would have told you that you were insane. You wouldn't have made that mistake."

"It wasn't a mistake," her father said. "It was a learning experience."

"It was impulsive, and I don't like her making decisions without thinking."

Diane hung over her toes, stretching out her back. "I just don't like this feeling, that I don't have a place to live."

"You do have a place to live." Her father peered under her hair. "We love you, and we love it that you're around. Stay here indefinitely. You're unbelievably welcome."

She wanted to burst into tears, or fall asleep. She wanted to get out of there. She sat upright. "You're very good to me," she said carefully, squeezing her father's hand. "I love you, too. I need my own place."

"I brought some clothes to the cleaners," her mother said.

"I wish you hadn't."

"No problem! Everything was covered in cat hair. I'd like to take you shopping tomorrow. I was appalled by the state of your wardrobe."

"When have you not been appalled by the state of my wardrobe?"

"Remember your old friend Leslie? I saw her today at the market. I told her you'd call. Her husband works on Wall Street, you know."

By this, Connie meant that Leslie's husband had access to men, appropriate ones, lots of them, some of whom *had* to be single. Diane pleaded exhaustion to end this talk. She took a shower in her old bathroom, noticing in the medicine cabinet a bottle of Herbal Essence shampoo that must have dated from 1978. It could be that, in this house at least, what she did and what she wore and whom she saw—her life, essentially—was rated PG, and could occur only if her mother had read a review and approved of it.

The Goodbye Girl had planted a new thought. In spite of an aversion to shared spaces, Diane turned to the "Roommates Wanted" section of *The Village Voice*. She began squinting at what had to be psychotic cases listed in 6-point type. If she couldn't read the small print, wasn't she too old to have a roommate? This had to be a bad time to start such a project—wasn't everyone busy with holiday parties and such? She snuck down to the kitchen and turned on her mother's computer; she composed a message to her sister in the dark.

"Dear Rachel,

"Connie and Gene are lovable, hospitable and caring. But they seem to think I'm home for life-coaching and dating services. Also, the commute is killing my back. May I impose on you for a brief time while I search for an apartment? My hours are odd enough, and I am out enough, that we may never meet. I am quiet and I will respect your household routine and try not to be any kind of a bother.

"Love,

"Diane."

She wondered what her sister's e-mail habits were like. Could she have an answer by the following day, meaning she should take her stuff to work?

She added:

"P.S. Whenever is convenient for you, but the sooner the better. I feel like I'm in the tenth grade and falling behind in math."

◆

On a frigid and windy Thanksgiving Day, Vladimir took the bus from Port Authority to Union City, New Jersey, for an early dinner at Bebo's. Vladimir had met Bebo in their first year in the architecture program at the University of Havana. Bebo wasn't Vladimir's only Cuban friend in the Tri-State Area, but he was the only one from that period that Vladimir was still speaking to. Bebo and Olga had two feral girls about a year apart, who spoke baby English and baby Spanish and vied for Vladimir's attention every other Friday night.

"Look how he still wears his hair," Bebo's father greeted him, grabbing his ponytail. Manuel was a pain in the ass, but he came by it honestly: he'd spent nineteen years in a Cuban prison for the crime of "Ideological Diversionism," for refusing to participate in the sugarcane harvest of 1970. He'd also been caught with forbidden books, among them *Animal Farm*.

"Come meet Olga's friend Carmen," Manuel said, and made an obscene gesture indicating an appreciation of Carmen's attractions.

Vladimir had no time to get annoyed, as the little girls threw themselves upon him and began to pull his hair while Carmen was presented. Carmen was plump and vivacious, no doubt available, wearing a short leather skirt. He was suddenly tired. He sat down on the couch, landing on a sharp plastic doll as the little girls kissed him savagely. Since the advent of these kids, it wasn't possible to see Bebo without them.

Carmen had just come back from Havana with news, letters and gifts. "When I got to my mother's," she said, telling her story directly to Vladimir as they moved to the kitchen and sat down, "I walked up the stairs. I greeted her, and we weren't in her kitchen for a minute—we hadn't even properly said hello—when there was a knock on the door: *toc, toc, TOC!*"

She looked at him, waiting for a reaction.

"It was the neighbor," she went on, grabbing his hand to squeeze it, as if terrified. Why was she touching him? He pulled his hand away. "She pushes her way into the house, points to me, and says to my mom, 'She can't stay here. You're only allowed to have two foreigners a year in your home. I'm going to report you.' " She looked up at him again. Olga must have told her about his situation. What did this woman want from him?

"Down, now," Bebo said, kindly and firmly, to the first daughter, who was standing on her chair. The child sent dishes and silverware clattering to the floor, but Bebo waited until she was seated before he picked them up. Everything with Bebo was relentlessly domestic; he seemed to go out of his way to emphasize what a good father he was.

Diane Kurasik was attractive, if poorly proportioned, and clearly she was interested. What was he going to do about her, now that they had won the bid? He wanted to talk to Bebo about it, but it was unlikely there would be an appropriate moment for a private chat amid all this family chaos.

"The Committee for the Defense of the Revolution has been watching her because my cousins stayed with her for two weeks last summer. So this bitch said I couldn't stay in my own mother's house. I'm a foreigner now."

"Where did you stay?" Olga asked, as she quieted the older daughter, who was bouncing around the kitchen.

"With my cousin, Jorge."

"How's Cousin Jorge?" Bebo asked, as the other daughter shrieked.

"He's something else," Carmen said, and pulled the sobbing child onto her lap, no doubt to show how competent she was in the child business. As if he cared. "All he talks about, he and his friends, is getting money, getting ahead."

The child struggled and escaped from Carmen's grasp. Vladimir smiled.

"You know, our generation, at least we believed in something," Bebo said, feeding the younger daughter. "In love, in friendship. In good design!"

"Good design," Vladimir said, trying to remember a time when it was all he cared about. He and Bebo rarely spoke about work; it raised awkward issues. Bebo was still making models. His career hadn't really taken off because of his English. Vladimir had stopped using Bebo because he often changed the design of a model when he thought he had a better idea.

"Coming next week?" Manuel asked. "We have an event in front of the Mission."

At the last protest he'd attended, the exiles marched in a circle chanting "¡Castro: traidor! ¡Asesino y dictador!" while the staff in the Cuban Mission office blasted the greatest hits of Van Van out the windows to drown out the protests. They also threw water on the protesters, which was why the City had moved all the protests across the street. Manuel and his friends, none of whom had done less than twelve years in prison, often planned events of this type. Vladimir didn't want to be rude, but the movement needed new blood and a different format.

"I want to do a silent protest," Vladimir said. "Think how effective it would be: gags and silence."

"How could there be a silent protest with Cubans involved?" Bebo asked, as his father roared, "We should be silent?" and the children screamed about dessert portions and Olga chatted with her friend about something else.

"Everyone is shouting, and nobody is listening. Nobody is hearing us."

Bebo and Manuel shrugged and Olga and Carmen continued their separate conversation. Nobody had a response. The chaos of the ravaged table gave Vladimir a headache, and it was getting late. He offered to take Carmen home, to be polite.

"She's staying here," Olga said.

"Unless you want to make her a better offer," Manuel said, and shadowboxed him in the groin. Carmen smiled up at him.

"Come on, then," he said without enthusiasm.

"Really?" she said, and gathered all her stuff into a heavy bag that he was soon carrying down four unlit flights of rickety stairs.

He had once tried to reciprocate all the dinners, and the shock— of the white neighborhood, the clean, white apartment, all the space he had to himself—had hit them in a bad way. This was when he'd been dating his neighbor Terry, a caterer who had a theory that what people really wanted was one perfect bite of a tiny, sculpted, labor-intensive still life. Bebo and Manuel had immediately inhaled the small plateful of beautiful, bite-sized hors d'oeuvres that had taken her all day to prepare. She had looked at them in shock. They had looked back at her with incomprehension. Three courses of small, elegant food with textures and layers and fresh herbs followed, and conversation ebbed: Bebo and Manuel really didn't have much to say in English, Terry didn't speak a word of Spanish and Olga was pregnant and still hungry. The whole thing worked only when Vladimir went to Union City.

Carmen chatted nonstop through the rain to the bus stop, on the bus and in the subway. She'd left Cuba in her early twenties, and had been living in Miami for six years, working most recently as a receptionist in a carpet showroom owned by an uncle's friend. She wasn't married and her mother was worried; she told him this while rubbing her bare legs to get warm. Why did anyone put up with the cold? She was eligible for citizenship, but hadn't done anything about it.

"Why not?" he asked, interrupting a story about her first experience of snow.

"I don't know," Carmen said, twisting the Virgin of Charity that hung from a chain into her cleavage. "I suppose I was hoping to keep my options open."

He had no patience for this kind of person. At one time, he would have given her a lecture about how lucky she was to have the opportunity and what an idiot she was to think a door to a Third World dictatorship was worth keeping open. There'd been a time when he thought he had to fight on all fronts. Now he just let it pass.

Her eyes widened when he led her into his apartment building. He made up the couch for her with pillows and blankets he kept in the coffee table, which he'd designed for this purpose. She went to the window. Before she reached his drafting table he said, "Don't touch that. Do not go anywhere near that."

"I just wanted to see."

"You wanted a place to sleep," he said. "Here it is."

She raised an eyebrow. He gave her a towel and a glass of water and closed his bedroom door. He wasn't inviting her into bed out of chivalry. No doubt Olga had explained his situation, reassuring her that he hadn't dated a Cubana since leaving the island. Manuel had no doubt joked about Vladimir's member, which only spoke English now.

The following morning, he hustled her out of the house at nine on the pretext that traffic would be terrible; if she wanted to get to LaGuardia for her flight at two she had to leave immediately. He hailed a cab and gave her the fare to LaGuardia, for surely she wouldn't get there any other way and he didn't want her turning up on his doorstep after missing her plane. She kissed his cheek with an offended little pout.

"DEAR VLADIMIR," began the new missile of rhetoric from Migdalia.

"Superfluous communication has never interested me. If you end our friendship, that's your problem."

The letter seemed to be sending sharp vibrations to his head and chest. Vladimir clicked the document off the screen and sent it to the trash.

It was the Monday after Thanksgiving, unseasonably warm, in the high 60s. Nonetheless, he had arrived to find that Chris had put Christmas lights on the shelves, without asking him. He wondered if he should sound Chris out about the Diane situation, but decided that the taboo on romance with a client was a preposterous, hypocritical American custom that no one observed and that didn't apply to him. They were both adults, and there was nothing preventing him from getting involved with her. Except, of course, the fact that he was married.

Assuming that he wanted to get involved. Vladimir peeled the lid off his coffee and searched for distraction on the Internet. More Cuban rafters had been picked up three miles off Miami by the United States Coast Guard. Several in the group had been lost in the waves; those who survived would be sent back, which meant either prison or retaliation—loss of a job, children denied access to school, pariah status, angry mobs besieging the house in acts of orchestrated harassment while the police sat by and watched.

On second thought, he pulled Migdalia's message out of the trash.

"Hatred has eaten away your entrails, causing an imperiousness that you don't recognize in yourself," Migdalia continued, and he looked around him, embarrassed. "The only thing that interests you is your odious little individualistic life."

"Hah!" he said out loud.

"So why do you bother to write?" she continued.

A good question. And why was he reading this bile?

"Who has brainwashed you with this propaganda? You think you are the one who opens my eyes? Incredible, the power that you attribute to yourself. When your fellow exiles in the Cuban American Mafia invade the island, where will you be? I ask out of curiosity only.

"Formerly your friend,

"Migdalia."

He wanted to slam her head into a concrete wall. *The Cuban American Mafia?* But anyone who wasn't specifically *in* the Revolution, according to the Supreme Leader in his speech of June 30, 1961, was *outside* the Revolution. And anyone who was outside the Revolution was allied with the Extreme Right Wing.

Chris entered singing, bearing a small tree on his shoulder. He set it down on the windowsill.

"You're blocking my view," Vladimir said.

"Where would you like the tree?" Chris asked.

"I don't know, but not there."

Magnus entered and removed his massive hip-hop parka to reveal a T-shirt advertising the now ubiquitous image of Che Guevara in the revolutionary beret.

Vladimir growled at him.

Magnus looked up. "What's the matter?"

"Would you walk around with an image of Hitler on your chest?"

"Good morning to you, too, Vladimir."

"You people. You see one movie, and you're blinded by love."

"You say terrorist, I say freedom fighter."

"Yes, but do you *know* anything? You're simply trafficking in a symbol that you received from somebody else. Somebody else who knows nothing."

"What the hell is he talking about?" Magnus asked Chris.

"Che Guevara threw homosexuals into concentration camps. Che Guevara gave the bullet to the heads of hundreds of people who weren't given fair trials, or any trials at all."

Magnus, a white kid from suburban Maryland, went into the pantry.

"Che Guevara shot people on his office in the way that you make coffee on your office," Vladimir called after him.

Magnus emerged with coffee and sat down at the model table with an arrogant flourish. "*In* my office, Vladimir. *In,* not *on.*"

"In *my* office, Magnus. *Mine,* not *yours.* I have a website for you. Find out what he really stood for, and then if you're still impressed by him, go ahead. Wear the shirt."

"It's just fashion."

You had to hand it to Fidel Castro: everyone still called it "the Revolution," that thing that hadn't moved in almost fifty years. And what a skilled politician he was! He had the island mesmerized watching the one hand, while with the other hand he exiled, jailed or executed anyone who disagreed with him, including his brothers-in-arms, the Heroes of the Revolution. He had his rivals murdered to turn them into controllable martyrs at home, and fashion statements abroad. Fidel Castro had made repression *cool*.

Chris had begun wrestling with a nest of electrical cords, to the accompaniment of loud choral music. Vladimir asked him to turn the volume down. He'd found out that Diane Kurasik was Jewish, as several of his American girlfriends had been. Jews were supposed to be such a minority in this country, so it was noteworthy that they kept turning up. American Jews never gave him a hard time about Cuba; if he told them that it was a police state, they didn't talk to him about free education and health care, or ask if he preferred Batista.

Diane and her light blue eyes with the dark blue edges were on his mind as he sat down and began to draw the lobby of the cinema on a roll of vellum. He had said he would call her, and he'd meant to, but he wasn't sure he was in the mood to go through all the preliminaries. Chris untangled strings of lights while brewing something aromatic in the pantry. Later, he began to attach ribbons and shiny balls to the tree.

Christianity seemed to be a collective decorative agreement in this country. One day, his first year in New York, Vladimir walked out of his apartment building and saw a woman with a dark check mark on her forehead. He debated telling her, but she'd crossed the street by the time he decided he would. On the next block, someone else passed by with a dark line on his forehead. In the subway, he saw three people smudged with x's. Were they marked for execution? No one was acting like anything was out of the ordinary! He was chilled. When he got to the office, he saw that the receptionist had the mark. He hesitated, and then walked down the hall with a dry mouth. But he had to turn around.

"Ah, Millie?" he said, pointing to her forehead.

"Ash Wednesday," she said, answering phones.

Of course! *Miércoles de Ceniza*.

Finally, at eight, he composed a brief message and sent it off.

"Dear Migdalia," he wrote. "Please reread the list of personal insults that you directed at me in your e-mail, and then tell me who is eaten up by worms of hatred.

"Farewell, Vladimir."

He sent the collected letters between Migdalia Rosario and himself to Bebo. On second thought, he decided to forward the exchange to a long list of people, Cuban and otherwise, with a note:

"Dear Friends, The debate that I am sending you requires no commentary. It is priceless. Please do not re-send this e-mail. It is for your consumption only. Best, Vladimir." He thought about including Diane, but decided that if she were a Spanish-speaker, he would know about it already. Americans who spoke Spanish were always so proud of themselves, they let you know right away.

AROUND THE CORNER from the theater, in a tiny basement apartment in a brick tenement, a male accountant at the tail end of middle age sat in front of two behemoths, sifting through a nasty, one-sided correspondence going back nearly forty years. The two enormous metal silos were telephone-switching equipment dating back to the early 1930s, and they lounged in the middle of his living room.

Ma Bell begat New York Telephone begat NYNEX; Bell Atlantic and NYNEX merged, acquired GTE, and begat Verizon; and Sid Bernstein, the resident, had been fighting with disrespectful representatives of these faceless corporations since he'd moved into this hole, early in the Nixon administration. He'd taken the apartment on the condition that the phone company remove the equipment. They've been slated to go for a long time now, the super had told him.

That was seven supers ago. He had protested: on the phone, by mail, in person, with a lawyer, with another lawyer, representing himself again, then with a slick class-action specialist who strung him along for a while but dropped him when he realized that there was no "class" for an action suit. Each time, he started from square one with a new company after a takeover; each time he went through the motions, being shifted and transferred and cut off. Each time he was told that someone new would look into it. Granted, his rent was quite low, currently $250 a month. And yes, it was the West Village, and his local phone service had been gratis for many years.

Never mind: Sid Bernstein had been sold a bill of goods by that first super. He'd been suffering ever since. He had headaches. He had nightmares. He would never have moved in had he known the silos weren't leaving. The space they took up, the evil lint and dirt they collected weren't enough: they vibrated and hummed, sometimes in the same key, sometimes not. Loose paper in the apartment ended up plastered to their rounded drum walls. Periodically, someone came to service the evil twins and he had to allow access to his apartment—always when he was at work, so that he couldn't talk to the serviceman. On more than one occasion, he'd taken the day off to be there to interrogate the serviceman, only to be told by a rude dispatcher when he called late in the day that the serviceman wouldn't make it. Some nights, only the idea that he might unleash something that could harm him—bacteria, electric shock, nesting rodents—stopped him from taking an axe to mutilate these filthy, throbbing metal monsters.

In nearly forty years, nobody had been willing to take responsibility.

The only solace in his life was the Bedford Street Cinema. It sat between his apartment and the office where he'd worked for more years than he cared to count.

He snared Diane Kurasik in the lobby. "You didn't respond to my memo."

"I'm sorry, Sid. I was waiting to put the suggestion before the Board at the next meeting. I'll get back to you when they've had a chance to consider it."

"How is an audience representative on the Board something that requires approval by the Board? This is taxation without representation."

"The Bedford Street Cinema is not a democracy."

"Tell me about it! How could you leave *Heaven Can Wait* out of the Lubitsch retrospective? That was a slap in the face!"

"Sid. The Board of Directors doesn't make decisions about pro-gramming."

"Does the Board make decisions about the theater?"

"Yes."

"Then I want to be on the Board. I've seen ninety-eight percent of the movies that have played at this theater over the last ten years. I have the ticket stubs to prove it. Can anyone else on the Board say that?" Some Board members attended only the annual fund-raiser. Some missed even that. So they were connected: big deal. It reeked of cronyism, kickbacks, patronage.

"Sid, don't beat me up today. I've had a bad week. I've had a bad month."

"I've had a bad life, Diane," Sid said, and stalked outside to smoke.

DECEMBER

THERE WERE SEVERAL responses to his group e-mail. "Dear Vladimir, I began reading, and had to stop after the first line. I was so nauseated I wanted to throw up," wrote one friend. "How sad this exchange!" wrote another. "Will the verbal carnage never end?" None of the non-Cubans responded. All were Spanish-speakers; but perhaps only a Cuban could be interested in this sort of thing.

He heard two sharp notes signaling a new e-mail: a letter that appeared to be from someone in the Cuban Ministry of Education named Elena Gutiérrez Pérez. He skipped down to the end—it was signed "Yasmina." He remembered Yasmina, Migdalia's friend and partner in crime in high school; her mother indeed had worked in the Ministry of Education. Elena Gutiérrez Pérez must have been Yasmina's mother.

"Dear Vladimir," Yasmina wrote.

"I have just finished reading your letter to Migdalia, and it seems to me that all you talk about is politics and cheap criticism. Where is the Vladimir that I used to know? May I ask, don't you feel any nostalgia for Havana? The streets, the happiness you shared with friends on the rooftops and the Malecón? It gives me much pain, Vladimir, that you are empty and spout pure Hollywood drivel. It would be impossible to hate you, because I have always treasured peace and happiness among my friends. I am not perfect, but I believe in the betterment of humankind. Only those who earn my respect can criticize my homeland. That word may sound foreign to you because you are among those who BUY respect.

"Until the victory forever, Yasmina."

He wanted to strike someone! She believed in the betterment of humankind! He stalked to the window. They would drown him in their rhetoric.

Enough of this! The sun was shining on the thick blue scales of the Hudson River. He needed a light American lunch with a new woman, preferably one who didn't speak Spanish. He called Diane Kurasik.

"Certainly," she said. "When would you like?"

"Now," he said, looking at the clock. It was ten forty-five.

"Okay!" she said, laughing. "Pick me up!"

He was immediately out the door in brisk December sunshine. There was nothing so clarifying as this freezing-cold air and the sharp blue sky. In a burst of energy, he decided to walk to the theater. He started walking downtown on Tenth Avenue. The streets were a maze of small, dirty walls of packed snow, topped with bags of garbage. He picked his way over the terrain carefully; loose trash and dog turds were scattered across banks of snow and the slush at the curbs had refrozen. As much as he loved the autumn in this part of the world, the winter took discipline, energy, strength to bear. As he caught sight of the marquee, he had a comfortable, familiar feeling. He was enjoying this project.

"FORGIVE MY DISTRACTION LATELY," Vladimir said to Diane as they sat down at a window table in a café around the corner from the theater. "I've been getting hate mail from Cuba."

"Really?" She was wearing her hair tied back today. "Is it polit-ical?"

"Everything is political with Cubans. Just the fact that I'm not there is political. The Cuban music I listen to is political, even if there are no lyrics."

Diane sat with her elbows on the table, chin resting on her hands. "Why?"

"It was made by musicians who aren't living on the island. You're either with the Revolution a hundred and ten percent, or you're an agent of the CIA."

They ordered lunch.

She looked up at him directly. "So why have I seen so little of you?" she asked.

He sighed.

"I'm sorry, was that too forward? Forgive me, sometimes I get impatient, and things just fly out of my mouth."

"No, I appreciate your honesty."

"I can't pretend not to be interested," she said.

"Thank you," he said, and looked at the sunlight slanting through the window onto the floor. The waiter brought juice to the table. "I'm glad you're interested. I'm interested."

"You haven't been acting interested."

Here it was, again. "It's not the way I like to begin, but I can't get around it. I'm married."

"Oh?" she said, both eyebrows raised.

"To a Cuban."

"I see."

"Who lives in Cuba."

She nodded.

"My wife will not grant me a divorce."

"Why not?"

"No reason."

"I see."

"Out of spite, perhaps."

She looked out the window. Had she lost interest now?

"Or for political reasons," he said, sipping juice.

She looked back at him. "Do you see her?"

"Not in years."

"She—your wife, what is her name?"

"María."

"María hasn't found anyone else?"

"She found my parents. They took her side! She lives with them. They're another story."

She laughed. "And what's *that* story?"

"You wouldn't believe it."

The lunch arrived.

"Try me."

"My parents divorced two years ago. But they live together," he said, digging into his omelet.

"Why?"

"He likes her cooking."

"And she likes cooking for him?"

"Him and his girlfriend."

Her mouth opened; she blinked and shook her head rapidly.

Which was worse: talking about his parents or talking about María?

"How bizarre." She was still looking at him directly; he considered this a good sign.

"It's very hard to find a place, and illegal to move."

"It's illegal to move?"

"Yes, but she could find a place. The ration card doesn't matter."

"Wait. They're on ration cards?"

This was news to most Americans. "Everyone is. And there isn't enough on the ration cards to live, to function. You need to supplement. Which they do, because I send them money. Well, I send money to my wife. But she's on the same household card."

"It sounds crowded."

"My sister and her husband and child also live with them. But it's a big house."

"Your mom couldn't get her own place to live?"

"She did, but somebody liked the idea of her apartment, and denounced her to the police. So they took her apartment away."

"What?"

"It's a long story. Still, my father has the frying pan by the handle." She squinted. "I mean, with a single phone call, he could have found her a place. I haven't spoken to him in five years. Since I moved here."

She considered this, browsing in her salad. "You know, Vladimir, I suspected that you were *interesting*. But I had no idea!" She laughed.

"So it's not that I don't want to get involved. I *am* involved."

She blinked rapidly. "You haven't seen your wife in how long?"

"Twelve years. All this time, we've been yelling at each other over the phone. It's not a good situation. And yet, there it is."

"So you must see other people here. Women."

"Yes. But there comes a time when even a woman who thinks she's not looking for something serious realizes that she can't stay on the situation. It's not natural."

"I'll tell you what's not natural. That a man like you—talented, successful, intelligent—can't talk some sense into this woman."

"That's flattering. You underestimate the power of spite."

"Twelve years?"

"All she has is this marriage."

"But she doesn't have it!"

"Exactly right. All she has is the bitterness. That's all my parents have. But it drives them, the hatred."

"It's perverse."

"Welcome to Cuba."

They ate for a few minutes. It was hard to tell how the facts had affected her.

"I'm sorry to hear all this." She stared at him with her blue, blue eyes. He hoped she was one of the complication junkies.

◆

THEY HAD ARRIVED before the lunch rush and had lingered afterwards, drinking tea and more tea. Vladimir wore an air of fatigued, melancholic superiority throughout, like Dirk Bogarde in *Darling*

(John Schlesinger, 1965). After his preliminary confession, as if by agreement, the conversation stayed in the present, avoiding personal topics. Diane told him about her real estate odyssey. Apparently Chris Wiley's romantic partner was a real estate broker; Vladimir said he would get his number for her. Vladimir followed her back to the cinema like a puppy, walking very close and looking at her a lot—a sudden, welcome turnaround that she needed time to process. Still: he was married.

The Bedford Street Cinema was playing *A Touch of Class* (Melvin Frank, 1972) as part of its "Manners in the Movies" series. When they hit the lobby, Vladimir went to look at the Cinema II space and Diane went into her office. She tripped over a suitcase: she'd forgotten that Rachel was expecting her. She should probably pick up some kind of house gift as a gesture: she would be staying open-endedly in the maid's room. Diane had thought she'd finished with her gift shopping (red scarves for everyone). But Chranukah wasn't for two weeks yet, and Rachel lived on Park Avenue. Did the doormen let you in without a gift?

She sat down at her desk to think.

Married. Granted, it wasn't good news. On the other hand, were there any men left at this age who didn't have baggage, often in two countries? Did it really matter, in the long run? Perhaps it mattered *only* in the long run.

Vladimir walked into her office as she was getting off the phone with a distributor. He stood in front of her desk. There was something in the air. She remembered the scene in *A Touch of Class* when George Segal comes to Glenda Jackson's office in a chaotic fashion showroom:

"Buying or selling?" her assistant asks him.

"Begging," he says.

Vladimir put his bag on her visitor's chair and watched her.

"How would you like to see a movie?" Diane asked.

"How would you like to see my apartment?"

She laughed long and hard at this one. "You know, it's three o'clock."

Vladimir took her hand to lead her away from the desk. "Yes."

"It's three o'clock and it's Tuesday."

They sat down on the sofa. "Let me look at you," he said. Vladimir Hurtado Padrón, of the dark eyes and the curly lashes and the heavy black eyebrows, gazed at her and began touching her face, her neck, her hair.

She wasn't expecting anyone, but her door was open. There was also the window from her office to the projection booth to consider, although Floyd wouldn't need to change the reels for another twenty minutes. In the meantime, here was Vladimir, alive and interested, impossibly and previously attached, running his hands through her hair.

She went to shut the door and he followed her. They stood at the door. Akira Kurosawa once said that sound and picture act as mutual multipliers. The combination of the sound of Vladimir's breathing on her neck and the sight of Vladimir's longing was multiplying her own longing, tremendously.

"Come home with me."

This could be just an average Tuesday afternoon for an attractive man like him. It could be that it was December—some people become needier around the holidays.

"I need a moment to think about this, Vladimir!"

"Oh."

"You duck phone calls and cancel dates and reschedule and then cancel again and get me all confused, and now suddenly you're here, and you're ready, with an absolutely *unbelievable* story, and I just need a minute to process it. Would that be okay?"

"Yes, okay," he said, sounding fatigued.

"Don't be depressed. Why don't you watch the movie?"

"No, I should get back to the studio. When will I see you?"

"Tomorrow night?"

She walked him out; as if by agreement, the space between them grew as they reached the lobby, and Vladimir waved as if he had just dropped by to look at the space.

Diane slipped into the theater just as the bored and married American George Segal brings the frustrated and divorced Brit Glenda Jackson to a London hotel room after a preliminary lunch.

"Look, I'm all for some good, healthy, uninvolved sex," she says, "but not in this overworked little joint where the sheets haven't been changed in three weeks and I have to be back at the office in— Christ, half an hour ago. But if you'd like to arrange a lovely week-*end,* somewhere where the sun is shining, by all means, *do.*"

Glenda Jackson was the Star of the Month because her oeuvre had particularly explored the darkness lurking beneath social niceties, and no one else had so perfectly embodied harassed intelligence. Manners were an issue every day at the Bedford Street Cinema: Diane found herself throwing out at least three customers a day for breaking the social contract—by talking; using cellphones, laptops, or video games; preparing food; changing diapers; or fornicating during screenings.

It was impossible to watch movies in theaters where she didn't have control. She'd seen her last first-run film at the Lincoln Plaza Cinemas, seated in front of a pair of pretentious yentas in late middle age parroting the *New York Times* review of what they were about to see, even as the film began to roll. Diane shushed them repeatedly.

"She is so *rude,*" said one of these women, loud.

"*I'm* rude? You're the ones behaving like you're in your own living room!"

"Pipe down, kids," said someone else.

"Well, you're just a bitch, then."

"Yes, I *AM* a bitch! I'm a bitch . . . *at the movies!*"

This got a laugh or two, and the women subsided for a moment. "Do you have a Kleenex?" said one to the other, as if they were on a bus. "I've been getting a cold."

"No, but I think I have a cough drop—where did I put it?"

At this point, Diane shone her flashlight into their eyes. There were sounds of shock and disbelief, and the ladies scurried out. A moment later, an usher with a flashlight of his own came and summoned her. There was a ruckus in front of the concession stand; the manager offered a refund, but insisted all three of them leave.

"I was doing what *you* should have been doing," Diane said. The movie was a Spanish costume drama at a so-called art house, not an action movie at the mall.

But this was surely last year's story of bad manners. In the meantime, she had better things on her mind, matters of courtship and excitement.

Vladimir had been standing right in front of her, touching her, ready to take her home. Why had she sent him away?

Even though Vladimir had promised to make the connection with Chris Wiley's partner, she called Chris directly and brought up the subject. Chris handed the phone to Paul, who was apparently sitting right there.

"Paul, I hear from Vladimir that you're a patient man."

"Vladimir said that? About me?" There was laughter on the other end.

"Maybe he didn't. Perhaps I just assumed it, because to do what you do in this market, I think you'd have to have the patience of a saint."

"I gather you've had a tough time of it. Would you like to stop by my office this week? When are you looking to move?"

"How does tomorrow sound?"

"My kind of client!" he said, and they fixed a date. "Vladimir is here, Diane. Would you like to talk to him?"

She felt flushed and dehydrated. "Sure." Had Vladimir talked to Paul and Chris about her? Was he that familiar with them? Or did he chat about his personal life mindlessly, like her sister?

A moment later he was on the phone. "Hi," he said quietly, and she heard rowdy laughter in the background. "Are we on?"

"Most definitely."

Vladimir hung up the phone in an optimistic mood. It was irritating to return to the conversation he'd just been having.

"We have a beautiful coffee-table book about Cuba," Paul had been saying. "All the fabulous pastel shades, and those great cars from the fifties. It's like a fantasy."

"It isn't *like* a fantasy, it *IS* a fantasy."

"But my friend Carl said it really does look like that. Everything in sepia tones, and old black guys in white linen suits carrying double basses through the streets. He just loved it. He collects fifties cars."

"Cubans drive cars from the fifties because apart from the Russian and Polish cars from the eighties, there are no other cars to drive. And you need a permit to have one."

"Like here."

"Does the U.S. government tell you if you have the right to own a car?"

"The Cuban government decides that?"

"Yes," Vladimir said, annoyed. Nobody listened.

He saw Paul processing the information. "Is that possible?" Paul asked.

"It's been possible for almost five decades."

"Well, Batista was terrible for the country, for the people, wasn't he?"

"Of course he was."

"You're not saying that Fidel is worse than Batista, are you?"

"These are the choices? Kleptocracy or dictatorship? Which would you like to live under?"

"We have a lot to answer for with the embargo," Magnus said piously.

"The embargo is the best friend Fidel Castro ever had!"

Magnus sat with his mouth open, as Paul asked, "Wait, you're saying that the embargo *helps* Fidel?"

"When anything goes wrong, Fidel Castro blames the embargo. There is nothing more bonding than a common enemy. If the U.S. ended the embargo, Fidel Castro would have no one to blame. He would fall flat on his ass."

"But when Fidel came to New York," Magnus said, as if it were relevant, "he didn't stay at the Waldorf-Astoria, he stayed in Harlem, right?"

"That's right," Paul said. "He stayed in Harlem, and he brought his own chickens with him."

Magnus nodded, eyes shining. "He took on *the Man,* didn't he?"

"Magnus, Magnus, white boy from the suburbs. You don't get it: Fidel Castro IS *the Man*. He *the MAN!*"

"Vladimir," Chris warned.

"So you're seeing this Diane person again?" Paul asked.

This was irrelevant, and typical of Paul. "I'll take the Fifth."

"Chris! He's taking the Fifth!" Paul roared with laughter.

Magnus was wearing baggy jeans and a T-shirt that hit his knees.

"So, Magnus, I see you're a rap star today. No more Revolución?"

Magnus cast a meaningful look at Chris, who sang, "Now, Vladimir, we must treat each other with respect."

Magnus whispered something to Paul, who looked amused.

"How am I not respectful?"

"Where I come from," Chris said, "everybody's *very nice*. They'll savage you the moment you leave the room, but they are *sweetness itself* when you show up. It's a good idea."

Vladimir had seen Chris upset when he walked into a store and wasn't greeted properly. "I'd rather they be rude to my face."

"No, you wouldn't," Chris said.

"I don't see why a T-shirt should cause unpleasantness," Magnus said.

"Then don't wear aggressive political statements. But if you do, be prepared to take responsibility for them."

Chris cast a baffled smile his way. No doubt there would be another lecture about American Business Practices, and he would be taken to task for his tardiness, again. Vladimir went to his computer, tuned them out, pulled up the latest nasty letter from Cuba and wrote rapidly without thinking.

"Dear Yasmina,

"It is unfortunate that Migdalia, violating a basic rule of formal education—that one does not share private correspondence—has dragged you into this sterile controversy. It is also unfortunate that in order to respond to a letter that was not sent to you, you are using your mother's e-mail address. As I prefer not to compromise your mother with this ridiculous dialogue, I will not prolong the ideological debate. It is absurd that you think that in order to love my friends who reside in Cuba I need to support the ruling dictatorship on the island. If one day you understand that I am not your enemy, that you have gratuitously insulted me, and that we can agree to disagree, perhaps you will be able to mend what you have so efficiently broken.

"Until that day comes, Vladimir."

He sent the letter off, to be read first by the censors in the Ministry of Education, then by Yasmina's mother, Yasmina's mother's friends and colleagues, then by Yasmina, Migdalia and every other defender of the bloody, pigheaded Revolution.

"Dear friends," he wrote, forwarding Yasmina's letter and his response in a new group e-mail to friends, Cuban and otherwise.

"Although I am aware that one does not share private correspondence, I couldn't stop myself from passing on this exchange. Please do not share it. Best, Vladimir." He sent this message off to his Spanish-speakers.

Now, to business: Diane smelled like citrus and was only an inch or so shorter than he was; she seemed a practical woman, but she had understandably been taken aback by his confession. Would she still be interested after she had "processed" the story?

What now? He had no idea what to do for the twenty-eight hours until he saw her again. He called Bebo. No one in the office spoke Spanish, but he went out in the hall for privacy. He described the situation.

"What if she's not interested?" he asked Bebo.

"They're all interested, Vladimir. You are just too interesting."

"I can't do this anymore. I think she's older than I am."

"Meaning?"

"I don't know, meaning more serious? She seems very reasonable."

"Well, that's good, isn't it?"

"What do I do? I'm completely distracted. I can't work," he said, although he hadn't actually tried. He thought of other women he knew, Ellen, most recently. She was ready to throw herself at him; he probably didn't have to give her a moment's notice. It depressed him, although it was flattering.

"So come help me: my car was towed."

"I don't want to help you pick up your car."

"So go with Olga and Martica to the pediatrician."

"I don't want to be involved with sick children."

"So go to the movies, then."

That wasn't such a bad idea.

DENNIS WAS OUT OF TOWN. There was Italian takeout for dinner, and Rachel's kids started off the meal demanding to see a new action movie that night.

"Everyone has seen it, Mom," said Jason, nine, who had his mother's thick, straight, dark red hair and freckles, and lived mainly inside video games.

Rachel was opening mail as she ate. "Oh yes?"

"We have been telling you *for three days now,*" said Cheryl, eleven, who had Dennis's dark blond hair and green eyes. She routinely pranced around like a sleazy pop star dry-humping for the MTV cameras.

"We'll talk about it after dinner."

"If you don't get those tickets over the phone *right now,* I won't eat!" Cheryl announced.

"Go to your room," Rachel said, and Cheryl flounced off.

"She's right, Mom," Jason said, looking up from his device. "The tickets are selling really fast."

"You, too. Go to your room."

He took his device with him. Their rooms hardly seemed like punishment.

"They're so spoiled; I don't understand it," Rachel said, writing something in her crowded date book and eating pasta with a bored expression.

Cheryl emerged dramatically to slam the hall door closed. Rachel let out a low chuckle and went to the phone to order tickets.

You rarely heard anymore about American children of privilege being subjugated to austere, punitive regimens on principle, like Rose Kennedy freezing her ass off in a French convent, or Christina

Crawford's bizarre, inexplicable incarceration for not writing thank-you notes soon enough, or the Lardner boys being chased out of doors in all kinds of weather by a Prussian governess, and sleeping on a screened porch year-round, including when it snowed.

"How is Dennis?" Diane asked.

"A bit cranky since the vasectomy."

"What vasectomy?"

"He had a vasectomy," she said impatiently, as if Diane should have known this. "About a month ago. Finally. I've been begging him for years."

"Why are you telling me this? How can I eat dinner with the man?"

"Oh, relax. It won't come up in conversation unless you bring it up."

"That's hardly the point. Would he want you talking about it with everyone?"

"You are hardly everyone."

"Well, thank you, but if you're telling me, your eight best friends already know."

"So what? When you get married—and you will—you'll understand."

Diane felt hot. What a patronizing (matronizing?) thing to say.

"What does that mean, 'and you will'? Says who? Where is it written?"

Rachel looked at Diane as if she might tell her to go to her room.

Diane had better be grateful. The forty-five-ish layout designer she'd met the previous day in the Flatiron District two-bedroom spoke very slowly, as if she were medicated, or underwater. Although Diane liked the location and the apartment, it was close quarters with a stranger—*Single White Female* (Barbet Schroeder, 1992) was a hard film to forget.

To see Rachel as Diane remembered her, at the age of sixteen—lounging on her bed on an average Friday night with a head full of hot rollers, drinking Tab, chewing gum, scarfing down cupcakes or

French fries, or both; watching *Wheel of Fortune* and listening to the dance station while simultaneously doing her homework, painting her toenails, tweezing her eyebrows and calling up all four of her best friends to gossip about Bruno, Massimo or Ioiahnn—was to understand that Rachel had an appetite for trash, trash in Sensur-round, trash in every orifice. To see her at the age of thirty-seven in a robe and curlers at nine a.m. getting ready for a committee meet-ing was like being in a time warp.

"Keep me company while I put on my face," she commanded, and Diane sat down on the carpet in her sister's boudoir as she put on makeup, blew on nail polish and fielded phone calls with the tel-evision and the radio on. Marcelina vacuumed in another room. *The New York Post* lay on the dressing table amid sticky lip-gloss wands, eyelash curlers, plastic toys, gum wrappers, candy canes, used cups and glasses, snapshots, magazine clippings and Q-tips. The doorbell rang, and Diane began to get up; Rachel signaled that she should sit. Rachel hung up the phone. It rang again immediately.

Diane had slept on a very uncomfortable foldout couch in the maid's room. She would get juice on the way to work, and of course arrange to be out every night. That day's lineup at the cin-ema included the wartime housing-shortage farce *The More the Mer-rier* (George Stevens, 1943); reminding Diane of her meeting with another potential roommate at ten-thirty. Rachel hung up, raised the volume on the TV and began stroking mascara on her eyelashes in front of a magnifying mirror.

"I'll be coming home late, so I'll need a key."

"I'll have to think about that," Rachel said, painting eyeliner on her lid.

"Do you really want me ringing the doorbell after midnight?"

Rachel opened up a drawer and pulled out a key. She held it up, looking at Diane in the mirror.

Diane took the key. "I'll be very quiet. As soon as I get a place, I'll move out and give it back."

Lara Freed walked into the room carrying a smooth caramel leather case. "Shake a leg, Rachel. Hey," she said, catching sight of Diane sitting on the floor. "What are *you* doing here?"

"I'm Rachel's sister. Perhaps you've heard of me?"

Lara had been Diane's best friend during and after college. They rarely spoke anymore. This was fine; Lara and Rachel had much more in common now.

"Did you pick up the tickets?" Rachel asked.

"I did, and I gave them to you."

"You did? What did I do with them?"

Lara opened the drawer from which the key had just been extracted, pulled out tickets and presented them to Rachel. She was dressed up in a tight tweed suit, a low-cut lace bustier underneath and high, high heels with pointy, pointy toes. What went on at these committee meetings? Diane couldn't wear shoes like this anymore. Lara removed a stack of magazines to sit down on a bench that Diane hadn't noticed. Her skirt fell open, exposing most of her legs. Lara had married a neckless, balding, golfing banker bore, and she believed that Diane was jealous of her. Lara's mother had approached Diane at Lara's wedding to say "I hope you won't be a stranger now, just because Lara's a married lady."

"So," Lara said. "What's new at the theater?"

"We're expanding next door, to add a second screen for new releases."

"*Good for you*," Lara said, as if presenting her with a consolation prize. "Do you have an architect?"

"We're using Chris Wiley and Vladimir Hurtado Padrón. They're terrific."

"Oh, no," Lara gasped, "not *Vladimir!*" She was smiling.

"You know him?"

"He did Sarah's place. He also did a number on Sarah's sister. You know he's married, right?"

Rachel was suddenly interested. "Who's married?"

"He's very attractive, Diane, but beware. He's a piece of work."

"Are you seeing this guy?" Rachel swiveled to face Diane directly.

"He's our architect."

"You didn't say he was attractive and straight and married."

"That's irrelevant, as far as the design is concerned."

A look passed between Rachel and Lara in the mirror.

"How'd it go with that divorced lawyer I sent you?" Lara asked.

"The guy who said, 'Every day I wake up and ask myself, *How can I be a better rock climber?*' Not well."

"Oh, I didn't think it would."

"So why did I have to go out with him?"

"I'd be a bad friend if I didn't pass on every possible lead."

Diane's single status hung in the air like a problem she was too vain to solve. If she could tell some rueful, self-deprecating story and play the Eve Arden role, these two would understand her and perhaps let her hang around. But it was clear that they would rather share intimacies about their husbands, their help or their children than include her by talking about politics, the weather, or even the real estate market. So she said goodbye.

Rachel walked her out; Lara stayed behind in the boudoir.

The front door closed behind Diane and she pressed the button for the elevator in the dimly lit hallway. On the way down in the wood-paneled box she wasn't sure if she was afraid that they would talk about her in her absence, or if she was afraid that they wouldn't even bother.

Although she had perfectly embodied the wisecracking working gal unlucky in love, Eve Arden had a happy second marriage with four children, many domestic pets and livestock. Never mind: Diane had a date that night. Moreover, she'd never aspired to be a married Committee Lady living very fancy with floor-to-ceiling taffeta curtains on the Upper East Side. So perhaps the situation that Vladimir had delineated was not a problem, but an *issue.*

And who *wasn't* a piece of work at this age?

In a gleaming glass office tower in Midtown, Diane underwent security measures and was sent upstairs with a badge and a computerized elevator key. Her potential roommate—a knife-thin, aggressively groomed editorial assistant in her early twenties in a miniskirt, fishnets and stiletto heels—met her at the elevators in front of the offices of a women's magazine. The party girl's impatience was palpable even before they reached her cubicle. The interview, if it could be called that, lasted less than three minutes. It felt like a mutual allergic reaction, or a bad blind date. Diane waited for the elevator feeling huffy that she'd wasted the time.

Fishnets, stilettos, miniskirts: once upon a time, in another life. Who could walk around like that now? On the way down in the elevator, a TV broadcast a chat show whose host was asking an actress how she kept her sex life exciting after fifteen years of marriage. Diane didn't want to share an apartment. With anyone, not even her best friend—whoever that was. Come to think of it, she hadn't spoken to Claire since right before her eviction—almost two months.

At the bank, a man cut in front of her on line, asking if she minded, as he had diarrhea and needed to reach a bathroom.

"Please go right ahead."

"Thank you." He grimaced, adding, "I ate too much beef last night."

What did intimacy mean anymore, when there was so much of it in circulation? What did friendship even consist of now, if everyone told everyone everything, and anyone dining at the next table heard about the mental illness in the family, the cheap behavior of the in-laws, the bitchy airs of the former friend? When everyone knew everything, what was there to talk about, really? Did the value of the information plummet with the range of its dispersal? Or was there just an insatiable appetite for more up-to-the-minute trashy details, not only about the stars, but about everyone?

Diane reached her office and sat down, already angry. Storm reported a toilet clog. Both cards in the suggestion box featured Sid Bernstein's spidery print with random words in block capitals, like notes from a serial killer. "A Concerned and Anonymous Film Lover," demanded to know why *Every Girl Should Be Married* (Don Hartman, 1948) and *My Favorite Wife* (Garson Kanin, 1940) were not included in the current series, and what the Management had against Cary Grant.

◆

VLADIMIR HOPPED on the downtown local train at six o'clock. He didn't want to be late. Diane hung up the phone as he walked into her office. She was looking hopeful in a bright green sweater and jeans, with her hair half up, half down. She suggested they see the movie first, and then have dinner. Why always a movie? He held her hand during the film, which was old, British and not funny. It was about a man and a woman in London both in love with the same guy—a loser, as far as Vladimir could tell. They had friends in common, and also shared an answering service as well as the lover. This movie was a waste of time; he asked to leave.

"I wouldn't put up with that," he said as they left the theater.

"What's that?"

"I wouldn't share a lover with anyone."

"You should talk," Diane said, and pushed open the door to the street.

This door was in bad shape, he noticed. They would have to replace it.

A VERY STRICT AESTHETIC was on display at Vladimir's apartment: white walls and black furniture, everything stowed away on shelves behind a wall of sleek, frosted-glass doors that reminded her of an interior in an Antonioni or Visconti film that she couldn't pinpoint. It was the nicest apartment she'd seen in a long time.

"You're very neat."

"I do my best," he said, and went to make some tea in the kitchen.

"I notice you have no extraneous paper around," she called.

"I keep things in files," he said. "It's better that way."

"Fellini had a problem with paper. He said it slowed him down. He threw everything out. Wouldn't even keep a letter. After he read it, he threw it out."

"That's good discipline," he said with approval. "Although you can get into trouble if you don't save your bills."

"It's hard to imagine Fellini paying bills." She walked to the window. He had a view of a baseball diamond and a schoolyard, lit by bright sodium-vapor lights shining behind a chain-link fence. It would be noisy during the school day, she supposed. It had begun to snow lightly.

He arrived in the living room carrying two cups of tea on a tray.

She sat down next to him on a black leather couch. His hair was down tonight, and it fell into his eyes. He was a darkly beautiful man, an architect with a sensitive face in a black turtleneck, but she knew next to nothing about him. He wanted to leave *Sunday, Bloody Sunday* (John Schlesinger, 1971) halfway through the film. This was all right—she'd seen it many times—but it didn't bode well. Diane was reminded of a first date in the mid-eighties whom she'd taken to an obscure and early Jacques Rivette experiment. On the street afterwards, the fellow had given her arm something between a squeeze and a pat, as if regretting to tell her she hadn't made the cut. Would he have been interested in her if they'd seen *Top Gun* (Tony Scott, 1986) instead?

This memory led to another memory of an erstwhile date, a tall, bald labor negotiator (specialty: Duke University Basketball) who'd told her that his all-time favorite movie was *Moonstruck* (Norman Jewison, 1987).

"I hate Nicolas Cage," she had said, without thinking.

He gave her a quick side-look. "People tell me I look like him."

"I don't mean what he looks like," she said. "I mean the essence of him." But, in fact, she wasn't attracted to the negotiator—not physically, and not to the essence of him. End of that story.

She'd been doing this for so long that perhaps this was *her* specialty: first and second dates with specialists. But why was she thinking about this now? Vladimir put his arm around her shoulders. She was attracted to Vladimir. She sipped her tea and looked around, refusing to be rushed.

"This apartment is like a gallery without the art," she said finally.

"I'm hardly ever here, so it doesn't really bother me."

"Don't you sleep here?"

"Sometimes," he said, after a pause.

Now, what did that mean?

"You could put a poster on that wall." She had just the one in mind: a poster for *Stolen Kisses* (François Truffaut, 1968), which was among the seven that she had put into storage in Queens when she'd been evicted.

"When I'm sleeping, I don't see it."

"And when you wake up?"

"I have work on my mind, and I get to the studio faster."

Another single man in his late thirties with nothing on his mind but the office? She had no way of knowing. Who would he spend the holidays with? His empty walls didn't say "Adorn me," they said "In the five minutes between work and sleep, he won't see you, either."

"Just trying to figure you out," she said.

He took her hand. "What can I tell you about myself, Diane?"

His sudden use of her name reminded her of an insurance salesman (specialty: *Peanuts* memorabilia) who had dropped her name so many times between the drinks and the main course that she had cut out before dessert, claiming to be in the throes of an asthma attack.

"What do you do for fun?"

"Well, I don't watch baseball, basketball or that thing you call 'football' in this country. I don't watch *real* football, either. That movie was the first one I've seen in a long time. I like music, but I may be the only Cuban who doesn't dance. I don't cook, so I eat most meals out."

She remembered what she had planned to say to him, about his situation, how she thought it was an issue, but not a problem. But she was sitting next to him on his sofa in his apartment at nine-thirty at night, wearing a smart new green V-neck sweater that she had bought for this very occasion. If she had thought it was a problem or even an issue, what was she doing there? She decided not to say anything unless he asked her. And why would he ask her?

"And you say you're not going back to Cuba?" she asked.

"Not until frogs grow hair," he said, and took the cup from her hands.

DIANE DECIDED to go straight to the cinema the next morning and skip the interrogation from Rachel. She spent the morning listening to Miss Dorothy Vail complain about her bursitis, tracking down the plumber, and contacting surviving members of the Hollywood blacklist for a panel discussion. She arrived at Rachel's apartment at two o'clock, wanting only a shower.

"Diane! Come meet my book group," Rachel called when Diane entered the apartment. A group of sleek women in tight pants, low-cut shiny sleeveless tops and serious jewelry were arranged languidly on the living room furniture, as if posing for an advertisement for an Italian liqueur.

"Oh, you told us about her," said a woman with long blond hair, capped teeth, full stage makeup and a bare midriff on display. "This is your older sister, the one who never got married."

Diane smiled. As a single woman, you often found it necessary to walk around armed and a bit mysterious, if only not to spend your days receiving instructions, criticism and pep talks, no matter how well-meaning. Of course, Rachel's friends had never been the well-meaning kind.

"So how come you never got married?" asked another camera-ready wife.

Diane wondered if people who asked this wanted her to burst into tears in front of them, and if she did, whether it would shorten the conversation.

"Well, there must be something terribly wrong with me." Diane walked past them, smiling; she wished she could shine her flashlight in their eyes.

She was out of clean clothing in every category. She'd rather buy new clothing than ask Rachel how to use the washing machine. Surely Rachel had no idea, and would give the laundry to Marcelina, and Diane couldn't bear to be dependent on her sister's help. She could wait to ask Marcelina when Rachel wasn't around. But Rachel was always around! Of course, it *was* her home.

Diane went to the scary, crusty maid's bath, where surely no one before her had ever taken a shower, and began to wash her hair. She had spent the night with Vladimir, connecting on various levels, not thinking about his wife in Cuba. Vladimir was attentive, but he wasn't particularly interested in kissing, she was disappointed to discover. She wondered if this was an issue or a problem.

Rachel was sitting on the pullout sofa when Diane returned from the shower in a towel. "So where'd you go last night?"

"Out," she said, meaning, "Get out of my room." But Rachel was planted.

"I think you were out with that guy."

"What guy?"

"The architect," Rachel said. "The married one."

Rachel wasn't moving. Diane hunted for clean underpants in her luggage, knowing that there were none to be had. Such a simple thing, clean clothing.

Cheryl arrived, wearing burgundy lipstick and a halter top. "You didn't come home last night," she said, looking at Diane's body as she pulled on the underpants, which happened to be ripped and sad-looking, as well as dingy.

"Diane has a crush!" Rachel told her daughter.

All her life Diane had waited for Rachel to be punished for her indiscretions. It never happened.

Cheryl squealed. "Who? Who is he? Is he cute?"

"Your mother was always immature," Diane told Cheryl. "But I expect more of you." She found a bathrobe, which she pulled on over the towel.

"Lara said he's gorgeous, with long black hair."

"Eeuuw!" Cheryl was up and moving again. "I hate long hair on guys!"

"Me too," said Rachel. "But look at your aunt!"

Cheryl left the room, bored by now.

"How was it?" Rachel asked.

"This has to stop," Diane warned.

"Ooh, I knew it! I could tell the minute you walked in! I'm calling Lara!"

"You're barking up the wrong tree," Diane warned.

"Okay, okay, so it wasn't the Russian architect," she said. "It was somebody else, then. So how was he?"

Inside Rachel beat the heart of a tabloid; Diane had never shared anything of value with her. She dressed and ran into the street with her hair in wet tangles; if she hustled, she might have time to buy underpants before her appointment with Paul Zazlow. On the way downtown, she called her friend Claire. She needed to line up another sofa bed.

JANUARY

VLADIMIR HAULED HIMSELF out of bed. It was January 1, his birthday—which, as luck would have it, was also María's birthday. Every year, he tried to focus on his new goals for the New Year, and got snagged on the fact of it. Sometimes he thought about how pleasant his life would be without the heaviness dragging him down. He could come and go, organize and protest, marry or just date, talk and disagree, without feeling ashamed, wrong, guilty, illegal. Was this too much to ask? On the other hand, every day he woke up not in Cuba was a gift.

During the run-up to Christmas, five separate Cubans, some of them living in the United States since the sixties who really should have known better, had sent him "*Feliz Pascua*" messages. Pascua was Easter. You really had to hand it to Fidel Castro, who had managed to eradicate nearly five hundred years' worth of Catholicism in a single generation. But how was it possible to live in the United

States for forty years and not know what the holiday celebrated on December 25 was called?

At the ink-black end of the day, he met Bebo and three friends in a café off Kennedy Boulevard in West New York, New Jersey, to talk about a protest for the anniversary of the Black Spring crackdown of March 18, 2003. Vladimir started the meeting by describing a terrific idea to come out of Holland, where activists placed seventy-five typewriters in front of the Cuban Mission to the Hague, one for each of the dissidents arrested. Each machine was loaded with a single page typed with the name of a dissident and the number of years he'd received in prison for crimes against the State, such as writing independent journalism, sharing books with others, composing poetry.

"We should make a portable jail and stand in it on Lexington Avenue," Bebo suggested.

"We'd probably need a permit for that," Vladimir said. "My experience with the City of New York has taught me that there's always a permit issue."

"Well, clearly, you would know better," Bebo said with sudden heat, and turned to look out the window. Had Bebo taken offense at Vladimir's mention of his experience? As if he'd been pointing out Bebo's lack of experience? That wasn't what he'd meant at all.

Miguel, an artist, suggested making a cage out of light and protesting at night—no permit necessary. Ernesto, a lawyer, suggested that they wear the black-and-white-striped uniform of convicts—he'd seen some as Halloween costumes at a party store. Oscar, a Spanish teacher, suggested they stage a hunger strike in front of the Cuban Mission.

Ernesto said it wouldn't bother him; the food he'd been eating lately was execrable. There followed a conversation about the intrinsic worth of Cuban food in Union City, West New York and Manhattan. No restaurant could compare with Miguel's mother's food; moreover, there was nothing special about any of the so-called Cuban restaurants, including the ones in Manhattan. In fact, Manhattan itself was overrated. You couldn't compare it to Havana.

Speaking of Havana: Oscar announced that the sister of someone he knew was going back in a week. This was a tricky proposition ethically, Vladimir said. If you had gained U.S. residency or citizenship by claiming that you were being persecuted politically, how could you go back? Each man at the table took the time to announce that he had never gone back, nor would he ever, as long as the *hijo de puta* was around. But taking advantage of others going back to send letters, medicines or presents to those left behind was something else entirely, Oscar said. If it was morally reprehensible to take advantage of someone else doing a morally reprehensible thing, then so be it, Miguel announced with a slap to the table that made the cups and glasses jump. If he could make a material difference in the lives of his mother, brother, nieces and nephews by sending them medicine, food and clothing, he would gladly have it on his conscience.

Vladimir had hit the limits of his patience.

"Look, do we agree on the premise that the protest should be silent?"

"I don't know how we can enforce that," Bebo said, "although I think it would play well in the media."

Vladimir suddenly remembered that he'd made a date with Diane.

He made excuses and propelled himself through the icy streets of West New York, the fluorescent-lit shabbiness of Port Authority, and the empty rattling bleakness of the off-hours downtown local.

"What's 'early' for you?" Diane said accusingly when he arrived in her messy office. "I've been waiting here for three hours."

He was hit with a wave of fatigue. Another *norteamericana* with a watch. He sat in her desk chair and looked over her scattered commotion. He could help her create a system to streamline the paperwork, but he had a feeling she was one of those people who are proud of their mess. This kind of person spends more time searching for her important papers than working on them.

"I'm here now," he said carefully. "Is it too late to see a movie?"

"You can see the next show of *Rear Window.* I've seen it about twelve times, once this afternoon. But you go watch. I have other things to do."

"So let's skip it," he said. "What would you like to eat?"

"I got too hungry, I'm sorry. I had a sandwich, I couldn't wait."

It hadn't been a good beginning with Diane. It felt off, somehow. Diane was a good person, but it was clear she wanted more than was available, in terms of time, attention, affection, energy. He was often at this juncture with a woman, but it usually took a few months to get to it. With Diane, it had happened right away: they had only been seeing each other for two weeks.

"I'm sorry. I worked all day on Cinema II, and I lost track of time."

"I guess as a client I should be glad. May I see?"

He rolled out his sketches. She came close to him, put an arm around his chest, and looked over his shoulder. She seemed less annoyed.

"I've been thinking about the movie theater as a sequence of spaces. You go out into public space to have a collective, but private experience."

She kissed his cheek, cast a lovely blue-eyed glance at him, and he pointed to a sketch.

"From the big street you stop in front of a small space, the tickets box."

"The box office," she suggested.

He nodded. "Then you pass into a bigger space: the lobby and the snack bar. Then you go through doors onto a narrow hall, and pass through more doors into a big space, the theater, where you sit on a small space, your seat, to get intimate with the people in the screen on a grand scale, while you ignore the people sitting next to you."

"If you're lucky enough to sit next to people who don't receive phone calls or kick your chair."

"Right. So I was thinking that perhaps it's the combination of big and small, intimate and grand, that makes the movies so powerful and popular."

She kissed him on the mouth. "This is what you did this afternoon?"

"That and answer hate mail from Cuba," he lied. "Most movie

theaters are burgundy, navy or gray. Why not go all the way, with black velvet chairs?"

"Very interesting," she said. "Who's sending you hate mail?"

He sighed. "Former friends."

"Do you want to talk about it?"

"Yes, but not now. I'm actually quite hungry." He glanced at her. "Would you like to watch me eat something?"

◆

ON A SLUSHY GRAY TUESDAY the following week, Diane took the Metro-North train into Manhattan from Glenwood, a dreary, generic suburb in Westchester with no real town. There, her friend Claire, whom she'd known since seventh grade, lived with her Big and Tall husband and bland suburban children on a cul-de-sac in a newly constructed Tudor mansion perched on a high, grassy mound. In spite of the many bedrooms, Diane was sleeping on a sofa bed in one of the living rooms—perhaps so that she wouldn't get too comfortable.

Claire's husband, Robert—a man whose taste in cinema was limited to the collected works of Bruce Willis—demanded all Claire's attention and time. Claire fed the children, and then fed Robert. Robert didn't cry when the ketchup was put on the wrong side of the plate, but on Diane's second night in residence, he demanded to know why they were out of beer.

"Because you've been drinking it all?" Diane joked, and saw Robert's face darken. That was the last family dinner for Diane; she was out as much as possible. Even so, she could imagine her suitcase of dirty laundry in the den igniting a row in her absence. Robert liked his underclothes ironed, so whatever time Claire spent with Diane was clearly wasted.

More and more people boarded the train; after the last Westchester stop, people had to stand. Not everyone in the suburbs was married, and not everything outside Manhattan was the suburbs. Perhaps she should leave New York City altogether. It was much too soon to show up at Vladimir's door with a suitcase, no matter how small. He seemed to be receding even as she got closer to him. He was consumed by work and she had every right to expect him to be: he was her architect, after all. Cuban politics seemed to spill over into every area of his life. *He* interested her, but perhaps the politics was too much. She wondered if she interested him. He didn't give much away.

There was a time when this topic would have been fuel for a lively conversation with Claire, over coffee. Claire used to be interested, even after her marriage. But somehow, boy problems at the age of almost forty had become too embarrassing to discuss out loud, more embarrassing even than boy problems had been in the seventh grade. Diane remembered the last time she mentioned to Lara the strange behavior of a man she was seeing. Without missing a beat, and looking her straight in the eye, Lara changed the subject.

You're impatient? Diane wanted to scream. Try *living* this life, the same damn thing over and over. Nothing, nothing, nobody! Eighteen months of bad first dates alternating with Soup for One. And then: A prospect! Excitement! A living male, stimulating and *unavailable*! Clearly there was some lesson Diane was supposed to be learning. Whatever it was, it eluded her. Discussing it publicly only left her open to pity, criticism or matchmaking. It was *unseemly* that she was still making the rounds.

At Grand Central, she realized that she'd left her keys in Westchester.

Paul Zazlow darted across the street to meet her. With the shock of straight dark brown hair flopping across his forehead, the cheekbones that could cut paper and an air of combined haste and languor, he reminded her of the young Alain Delon. The tight-fitting pale gray suits and shiny black shoes added to the illusion, and initially, as they toured the lower end of Manhattan properties with fatal flaws, she'd felt as if she were in a small European movie full of intrigue and possibilities. A month into the process, with three deals that had fallen through, Diane was impatient with him, although it wasn't his fault.

"Nice sweater," he said as he opened the lobby door.

"Sarcasm?" She'd worn the green sweater nearly every day for two weeks.

"No, it's beautiful. And fragrant."

"Paul. I can't handle one more night on a sofa bed without some kind of hope."

"I have a feeling in my bones today."

Paul often had this feeling in his bones. The building had been a children's hospital in the nineteenth century; it was now a marble-paved luxury rental with historical plaques in the lobby. They waited for the elevator.

The apartment was a studio triplex, Paul noted.

"A *what?*"

"That must be a misprint. Let's take a look."

Upstairs, there was a landing pad, about ten feet by ten feet, with a spiral staircase to another level, which was eight by eight, but had a tiny bathroom. Up another spiral staircase sat a doll's kitchen and a four-by-four space—perhaps for a single chair to overlook the levels below. It was a studio triplex.

"I don't think I could have a complete thought in this space," Diane said.

Normally, Paul countered ambivalence or criticism with some unique asset she hadn't noticed, but apparently he couldn't argue with that.

An hour later, they were in a pirate's kitchen on the Upper West Side, where a picturesque chest overflowing with gold coins, jewel-studded medallions and strands of pearls sat on the counter next to the fridge. A mermaid was painted on the door.

"This is to rent or to buy," Paul read from a sheet.

"Can I buy the place with sunken treasure, matey?"

"You've got to get realistic, Diane," Paul said, leaning against the mast. "You're not going to find what you want at the price you want. You'll have to make some compromises. Take out the nets and the sails and this could be a great kitchen. Think what Vladimir could do with this space."

What did Paul know about her and Vladimir? She ignored the insinuation.

"Where's the stove?" she asked.

"There's no stove?"

AT THE OFFICE, her mother called to make plans for Uncle Mort's birthday.

Diane cut her off. "I don't *think* so."

"Are you still upset about that?"

Diane didn't respond.

"What about Saturday night? We're having the Steins over for dinner, you know how much they love you."

"Can't do it, I have plans."

"And Sunday morning? We could come to Westchester, take you and Claire and the kids out for brunch?"

"That's a sweet invitation, but I don't know what Claire's plans are."

"Or the following Tuesday, we could come in for dinner in the city?"

This could go on and on. "Mom, I'm running late. I really must go."

The phone rang again.

"I was just handed two theater tickets for tonight," Dorothy announced, "and I can't think of anyone I'd rather go with than *you!*"

The only thing Diane hated more than live theater was being at Miss Dorothy's Vail's beck and call. "I am so sorry, Dorothy, I have plans."

"No, you don't."

"Excuse me?"

"I happen to know that you don't have plans. I looked in your date book yesterday when I was visiting."

"Did you happen to notice that that date book was business-only?"

"Fifth row center," she continued. "I don't want to make a point of it, but it's getting harder and harder for me, going places alone."

This woman was really turning into a second job.

"I am so sorry, Dorothy," Diane purred, "but the plumber is here, and I must get back to work."

In fact, she did have plans: she was seeing Vladimir that evening for an early movie and dinner. There was an unspoken agreement that she would spend the night with him on weekends, but not weeknights. She had a seventy-five-minute trip on Metro-North to consider now. She didn't want to crowd him, but if he expected the evening to end at his apartment, it would have to be a sleepover. She wanted to clarify things, but each time she brought up something practical, Vladimir changed the subject.

She reserved seats in the back, and at the end of the day, Vladimir arrived and they installed themselves just as the lights went down. They saw *Spring, Summer, Fall, Winter . . . and Spring* (Kim Ki-duk, 2003), a Korean film about a Buddhist monk and a boy he is raising in a one-room monastery on a raft in the middle of a lake. Each season deals with a different stage of life—the natural cruelty of the boy in childhood, his sexual awakening as an adolescent, the young man's return to the lake after experiencing torment in the world outside, and so on. With next to no dialogue, simply through interactions between the characters, the breathtaking natural scenery and animals, the film cleverly raises questions about large moral issues—cruelty, passion, responsibility—without passing judgment. As with the first time she'd seen it, the film's simplicity and intimate connection to nature felt like a thorough vacation to Diane. This time, she decided that one-room living was actually desirable. When the lights came up, she was refreshed and ready to talk. Vladimir was asleep.

"How could you?"

He yawned. "Monks in a lake? Very easily."

Over dinner, she asked him about his favorite movies.

"No offense to you, your profession, or anything, but I think that movies are a waste of time."

"Oh, come on. You must have some favorite movies."

He shrugged. When she pressed him, the names Schwarzenegger, Norris and Willis surfaced. She looked at him. This would be a problem—not just an issue: a *problem*. She was currently running a series of films with intriguing elements of set or production design;

many of these would appeal to his architectural side. The following week, in a double feature of films using color in unusual ways, she would show *Hero* (Zhang Yimou, 2002), a gorgeous martial arts epic featuring Maggie Cheung and Zhang Ziyi in an airborne sword fight amid a whirlpool of red and yellow leaves. She had paired it with *Gattaca* (Andrew Niccol, 1997), a sci-fi thriller that appeared to be set in an Armani showroom of the future as seen through a beaker of urine.

She invited him to see either or both.

"We had a visit today from your friend Paul," he said in response. "Does he ask you about me? Because he asks me about you. And he keeps talking about how beautiful Havana is."

"Speaking of Havana," she said, dipping a piece of raw salmon into dark sauce, "we have a screening of *The Buena Vista Social Club* coming up. Would you like to see it?"

"I saw it."

"Did you like it?"

"Some of them signed the petition supporting the Regime's incarceration of journalists and librarians in 2003," Vladimir said, polishing off his rice.

"The musicians?"

He nodded. "Either they signed the petition, or they woke up one morning and discovered, mysteriously, that they had signed the petition. Either way, it doesn't matter."

"Doesn't it?"

"They're dependent on the Regime's favor, in order to make records, to leave the island and tour."

"Did you like the film?"

"I cannot tell you how mad that petition made me."

He was there, vividly, and yet he was not quite interactive. She was dating a hologram.

◆

CHRIS LEFT HIS SUITCASE in the dark foyer and walked to the back of the apartment.

Paul was propped up on pillows in bed. He peered at him from behind the tent of *The New York Times.* "You look like the cat that swallowed the dog."

Chris took off his shoes. "I bought a house."

"You what?"

He tried not to smile. "A house. With a front porch and a back-yard."

Paul batted through the pages and settled on one, rattling the newspaper into place and doubling it up to read above the fold. "A house. You bought a *house*? I don't buy a jacket without discussing it with you."

"I've discussed it with you."

He tossed the paper aside. "And I told you I don't want to live in Atlanta."

"And that was the end of the conversation. So I made the bid without you."

"You are aware of what I do for a living?"

Chris took off his jacket. He'd expected personal irritation from Paul, but he hadn't counted on professional pique.

"How could you think of leaving this?" Paul flung out his hand.

"This? This urine-soaked alley crisscrossed by scaffolding and garbage, bombarded by handbag vendors and teenage tourists? This noisy, overcrowded, hyped-up zone of boutiques selling Italian shoes and Japanese makeup and ten-dollar tomatoes? Tell me what's so great about it."

The newspaper fell to the floor. "Have you spoken to Vladimir?"

"Of course not. You're my first stop."

Paul was motionless, blinking.

Chris pulled a chair over to the side of the bed and perched there.

"You think you should maybe talk to him?" Paul asked. "I mean, isn't he your partner?"

"I don't think it would ultimately affect the partnership. I'll be going back and forth. When I'm not around, he and I can do every-thing over the phone and on the computer. And I can start devel-oping business in Atlanta."

"I see. How much time do you think you'll be spending in Dixie?"

"I have to go down to take another look at it before the closing, and talk to some contractors. I want to be there for the home inspection."

He saw Paul's key-driven mind kicking into gear. "It needs work."

"Major, major work. I thought I'd go down on Thursday nights, for the weekend, while the work is going on. You are invited for any and all of it." He nudged Paul aside and sat down on top of the covers.

Paul made room for him. "How would we get there?" he asked, raising an eyebrow.

"We would fly."

"We would *WHAT*?"

"We would fly," Chris laughed, and ran his fingers through Paul's bangs.

"We would voluntarily put ourselves in a metal tube that goes up in the air? Twice in a weekend? Why would we do that?"

"Come on. It's not so bad."

Paul tossed the covers aside and got out of bed; he was winding himself up for a fight. "You knew what I would say, and you went right ahead anyway."

Paul could be such a handful. "We've been through this. I need a slower pace. I need more space, greenery, conversation. I need a porch."

Paul was stalking the confined space at the foot of the bed. "And who will you be having conversations with on this porch? Your neighbor, Mrs. Magnolia Peach Pie, who has a vested interest in making your life a living hell so you move out and some nice clean straight couple moves in?"

"You haven't seen the neighborhood, friend."

"Gay neighborhood?"

"Mixed. In all senses."

"In *Georgia*? You're insane, friend."

"I'd respect your opinion if it was actually based on anything. I think if you visited, you might change your mind, but I'm not pushing you." Chris got off the bed to get something to eat. "I want to be with you, but I'm not willing to stay here full-time."

"What does that mean?"

Chris paused. "That means I'll be traveling, and I hope you will, too."

Paul went into the bathroom shaking his head.

When Chris saw impatient-looking boys in tight jeans on the streets of New York, he was reminded of himself in his early twenties, avid for the next experience. He'd been aggressive, hardworking and driven in his professional life; he'd been shallow, arrogant and naïve in his personal life. Currently, he was politically gay, socially gay, *demographically* gay, but sex itself had little to do with it. Where had all the sex gone? Increasingly, impatient-looking boys in tight jeans walked right past him, not even making eye contact. Fatigue and irritation outweighed desire much of the time. Had he been drained of all hormones? Did he care? Was this a natural effect of age, or monogamy, or was it just Paul? Paul was seriously gorgeous, but so annoying on occasion that Chris had to remind himself to open his mouth to avoid clenching his teeth. Periodically, Paul did absurd things—tossing liquids out the window, going out in January without a coat, crossing against the light in the middle of the block while traffic whizzed all around him—that Chris suspected were intended to elicit an alarmed response from him so Paul could then accuse him of behaving like a Jewish mother.

"What do you get *out* of this?" Chris asked him each time.

"Just that! The way you say 'What do you get *out* of this?' makes me happy! I don't know why!"

Paul returned, still in a snit. He picked up the newspaper and rattled it.

"An unexpected turn of events," he announced, getting back into bed.

FEBRUARY

AT SOME POINT much too early in the morning, a phone rang very near her head, and Diane was jolted awake. Vladimir reached over her to pick it up. He listened, cursed, rose and took the phone out into the living room. He spoke in loud and emphatic Spanish. She had taken French in school, but she was able to recognize a few words, like "María" and "*cojones.*"

She looked at the clock. It was seven a.m. This was too early for phone calls, weekday or not. He walked back into the bedroom and turned on the lamp.

"What happened?" she asked.

"Javier didn't come home last night, so they're hysterical."

"Who's Javier?"

He sat down on the bed. "My son."

The lamp was awfully bright.

"You have a son?"

"Yes, I have a son."

"What?" When had he planned to tell her this?

"I have a son. He's seventeen."

"He's *seventeen*? You have a son who's *seventeen*?"

He cast a dark, impatient look at her. "*Cojones,* Diane!"

This was said in the same tone of voice as "*Cojones,* María!"

She had to be careful. "Okay, what happened to your son?"

"They don't know, so they call me, like I can do something about it. From here. He's probably getting laid."

"If he did . . . get laid last night, where is he now? Wouldn't he go home?"

"How would I know? Why do they call *me*? What can I do about it?"

"Well, he *is* your son."

"Yes, Diane, he is my son," he said at top volume. "And we have as much in common as any two people who've had dinner together twice."

He stalked into the living room. She lay back down. She heard him turning on his computer. Vladimir was always working, always angry—at Fidel Castro, a contractor, an electrician, the bank, his father, his mother, his wife, his sister, the Cuban people for being so easily manipulated, the American people for being so naïve, the Miami Cubans for living in nostalgia, the substandard and ungrammatical Hispanic press, the substandard and vulgar Hispanic TV, the Spanglish spoken on the streets of New York. He was in regular conflict with old friends who remained in Cuba, and old friends who'd arrived in America and hadn't pushed themselves. He'd begun to play chess obsessively with a computer program, referring to the opponent as "Castro," whether he won or lost. Diane was walking on eggs with him at all times.

"He's *alive,* Diane," he called.

She knew who *He* was. Fidel Castro hovered over every conversation, in the tradition of the one-issue man. She stayed in Vladimir's bed a while longer. She needed a shower. Would he consider it pushy if she asked to leave a few things in the bathroom? What if she just hid them under his sink? What could he do to her?

"How is it possible to be immersed in something that makes you mad all the time?" she asked, and was pleased that he actually looked up.

"That's a really interesting question," he said.

But he didn't answer it.

Akira Kurosawa had reported in his memoirs that he always felt more loneliness at being separated from his film crew than joy at being reunited with his family. How had this gone over with Mrs. Kurosawa?

"Will you come this Friday for the panel discussion?" she called.

"Ah, no. I have a friend coming into town from Paris."

She rolled over. A friend?

"So I won't be making plans for this weekend."

She decided to deal from strength. "So come to the movie tonight."

"I have to work late."

"Come to the late show."

"Why don't you come over here after the late show?"

She breathed in. "So does this go over well in Havana? 'I'm married in absentia, and I'd like to see you tonight *after* the late show?' "

He looked exhausted. "I am running behind in the construction documents. *Your* construction documents."

"Would this friend from Paris be Terry, the chef and former neighbor that you dated for two years?"

"Yes," he said, typing.

She stepped into the shower. In *The Grifters* (Stephen Frears, 1990), which would play that night in the "Cynics, Shysters and Con Men" series, a young and eager John Cusack receives advice from a card shark in a white suit who tells him to stick to the short con, and never take a partner—partners are out to fleece you. "There's nothing to whipping a fool. Fools are made to be whipped. But to take another pro, even your partner, who knows you and has his eye on you: that's a score, no matter what happens."

Diane had been dating for twenty-five years. What was she, if not a pro? She was a pro, and yet she never seemed to get any better at it. How had she not seen this? What had they been talking about for almost six weeks?

When she emerged, wearing a sweater from his collection, he was at his drafting table looking handsome, talented and absorbed, with his magnificent hair restrained by a No. 2 pencil. If she had to design a model boyfriend, in his totality, her ideal probably wouldn't come out like Vladimir, even without a child involved. But that wasn't how it worked. You had to deal with who showed up. And here he was. Intractably married, with a seventeen-year-old in a different country. He continued to focus on the Internet.

Finally she said, "Do you have a picture of your son?"

He slid off his stool and pushed open one of the frosted-glass doors of the cabinet he'd designed. He pulled out a framed picture.

It was the whole family, in front of a cake.

"This is Javier." He pointed to a twelve-year-old who looked like him: The boy was surrounded by laughing people. "That's my mother," he said, pointing to a woman with short maroon hair. "And that's María." He pointed to an overweight women in a sundress. He put the photo back on the shelf and slid the door closed. And that was that.

He was married, with a child. Not a child, a teenager! What else was he hiding in these cabinets? "Tell me. I want to understand the situation."

"María and I talk twice a month. She poses questions, and then answers them, and then shouts at me for not getting involved."

"And Terry?"

"Terry comes into town now and then."

"Is she staying here?"

"No," he said. He didn't sound quite sure.

She walked to the window. Most Americans didn't like anyone to rain on their parade. But cynicism of the lyrical variety—Billy Wilder, Joseph L. Mankiewicz, Spike Lee, David Mamet—was a homegrown tradition rarely acknowledged or celebrated; Diane had programmed the current series to run when everyone else was promoting Valentine's Day schmaltz. She was showing *Witness for the*

Prosecution (Billy Wilder, 1957), a film so cynical it made *Double In-demnity* (Billy Wilder, 1944) look like a bedtime story. In the film, Marlene Dietrich delivers the definitive con by using her reputation as a dragon lady to make people see what they expect to see. People are often misled by their own expectations. Look at her expectations of Vladimir—she hadn't asked him about children, or other women, because it hadn't even occurred to her that he might have any stashed away. Few people were as solitary as she seemed to be.

"You're forbidding me to see an old friend?"

"Of course not. A man cheating on his wife is one thing. But a man cheating on his girlfriend and insisting he has every right to do so . . ."

"What cheating? Who is cheating? We are *having dinner!*"

"And after dinner?"

"That doesn't affect you and me."

"I don't like this situation, Vladimir. If you hadn't mentioned it, I'd be none the wiser. But since you mention it, sorry, I can't sign up for that."

American prude, she thought, and walked out into the hall. She pushed the elevator button. Okay, then. She'd find somebody else. Single, straight, monogamous men over thirty-five were just growing on trees in New York, after all. There was a terrible pressure in her head. She'd made a nice exit; she couldn't very well ring the bell and ask for aspirin now. She had just stepped into the elevator when he walked out barefoot and blocked the elevator door.

"She's not staying. It really is just dinner."

He had, it seemed, gone out of his way to make her nervous about this woman. Why? He began to squeeze her upper arms. "Come on, Diane, I have a crust on you."

She began to laugh. "*Crush.* You have a *crush* on me?"

She noticed again the deep, abstract headache in the center of her forehead. It was an oppressive fog, and she would carry it home with her.

Not home: Glenfield, Glendale, Glenwood.

"Do you have aspirin?" she asked, and he led her back in.

—

"BEYOND THE PAIN and humiliation," Javier asked as he dropped the fifth enormous rock on the left side of the field, "is there a point to this exercise?"

"Hurtado: Do you want to spend all of tomorrow picking up these rocks and bringing them back over there? Then shut up."

In fact, the whole month had been a series of outrages, frustrations and disappointments. But he had a pass to go home at four p.m., his first pass in six weeks.

Just after dismissal, Javier saw Martínez, the drill instructor, leaning over Yusleidis in the corridor; he had one hand on the wall, and one hand on the front of her neck. A cold electric current ran down the front of Javier's own neck.

"Hey!"

After a moment, they both looked over at him.

Javier controlled his anger, as he had learned to do. "I will see you in your office, now," he ordered Martínez—an adult, a Sergeant, and the Officer in charge of Javier's own barracks.

Martínez raised an eyebrow, then threw his head back laughing.

Javier told Yusleidis to go wait for him outside the cafeteria. When he turned to go, she held his hands, detaining him; he told her they would talk later, and followed the swaggering Martínez down the hall to his office.

The sergeant sat at his desk under a photo of Fidel Castro delivering a lecture. Javier did not sit down, nor did he stand at attention.

"Yusleidis is a sophomore and you're a drill instructor," he said. "Even if you aren't bright enough to teach anything, you're a figure of authority here."

A smile displaced the man's enormous mustache. "You're a bigger fool than I thought you were," Martínez said. He might have been over thirty, at least six feet three and the Commanding Officer of his unit, but his smirk enraged Javier.

"I'm not talking to the officer," Javier said. "I'm talking to you, the man—if you *are* a man." Javier had had several years of karate and a few months of aikido. But he wouldn't physically attack him: that was the lowest of all forms. "What were you doing to Yusleidis? Account for yourself!"

Martínez came around the desk to swat at him. Javier leaned back, caught the slapping arm in one hand and pressed against the elbow in the wrong direction with the other. This caused a sharp pain, which registered on the officer's face as surprise and fear. Fidel Castro continued lecturing on the wall.

"Stop!" Yusleidis burst into the room, her heart-shaped face aghast.

Javier released his hold. Martínez held his right elbow in his left hand.

"I'm leaving," Javier said in a cool voice. "Keep your hands off her."

He led Yusleidis out to the hall as Martinez shouted: "YOU WILL STAND BEFORE THE TRIBUNAL IN TEN MINUTES TO ANSWER CHARGES OF AGGRESSION AND LACK OF RESPECT TOWARD AN OFFICER!"

This is the end of my military career, Javier thought, and kept walking. He didn't want a military career. But was this the end of *any* career?

Yusleidis stopped him. "Didn't he just say you had to stand trial?"

"If I'm expelled, I'm expelled. I don't have to hang around waiting to hear them tell me. What more could they do to me?"

She inhaled. "Listen, Javier. You shouldn't have done that."

He looked at her. "How did you let yourself get into that situation?"

"You know, I can take care of myself."

"I'm sorry I protected you, if you were so interested in that toad."

"Fuck you, Javier."

He stared at her, without comprehension. She turned around and walked back. She walked back to the administration building!

Javier passed through the gates before someone noticed and dragged him back into the cesspit of stupidity that was the Camilo

Cienfuegos Military High School of Capdevila. He kept up a good pace until he got to the roundabout, where he waited on a line beneath a billboard that read *SOCIALISM OR DEATH*. He was starving again, and he reflected that one didn't really have to choose.

He'd managed to sneak out each weekend of detention to visit Yusleidis, whose family lived about two miles down the road from the stinking institution. For six weeks, she'd been driving him crazy in her room. He'd been so close to getting her to complete the transaction. Now this. There was a shortage of females at the school, about one girl for every four guys. Of the girls they had, very few were attractive; Yusleidis had her pick of any *camilito* she wanted and, apparently, any officer, too. Javier had shaved his head the previous weekend out of boredom and a misguided belief that it would make him look cool. Did his new look have anything to do with her behavior?

There was a long line of people trying to get downtown for Friday night; he waited two hours before he could get on a truck, and it broke down halfway, so he had to wait another hour. His hunger was acute. By the time he got to Miramar he had no desire to be home. He got off six blocks farther and went to see Paco, who knew all the dance moves. With his white, white head and surfeit of ears, Javier had better learn to dance really well.

Paco and Néstor were smoking on the front steps; they pointed at his head and laughed. They were on their way to a concert, and he joined them; nobody had a ticket—they were going to talk their way in. Néstor was very good at that. The group began walking to the Karl Marx Theater in high spirits.

A big crowd had already gathered in front of the theater, and Javier saw a police officer's gaze lock onto Néstor; it would be only a moment before he started harassing him, demanding to see his ID card. This happened every time he was out with Néstor now: Néstor was black and wore his hair in long braids and had grown about a foot since Javier had seen him last. But mainly, he was black. As he predicted, two cops pushed their way through the crowd and stood in front of Néstor.

"I-car," demanded one cop.

"Hmm?" Néstor asked.

"I-CAR," demanded the policeman again.

Néstor was mystified.

"He wants to see your ID card," Javier said, "but he doesn't know how to pronounce it. Isn't that right?"

"*YOU!*" the cop yelled at Javier, pointing his nightstick at him. "*I-CAR!*"

"Okay, okay," Javier said, as he and Néstor produced their ID cards.

People around them were scattering to avoid the scene.

"What's this?" The cop pointed to Javier's ID card. Javier had replaced his awful ID picture with another photo, in which he looked better. He realized his error: he'd replaced the official black-and-white photo with a color snapshot. Also, the official raised seal was missing. He was trying to explain this to the one cop; meanwhile, the other cop was handcuffing Néstor.

"Why are you handcuffing him?"

"He's a citizen with characteristics," said the second cop.

"He did nothing!" Javier shouted, and before he realized it, the cop had slammed his head onto the hood of the police car.

"Spread your legs!"

He opened his legs and exchanged a terrified look with Néstor, whose head was also on the hood of the car. Javier began to sweat.

The cop kicked his right leg open farther.

"*Ow!* My legs are spread! They're spread!"

"Shut up, *camilito*," said the cop, and kicked his left leg.

Who was watching? Did it matter? They could do anything they wanted.

THERE WAS AN IMPASSE at the police station: they had no place to put juveniles. After twenty minutes of standing in handcuffs in the middle of the station, Javier and Néstor were led down a series of ever-darker hallways and finally pushed into a fluorescent-lit cell that stank of urine and sweat. A mulatto with a snake tattoo climbing up his neck watched them with wordless hostility from one corner, where he sat on the floor. The jailer locked the cell.

Whatever they did now was critical, Javier decided. He reached into his shirt pocket and pulled out a cigarette.

"Are you out of your mind?" Néstor pointed to a No Smoking sign on the wall, next to a photo of Fidel making another point, finger in the air.

Javier lit the butt with one eye closed, looking straight at his cell mate, who was thin but strong and had the most enormous Afro he'd ever seen.

"HEY!" someone yelled. "Who's smoking?"

The cop who had kicked his legs and handcuffed him arrived at the cell. Javier blew a stream of smoke in his direction and then slowly ground the butt onto the floor. The cop opened the door to the cell. "Little *camilito* with a big attitude," he said, and slapped Javier's face hard. He locked the gate.

"His grandfather is a Colonel," Néstor called after him.

"Shut up," Javier whispered.

Their cell mate had a very heavy aura about him.

"What are you in for?" Néstor asked the fellow.

What the hell was Néstor doing? They were dead meat!

"I won't bother you," the cell mate said, slowly. "Don't you bother me."

Javier and Néstor sat on the floor, not looking at each other. Néstor was shivering.

Now that Javier was taller than his grandfather, it made no sense that Pucho hit him. Pucho knew how much he resented it. He knew he'd taken karate, aikido. The entire household made no sense. Ever since his grandmother Alicia had moved back in after the divorce, Mercedes, Pucho's girlfriend, sat on the patio all day like a queen while his grandmother cooked meals and cried in the servant's room. His aunt and her husband had nasty, screaming fights. His five-year-old cousin, Hanoi, was all over his things, ruining important cassette tapes and getting guava paste on his books. His mother was constantly hounding him. Whatever he was doing, she was there to tell him he should be doing something else. There wasn't a moment of peace.

After a period that could have been five minutes or three hours, the two cops who had arrested them came in. They had been drinking.

"Get up, Aurelio," they said to the cell mate.

The man in the corner didn't move, but glared to tremendous effect. The one who couldn't talk yanked him to a standing position. Javier began to shake. Aurelio let out a growl, threw himself at the cop and knocked him across the cell. Aurelio would not leave the cell! He was giving the cop hell! The second cop came in, leaving the door ajar. It occurred to Javier to use the moment to escape. But they had his ID—what was the point? He and Néstor backed up against the wall to avoid getting hit in the commotion.

The cops dragged the man out of the cell to a little clearing, where all three of them caught their breath.

"What's the matter, Aurelio, you tired?" They began taking turns, one to hold him down, the other to kick and punch him.

Javier walked a few steps, sank to his knees and began to heave.

After what seemed like an eternity, they threw Aurelio back into the cell. He stayed where he fell, bloodied and panting, beneath the fluorescent lamp.

"Are you okay, brother?" Javier asked, and gave him his handkerchief.

Aurelio took it with a slight nod and dabbed at his nose and mouth. It suddenly occurred to Javier—and apparently to Néstor at the same time, because they exchanged a petrified glance—that they might be next. Aurelio was sleeping—or had he passed out? They were sitting on the urine, blood and vomit of other prisoners. Tension mounted.

"I cannot believe this is happening," Javier said, sitting back.

"This is exactly how I imagined it," Néstor said.

They shifted uncomfortably on the floor. Javier wanted to sleep. He wanted a very long shower. He had probably been expelled again, the second school in two years. He had done a very stupid and unnecessary thing; it was Forgery, or Destruction of State Property, meaning official punishment as well as whatever Pucho would mete out. Yusleidis had clearly moved on. The fluorescent light was relentless. He had reached the nadir of his life.

—

"You," an unfamiliar cop said, pointing at him.

It was morning; he'd fallen asleep leaning against the wall.

Néstor was gone. Aurelio was gone. The cops from the previous evening were gone. The taste in his mouth was atrocious. Javier stood up, and was taken through a series of halls and offered a chair in a room with a row of desks and a partition, beyond which were seats for the public.

"I hear you have a big mouth and an irregular ID card," said a new cop, a thin white man with a reddish mustache.

"I can explain," Javier said, and saw Pucho beyond the partition, wearing an olive green uniform that didn't fit him anymore and a thick, official face.

The floor of his nadir had just dropped.

"You say this is your ID card," the cop said, "but you could have stolen it."

If Pucho beats me today, Javier thought, I'll deserve it.

"I'll identify him, Officer," Pucho called, and stepped up to the partition, showing the cop his National ID card and Army ID card.

There was a dialogue, during which the cop justified taking Javier into custody, and Pucho agreed with the decision; the cop held up the evidence to examine it in the light, and Pucho praised him for his care in observing procedure; the cop explained the policy on forged ID cards and Pucho commended him on his diligence.

"He'll be hearing from me. He's my grandson," Pucho said. "I shouldn't have to do this, but his father is a nonperson. Antisocial scum."

The cop applauded Pucho for not being afraid of old-fashioned discipline, and Pucho accepted the compliment and griped about the decline in parenting standards, all the while fingering the buttons on his jacket and clearing his throat violently, a noise that Javier could not, could not stand. After fingerprints, photos and signatures, Javier was released into the custody of his grandfather, who marched out of the station as if about to inspect a line of troops.

The light outside was blinding.

Pucho glanced at Javier with disdain. "Tuck in your shirt: you'll get a demerit."

Another issue to deal with. Javier got into the Chevrolet.

"You may be the luckiest moron I know. We're visiting Mercedes' sister in the hospital. You and I will have a long talk when I get back."

Terrific. He could now sit at home and anticipate the humiliation.

"And I don't need to tell you that you can't go out," Pucho said, pulling up to the house, where Mercedes waited, wearing her lemon-sucking face. "You'll be arrested again for not having ID. I'll see you this afternoon."

Mercedes didn't look at him as she took his place in the passenger seat.

He walked up the steps into the house and opened the front door.

"Oh my God!" His mother fell to her knees at his feet, sobbing.

"Is that necessary?" he asked.

In one motion she got up and slapped him across the mouth. This was really too much. She was yelling again. He walked out of the house, although he badly needed to use a bathroom and hadn't eaten since lunch the day before. He had to get this uniform off, and he wanted to sleep, in a room without light.

Paco was sitting on his stoop playing his guitar.

"What happened, brother?" he asked.

"I'll tell you if you let me take a shower."

Paco led him inside, past his sister and her boyfriend, his grandmother and the television, which was showing another Roundtable Debate. Nobody ever mentioned how the table itself was rectangular, or how nobody disagreed. There wasn't much hot water or soap, but Javier felt so unclean he stayed under the cold water for as long as he could. Joining Paco in his room, he gave him the details of the night before. Paco was riveted. Javier felt a little better, but he couldn't turn the experience into a lighthearted tale.

"What did they want in the first place?" Paco asked.

"They had it in for Néstor. And he's so naïve, he doesn't get angry."

"He's not naïve, he's dense," Paco said, and picked up his guitar. He was always playing the same irritating song that he had written.

"But he should get angry!" Javier said, feeling hot all of a sudden. "We all should! I don't know what is Left or Right anymore, but wherever Fidel Castro is located, I am 180 degrees at the opposite pole."

Paco's face was immobilized. "You didn't just say that."

Just because Paco played the guitar and wore his hair long, and just because they had drunk rum and talked about girls together, what made Javier suppose that Paco, son of high-ranking Party members, would be receptive? And where was Paco while he and Néstor were pressed facedown on the squad car?

"No, I didn't say that."

"Good, I didn't think so. You going to that party tonight?"

Javier wanted to sleep for five or six years. "No, I think I'll skip it."

"Okay. See you around."

WHEN JAVIER WALKED IN, his grandfather was strutting around the kitchen.

"What did I tell you about going out?"

Bang. A blow to the head.

"Do it again," Javier told him, and his grandfather lifted his hand in a gesture of dismissal. "Do it again, Pucho. Come on, right here. I will knock you flat on your nasty, fat, arthritic ass. Watch me."

"Listen how he talks to his grandfather!" Mercedes squawked.

"Shut up, you lazy bitch," Javier told her.

Pucho came at him in a rage. Right there, in the middle of the kitchen, in front of his mother, his aunt, his grandfather's whore, his cousin and his grandmother, the usual passive spectators, he performed the move he had chosen. It was quick, it was light—it was almost like dancing. Pucho lay on his back on the tiled floor, stunned.

"I have had," Javier said, controlling himself, "*a very bad day.* I am going to sleep now, and I expect you all to leave me alone."

He walked upstairs. Aikido had really taken his skills to a new level.

He still hadn't eaten anything.

Alicia came to his room and sat on his bed as he stewed in his mess.

"Your father was exactly the same at this age," his grandmother said, a hand on his shoulder. "I don't know how many times he was arrested and for what."

His father: antisocial scum or misunderstood saint, depending on whom you asked. "What about Nadia?"

"She got yelled at," Alicia said. "But he never hit her. Vladimir really got it."

And then he got out, Javier knew.

Which raised the inevitable, inconvenient, unanswerable question:

How could he leave me here?

MARCH

ON A BLUSTERY SUNDAY MORNING, Vladimir made coffee and dialed Cuba. The baseball diamond across the street still had a crusty edge of old snow that attracted paper and soot. The trees had begun to show signs of awakening, but actual leaves had not yet appeared. He got through after about fifteen minutes.

"Talk to your sister," Alicia said. "All I asked is for help with the shopping. She's behaving as if I constantly demand favors!"

He held the phone away from his head.

Diane perked up; she was reading the newspaper on the sofa.

He cleared his throat. "If you speak to me in a reasonable tone of voice about neutral topics, like what's new, how's the weather, then fine. But if you continue to scream, I'm hanging up."

Alicia continued to scream.

"I have a new way of handling this," he said in English as he hung up.

Diane stared at him. "Did you just hang up on your mother?"

He smiled. "Yes, I did."

"Just like that? What was she saying?"

"She wants me to get involved with some drama with my sister."

"So you hung up on her? You could have said no."

"I've been saying no for about twenty years now. She doesn't hear me."

The phone rang, and he picked up. It was Nadia. He held out the receiver, so that Diane could hear the torrent of Spanish from the other end.

"No, really. I hung up on her, and I'm hanging up on you," he said, and hung up the phone. He looked out the window and laughed. "I don't know why I didn't start doing this *years* ago." Diane hung her head as if she were the guilty one, and looked up at him with a fearful expression. She could be so very beautiful. A shame she was always wearing the same thing.

"I think it's time we went out," he said grandly. "It's a new day, and there's so much to see in the world."

The phone rang as they collected their coats. María left a message on the machine in violent, sputtering Spanish. He waited for her to finish, and then erased her voice with a feeling of satisfaction. As gusts of wind assailed them on Hudson Street, his cellphone rang. María began to shout and he interrupted her.

"It would be no trouble to me never to speak to you again, so don't threaten me. And if you cry"—he turned to Diane, nodding: María was crying; of course she was—"I will end this conversation right now. So it's really your choice."

He waited. She continued to sob. "Okay, then." He hung up the phone, and took Diane's hand to stroll with her up the avenue.

"What was all that about?" she asked.

"They want to drag me back into their arguments, their stupid neighborhood soap operas. The fact that I won't listen to my mother talk about third parties is almost as bad as the fact that I don't visit."

"Yes, but what specifically was the argument?"

"Who cares?"

"I care," she said, as they crossed the street.

His new theory was that the soap operas on TV and in the households were the only thing that sustained them all amid the vast failures of the Revolution. No food, no space, no peace, no books, no freedom, no progress, no repairs? No problem: as long as they could have their daily melodramas over petty bullshit, and drive each other insane, they could survive. Trash swirled in little eddies on Hudson Street.

"I'm starving," he said as he opened the door to the coffee shop. "Did I tell you that Chris had an affair with Jan Mattias a few years ago?"

"Well, that would explain things," Diane said.

VLADIMIR HAD FIRST come to the United States after winning a design competition sponsored by the University of Illinois. The invitation for postgraduate study came right after his final year in architecture school; perhaps he was too young to realize how good his luck was. After the fellowship ended, he had returned to Cuba with dread, sweating the whole way home. Nothing good could come of it, but he felt he had no other option. Gravity was stronger then.

It was like volunteering to stand in a cage. María was a bottomless pit of need. She had gained at least thirty pounds and was a seething, sobbing mess, impatient to pretend that he had never left. Javier was almost three, and had not yet learned how to pass half an hour without falling, screaming or crying. Pucho was still in his Army job and the house was organized around his schedule and moods. After two years of living his own life in a place where anything seemed possible, Vladimir was acutely aware of the narrowness of the place they expected him to squeeze himself back into in order to live.

His father took him aside the night he came back home.

"I don't have to tell you that they still have a file on you," Pucho said, sitting down on his chair on the patio and lighting up a cigar. A fight broke out in the kitchen. "You'll be followed. This house will be watched. The entire family will be watched." He waved the match out and exhaled.

Javier let out a howl from the kitchen.

This was a scene he hadn't missed: Pucho holding court from the only unbroken chair on the humid patio, while melodrama raged in the kitchen.

"What's the matter now?" Pucho called, but no one responded. His face had gotten thicker in the two years Vladimir had been away; he'd become a caricature of himself, with heavy jowls and dark, three-dimensional pouches under his eyes. He turned his attention back to Vladimir. "I don't care what you did in Disneyland. You're under my roof now, and I will not have you blight our careers or compromise our lives with your selfishness again."

Javier climbed onto Vladimir's lap and squealed. María arrived and perched her heavy haunch on the arm of Pucho's chair. Vladimir's throat was beginning to close. Javier was now banging his head on the table repeatedly.

"Javier!" María shouted and dragged him upstairs. To their room, where Vladimir would have to go and make some kind of peace with her shortly.

"Vladimir, come take a look," his mother called.

She led him to a corner where she'd been working on a perfectly proportioned replica of the Cathedral of Havana. He bent to look at the colonnades and the cobblestoned square. "I have to be careful, or someone will destroy this. Either Javier or Pucho, I don't know who."

He sat down with her at her workbench. His mother had taught him how to measure, how to draw straight lines, how to think about space and how to make models, using pieces of cardboard dipped in tea for roof tiles. There was a time when she'd had an entire construction crew at her disposal, but her responsibilities had diminished year by year, even though there were buildings collapsing at least once a week and the need for architects and preservationists was visible on every street. She'd once been a gorgeous woman with magnificent posture and long black hair. She still stood up straight, but her hair was short now, a strange burgundy color, and she had dark, nearly navy blue blotches under her eyes.

He wanted to cry.

"How can you stand it anymore?" he asked her.

She looked at him directly. "What are the alternatives?"

He'd had alternatives! What had he been thinking?

◆

WHEN THEY CAME BACK to Vladimir's apartment after breakfast, the phone was ringing, and Diane picked it up before Vladimir could stop her. She'd arrived the previous week with misgivings, apologies and the smallest of suitcases. She really shouldn't be picking up his phone without permission, but clearly something was wrong down there and his attitude was not helping. Also, she was curious.

"*¡Oigo!*" said a male voice.

"Hello. I'm sorry, I don't speak Spanish."

There was a pause, as gears shifted into English. "Who are you?"

"This is Diane. I'm a friend of Vladimir's."

The voice was deep and energetic. "This is the new woman?"

"You must be Javier! I've seen your picture. How do you do?"

Vladimir went to his desk, holding his hands away from his body, as if to say, I want nothing to do with this.

"Why my father hangs up the phone?" Javier asked.

"He's annoyed."

"Always he's annoyed."

She thought about this. "That's true. Tell me about you?"

He released a dark, humorless laugh. "I am on trouble all the time."

She sat down to listen. "Do you want to talk about it?"

"Yes. You're a good person to talk. But not by phone. When we meet?"

"When are you coming, Javier? I don't think I can go there."

"What's he talking about?" Vladimir asked, organizing his desk.

"Tell my father," Javier was saying, "I come to you in this summer. They want me to go to the Army. I am not a *militar*, Diane. Even my grandfather knows this. But he makes me to go to the *militar* school."

"What are your alternatives?"

"I can't talk now," he said rapidly.

"Did someone just walk in?"

"Yes." He sounded under pressure.

"Your grandfather?"

"Listen, Diane, I like to talk to you again. When you call me?"

"When would be a good time?"

Vladimir took the phone out of her hand.

"Wait," she said, surprised.

He held his hand up and began speaking in rapid, incomprehensible Spanish. He hung up the phone, dialed the number a few times, and then got through. He listened for a long time. At one point, he laughed very hard. At another point he put his hand over his eyes. Whatever it was, it was very funny or very bad, and he probably wouldn't tell her. Why hadn't she asked Javier yes-or-no questions? Why hadn't she taken Spanish instead of French in school? Billy Wilder learned English when he first came to Hollywood by committing ten new words a day to memory. She could do that with Spanish. Why hadn't she started already?

Vladimir hung up, shaking his head, smirking. Now he would go to his desk and answer only the questions he wanted to answer.

Diane pursued him to his computer. "What happened?"

"Big trouble. It's too long to go into, but funny. I was cracking down."

"Cracking *up*. Cracking *down* is what they do to the dissidents."

"You're learning, Diane," he said laughing, but she heard the distinctive volleying notes of an Internet chess game, and the conversation was over.

Diane had no problem imagining living in Vladimir's cool, open apartment. It was difficult, however, to imagine living there with Vladimir, even though this was what she was actually doing. They came home, separately or together, after eleven p.m., and he went directly to the computer to read updates on Cuba and play chess with international strangers. He was on the Internet by nine every morning, and often departed before she was fully awake, leaving very little time for talk, much of which concerned the longevity of the *hijo de puta*. He had yet to attend another movie. Was he avoiding her?

It was March, her annual chance to right the wrongs of Hollywood history, in the series "And the Envelope, Please . . ." As Neal Gabler argues in his brilliant treatise *An Empire of Their Own,* the dysfunctional, status-hungry Jewish tyrants who created the Studio System of old routinely turned to the classical stage and tragedy to give their new media more "class." So when the industry got together to bestow awards on itself, the serious, high-art stuff naturally won the awards. The tradition continues, even though film stars represent the "class," if not the deities, of the current era. Thoughts of golden-idol worship were inevitable, especially during Awards Season.

Her new cellphone rang for the first time. She hadn't given the number to anyone except Cindy, to use in case of emergency only, and Vladimir, who was sitting across from her, not communicating. This had to be a wrong number.

"That bastard Mattias has been blacklisting me in Hollywood for the last ten years." She sighed. Daniel Dubrovnik, time-consuming Board member number two.

"How did you get this number?"

"Dorothy gave it to me."

She closed her eyes. It was just a matter of time before the daily assault on her time went mobile.

Daniel was hopping mad: How else could she explain industry-wide lack of interest in his scripts after twenty-five years of award-winning work?

"Assuming that you're right," Diane yawned, "why would he do it?"

"Jealousy, Diane. I have *ideas.* Jan Mattias is essentially in *real estate.* He buys *properties.* He hasn't had an original thought in his life. I know for a fact that he's had face work done. He's even had body implants."

Diane promised to consider options for Daniel, and hung up; he'd been unraveling in slow motion over the last year, she supposed, but she couldn't take him seriously.

The interesting downside of fame that Richard Schickel explores at length in his harrowing book *Intimate Strangers* is the ill will ordinary citizens bear the celebrities they worship. The bigger the fame, the bigger the resentment. Vladimir was right: bigness certainly was a factor in the movies, as in life. Would the Taliban have blown up the colossal Buddhas carved into the cliffs of Afghanistan if the statues had been just a little smaller? Dorothy and Estelle talking about the star-studded MGM commissary sounded like a scene out of *Mean Girls* (Mark Waters, 2004).

"Why don't you do like I do?" Vladimir asked. "Just hang up the phone."

"You make a fine point. By the way, Javier wants to come here this summer."

"Yeah, right," Vladimir said, typing.

"Why not?"

He was about to say something but stopped with his mouth open. He looked cornered. "A family visa is next to impossible to get. He would need a formal invitation from an institution that would agree to pay all his expenses."

"From Wiley Hurtado Padrón Architects, for example?"

"They'd see through that."

"The Bedford Street Cinema's International Internship Program?"

Vladimir smiled at her with his eyes only.

"He sounds like fun. He sounds like he could use a visit with you."

Vladimir grunted, and made a move on the electronic chessboard.

"His grandfather wants him in the army, did you hear that?"

"*Cojones,*" he said, shaking his head, staring at the screen. He held up his hands, as if to say, What can I do about it?

"I'd be glad to supply the letter. You tell me what to say."

"Thank you," he said, and squeezed her hand dismissively while waiting for his opponent to make a move. "I'll send you a letter tomorrow."

"And give me his phone number—he wants me to call him."

Vladimir dropped her hand.

"He needs someone to talk to."

A look of disgust made a mash of his handsome face. Clearly there was a long, nasty history, but why let it seep down on the kid? Vladimir was now fully absorbed in his game. The following day, she would sign a year-long lease for a studio Paul had found in Brooklyn Heights. Without a fixed place to keep her clothing and a bed that she could sleep in without apologizing, she couldn't plan further than a day ahead. Regardless of what happened with Vladimir, she needed her own place. She settled back in to read the rest of the paper. Vladimir wasn't unpleasant, but he wasn't ideal.

◆

ON THE INTERNET when Vladimir got to the studio: He Who Must Not Be Named was still alive. Magnus wore two earrings that day, one in each ear.

Diane had been in residence in Vladimir's apartment for a week. Vladimir wanted to enjoy having her around, but she often seemed to be waiting for him to say or do something, and this made him uncomfortable. She was sloppy about her clothing, papers and personal space. She took forever in the shower. His thoughts went through the same loop over and over: Where is this going? This can go nowhere, so what's the point?

The phone rang. It was Rosa, an old friend of his mother's.

"Vladimir, I just got out. I'm visiting my son in Miami. I'm worried about your mother. You must call her."

"I do call her."

"No. You must call her every day and say something nice. It's the least you can do. She deserves better."

"I will call her when I like, how often I like, and tell her what I like."

Rosa began to cry. These women! It was all he could do not to slam down the phone.

"Vladimir, he's cruel, your father."

"Exactly! And she chooses to stay with him. That's her business. Not yours."

"She's really desperate to get out. She told me to call you."

"Wait: She told you to tell me that I wasn't calling enough, or that she wants to get out? Out of the house? Or out of the country?"

"Yes, yes!"

"Yes *what*, Rosa?"

"All of the above. But she would settle for a nice phone call."

He hung up. He stalked around the office.

Magnus looked up from his model making. "What did I do now?"

"The *bullshit. The BULLSHIT!*"

Vladimir went back to the phone and stabbed in the number. He couldn't get through. His anger abated somewhat as he dialed the number repeatedly while downloading new software, chewing gum violently and reading editorials he agreed with on the Internet.

AFTER VLADIMIR RETURNED from America, the family watched him for signs of corruption, freedom, ideological diversionism, despair. He did despair: he was back in the purview of the Neighborhood Watch Committee, standing on line for two hours in the hot sun in front of stores with no food. The loudspeakers on the street broadcast the Leader's speech, so even if you avoided the demonstration, or didn't watch it on TV, you still had to listen to it. Every thought was—forget judged!—*interrupted*.

Within a week, he could barely function. They drove him out of bed with their hectoring in the morning. He received advice at the dinner table every night from his father, his mother, his sister (then nineteen), his grandmother (whether or not she was lucid), and his wife (a woman who had never worked a day in her life). He was sick of everyone, most especially María, who struck him as unbelievably childish, vulgar, impulsive and fat. Why had he agreed to this marriage?

After a month of this, he went to the university with shaking hands. It was August by then, and his old mentor was scheduling classes. He assigned Vladimir a third-year studio. There was a brief armistice in the house; Pucho poured him a glass of Havana Club to toast his new job. Vladimir sipped the rum warily and faced his family in silence, preparing himself for the next bad scene, which came in short order—Javier sent dishes smashing to the floor. Not an hour went by without shouting or tears. How could he live another day in this intolerable heat, harassment, proximity, friction?

Vladimir's classroom was an enormous ballroom with twenty-foot ceilings, Corinthian columns and formerly magnificent marble floors. His signature was constantly in demand for petitions. There were routine departmental meetings during which the staff was told to work the Bay of Pigs Invasion, the Battle of Ideas, the Duties of a Revolutionary, etc., into the day's curriculum. The section leader said that she couldn't be sure his job was secure if he didn't attend Committee meetings, sign petitions and march in weekly demonstrations.

Within a week of the start of school, Vladimir noticed nests of twigs, dolls and patches of fabric at the bases of the columns in his classroom and in spots around the building. When he mentioned it in the staff room, he was hushed by one colleague, and cut dead by another, who walked away while he was speaking to her.

Vladimir happily reconnected with Bebo, who was also teaching in the department. They began having lunch. Some days they split a plate at the cafeteria; at the end of the month, they ate cones of peanuts in the park. Vladimir was determined not to go home for the midday meal.

Two months into the term, one of the deans collapsed in the lunchroom, poisoned by a teacher, who confessed she'd put a drop of smoked cod oil in his coffee in order to get him out of her hair. The dean, who was allergic to fish, died. The teacher was sent to prison, but the little offerings on the columns, stairwells and windowsills remained. Vladimir was afraid to leave a cup of water unattended when he went around the room assessing student work.

After dinner, he often sat with Bebo on the lip of the old dry fountain across from Bebo's building in Centro Habana. Sometimes there was rum; usually not. Bebo had had little action, and was impressed that by law, a twenty-three-year-old like Vladimir could demand sex from his wife every night.

"That assumes that I want it."

"How could you not?"

"Eat a meal with her and then tell me you're still interested."

Every day, he looked at María—truly looked at her, sifting through her features, statements and movements—trying to find something attractive about her. In fact, he'd never been particularly attracted to her; he'd started talking to her that first time because she happened to be standing there and he'd just been stood up by someone else. She'd been a bulldozer from the beginning; she'd introduced him as her boyfriend on their second date. In fact, he almost got rid of her the second month when he overheard her referring to Pucho as her father-in-law when talking to a friend. Perversely, Pucho had started taking Vladimir more seriously with the advent of María. When Vladimir mentioned seeing other people, María went on talking as if he hadn't spoken. He'd tried to break up with her on three separate occasions by the time she told him, not bothering to hide her satisfaction, that she was pregnant. It was too heartbreaking to think about.

One night María appeared as he and Bebo sat smoking on the steps by the fountain across from Bebo's. She stood with her hands on her hips.

"What are you doing, talking to this loser," she demanded. It was unclear if she was addressing him or Bebo. She had put on makeup for this scene, and it was melting in the heat. "You should be at home, with your wife and family."

He hated her smug passivity.

"In that airless house? With the patriarch behaving like a pig? No thanks. You go: you seem to be in love with him."

"Ha!" A single note of amazement came from a woman in the second-floor window who had been following their discussion.

"Catch you later, brother," Bebo said, patting his shoulder.

"You're a disgrace," María said, raising her voice.

A small crowd had gathered. He wondered if she would become physically violent and make it a show.

"That's right. So why not divorce me, if you're so ashamed and unhappy?"

At this, the first mention of divorce, she burst into tears, just as she would with every subsequent use of the word. She doubled over as if he'd punched her in the stomach. An audience member came to her aid.

"Yes, *you* deal with her," Vladimir told the spectators, and walked off. "I have no patience for her anymore. She's a black hole."

There was whistling and shouting in his wake.

What a mistake, what a weight, what a burden she was! He left the scene, but of course she followed behind him whimpering as he stalked to the Malecón. When could he have a moment of solitude in this fucking country?

The temperature had dropped; a clap of thunder was coming soon. She put her sticky arms around his neck. He peeled her hands off and walked. All he wanted was to sit on the wall and think. But she wouldn't even give him that much space.

Countless people were embarking from these rocks on rafts and tires to reach freedom. An unknowable number had already perished in the process. What was he doing here? He could have stayed in Chicago! He would have been illegal for a time, but so what? He would have been illegal till he was legal. Cuba was perhaps the last bad place you could be from, according to the U.S. Immigration and Naturalization Service: there were special provisions. You could essentially defect without having to prove you were politically persecuted. They knew all about Fidel Castro at the INS.

He had come home because he was sick of the drum beating constantly in his head: *bad son, bad husband, bad father.* But all he wanted now was to get away. It was all a big mistake—this girl was a cow! She wasn't even such a great mother: all she did was yell. She spanked Javier with a hairbrush at least once a day. She kissed the child on the mouth! Vladimir was appalled. He wanted to hit her each time she hit the child. They had arguments at night. She asked him, again with the triumphant smile: When had he changed a diaper? When had he picked the child up after a fall? When had he done anything for Javier? What gave him the right to have opinions on how she was raising the child?

Each time he tried to reach within himself to find love or tenderness or at least the resources to deal with the revulsion, she did something more revolting. How could he ever respond positively to her? He hated the sight of her! He hated the sight of her laughing with his father. He didn't want to, but he hated Javier, too. Just for being there, taking up space, making noise, causing chaos.

He'd had friends, and yes, girlfriends in America: he wasn't made of stone. But things were different there, lighter. Perhaps even *too* light: some people saw their families once a year! People lived alone, with space, with peace and quiet. They weren't bombarded all day long by the needs, shouts, smells and sweaty hands of four generations of demanding family members.

The clap of thunder he'd been expecting shook the waterfront, and the rain began in earnest. He was shortly drenched. He turned and walked straight home, with María alternately trotting at his side to beg his forgiveness, and falling back to groan excessively and curse him out. When they reached the house, he waited outside; he saw her answering questions in the front room. He debated going in for a towel, but decided to skip the interrogation. Any day now, he expected a lecture from his father on how to satisfy his wife.

He ran to Bebo's and whistled, but no one came out. He spent the night lying sleepless in the darkness on a wet concrete bench outside his classroom. Perhaps there wasn't such a thing as true love. But there had to be something better than this!

IT TOOK A FULL HOUR to get through to Cuba; by this time he had forgotten why he was calling. His father answered.

"Put Mom on," Vladimir said.

"Who is this?" Pucho asked.

Vladimir felt a familiar metallic taste in his mouth.

"Well, let's see. How many men call your home asking for 'Mom'?"

Of course, his father could simply hang up the phone. But he didn't.

"Alicia!" he roared. Vladimir waited. He wondered if his father would speak to him. Pucho had stopped speaking to his own father over politics, so there was historical precedent for this. Vladimir's mother came to the phone.

"Rosa called," Vladimir said. "She tells me you're unhappy."

There was silence. Then: "Oh, Vladimir."

"Just answer yes or no. Do you want to move out?"

"Yes."

"Would you like to go live with your sister?"

"Yes. But there are technicalities."

The situation had to be pretty terrible if she wanted to move in with her sister and brother-in-law in the middle of nowhere in La Lisa.

"Put him on the phone."

The phone switched hands. "What," his father said.

"What kind of technicalities?"

"Ana won't take her," Pucho said.

"That *cannot* be true. Put her on," he said quickly, before his father got wound up. "Mom? Is it true what he just said?"

"Pucho said there may be a problem getting me on her ration card."

"Put him on."

The phone switched hands again.

"What," his father said.

"You can make a single phone call and get Mom on Ana's household card."

"Maybe Ana used the ration card as an excuse because she didn't want your mother moving in. I don't think she has much space."

A searing pain sliced his chest. "You should be ashamed of yourself!"

"Why? I'm doing her a great favor, letting her live here."

"Bullshit," Vladimir said, trying to control his anger. He hung
up and began dialing his aunt's number.

He got through half an hour later. "Are you up-to-date with
Mom?"

"She's living with that monster and his girlfriend."

"Would you be able to take her in?"

"I would love it!"

"She said there was a problem with the ration card."

"There won't be a problem," Ana said. "I know some people.
She could move in this weekend."

"Good. Thank you."

"We miss you, Vladimir! Why don't you ever come back to
visit?"

"You don't have the time to hear that list," he said.

Placing his next call, Vladimir got through to Cuba on the third
try.

His sister answered. "So you don't have a grandmother now?"

Vladimir was immediately on guard. He smelled sulfur, sewers.
"What?"

"I read your application to that foundation for a grant," Nadia
said.

"What?"

"Are you alive? Most people hear these things about themselves
only after they're dead. And you wrote that stuff about yourself? It's
sickening."

"How is it possible that you read my grant application?"

"Tell me, Vladimir, if you have truly moved on to a new world,
why is your Yahoo password *c-u-b-a*?"

He would not stoop to their level. "Put your mother on the
phone."

Alicia thanked him when he told her the news. He really should
call her more often, he reflected. She did deserve better. If only all
these other vipers weren't there.

He hung up, changed his password, and called Bebo to tell him about Nadia's e-mail trespass.

"That's *my* password," Bebo said, not at all surprised.

It was probably the password of all two million Cubans in exile.

In his e-mail in-box, there was a letter from Elena Gutiérrez Pérez—no doubt another projectile of rhetoric from her daughter Yasmina. He opened it: it was from Elena Gutiérrez Pérez herself. She was writing to tell him that he had insulted her by implying that his correspondence with her daughter over her e-mail account could in any way compromise her. She had a spotless reputation, she wrote, as the Administrative Secretary of the Deputy Chief of the Ministry of Education; she was also a Member in Good Standing of the Federation of Cuban Women, and a Sector Chief of the Committee for the Defense of the Revolution. Anyone reading his letter could come to only one conclusion: He was a disgrace to his country.

Cojones!

◆

IN SPITE OF having campaigned with all his strength to go to La Lenin, the top nonmilitary high school where all his friends went, Javier was now enrolled in another *camilito* school. His grandfather had granite wrapped in flan where his brain should have been.

"Why am I in a military school if I'm not going into the military?"

"Everyone does military service," Pucho said. "And so will you. You'll have a head start by being a *camilito*."

"If you do well in the exams," Javier said, "you do one year in the military instead of two, and then you go to university."

"So do well in the exams," Pucho said, as if the idea were preposterous.

He would get into university, if only to fuck his grandfather over.

His standing at the Camilo Cienfuegos Military High School in El Cotorro was worse than at the one in Capdevila. He was given an extra conduct card, as his bad acts couldn't fit on one card. It read:

REPORT	DEMERITS
Late to Formation	1
Personal Hygiene (dirt on boots)	1
Talking Back (to Lieutenant)	3
Sleeping in Class	2
Speaking in Class	2
Absent from Class	3
Smoking in an Inappropriate Area	3
Talking Back (to Captain)	4
Exposing Member in an Inappropriate Area (urinating behind Auditorium)	4
Lack of Courtesy (not saluting an Officer)	4
Talking Back (to Colonel)	5
Yawning in Class	2

At the weekly court-martial, where student conduct was tabulated, he was told to reflect on his contribution to the Revolution, and was sentenced to weekend drudgery. At the barracks, a mimeographed sheet lay on his bed. It read:

Year of the XXXXV Anniversary of the Victory of Playa Girón, The First Great Defeat of Imperialism in Latin America

Your presence is requested next Monday, April 12th, at 15:30 hours. The purpose of this meeting is the interview of the candidate [here the name Javier Hurtado Casares was written on a blank line in pencil] on his qualifications to be a member of the Unión de Jovenes Comunistas (UJC), in the Province of Ciudad de la Habana, Camilo Cienfuegos Military School, El Cotorro Section.

Public humiliation for two conduct cards on a Thursday, and then UJC membership the following Monday? Not possible.

On Monday afternoon at the appointed time, he showed up at

the designated classroom, and he tried to be neat. Leticia Gómez, the Section Leader of the Juventud at the school, was sitting with the Principal and two men in their early twenties at the front of the humid room. Javier saw Pucho chatting with his Marxism teacher, who had caught him smoking in an inappropriate area. The meeting began with formal introductions, and he began to sweat on his forehead.

"As you are fully aware," the UJC Municipal Director said, "being a Member of the Union of Young Communists is an honor. Joining is voluntary and selective. Your record has been examined, and a recommendation has been made to the Chief of the Base Core."

Javier felt sweat on the back of his knees.

The UJC officer then read aloud a list of Necessary Attributes of a Communist Youth, adding, "To be a part of the New Generation of Rebel Youth, you must always be in the Vanguard, mindful of the legacy of Our Heroes and Martyrs, who started the unceasing Struggle against Imperialism. Leticia, would you like to continue?"

Javier felt sweat breaking out under his arms and on his back.

"You must train yourself to think proper thoughts, to have co-herent ideas," Leticia Gómez declared. "You must understand your role and have total consciousness of what we defend. You must be efficacious in each and every working day!"

His mouth and throat were dry.

"You will join the struggle of anti-imperialism, without forget-ting, as our dear Commander-in-Chief, Fidel, has taught us, the se-cret lies in the Unity of forces, now more than ever!" She finished on a ringing note, and there was a round of polite grunting. The Division Director suddenly focused on Javier.

"Your father is a traitor and a worm. What do you think of him?"

Javier cleared his throat. "I don't see how that's relevant."

"*We* decide what's relevant," the Director said, leaning forward for emphasis. "Why do you want to be a member of the Juventud?"

"I don't."

He felt, rather than saw, his grandfather sit up and look around, as if to catch someone's eye whom he could command to change what was wrong.

"I don't think I can be the kind of candidate you're looking for," he said, sweating in his groin now. "I respect the institution, so I don't want to waste your time. I'm just not that kind of Revolutionary material."

There was silence in the room. Leticia looked at him as if he'd announced he slept on a bed of live snakes. The Principal nodded; he'd been the one who caught him urinating behind the auditorium. "Thank you for your honesty," he said. "Are you sure?"

"Completely sure."

The Principal cast a glance over his head. "Well, then, that's all."

Everyone got up to leave. Pucho continued to sit at the school desk. Javier walked out of the classroom without looking at him.

He went to his barracks, where two guys were playing cards on the shady side of the room. He lay down on his bed and waited. He was starving. His life loomed ahead: hunger, boredom and confrontation. It was just a matter of time.

The barracks doors banging open sounded like gunshots.

The card players scurried to attention. In his uniform, with magnificent posture, Pucho entered, looked them over in an arrogant fashion, and passed on to Javier's bed. How wonderful to walk into a room and make everything stop.

Pucho waited, giving him the stony, fleshy stare.

Javier sat up, but didn't stand. He pulled his new conduct card out of his pocket and held it out for demerits.

"Outside." Pucho pivoted and left the barracks with a banging of doors.

Javier found him sitting on a bench outside the dining hall.

"You humiliated me in there," Pucho said.

Javier sat down next to him. "I was trying to do the honorable thing."

"Joining *is* the honorable thing. You'd make contacts, you'd get points."

"It would be hypocritical for me to join."

Pucho gave his head an impatient shake. "You could be a great

Revolutionary, if you tried. You don't try. And I don't understand why."

The school's stray trotted over. Pucho clapped his hands at the dog to make it go away. The dog followed the order. "Do you know what I had to do to get them to consider your application? After you were expelled? Twice?"

"If you had asked me, I would have told you that the *last* thing I want is to be a member of the Juventud. But you never ask!"

"You think you're smart, but you're only hurting yourself. Pretty soon you'll be putting your family in jeopardy." He stood up. "I think you fucked yourself but good this time. But go to the Principal and tell him you're sorry."

"For what?"

"Do what I tell you. No arguments."

"I'm not a Young Communist, I don't know how else to say it! And there's nothing you can do to make me one."

"*Cojones!* You never learn."

◆

"WE WANT A PEACEFUL EVENT," warned a young, stocky cop with an Irish name and an open face, who was guarding the barricades across from the Cuban Mission.

"This protest will be silent," Vladimir announced.

Relief and surprise passed over the cop's face.

Vladimir wore a sign with a photo of Blas Giraldo Reyes Rodríguez. *CRIME: LENDING BOOKS. SENTENCE: 25 YEARS IN PRISON.* He held high another sign: *DICTATOR-SHIP FROM THE LEFT IS STILL DICTATORSHIP.* He felt a current of electricity shoot through his chest as he and the others in his group covered their mouths with duct tape and began to walk in an oval at the curb on Lexington Avenue.

There were ten people in Vladimir's group; Manuel's group, the Sons of Martí, had refused to participate, but some of the *sons* of the Sons of José Martí had joined them. Just before noon, a flock of women arrived: mothers, sisters, daughters and wives of Cuban political prisoners. He eyed one who was holding a megaphone and pointed to the tape on his mouth; she set it down at the curb. So far, so good. A lone cameraman from Univision filmed. None of the English-language media he'd contacted had come. This was the flip side of democracy: people were free to pay no attention.

At twelve-fifteen, a stereo speaker appeared at a window across the street, and the hectic sounds of a Van Van song filled the air.

Bebo ripped off his duct tape and screamed: "*¡ABAJO CAS-TRO!*"

Vladimir watched as every last silent Cuban stripped off his tape and cried: "*¡ABAJO CASTRO!*"

The woman scrambled to retrieve her megaphone and began the chant: "*¡CASTRO: TRAIDOR! ¡ASESINO Y DICTADOR!*"

Vladimir broke out of the oval in disgust.

"You had a good thing going there," said the cop. "What happened?"

He peeled tape off his mouth. "You don't know how many meetings. We agreed!"

"It's your right. Constitutionally."

"But in a place of freedom, where everyone has the right to scream, you must be silent in order to be heard. It's a question of tactics."

The cop nodded, then swiveled back to supervise the noise.

¡CASTRO: TRAIDOR! ¡ASESINO Y DICTADOR! rang in his head as he boarded the subway. How could there be democracy with such a stubborn people? He wouldn't speak to any of them, ever again. He was through with cooperation and compromise. Perhaps he was through with Cuba. It was too heartbreaking, too annoying. Nothing ever changed.

◆

"So this is Tara," Paul said as he strolled into and out of rooms, testing doors, windows and appliances, getting in the way of the contractor and the home inspector at every turn. Chris was losing patience. When a neighbor stopped by to introduce herself, Paul opened his arms wide and cried, "The Hospitality Committee!"

Perhaps the porch only made sense without Paul.

On the flight home, when the Fasten Seat Belt sign was extinguished, Paul loosened his grip on Chris's wrist and said, "Vladimir really knows what he's doing with indoor-outdoor transitions. I think you should ask him for help when you design the porch."

Chris cast a look at him. Now, what did that mean?

Paul reclined in his chair and put on a navy blue eye mask with ceremony. "You still haven't told him, have you?"

In fact, he hadn't. He had a stable professional situation with Vladimir, and a stable personal situation with Paul. What was he doing throwing away money and antagonizing people for a porch? There were porches within driving distance of NoHo.

Chris pulled out his phone in the LaGuardia baggage claim.

"Who are you calling?"

"Sheilah and Julius," he said. "To let them know that we're okay, and to make plans for tonight."

"I cannot take another tofu casserole," Paul said, "and I don't want you cooking again. They don't appreciate it."

Sheilah was a social worker and Julius was a retired illustrator; they were Paul's parents, and Chris wanted to see them more than Paul did. They routinely marched against war, government wiretapping and the like in their orthopedic sandals and socks. There was always a lively chat going on in their tiny, overcrowded apartment on Amsterdam Avenue. Chris liked the fact that anything that might come up in conversation there was always normal to talk about.

Each time Chris suggested a trip to the Upper West Side, Paul said, "You just like them because you share a common enemy." He made scathing remarks, often to their faces, about their hair (long), their clothing (hemp), their food (vegetarian), their housekeeping (lax) and their pieties (liberal). Each time they left, Julius told Chris, "Come back soon. But don't bring that snotty little twerp you hang out with next time. He's such a drag."

And Paul would stick his tongue out or make an obscene noise.

By contrast, Chris's father—dead five years now—had stopped speaking to him fifteen years earlier. Chris supposed his father had known about him long before he had. His mother had always kept the door open for him, and true to form, they had never discussed the Topic. When she came to New York (his father never joined her), Chris introduced her around to all his friends and colleagues. Charlotte was chatty, affectionate and polite; at an AIDS benefit held in a restaurant he'd designed, he caught her smiling fiercely. She was proud of his professional success. And the topic of gayness just never came up. Each time he visited, his sister-in-law would ask brightly, "Will you be bringing anyone along?"

He never had. But it was unnatural not to bring Paul after all this time.

Chris's mother was an hour away by car, his brother twenty minutes by car. He would get back in touch with old friends, but would old friends be interested in double dates with him and Paul? Did he care? Was there a home in Atlanta (other than his own) where anything that might come up in conversation would be considered normal to talk about?

APRIL

"What happened to your eyebrows?"

Vladimir had arrived home on a rainy night to find Diane on the floor, sweeping shards of glass into a dustpan.

"I'm sorry, I just wanted to make a pot roast. Everything went wrong," she said, and burst into a brief volley of sobs. He held her close. He had never seen her cry before. Fortunately, it didn't last long. He brought her to the bathroom to treat her wounds.

"Vladimir, the studio in Brooklyn fell through," she said, and he fought off a brief impulse to flee. This soon-to-be-available apartment was the reason he'd agreed to let her stay without an exit date.

"What in hell does that Paul think he's doing? This is the third apartment in a row to fall out? You need a place to live!"

She looked conflicted. He knew she didn't want to live in Brooklyn.

They went to the Chinese place on the corner. He didn't want to know if the pot roast had some significance. Desperately, he did not want her to push the issue. Yes, they'd been seeing each other for several months. Yes, she would soon be turning forty. Yes, if he wasn't serious he should tell her.

"I want to point something out to you," she said after they ordered.

"I don't want to talk about it."

She stopped playing with her chopsticks. "How do you know what I'm going to say?"

"I don't want to talk about anything in a serious way tonight, Diane."

"I think the María situation is not a stalemate."

"Why? We've been married for seventeen years, and I've been begging to get out for sixteen of them. Why should it change?"

"Because things change. They *do*," she said, when he objected. "When did you last talk to her about it?"

"I wrote her an e-mail. In the fall."

"Did she answer you?"

"Always. Long, nasty letters. Terrible punctuation and typos, practically illiterate, stream of consciousness. In every letter she says no."

"What if *I* talked to her?"

He laughed. "You're brave even to consider it."

"Does she speak English?" He shook his head. "We could get a translator here. What about your friend Bebo?"

"*¡Comemierda, carajo!* I'll never speak to him again. Also, his English is bad. But his wife is fluent." He suddenly felt hot. "What would you say?"

"I would just pose a few new questions, to open doors in her mind."

Her left eyebrow looked like straw. Diane was messy. Diane was clumsy. Diane gave him hope.

"May I ask you to stay out of the kitchen?"

"It's not usually that bad," she said.

FROM CHRIS's bored expression, Vladimir knew he was very late. A group was gathered in front of the screen at the Bedford Street Cinema. He made sure to greet Diane as if he hadn't seen her since the last meeting.

"I think we may have to cancel the blacklist panel," Diane said. "Two of our panelists have cancelled because of illness."

"I'd be glad to step in," said the mousy little man who stared at Diane with an open mouth at every meeting.

"Jan Mattias hates the design," said Jack Lipsky, Diane's boss.

Vladimir didn't get upset about these things anymore. "Which part?"

"He didn't say."

"Has he seen it?" Diane asked.

"I didn't show him anything," Vladimir said, and Chris began blinking. Vladimir had learned this was a sign that his partner was angry. "We should feel him up about that."

There were a few giggles. "Feel him *out*," Chris corrected.

"Out, up, in, through. Find out what is the bee in his bucket."

"I'll do that," said Diane, and went to the last row with her phone.

"You know, Vladimir, I used to go to Cuba in the fifties," one of the old actresses said. "The Hotel Nacional was so glamorous. You wouldn't understand. How glamorous it was, all the chic people."

Chris raised an eyebrow at him. Vladimir knew that to most of the Americans he met, he represented all of Cuba; for many, he represented all of Latin America. On some level—no, on many levels—this was tedious.

"Herb and I stayed at the Hotel Nacional in 2001," said the other actress. "It's not the same. But we went to the cigar factories, and we saw them reading Dickens to the people. The people are happy in Cuba. They love the Revolution."

"Where did you get this fiction?" Vladimir asked.

"The tour guide," she said, smiling.

The tour guide. When feeling optimistic, Vladimir believed in fighting on all fronts. But talking was a waste of time, especially talking to Americans, who lived in a kind of national kindergarten, where no one was allowed to say anything unkind and everyone pretended to clean up. He'd said it all, he'd heard it all. He was done with *discusión,* which was harsher in Spanish, closer to *argument* than to *conversation.* No more talk!

Diane trotted back to the stage. "Jan seems to think the entire concept is wrong. I asked him if he was talking about the layout, or the look. He said both. But since he hasn't seen your drawings, I don't know what he's talking about, and I propose that neither does he. So let's continue. If he has a specific objection, he can raise it."

Chris sent Vladimir a we'll-talk-later look.

"Jan said he'd step in on the blacklist panel," Diane said.

The mousy man blew a gasket. "YOU HAVE *GOT* TO BE KIDDING ME! WHAT THE HELL DOES JAN MATTIAS KNOW ABOUT THE BLACKLIST?"

"Daniel, calm down," said the older woman.

"That bastard isn't going anywhere *near* the panel. Diane? Do you not see how obscene that is? *Diane?*"

Diane made a calming hand gesture and gave this man a steadying look.

"So when are you going back to Cuba?" asked the tiny blond donor.

"I'd rather have my liver picked out by birds of prey."

THE YEAR AFTER Vladimir had made the error of returning to Cuba, salvation arrived in the form of one of his University of Illinois professors, who came to Havana with a historic-preservation tour group. The professor gave Vladimir an application to a state-of-the-art research unit in the Department of Architecture and Spacial Design at London Metropolitan University. Vladimir filled out the form, using his aunt's Miami address. He asked the professor to mail it from the United States, as the Cuban postal system, like the Cuban Revolution, was a mire of stagnation. Two months later, his aunt called with good news and sent him his acceptance letter with a friend who was visiting Havana.

When Vladimir applied for an Exit Permit, the functionary at the Ministry of Culture looked up from his file and said, "But you just got back."

He cleared his throat. "This unit studies materials and manufacturing processes. It's really what I'd like to specialize in, and there's nothing like it at any of our universities."

The functionary leaned back in his chair and smiled. "You're applying for school, and my son's in school! He's nine. He's desperate for a backpack."

"Really," Vladimir said.

"Yes. And my girl is twelve. She's been begging for a Walkman. Well, I'll look over your paperwork here, and get back to you."

The following week, Vladimir arrived at the office with a backpack and a Walkman that he bought at the Dollar Store with money he'd earned making models for his professor's firm in Chicago.

"What a coincidence," the functionary said. "I was just looking over your file, and here it is, your Exit Permit." He pulled a rubber stamp and an ink pad out of his drawer.

A month prior to his departure for the United Kingdom, Vladimir received a visit. His father greeted the officer of the Ministry of the Interior cordially. His mother brought coffee out to the patio on a tray, and in the guise of one paying a social call, the officer questioned Vladimir about what he planned to do in London, and if he would represent Cuba in a positive manner.

Since Vladimir hadn't mentioned his plans to anyone in the house, there was utter silence on the patio. "I think I was a great ambassador for the Nation in the United States," he said with conviction, "and I will continue to present a positive face when I go to the United Kingdom next month."

Pucho's eyebrow rose at his use of the word "when" instead of "if." His sister, Nadia, followed the conversation as if it were a tennis match. María sat next to Vladimir on the sofa in rigid corpulence. He could hear her breathing.

"It has come to our attention that you haven't attended Departmental Meetings or Rallies. Your Section Supervisor wrote in your Report that your colleagues have doubts about your fealty to the Revolution."

"No one can question my patriotism," he said with fervor, and it was true. He loved his country. Not the demented dictator, but the country of Cuba. Cuba itself!

"And this Report we have?"

Vladimir leaned forward. "May I tell you something in confidence?"

Everyone leaned forward. Javier ran through the patio naked, and everyone ignored him. Vladimir kept his voice low, as if he didn't want his wife to hear, although she was sitting right next to him. "The woman who wrote that is still upset that I turned her down in our first year at university. What do you think she's going to say about me, now that she's in a position of power?"

The agent seemed satisfied by this, and finished his coffee. Fresh gossip was perhaps the only thing that could neutralize a bad Committee Report. There was handshaking. Pucho behaved as if the visit had been a special consideration granted to Vladimir because of his own rank in the Army.

All hell broke loose on the patio when the front door closed.

"He's leaving!" María shrieked. "He's just going to walk out again!"

"It's a two-week course, you pinhead," he told her.

"Don't talk to your wife like that," Pucho shouted.

"Who are you to tell me how to talk to my wife?" he said, and stood up.

The last time his father had hit him was when he was thirteen. Was it a coincidence that that was the first time that Vladimir had hit back?

Pucho kicked the coffee table across the patio. Cups and saucers scattered and shattered all over the floor. Alicia began to cry over the family dishes.

"That was helpful," Vladimir said.

His father went upstairs to his bedroom and slammed the door. Vladimir bent down with his mother to help her clean up the mess.

"Let him go," Nadia said. "He isn't really doing anyone any good here."

Javier screamed and began banging his head on the wall. María yelled at the child, at Vladimir, at Alicia.

Vladimir walked out of the house. This was truly somebody else's life. He pitied the poor man whose life this was.

When he received his visa to enter the UK, María threw another tantrum. She stole his plane ticket and sliced three pairs of his pants with a pair of scissors as he packed. His mother sewed his pants while his wife oscillated between tears and rage, cursing loudly enough for the entire neighborhood to hear. Meanwhile, on the patio, his father picked his teeth, calling Vladimir a lazy imperialist, a collaborator, a spy.

They had hounded him out of that country! How was it possible that they were all still surprised that he'd stayed away?

◆

DIANE LEFT VLADIMIR on a Sunday at noon to see *Raise the Red Lantern* (Zhang Yimou, 1991), a harrowing evocation of feudal China, where a nineteen-year-old university student (the incandescent Gong Li) is forced to marry a powerful lord who already has three wives. The jockeying for position among the wives is fierce as, each twilight, the women attend a ceremony in which the lord announces with whom he will spend the night, and red lanterns are raised in front of that woman's quarters. There is much scheming, antagonism and treachery among the wives and the servants to obtain the favors of the Master, who is glimpsed only at a distance, often through silk curtains. Even though "Fourth Mistress" is too smart to buy into this poisonous system, when she begins to play the game, it soon turns deadly.

The new series at Bedford Street, "Pageantry and Cruelty," featured films of the last fifteen years from China, Hong Kong and Taiwan. These were, for Diane, what the old Hollywood musicals had been for many: pure spectacle and escape. She had a magnificent lineup—a pity she couldn't interest Vladimir in anything.

THE INTERNATIONAL INCIDENT was planned for that afternoon at five. Olga arrived a few minutes early; she was tall, lively and curious, clearly amused by the assignment. Diane was looking forward to getting to know her; she would clearly have to organize something herself, as Vladimir was not the most inclusive social secretary. It took many attempts to get through to Cuba. When they finally had María on the line, Olga introduced herself, and then made a master-of-ceremonies gesture to Diane.

"Hello, María, it's Diane Kurasik," she said, and Olga translated. "I wanted to talk to you about . . . your life. I wondered what you have planned."

"My life?" Olga held the phone away from her ear; María was apparently laughing.

Vladimir leaned against the windowsill with a stony expression.

" 'Excuse me, but who are you to ask about my life, my plans?' María asks," Olga said.

"Vladimir and I are seeing each other. He tells me that the situation is hopeless, that you haven't seen him in twelve years, that you'll never give him a divorce and all you have is spite."

Olga translated with a diplomatic face. " 'That's right,' she says, and asks, 'You want to marry Vladimir?' "

"Vladimir's marital status doesn't really affect Vladimir and me," Diane answered, wondering if that was really true or only true legally. "If I needed to get married, I would have gotten married a long time ago."

Vladimir was looking out at the empty schoolyard. He interrupted Olga to correct a translation.

"So I was just wondering," Diane continued. "When will you be happy?"

" 'Happy? What kind of an idiot is she?' María asks."

"I'm just trying to understand you."

"She says she'll be happy when Vladimir returns," Olga said.

"Vladimir has a business and a life in New York. He's on track to become an American citizen," Diane said slowly. She waited for Olga to finish translating before adding, "Vladimir is not going back to Cuba. Not now, not ever."

Vladimir continued to look out the window.

"So María," Diane said, "you need to find another way to be happy."

There was silence. Olga said, "She says, 'You think I give him a divorce, and make your life easy?' "

"I am irrelevant here," Diane said, thinking that this was the truest thing she'd said out loud in a while. "Maybe it will work out with me and Vladimir, maybe not. To be honest with you, it doesn't look so hopeful."

Olga translated, not looking at her or Vladimir.

"So stop thinking about Vladimir," Diane continued. "You need to think about yourself. What will make *you* happy?"

No response.

"Okay, that's all I wanted to say." She stood up to look out the window.

Vladimir took the phone and spoke quietly. He hung up.

"I thought that went very well!" Olga said.

Vladimir thanked Olga and retrieved her coat from the closet. Olga wound a scarf around her neck and walked out into the corridor. "Next time, bring this lady to dinner. Bebo and the girls are dying to meet you, Diane!"

Diane thanked her and said that she would call her soon. The elevator arrived, and the man she was living with and still couldn't call "boyfriend" closed the door and went directly to his computer. She heard the unmistakable sounds of a chess game beginning. A low-grade depression seeped into the room. She'd hoped that breaking the impasse in Havana would lead to progress in New York. But it seemed they had nothing to tell each other.

Diane walked uptown in the frigid darkness, too cold and numb to take the time to inspect the wind-tossed boughs of the trees for the presence of leaves. She returned to the theater to see *Farewell My Concubine* (Chen Kaige, 1993), a ravishing film so tough it was like being dragged across a gravel parking lot by your hair.

◆

ON THE WAY to meet Vladimir for lunch, Chris saw a man who had decorated a car with vitriolic statements: *ABEL NESKIN: THIEF, LIAR, SCOURGE OF THE CITY* was written in a shaky hand on cardboard; evidence photos curled under Saran Wrap. *ARREST ABEL NESKIN, MAN OF FALSE PROMISES AND BAD FAITH!* The offended party perched on a stool outside his station wagon, wearing more signs on his coat. Most people saw the shopping cart and the cat on a leash and looked away. Chris didn't want to get involved, but he couldn't walk by this man without acknowledging him. It was rude.

"Good morning," Chris said and nodded. That was the way he was raised.

"A POX ON ABEL NESKIN!"

"Thank you, you too," Chris said, and entered the restaurant, nearly colliding with a professionally dressed woman on a cellphone using variations of the word "fuck" as a noun, a verb and a filler for other words she didn't seem to have access to.

Atlanta would be better.

Vladimir was sitting at the bar, reading a newspaper, oblivious. His curls, as usual, stuck out in all directions, genius style. They went to a table in the back.

"How's Diane?" Chris asked, making small talk.

Vladimir exhaled and shifted in his seat. "I think Diane and I are—how do they say in the tabloids? Not longer a subject?"

"No longer an item?"

"Yes."

"Oh no! I'm very sorry. I thought you made a great item."

"I haven't talked to her about it yet. But I wanted you to know, because I don't want there to be any misunderstandings on it."

Chris laughed. "You think you should talk to her about it?"

"Of course." An impatient look passed across his face. "But it's awkward. She still hasn't found an apartment. I want to light a fire on Paul's ass. Anyway. It's not a topic of conversation."

"No, of course not."

He looked like he still had more to say.

"I tell you only because we all work together." Vladimir looked as if he might be tempted to say more, but thought the better of it.

"Well, if you ever want to talk about it, you know I'm here."

Vladimir gave an impatient smirk.

The waiter took their order.

Chris laced his fingers and took a deep breath. "I asked you to lunch because I wanted to talk to *you* about something." It felt like he was about to break up with someone. "It's something that will affect the partnership, but ultimately I think it will benefit the partnership."

Vladimir looked up. Better to just come out with it.

"I bought a house in Atlanta."

"That's nice. You *WHAT*?"

Chris laughed. "I bought a house in Atlanta."

Vladimir let out a low chuckle.

"I bought it as a kind of a weekend house, but I hope, ultimately, to settle there."

Vladimir began buttering bread rapidly. "Does Paul know?"

"You know, you and Paul are very much alike."

Vladimir looked disgusted. "Please. Paul is behind you in this?"

"Paul thinks I'm insane."

"Paul is right. But never mind, you want to be there. You want to make a transition from here to there. You want to end the partnership."

"No. I don't. Look: I'll be here three or four days a week. Everything we do together we can still do together. And the things we do separately, we'd be doing them separately in any event. We can communicate over the phone and by e-mail. The only difference is that I would be down there some of the time."

"You want to get some work going there."

"Yes. There's better work to be had down there. And you'd be part of that, too."

"But ultimately, you want a second office there, and you would spend most of your time there. That's what you're talking about, right?"

"Ultimately, yes."

"Paul knows about this?"

"Forget about Paul! Paul is irrelevant to our work."

Vladimir popped an enormous piece of bread into his mouth. "I see."

"Vladimir, you are my all-time favorite colleague. I don't want to end the partnership. But I can't live in this city full-time. It's eating away at my insides."

Vladimir nodded and chewed morosely.

"If you saw the house, the neighborhood, the type of work available to little guys like us, I think you'd understand."

He nodded. "Maybe I should move there, too. Nothing is keeping me here."

"Now, that's the spirit!"

"Do they have indoor plumbing?"

ON A STORMY FRIDAY in late April, Diane saw a furnished studio with kitchenette in the Commodore Club, a former single-room-occupancy hotel northwest of the theater district that had been spiffed up into "luxury rentals." Moving out was taking a step backward, but until Vladimir wanted to talk to her more than he wanted to play chess against Castro, Diane had no choice. When she told him, he nodded. He seemed relieved, but he didn't take the opportunity to define their situation in any way. This was all right: she could use some time to herself, a place to be without feeling like she was in the way, or had to be grateful just for being allowed to perch there.

"This makes sense, considering," Paul said the following day, when she signed a month-to-month lease on her way to see more options for the long term.

Considering what? He seemed to be scanning her face for emotional clues. When they hit the sidewalk on Tenth Avenue, he said, "Diane, we don't need to schlep around today. Why don't you take a break, put your feet up?"

What did he know that she didn't?

Her furnished room with kitchenette on the third floor had a view of a brick wall and was bathed in a red glow from the neon sign of a take-out kebab shop next door. She dialed Chris's number and hung up before the phone began to ring. She had no idea what she would ask, or how. Periodically, an ambulance careened in or out of the emergency room of St. Clare's on the next block, with sirens and lights. She wished she had a plaintive saxophone score to accompany her in this sickly green, rainy-day room, instead of the chatter and cigarette smoke of a support group congregating in the alley downstairs beneath her window.

If Vladimir had wanted his place to himself, or time to himself, that would have been fine. If he'd wanted to get rid of her, that would have been . . . not *fine*, necessarily, but worthy of discussion. He never mentioned it. She had no idea where she stood with him; it was irritating that she would now have to badger him to find out. It could be worse: Ernst Lubitsch learned he'd been fired as Chief of Production at Paramount from the masseur at the Beverly Hills Hotel.

She sat on the king-sized bed, flipping through five hundred channels on TV as her fatigue and disappointment mingled with the sounds of the city flooding the room. She ate too much greasy take-out food. She didn't sleep very well.

Meanwhile, at the cinema, construction had started. She saw or spoke to Vladimir at least once a day. He was absorbed in the details, calling when he needed information or decisions, saying goodbye in a friendly but uncommitted fashion. He was on good behavior now, not displaying anger or temper at anyone. At one point, he asked her opinion on a fabric, and performed something between a squeeze and a shake to her right hand. And then he was gone.

Truffaut once said that in matters of love, women were professionals while men were amateurs. "Women live their love stories in a double sense: they experience them and reflect on them at the same time. Men do not reflect upon what they're feeling . . . until it's too late." Clearly, Vladimir had not given the matter of Diane much reflection.

Bobby Wald arrived the first day of construction to announce that he had quit his job, was suing his boss, planned to open his own shop and was available for work in the meantime. His work was meticulous: she had seen photos. She walked him back to introduce him to the chronically understaffed Joe Franco; they both thanked her.

On a reduced schedule designed to accommodate the construction, Diane was currently running "With You / Without You," a series of movies about or starring couples that couldn't stay together or apart. That night, she was showing *Too Many Girls* (George Abbott, 1940), the RKO picture on which two unknown contract players, Lucille Ball and Desi Arnaz, met and fell in love. "Too many girls" was, indeed, destined to be one of the problems with Lucy and Desi's marriage. In spite of his flagrant and constant infidelities, Lucy reconciled with Desi the night before their divorce decree became final. Their first divorce.

Lucy and Desi were an interesting example of a couple better together professionally than personally. For years, Lucy desperately wanted to work with Desi so that he wouldn't take his nightclub act on the road. Keeping him at home meant she might get pregnant as well as stop him from carousing. In fact, the more they worked together, the further apart they grew. And though he did get her pregnant, he never did spend much time at home. "Why does she get so upset?" he once said to a friend. "They're only hookers."

During the day, Diane was on edge from the demolition; at night, she walked through the hyped-up, overemphatic entertainment district to her private eye's lair and turned on the TV. Even if you have a lot in common with someone, it doesn't always work. During her brief marriage to older man-about-town William Powell, party-girl Carole Lombard suffered toxic poisoning, malaria, pneumonia, influenza, pleurisy and chronic anemia. She famously said that George Raft was the sexiest man in Hollywood, but she remodeled herself as one of the guys in order to go fishing and play poker with her second husband, Clark Gable, "the King of Hollywood" at the time. Still: Gable was uncultured, limited and legendarily cheap with waitresses and cab drivers. Lombard had the shock of her life when she saw his false teeth grinning up at her from the nightstand on their honeymoon night. She died in a plane crash two years later, at the height of her fame and his. Who knows what might have happened?

Vladimir seemed to have no trouble staying apart. Wounded pride was a waste of time; after all, she hadn't been 100 percent head-over-heels for him, either. If it wasn't right, did it matter whose decision it had been to part? Not that they had actually "broken up." But a man who sees you every day and doesn't make a plan with you for *any* night is a man who has no plans. She wouldn't give in to resentment or sarcasm. She would just change the dynamic between them.

Now, how would she do that?

◆

AN INSTANT MESSAGE flashed on Vladimir's screen: it was Carlos, an old friend from university he'd lost touch with. Carlos had been living in Holland for four years, was engaged to a Dutch woman, on track for Dutch citizenship. Vladimir congratulated him.

"I'm thinking about going back," Carlos wrote. "I wanted your opinion."

"No!" Vladimir shouted, and wrote back, "Absolutely not!!!"

"My mother has colon cancer," Carlos wrote.

"I'm very sorry to hear that. Send your fiancée."

"Remember Simona? She went back and got out. Three times."

"Simona is a woman! She's no threat to them. You're a man, you're a teacher, you signed every petition. You're on every list. Don't do it!"

Carlos logged off abruptly.

"Hey, Vladimir," Magnus called out. "How's Diane?"

"Hey, Magnus," he responded, picking up his keys. "You like your job?"

Chris gave him a series of looks—anguish, anger, impatience— and Vladimir left the office with a feeling of extreme unease. A biting April wind blasted east from the Hudson, scattering trash into his path and soot into his eyes. Why could he see the tragedy awaiting Carlos while Carlos could not? The clocks had been set ahead, and although it was cold, he decided he would walk home in the late-afternoon sunshine. He needed a break. As he walked, he compiled a list of unusual escapes from the island of Dr. No:

- The Cuban woman who shipped herself from the Bahamas to Miami in a DHL box. How she got to the Bahamas was not revealed.

- The 1951 Chevrolet truck that a group had reengineered to drive across the Florida Straits in 2003. The twelve people aboard were caught a few miles off the coast of Miami and deported. The truck was sunk.

- The various hijackings of the Havana Bay ferryboat, including the original successful attempt in 1994, when many passengers apparently cheered upon hearing they were hostages on their way to Miami. After that incident, the authorities had gotten wise.

- A bride and groom who hopped on the ferry at the last minute, carrying a cake and a case of beer. As they pushed off from the dock, the groom took a gun out of the cake and announced the hijack. When the ferryman said he had only enough gas to get to the other side of the bay, as per the new, tighter security, the bride walked in with the case of beer; each bottle was filled with gas. The hostages cheered. This attempt was also a success.

- The last attempt in April 2003, when the hijackers ran out of fuel and had to dock the ferry at a Cuban port. Officials stormed the boat and arrested all three hijackers. At a summary trial, all three received death sentences, and eight days after they were caught, a firing squad shot them against a wall, in the Revolutionary style.

On some level, hadn't the Revolution won? It was all he thought about.

He walked into his empty apartment with relief. Perhaps if he didn't see Diane every day, he might have built up something like a need for her. But there she was. Although she hadn't pressed him for definitions, every time he saw her, he feared that she might. If the situation had been reversed, he would have wanted some kind of explanation. But more than anything, he didn't want a scene. He didn't want to talk about anything. The business about not needing to get married hadn't fooled him.

He checked on the health of the Grand Bearded Diva. Alive, the son of a bitch. A message from his sister, Nadia, was in his in-box. He almost deleted it, but a perverse need to know overrode the impulse. He opened it.

"Vladimir,

"I will do the paperwork and let you know what you need to do to formally end our marriage. Your soon-to-be former wife, María."

He stared at this. He leaned back.

There were kids playing on the baseball field and the sun was still shining.

Now what?

◆

DIANE WADED through stationary cars in the midst of tunnel traffic on Seventh Avenue South, looking at passing pedestrians, wondering where her next date was coming from. She felt an odd vibration on her hip: her mobile phone was ringing. It was Jan Mattias: the Bedford Street Cinema had been nominated for a Best Repertory Cinema Award from the National Film Critics Guild. Would she mind if he accepted the award if they won, as his work behind the scenes had led to the nomination?

Each time she spoke to Jan, she remembered *You'll Never Eat Lunch in This Town Again.* "Men brought up in California are different from all other American men," Julia Phillips had written. "For one thing, they are better-looking and in better shape. They also tend to be weak in ways that are very subtle."

"By all means, go," she said, wondering what Jan got out of the Florentine maneuvers. She hadn't even known there was a National Film Critics Guild.

Three people had mentioned the same online dating service in two days. She supposed that a computer match or even a random se-

lection of men on the street couldn't be worse than the dates that
had been sent her way by people who theoretically knew her well.
Still, the Internet was not her medium.

She felt the odd vibration again. Her phone. It was Daniel Dubrovnik, calling to tell her that Jan Mattias would be calling her.

"He just called. He asked to accept an award and I told him yes."

"No! *I* should be the one who accepts the award for Bedford
Street. I'm a member of the National Film Critics Guild."

"Daniel, let it go," she shouted over rush hour noise. "This ri-
valry, or anger, it's just not good for you. Stop trying to involve me.
You know I can't get involved."

She hung up before he could get further wound up or ask her
out again.

There were those who believed you could "make a go of it"
with anybody. Each time Joan Crawford married, for example, she
changed the name of her Brentwood estate and installed all-new
toilet seats. Of course, marriage in those days was different, a conduit to sex, even in Hollywood. Doris Day shocked everyone in the
1980s when she announced that she believed in both premarital sex
and cohabitation: had she lived with any of the fellows she'd dated,
she never would have married them, and could have saved herself a
lot of heartache.

Her hip was vibrating again. It was Vladimir. He suggested
dinner.

It was Friday night at six-thirty. She looked around at the stand-
still traffic, which felt symbolic of everything that wasn't working
the way it was supposed to.

She met him at a restaurant near his studio. The place was loud,
the food was greasy. They ate too much, said very little and returned
to her room-with-kitchenette. Physical contact ensued and it was
brief, impersonal and uninspiring. He left for his apartment where,
he said, he wasn't bothered by neon or noise, and where he had the
Internet. If nothing else was clear, it was plain that he didn't want
her to join him.

She sat cross-legged on the bed in the red neon glow, flipping channels. She'd been switching gears, ready to move on. She had been ready to move back to being single again. How had this happened? And what did it mean?

THE FOLLOWING AFTERNOON, a vibrant Saturday with the feeling of real spring suddenly pulsing all around, Diane went to a hairstylist, taking with her various magazine photos. She watched passively as two feet of hair dropped to the floor.

"It was time," she said, shocked and amazed.

"Do you want to keep this?" the woman asked. "We could donate it."

"Donate it. If I'm not going to wear it, I have no place to put it."

She walked out of the salon, determined not to look at her hair in every store window. She barely recognized herself in the mirror of a shop display. She looked older. She looked like an anchorwoman on her day off.

ON MONDAY MORNING, after making sympathetic noises to Dorothy Vail, who had health insurance headaches she needed to complain about in an extended phone chat, Diane called a distributor whose copy of *Who's Afraid of Virginia Woolf?* (Mike Nichols, 1966) hadn't materialized. The intense bickering in the film was widely reputed to have turned into a real-life habit that drove Elizabeth Taylor and Richard Burton to their first divorce.

"I have it in writing," she told the distributor, "and it's on my calendar. So make it appear by tomorrow, as agreed."

Rachel arrived at her desk. "Look at you! I never thought I'd see the day! Oh, Diane, it's stunning. Do you love it? I love it! Why didn't you tell me?"

Diane tried to smile; she had complicated feelings about her hair.

She took Rachel to look at the construction zone.

"*Oh my God! That's Bobby Wald,*" Rachel gasped, peering through an opening in the plastic sheeting at the former heartthrob methodically cutting wood on a table saw. "I had such a crush on him. He waited for me after the seventh-grade play and gave me a lily."

"He did?" That was the spring that eleventh-grade Bobby Wald had touched Diane's ninth-grade knee in the bleachers. "Well, here's your chance, Rachel."

"You mean here's *your* chance, Diane."

"Not my type."

"Where *is* Vladimir? It's bizarre that you haven't introduced him to us."

"He's not here. We're in the midst of a re-think."

Before Rachel could interrogate her, Vladimir arrived, looking like an unwashed student on the last day of finals. Rachel was clearly unimpressed, but Diane felt her throat constricting.

At that moment, Cindy arrived in the construction area with a phone and Diane was able to excuse herself. The distributor apologized. Would she settle for *Cleopatra* (Joseph L. Mankiewicz, 1963) instead? Rachel was engaged in conversation with Vladimir, leaning toward him, twirling her hair, smiling; Vladimir had an expression of long-suffering on his face. *Cleopatra* was the movie that brought Burton and Taylor together for the first time, ended both of their marriages to other people and nearly bankrupted Twentieth Century–Fox in the process. *Cleopatra* was fine, but it didn't feature Elizabeth Taylor shrieking like a banshee and swinging her rear end to "rock 'n' roll," which Diane was in the mood to watch, for some reason. She hung up.

"What can I do for everyone? Vladimir first. Business is business."

"I just need you for one minute," he said.

"Really?" Rachel flirted mindlessly. "Surely you need more than that."

"He actually means that," Diane said, following her architect through the plastic sheeting, annoyed to be playing Eve Arden again.

As the three of them walked into the construction zone, Bobby Wald greeted Rachel like a Saint Bernard. "Well, of course you're married with children!" he told her, and they were off and running. Diane again felt the burden of her status like a heavy, ugly, pointy sculpture that she wanted to just abandon by the side of the road, but had to carry around with her, for some reason that was never named.

"Let's talk about the screen," Vladimir said.

As always, she wished he were more interested in her. He hadn't mentioned the hair, hadn't even looked at the hair. Which possibility was worse: that he noticed it and didn't like it, or that he just didn't *see* her?

"Do you approve this angle for the proscenium?" he asked with his eyes fixed on the floor.

What had this been about with Vladimir? Certainly, he was nice to look at, intriguing, talented. She missed the calm of his apartment. But did she miss him? She tried to pinpoint a lighthearted episode, but could remember only a general feeling of standing around, waiting for him to look up from his computer—a fairly representative moment, come to think of it. And, he hated movies. Perhaps Vladimir's potential had been more interesting than he himself had been.

"Sure. Anything else?"

He squatted to spray a line of fluorescent orange paint onto the floor to mark the angle. He rose, his mind clearly elsewhere. "I'll keep you posted."

And he was off.

"So listen," Rachel said in a deal-making tone. She invited Diane to dinner with Dennis and a colleague of his from Los Angeles who was in town on business.

"Say yes," she insisted, and Diane said yes before even thinking about it.

"Great," Rachel said. "After all, you have nothing to lose."

DIANE SPENT THE AFTERNOON sorting piles of new releases on DVD, while listening to Daniel Dubrovnik rant on the speakerphone about Jan Mattias, and waiting for the plumber to come fix a faucet in the men's room. By the time she arrived at the restaurant all she wanted was a shower and a bowl of Cream of Wheat. Dennis gave her a grateful kiss on the cheek.

The fellow had a loud voice, and he ended most sentences with a forward thrust of his head, and the phrase "Know what I mean?"

"Yes, I do know what you mean," she said each time, looking at Rachel, who avoided her gaze. The meal flew by with all the buoyancy of major dental work. Dennis's colleague had the distinction of being involved in the Industry, on the insurance-litigation end, and dropped some names, including MGM. Diane mentioned her favorite pair of starlets, Dorothy and Estelle, and the bond they'd forged on the lot at MGM.

"Are those people still *alive*?"

"Alive and hoofing."

"Your end of the biz is really the end of the line! Know what I mean?"

"No, I don't know what you mean." She turned to face him directly. She sensed her sister and brother-in-law solidly behind her, for a change.

"You're a good sport," Dennis said as he put her into a taxi afterwards.

"Yes. And you owe me. Know what I mean?"

When she arrived at the Commodore Club at ten p.m., the place was blocked off by yellow crime-scene tape and lit up by a herd of police cars with flashing lights. All she wanted was a shower and a large dose of bad TV. There were purposeful people in suits and latex gloves. She shivered in a trench coat: the temperature had dropped at least 20 degrees.

"There was a shoot-out," the doorman said, but it had been nothing fatal. A drug ring operating out of the fourteenth floor had been caught in a sting operation. The police weren't letting anyone back into the building for the foreseeable future.

She deflated completely. She could have called Rachel, her parents, Lara, or even Dorothy, who had repeatedly offered to put her up. She could have used the crime scene as an excuse to force the issue with Vladimir. But if she had learned anything from him, it was that there was no asking him questions he didn't want to answer.

The hell with Vladimir. She should just move on.

Bobby Wald greeted her in plaid pajama pants and an undershirt. "Come on in," he said, and gestured to a spot on a leather couch in front of an enormous TV.

"I hope you like wrestling," he said, and offered her a beer.

She wondered why he wasn't wondering why she had called him. She sank down into the sofa, exhausted.

"Look!" He handed her a cold, wet brown bottle and sat down on the other end of the couch. "The number one pro wrestler in the world, Diane!"

"Really," she said, taking a swig of beer, completely numb, feeling her systems switching down, switching off. "Could I use the ladies' room?"

Perhaps she needed to give up some idea in order to move forward. She wondered what it was. The idea of a leading man leading her off? She'd thrown that one overboard ten years ago. She was down to ONE HANDBAG, watching pro wrestling on TV, making conversation with a man she'd rather avoid. What else could she give up? Another day, a different problem in the theater, another preliminary conversation with an unfamiliar man, another endless phone call with Dorothy, a different uncomfortable sleeping arrangement. This life seemed like a rehearsal for a show that wasn't going to go on.

She slept on the sofa, Bobby slept in the bedroom. The next morning, she thanked him and went back to the Commodore Club for a shower. When she opened the bathroom door, she saw an enormous black water bug lounging on the sink. It was her fortieth birthday. If her life were a movie, she wasn't sure she would want to watch it.

MAY

In one miraculous week, Javier managed to avoid getting caught smoking, urinating, or talking back. He had enough white space on his conduct card to merit a weekend home. Standing in the back of a truck, halfway to Miramar on Friday night, he realized he had no interest in *being* home for the weekend.

He hadn't bothered to make friends at El Cotorro, and since he often had a cloud of punishment hanging over him, most of the *camilitos* avoided him. However, he'd met a twelfth-grader named Sofía, with whom he was studying. Sofía had caramel skin, hair and eyes. No chest, it appeared. That was all right; she laughed at everything he said. It looked promising.

If he kept going on this truck, he could surprise Sofía at home, assuming she was there. What he would do after that, he had no idea. He skipped Miramar altogether, went through Vedado and got off on Calle Neptuno in Centro Habana. He walked toward her address, making sure that his shirt was tucked in and his fly was not undone. His hair was growing in. At her building, the Vigilance stopped him. She'd never heard of Sofía, or seen anyone of her description. He asked at a few nearby buildings, in case he had the number wrong. No luck.

Had she given him a false address? This made no sense. He started walking toward Néstor's apartment. A block later, he felt a hand on his shoulder. He turned around.

"Javier!" Milady said.

He hadn't seen her in a couple of years, since the School in the Fields, where he had succeeded in making out with her behind the toolshed on several occasions, getting thus far and no further, the story of his life.

"I've been missing you!" she said, kissing his face in various places.

"Really?"

"Yes," she said, sidling up and pulling him toward the wall, where she pressed herself up against him and kissed him flush on the mouth. He had his back against the wall and his front against the lushness of her body.

This was nice. This was weird. This was—wait—out of nowhere.

"What if I had walked on Concordia instead of Neptuno?"

"Then you would have missed me," she said, putting his hand on her left breast.

His mind went blank.

"Milady, what are you doing?" he asked, and someone dumped a pot of water out a window. It landed four feet away and a drop hit his upper lip. What? Was that directed at them? For kissing? He hoped it was water.

"Come here," she said, and led him into a courtyard, through a narrow passageway, up two flights of spiral stairs, across a shaded balcony, up another flight of stairs, through a black door, and onto a tiny roof deck.

It was a nice view. It had no railing.

To the left, there was a red bucket of stagnant water, an old rolled-up rug, dead plants in pots and a broken wooden chair. To the right, there were two long aluminum-and-plastic chairs for sun-bathing. Milady was stretched out on one, holding her arms out.

"There's no railing," he said. "This is dangerous. Someone could fall off the roof."

She smiled at him but didn't say anything. What was this place? Breathing slowly, he lowered himself on top of her and began to kiss her.

Was this her apartment building? Darkness had only just started to fall: could anyone see them? At this point, she had pulled off his shirt and her own, and was unbuckling his belt. Would she stop him, as she had at the School in the Fields, by saying that her parents insisted she be a *señorita,* and had ways of finding out if she had done something. Who had thrown the water, and why? Had Sofía given him the wrong address on purpose?

Milady had his pants off now, and had rolled up her skirt. She began clawing at his underwear. He pulled away. He was in his underpants, half-standing, half-sitting on an open roof without a railing in the middle of Centro Habana with a massive erection.

"What if someone comes up here?"

"I locked it from the outside," she said, and pointed to the door.

She had been here before. He looked around, checking out the sight lines from other balconies and windows. It was unlikely, if they stayed down on the chaise, that anyone could see them, or anyhow, see all of them.

Would she have come up here with anyone passing by?

He couldn't afford to think this way. When would he be in this position again? He readdressed himself to Milady, who was clearly not a *señorita* anymore.

Afterwards, he kissed her as she fiddled with the straps to her bra. She smiled, and barely spoke as she led him back, down, across, out and through to the street. The goodbye—considering the tone of the hello—was pretty offhand:

"See you, Enrique," she said.

He looked at her. She was fussing with her hair. "It's *Javier.*"

"I know!" she said, laughing, and patted him on the cheek.

He walked the rest of the way home in raw, abstract confusion. He wanted to be happy, but he felt . . . not happy at all.

A fight was going on in the kitchen between his mother and his aunt over who was supposed to buy the cooking oil, as there was none.

"I'm home," he said, and sat down on the tiled floor in the living room. He was trying to figure out what had just happened.

Pucho arrived. He walked around the sofa slowly. He stopped in front of Javier. Javier refused to be afraid.

"What the hell are you doing, sitting on the floor?"

He'd spent his strength on the roof. "I'm just sitting here."

"You're getting your uniform dirty. It's a disgrace."

"Is combat a disgrace? Because it would get pretty dirty in combat."

"I told you to apologize to the Principal. Why didn't you go?"

Justification was the prostitution of character.

Pucho leaned down and shouted, "I ASKED YOU A QUESTION."

There was no winning with a person like this. He could be successful only if he redefined the argument. And such a thing was not possible: he lacked the verbal skills. Pucho hadn't actually struck him yet: real progress. Still, the lowest form of behavior is to attack—verbally or physically—without provocation. He'd been meaning to tell Pucho all these years: You are dishonorable.

But all he managed to do was labor to his feet and climb slowly upstairs to his room, a coward. There, he reviewed each thing said and done that day, replaying the frustration, amazement, triumph, shock and humiliation, over and over again, until he fell asleep, disgusted and exhausted.

◆

ON A WARM, sunny day, Vladimir watched the boats on the Hudson from his seat on the train. He was going to Westchester at the request of Corinne, a problem client from his previous partnership.

She'd once asked him to help her "finish the look," and had re-arranged throw pillows on her couch and books on her coffee table for forty-five minutes, asking him in utter seriousness each time, "How's that? What about here?" On one occasion, she'd pulled her gardener aside and demanded that the sunflowers face the house. Today, she needed advice about displaying her art collection.

Was this fear, underneath it all? In the country with the most wealth and freedom in the world, the wealthiest and freest people were consumed with anxieties. Still: she paid her bills on time, it was a gorgeous spring day and he could use a field trip away from the site, the ever-present Diane and the put-on smile that didn't conceal her disappointment. The night at her depressing new apartment had been a big mistake, a weak moment. He wouldn't call her again.

At the station, Corinne leapt out of a white BMW convertible, and if he had any lingering doubts, they were put to rest when she pressed the length of her entire body against him and kissed both of his cheeks, leaving a wet substance behind. She chatted nervously as she drove to the house. Her face looked distorted. Some kind of medical intervention was no doubt involved.

He had designated his mother as his representative in the matter of the divorce, and she would go with María on Monday afternoon to sign the papers on his behalf. Next week, if all went well, he would be divorced. He wouldn't believe it till he saw it in print. He hadn't told anyone. He didn't want to think about Diane, or any-body else, either. And certainly not Corinne, whose enormous, glossy, peach-colored lips looked like an experiment that had gone very wrong.

They arrived at the house, a hideous redbrick box on a mound barely big enough for a strip of grass on either side. "I have lunch set up outside," she said, leading him to the back. He wasn't surprised to find a pair of white stone dolphins cavorting in an enormous fountain in the center of a lawn he'd advised her not to mess with.

Artfully arranged food and color-coordinated linens were spread out on the patio table, and as Corinne confessed unhappy details about her marriage and teenage eating disorders, his mind wandered back to Havana and 1994, the heart of "the Special Period," when everyone had cabbage and soy for dinner every night because there was no meat, chicken or fish to be found in the entire country.

The smell of mowed grass wafted over the table, reminding him of where he was.

"You haven't said anything," she said, spooning more food onto his plate. "Say something! Or I'll think you think I'm revolting."

He tried not to look at her enormous bee-stung lips. "I think eating disorders are a First World problem," he said.

"What do you mean?"

"If you grew up, as I did, in a place where there was no food and you were truly hungry, you'd understand why I have little patience for this issue."

"But I *was* truly hungry! I still am!"

"You're not hearing me, Corinne. We had no food."

"That's exactly right! I had no food!"

If only he could enjoy absurd situations like this. After lunch, he looked at her art and recommended a lighting designer. He could have done this over the phone. He deflected all inquiries into his private life, alluding to "a complicated situation."

"Well, I'm married, too."

"Actually, I was referring to a different complicated situation, although my marriage is also complicated."

"What a pity, Vladimir." She squeezed his arm and pouted obscenely.

He watched the Hudson River from the train, vowing never to make another house call once a job was finished.

AFTER RETURNING for an unproductive afternoon at the studio, Vladimir decided to walk home. It was high spring, and everyone was outside enjoying the city. He stopped at a new watering hole in the Meatpacking District on the way. He spent a few moments assessing all the synthetically smooth young women flashing bare shoulders and tattooed midriffs. Where to begin, and did it matter? He introduced himself to two young ladies perched on stools at the bar. They were Brandy and Clarissa, in their mid-twenties, self-assured and tattooed, both of them; one had straight red hair, one had straight blond hair. He ordered rum on ice.

"I like rum," said Clarissa. "Where are you from?"

"Cuba," he said, wondering if he wanted to get into it.

But he had to fight on all fronts. So he asked them what they thought of the fact that the United Nations Commission on Human Rights was made up of nations like Cuba, Libya, China, Saudi Arabia and the Sudan.

"Well, I hadn't really thought much about it," Brandy said, exchanging a glance and a titter with her friend.

An overgroomed young man in a tight shirt sidled up and introduced himself to the women as Wade. Clarissa shook his hand.

"I'm Clarissa, and this is Brandy. And this is Vladimir. He's from Cuba."

"Cuba!" said Wade. "Tell me: are there any worthwhile beaches?"

"Worthwhile?"

"You know, *hot*. Is it a happening place?"

"If you aren't Cuban, perhaps it is a happening place. Are you an American citizen?" he asked. All three nodded. "Your president has cracked down on travel to Cuba for Americans. So, worthwhile or not, you can't go without special permission."

"Don't blame me, man, I didn't vote for him."

"Did you?" Vladimir asked the women.

"I didn't vote," said Brandy.

"What?"

"Me neither," said Clarissa.

"What?"

"Me neither," said Wade.

"WHAT?"

"I'm not registered," Clarissa said.

Vladimir was thunderstruck. *"WHY?"*

She shrank back from him.

"And what's your excuse?" he asked Wade.

"Ran out of time, man," he said, running a hand through his sculpted hair. He changed the subject to a sitcom he'd seen the night before on TV.

Vladimir interrupted him to give an impassioned lecture, to which all three listened wearing the same alarmed smile.

He paid and left them to giggle about him in his wake.

Americans. Lazy, narcissistic, sugar-sucking, SUV-driving, spoiled children, spending all their free time in front of the TV or at the mall. If they hadn't done something, well then, perhaps it didn't need to be done!

He resumed his walk, irritated. That morning, he had finally received the paperwork for American citizenship. Five years he'd waited—twelve, if you counted the time he'd spent in the UK—but he had put the papers aside for later, surprising himself. Now, as he passed through teeming New York nightlife on Hudson Street, he was awash in sudden, unexpected sentiment. Normally, he fought nostalgia like a disease. But in a single month, the compass points of his existence could change. He could become legally divorced and un-Cuban. He might not recognize his own life.

Why did he have to leave? Castro should have been the one to leave. Why should he become American? The culture was passive, callous, unthinking. Americans had all the freedom and luxury in the world, and what did they do with it? They watched TV. They went shopping. *They watched TV shows about shopping.* They took vacations. But they were just *too busy* to vote. He'd given up his language, his city and his culture. He routinely responded to bizarre, inept pronunciations of his name. Sometimes, to speed things up, he himself gave the Anglo mispronunciation of his name. The only Cuban thing left in his life was his nationality.

If he didn't become an American, he would have to renew his Cuban passport: an absurd, masochistic exercise. The rates had gone up. It was now $350 for a document that entitled him third- or fourth-class citizenship in his own country, opened no doors abroad and raised red flags at every airport. He crossed Bedford Street and thought briefly about Diane. What had she said to María? Was it what she had said, or the fact that it wasn't he, Vladimir, who had said it? Diane would be at the theater. But he didn't want to see her. Even if she had voted, even if she didn't drive an SUV or watch TV.

It was a lush Friday night in May, and he could do what he

wanted, say what he wanted, go where he wanted, read what he wanted, *think* what he wanted. The nostalgia had been a momentary weakness, brought on by a bad drink. America was a good idea, even if it was wasted on some people.

When he got home, he pulled out the citizenship paperwork and called the woman who let his mother and his aunt use her telephone.

"Catalina isn't here," said whoever answered. "She's having an abortion."

He was incredulous. "Do you know who this is?"

"No. Who is this?"

"You don't know who I am, and you tell me she's having an abortion?"

"What do you want? She'll be back later tonight."

"I'm looking for Alicia, the sister of Ana, the woman who lives across the hall. Could you go and tell her that I'll call back in five minutes?"

"I guess I could do that."

He hung up without much confidence that she would. He walked around his living room, and caught sight of Diane's sweater on his desk chair. Every day, he meant to put it with his bag and blueprints to take it with him to work. But he forgot every day. He dropped it on the dry-cleaning pile.

He called Cuba back, and Alicia picked up.

"I have good news and bad news," his mother said. "Which do you want first?"

"The bad news."

"Your friend Carlos is back."

He shut his eyes. "I can't believe it. I told him not to go."

"His mother is very ill."

"He told me." He hoped his mother wouldn't press the issue. If she ever became ill, she should just be prepared. He wasn't coming to see her.

"They left a note on his mother's door saying, 'If you do not present yourself at the Ministry of Immigration by tomorrow at five o'clock, you will be declared a fugitive from justice, and we'll issue an all-points bulletin.' "

"What did he do?"

"He went! They took his passport and his Dutch residency card, and they asked him questions for two full hours."

"What did they ask him?"

" 'What are you doing in Holland?' 'Where is your brother living?' 'What kind of sociology are you teaching?' "

"What do they care what kind of sociology he is teaching?"

"Can you imagine? Also, they said: 'Your mother takes in more foreigners than she's allowed. You wouldn't want her to do anything that might put her medical treatment at risk, would you?' "

"No!"

"Yes. Then they said: 'You didn't do your military service or social service. We'll keep your passport and your Dutch residency card until we resolve some issues.' That was Monday. He's supposed to leave tomorrow, and they still haven't returned his papers."

He looked out at the baseball diamond, where some teenagers were congregating. Smoke drifted up toward the sodium-vapor lights.

"What's the good news?"

"I am holding in my hand a passport for Javier Hurtado Casares."

The name sounded familiar.

"What?"

"A passport, with an American Visa. Valid for three months, beginning June third. For Javier."

Vladimir breathed in. He would soon be a divorced American father with a teenage roommate. The speed with which his life was changing was just astonishing.

◆

WITH NO FOREWARNING to Diane, Dario Travisini brought a friend to the Renovation Committee meeting. Since the friend was a

French movie star who had worked with everyone from Claude Chabrol to Louis Malle, everyone overlooked the lapse in protocol and tripped all over themselves to welcome her. Catherine Merveille was petite and was dressed in black jeans and a deceptively simple gray linen jacket; she behaved like a college student glad to be given the opportunity to sit in on a meeting in a field she wanted to enter. She shook hands graciously, accepting praise as if she'd never heard it before. Her hair was fluffy, shoulder length, more salt than pepper; she wore massive silver jewelry and carefully applied light makeup. She had allowed herself to age, but she seemed to be conducting the energy of the universe through her body. Everyone leaned in to watch her; she had that inexplicable quality that made every last raise of her eyebrow riveting. Dorothy and Estelle were unusually quiet.

"You look fabulous, Miss Merveille," Jan Mattias said. He had started the meeting with a big ceremony, presenting Diane with a small glass cube, the Best Repertory Cinema Award from the National Film Critics Guild, while Daniel Dubrovnik glowered at him and cleared his throat violently.

"Sank you, I am just recovaired from *un accident de voiture*," she said, and there was a furor at the table as everyone offered sympathy and alarm.

"*Non*," she said definitively. "It was zhe best sing zhat ever 'appen to me. Before, I was bored wiz life. Now, I see zhat every moment in zhis life is a gift. Zhe surgery took sixteen howers. I do physical serapy for ten month. Zhe surgeon—young man, a fan of my film—ask me, while he is in zhe neighborhood, eef I want reconstruction of zhe face."

She paused.

"I was offended. Why would I shange my face? I earn zhese lines! Ow can I take on a role of one who has suffaired eef I erase all zhe living from my face? All zhe actress who do not shange in sirty-fife years. You honestly belief a word of Deneuve? Zhere is nussing *real* zhere."

"You're so right," Jan Mattias said, taking her hand. "We're all such phonies."

"Appropriately enough, Catherine, our theme this month is 'Age, Hollywood, and the Worship of Youth,'" Diane said, and Catherine gave her an encouraging smile. "Perhaps you'll stay for a screening—we have *All About Eve* and *Death Becomes Her.*"

"Here's our architect," Estelle said, as Vladimir bounded down the aisle, forty-five minutes late.

Vladimir, man of many mysteries: Why hadn't he just broken it off? Was he stringing her along because of the project? Did he think she hadn't noticed? She was actively dreading a blind date that evening.

"Look what I found on the Internet this morning." Vladimir passed around a photo of a 1957 Buick being driven over water from Cuba to Florida. "They should hire these people at NASA! Instead, they deport them to Cuba. It's like a death sentence."

"¡Ah, cubano!" said Catherine, and began speaking to him in fluid Spanish.

Vladimir's usual frustrated expression was replaced by a rapturous glow. He and Catherine began to chat, and the exchange went on for some time. They interrupted each other—apparently to compliment each other—and laughed as if passing back and forth some kind of private toy.

So this was what Diane needed to get Vladimir's attention: she needed to speak fluent Spanish and be a legendary if faded French film star wise in the ways of men. Oh yes, and radiate the energy of the universe.

"I hate to interrupt," Diane said, careful not to display anything like jealousy. "But we really do need to get to business. Vladimir, why don't you give us an update?"

He smiled at Diane as if he were sorry for her, and directed his comments to Catherine, whose face had an intense expression, fascinating even in repose.

Diane wanted to flee. She wanted to set fire to his hair.

Vladimir finished, answered questions and rose to leave.

Catherine popped up. "I weel walk wiz you," she said, following him.

Jan, Daniel and Dario jumped up to follow the legend. Diane remained seated with Estelle and Dorothy. In her mind was the image of Bette Davis, as an aging star of the stage venomously chewing chocolates and knocking back highballs before her fortieth birthday party in *All About Eve* (Joseph L. Mankiewicz, 1950), working herself into a jealous rage over the seemingly naïve and worshipful young actress who insinuates herself into her life.

Catherine Merveille had to be at least seventy.

"That's some routine," Dorothy said.

"You know, Sam Goldwyn insisted that each Goldwyn Girl had to have beauty, personality, talent, self-confidence and ambition," Estelle said. "White hair and eye bags weren't part of the contract."

"Well, you girls don't have to worry," Diane said. "You look fabulous."

"Pfff," said Dorothy, who was recovering from an eyelift, her third.

"So, Diane, what's the story with Vladimir?" Estelle said.

"So, Estelle," Diane said with a smile, "let's talk about the name of the theater."

"I was talking to Chris," Estelle continued. "And it appears that after a long stalemate, Vladimir's wife in Cuba is granting him a divorce."

Diane tried to keep her face together.

Estelle and Chris were privy to this information, but Diane was not?

"I was thinking 'the Estelle DeWinter Greenblatt and Herbert Leonard Greenblatt Theater at the Bedford Street Cinémathèque,'" Estelle said.

Dorothy shot Diane a look. "Is the marquee big enough for all that?"

"We'll make the letters smaller," Diane said. "Let's move on. I'd like to make sure that all the principals are here for the opening. Will you two busy socialites consult your calendars and give me possible dates in September?"

DIANE SAT flipping through magazines as Dorothy and Estelle discussed the opening gala while having their nails done. *InStyle* magazine was precipitating a flashback to her unfinished graduate school thesis comparing contemporary celebrity worship to ancient Roman religious practices. She'd left grad school before the advent of *InStyle*. But here, surely, was the contemporary equivalent of a Roman ritual: an authorized mediator (the magazine) prescribed rites and offerings ("Stella McCartney T-shirt, $375") to the people, so that wishes would be granted ("Get Gwyneth's Hot New Look for Spring!") and affliction-specific prayers could be answered ("Fabulous Jeans to Minimize a Droopy Butt!"). If you bought the table settings and followed the menu, you, too, could give a perfect Asian theme party like Madonna. Perhaps you could *be* Madonna.

Dorothy asked, "Was he trying to make you jealous with that aging French tart?"

"Whatever," Diane said, wondering which god she should make an offering to in order to speed up her application to the co-op board to buy a fourth-floor studio with kitchen alcove in the Gramercy Park area. Vesta, goddess of the home? Mars, god of war? The apartment was unlisted, as of now—Paul knew someone, had done something to keep it secret. When she walked in, saw the view of treetops from the nice, if small, hot-pink-painted kitchen, she'd said yes before even looking at the closet space or bathroom. Paul dialed his omnipresent cellphone and commenced negotiations with the seller in a polished fashion. He was leaning on the windowsill, with one hand in his shiny black hair; she noticed again how magnificent his features were. He wheeled around to give her the thumbs-up with a triumphant smile, keeping his voice steady and normal.

He put his arm around her and steered her to the living room, where he sat down with her on the sofa and held her hands. "Now we just have to get past the board," he told her, and repeated the list of items she would need to put together for the co-op board package. She had assembled these letters and documents four months earlier, at his suggestion. "We just have to hope that she doesn't get cold feet and decide to list the place before we get a contract," he said, and crossed his fingers before kissing Diane goodbye on both cheeks.

It occurred to her that she had spent more time with Paul than she had with Vladimir. Paul had made it clear that she was his favorite client, even if he never made a cent from her. Paul was funny, gorgeous, expressive and Jewish. In a different generation, she would have married Paul. They probably would have had two teenagers by now.

"I THINK YOU might like to meet my nephew," Estelle was saying.

"That's a great idea," Dorothy said, and patted Diane's hand, smudging coral nail polish in the process. This meant that Miss Vail's polish had to be redone.

Was it the essence of the star—as displayed on the face of the star—that the audience fell in love with? Or was it the face itself? And if the face itself was succumbing to forces of nature, did you still want to watch it? According to Catherine Merveille, the answer was *oui*: the audience wanted to watch her real face as a conduit of her authentic self. Of course, this was not the ruling local aesthetic. And not just for women: Connie had once confided that she'd never gotten over seeing her childhood crush Ray Milland playing the aging, disapproving patriarch in *Love Story* (Arthur Hiller, 1970).

Estelle wanted the Grand Reopening to be on September 18. Estelle had stopped working at the age of twenty-eight; thus she was immortalized in celluloid at what Paul Veyne once called "the canonical age," the age at which one has achieved full maturity, but before time has altered the facial features.

"Nothing sooner than September twenty-ninth," Dorothy insisted. Dorothy had continued working, playing spinsters, mothers and grandmothers. "The invitation will get lost in the backlog of mail when people come back home from Labor Day weekend."

Estelle deferred to Dorothy: Dorothy had recently played an egomaniacal matriarch in an episode of *Law & Order;* she was more current.

Bette Davis went directly from vamp to camp in grotesque films such as *What Ever Happened to Baby Jane* (Robert Aldrich, 1962) and *Hush . . . Hush, Sweet Charlotte* (Robert Aldrich, 1965). On the other hand, Katharine Hepburn won three of her four Best Actress Oscars after the age of sixty. But not for playing "*the girl.*"

The theater was closed for electrical wiring, and Diane took the rest of the day off. Something was happening around her eyes, in addition to the usual bluish circles—the structure underneath the skin was beginning to slide downward. She sought advice at a cosmetics counter in SoHo. A tall, languid saleswoman not much younger than Diane said, "Some of our clients with mature skin like this product."

Mature skin? *Mature?* She slid off the stool in a huff. At a different counter, she found someone older than herself and submitted to the woman's ministrations, watching in the mirror as a more professional, fully awake Diane emerged. She dropped a small fortune on eye cream, makeup and brushes.

Outside, she caught a look at herself in a storefront in SoHo: a painted matron in gaudy, unnatural colors amid a sea of teenage sprites. What if she ran into someone she knew? Fear and cowardice were written all over this carefully applied new face.

She walked uptown toward Union Square, wiping off the paint and contemplating the intersection of fate and human choice. What would have happened if Fred MacMurray had decided to just stick to playing the saxophone? What would have happened if Carole Lombard hadn't had a car accident at the age of eighteen that forced her to develop a personality for fear that the nearly undetectable scar on her face would end her career in pictures? What would have happened if Mike Todd, Elizabeth Taylor's third husband and reputedly her "one true love," hadn't died in a plane crash?

Spring was everywhere; every tree was bursting into song under a crisp blue sky. What would have happened if she hadn't run after Vladimir at that first meeting? If she hadn't pushed for him to get the contract? If she hadn't asked to stay in his apartment, hadn't set up a phone call with his wife, made offers to employ his son? What would have happened if she had married Eric Mandell, her graduate school boyfriend—a good man, a generalist who, seven months after they broke up, married a talent agent and sired two kids right off the bat and apparently went into computer animation somewhere in greater Los Angeles? What would have happened if she had followed Paolo, the Italian sound engineer, back to Cinecittá? She bought a pair of turquoise Capri pants in an uplifting sixties swirl pattern that reminded her of her youth. She wore the pants out of the store, leaving her jeans in a trash can on the corner.

At the appointed hour, as if girding herself for battle, she yanked opened the door of the establishment the blind date had chosen. She saw him at the bar, a Rachel classic: an investment banker in his mid-thirties with suspenders, tweezed eyebrows and a smirk. She tried not to judge; everybody has something to teach you. The key was figuring out how to steam through the small talk and bullshit to find whatever that thing was. She introduced herself, and waited to hear the Specialty. As the drinks arrived, he told her that he'd been sexually abused by his stepmother, who had seduced him at the age of seventeen. So much for small talk.

Diane looked across the restaurant at all the regular people who knew and liked each other already, and was viciously jealous.

She pulled the rudder of conversation firmly in another direction. This guy could learn a thing or two from her.

"Did you know that Jimmy Cagney spoke Yiddish?"

"I didn't know that."

"He grew up on the Lower East Side. He said that if he hadn't learned Yiddish, the family would have starved. Because he was the youngest and good with languages, the family designated him as the Yiddish speaker, and he did all the shopping."

"Interesting. So my stepmother has been calling me lately," the blind date said again.

She leaned forward. "This is not the appropriate forum for that story."

A look of anger passed across his face. "And what would that be?"

"You're in therapy?"

He opened his mouth, and then nodded.

"So talk about it there. Check, please?"

"You're dismissing me because I was abused as a child?"

"That doesn't sound like sexual abuse—that sounds like a letter to *Penthouse*."

She dropped a bill on the table and left the restaurant without a backward glance.

She took the No. 1 train uptown. Had she been hasty? Had she been rude? She had no patience anymore. She had once spent an entire summer in despair over the movie *Stevie* (Robert Enders, 1978), in which Glenda Jackson portrayed the British poet Stevie Smith, who turned down a proposal from a lightweight, anyone-for-tennis type, only to spend the rest of her life alone, starving for affection.

Diane stopped at a corner bodega for a sandwich and some flowers to brighten up the private eye's lair.

"You don't need these wrapped, right?" the cashier said. So it was visible: she was alone and depressed—who else could she be buying flowers for?

"Oh, but I *do* want them wrapped. Nicely," she emphasized, looking at her watch, as if she were late for a date. Diane was sick of defending herself in her mind as a legal entity. No husband? No children? Forty years old and unwilling to accommodate the only single man in the room? The counterman wrapped the flowers in silver paper indifferently, as if he didn't believe her. Every last stranger was a life critic.

Back at the Commodore Club, Diane faced the TV in her room, switching channels with the remote control, drowning out the sounds of the city entertaining itself and the couple in the next room with kitchenette entertaining each other. She was thinking about the studio with the hot-pink kitchen in the same way she had yearned for Vladimir in the fall, when he wasn't calling her. It was unrequited love for an unlisted apartment. And as with all unrequited love, the energy had nowhere to go, so it rained back down on her, saturating her with prosaic, unfulfilled wishes, intensifying the want. How many apartments could fall through? Could she bribe someone to get this new apartment? *What would it take?*

At midnight, she dialed Paul's cellphone with a shaking hand. His voice mail answered.

"Paul, it's Diane," she whispered. She might come unglued at any moment. "I will pay anyone any amount of money for the Gramercy Park area studio. I must be approved, Paul. I cannot go on like this anymore. ENOUGH."

JUNE

UNTIL HE SAW Javier in the flesh, Vladimir wouldn't believe he was coming. Anything could happen. They might revoke his exit permit, or cancel the flight; he might have gotten lost in the Miami airport. Vladimir had no sense of Javier's abilities. He knew he'd been expelled from school, but insubordination in Cuba didn't indicate a lack of intelligence. He waited in a small knot of people at the end of a long passageway at LaGuardia, wondering if they would recognize each other.

Vladimir had to smile: Javier was the last person off the plane; he wore combat pants, a blue T-shirt and a bewildered expression. His hair was in short curls and he seemed to be moving in slow motion. There was instant recognition. They embraced awkwardly among the crowds in the passage, and proceeded together to the baggage claim.

Javier retrieved a small, old-fashioned gray-blue suitcase that Vladimir remembered from his own childhood. It weighed a ton, and Javier insisted on carrying it himself. Vladimir steered him to

the taxi line and they chatted lightly about air travel for a few minutes until it was their turn. A cab pulled up.

"We're taking a taxi!" Javier enthused.

"Get in," Vladimir said, and gave the driver his address.

Javier immediately tried to start up a conversation in English
with the driver, but the man was talking on the phone and wasn't
interested. As the cab merged into traffic on the highway, Javier
pulled something out of a shoulder bag.

"Here's something from Mom," he said, switching back to
Spanish and handing Vladimir an envelope. Like everything else that
came from Cuba, the envelope was open for all the world to see.

It was the divorce papers.

"Did you see this?" Vladimir asked.

"No," Javier said, looking out the window. He was a terrible
liar.

"Your mother didn't tell you what this was?"

"Oh, yeah," he admitted. "You're divorced. Congratulations."

It was hard to know how to take this. Vladimir felt heavy ma-
chinery clicking into gear: It was possible that he had spoken to his
son for all of half an hour in the course of the last year. And this had
not been an unusual year.

"So tell me what's new."

"*This* is new! New York is very, very new!"

As the Manhattan skyline appeared over the Triborough Bridge,
Javier drank in the city. The cab rocketed down the FDR Drive and
the boy peered out at the gritty and glamorous panorama of the East
River and asked: "What's that? Is that a haunted castle? What's
that?" The traffic slowed, and the driver turned off the highway,
taking side streets through the East Village. The sight of Cooper
Union, where he'd prepared for certification exams, brought
Vladimir back to his own first days in New York, when he'd spent
hours in the street, studying steel, stone, cast iron and neon.

As they stopped at a light, he looked over at Javier, who had a
rapt expression, as if he were in thrall, or in love. The cab started up
again.

"Is it true about Michael Jackson?" Javier asked.

—

VLADIMIR GAVE JAVIER a tour of the apartment. Javier seemed genuinely impressed by the building, the lobby, the view and the furniture that Vladimir had designed. He showed Javier a section of his closet and a drawer in his bureau that he could use. He showed him the bathroom, and Javier opened the medicine cabinet. Before Vladimir could tell him it was rude to go through other people's medicine cabinets, he asked, "What's this?"

He held up one of the expensive skin products that Terry had insisted he use. "I don't know. A woman bought me those. I don't really use them."

"Diane?"

"No. One of Diane's predecessors."

Javier nodded, looking at him directly. What was the kid thinking? What had María told him? Would he hold it against him, the fact of his personal life?

"When can I meet Diane?"

"Diane. Well, Diane and I are sort of . . . over."

"Oh," Javier said. He seemed disappointed.

"But I see her all the time. At the movie theater."

"Can I meet her anyway? I'd like to see the theater. And since she sent me my invitation letter, I'd like to work for her. It's the least I can do."

Vladimir smiled. That sounded like something Alicia might say.

Vladimir bent to wash his hands. Javier looked like a younger version of him, with María's round brown eyes. He wondered how much of María had been passed on to him.

"So you have a new girlfriend now?"

Was Javier taller than he was? "Who wants to know?"

Javier looked wounded. "Just asking."

"Well, not that it's any of your business, but no," he said, drying his hands.

They walked out of the bathroom. "What's this?" Javier asked, pointing to a pile of mail on the table by the door.

"Mail."

"*Mail!*" he said, astounded.

Vladimir laughed. "Prehistoric man has awakened in modern times!"

"Go ahead and laugh. I'm the newest model from Cuba."

"Are you hungry?"

"We just established that I'm coming from Cuba. What do you think?"

"How about a steak?"

"You're kidding, right?"

"There's a place that I think you'd like."

"A *restaurant?*"

"Yes. Why don't you take a shower before dinner?"

"Okay!"

"Do you have anything to wear?"

Javier inhaled.

"Don't worry," Vladimir said. "We'll get you some new clothes, maybe tomorrow. In the meantime, how about this?" He pulled a shirt and jacket out of the closet and laid them on the bed. "You want pants, too?"

"The whole uniform," Javier said, holding the jacket up to his body, looking in the mirror, nodding seriously. "Is this what people wear to restaurants in New York?"

"Yes. So, would you like to take a shower?"

"Okay!" Javier said, and didn't move.

It was a three-month visa.

Vladimir felt crowded already.

IN A LOUD, clubby steak house in Midtown that had left a lasting impression on him when a client had treated him to dinner his first year in New York, Vladimir led his new son through rituals that had become second nature to him. The waiter handed Javier an oversized leather-bound menu; he took it in his hands as if it were a breakable object that he didn't know what to do with. He looked much older in Vladimir's blazer and button-down shirt. On the other hand, he was wearing four rings on his fingers, a rope bracelet on one wrist, a beaded bracelet on the other wrist, and several neck-laces that hit his chest at different points—not exactly a mature look.

The waiter returned. "May I bring you something from the bar?"

"What would you like?" Vladimir asked Javier.

"I'll have what you have."

"Two ginger ales, please," Vladimir said.

"You can drink, Dad," Javier said when the waiter had left.

"Yes, but you can't. I think the drinking age in New York is twenty-one."

Javier nodded.

"I have some rum at home," Vladimir told him. "We'll toast your arrival when we get back."

There was an explosion of raucous laughter from the bar.

What if someone he knew came over to the table? Javier was too big to hide now. He had to remember not to introduce Javier as his new son. But wasn't it true? Thus far, there had been no discussion, no resentment. It would just be a matter of time.

"By the way, since you're old enough to drive now, I think you can call me Vladimir."

Javier looked down at his lap with an open mouth. Then he cocked his head and studied Vladimir. "Is that what you want me to call you?"

"Would it not be weird and hypocritical for you to call me Dad?"

"It's what I've always called you."

"Well, whatever makes you comfortable," Vladimir said, un-comfortable.

He was in it now. He was *Dad* now.

Javier opened the menu and his head dropped low. He inhaled, and looked up, near tears. "Dad, can you afford this?"

"I don't get paid in pesos anymore," Vladimir whispered back.

JAVIER SNAPPED to attention when the waiter put a plate in front of him.

"*Oh my GOD!*" he said, staring at the steak.

They really could have split a steak, but Vladimir wanted the kid to have his own. "I promise you, these are not normal portions. Don't hurt yourself; we can take home whatever we don't eat and have it tomorrow."

"This is more meat than we saw all last year, for all of us."

Now Vladimir felt awful. Perhaps he should have made a more gradual introduction. But Javier's mood seemed to lift as he picked up the heavy, wooden-handled knife; he held it as if examining a valuable armament. He cut a piece of sirloin and said, "Did you know we were almost arrested last year for having meat in the freezer?"

Javier told the story and ate very slowly, appearing to get pleasure from every bite of meat. He quizzed Vladimir. Was this a typical restaurant in New York? How often did he go to restaurants? Was it true that there were no ration cards? Who were these other people? Why were there no women? Was it true that New York was super-dangerous? What did he need to know to avoid getting into trouble with the police in New York?

"Well, don't steal anything, that's a start," Vladimir said.

"No, I mean it."

"I'll tell you something sad," Vladimir said, and Javier leaned forward. "I felt safer, less frightened and less conspicuous as an illegal alien in New York than I did as a full-fledged Cuban citizen in Havana. You will not be stopped just for walking down the street. You will not be stopped for speaking, or walking into a hotel, or carrying bags on the street. It doesn't happen. Maybe if you're black, maybe in the South. But not here."

Javier seemed about to say something, but continued to listen.

"You want to speak ill of the president? Go ahead. If you're entertaining about it, they'll give you a TV show."

This elicited a burst of laughter.

"This is New York! You can speak ill of *FIDEL CASTRO, SON OF A WHORE!* And no one will even look at you!"

Javier looked around, amazed. Nobody was looking. He continued to laugh and eat, laugh and eat; he was sucking down steak, spinach and potatoes as if he hadn't eaten in months. He probably hadn't.

"You can read what you want. At home, and even in public. I have books that could land you in jail in Cuba. Walk down Broadway holding them up. Nothing will happen. Most important, no one can tell you what to think."

Javier nodded.

"Actually, that's not true. Everyone tells you what to think, all the time, including the government. But you can tell them all to go to hell."

"Why is nobody smoking?" Javier asked, looking around.

"It's illegal."

"They can't tell you what to think, but they can tell you not to smoke?"

"In restaurants, in New York City. It's a law. It's controversial."

Javier had a disconcerting habit of staring at you directly with the big, round eyes. He cleared his throat. "*FIDEL CASTRO IS A SON OF A WHORE*," Javier tested, in Spanish, grinning like a maniac. Then he burst into waves of excited laughter, and knocked on the table three times, the way Pucho used to. A passing busboy smirked, and the people at the next table paused, considered them, and resumed their own shouting.

"Oh, that felt good," he said, sitting back, looking flushed and sated.

When the bill came, Javier looked down, as if in acute embarrassment. "Did we need special permission to be here?"

Vladimir put a credit card on the tray. "You've got a lot to learn, kid."

Javier held his doggie bag close to his body as they rose from the table. He looked sophisticated in his clothes, Vladimir decided—older than seventeen, in any event. On the way out, Javier stopped the maître d' to shake his hand.

"Thank you very much," he said in English. "It is the mostest delicious dinner. The mostest meat I ever see."

Then he got caught in the revolving door.

"Perhaps we can look into some English classes while you're here," Vladimir said when they reached the street.

AT HOME, Javier presented him with a bottle of seven-year-old Havana Club.

"I don't want to offend you," Vladimir told him carefully, "but I can't accept anything from Pucho."

Javier nodded. "You have a problem with your father."

"Yes, I do," Vladimir said. Before the boy had a chance to say the same thing about him, he added, "I understand you have problems with him, too."

"Yes." It was clear they had too much to talk about, none of it good.

"Here, have some rum," Vladimir said, pouring two glasses. "It's not Cuban, but it will do. Welcome."

"Here's to you, Dad. Thank you for inviting me."

Vladimir inhaled, helpless. Did he have to be so endearing?

Javier pulled out a pack of cigarettes.

"May I ask you not to smoke?"

"It's against the law in apartments, too?"

"No, everyone makes his own rules about his own home."

Javier looked as if he might get combative. "You forbid me to smoke?"

"Oh, no. Do what you want. I just can't take the smell in the house. You can go out on the fire escape if you'd like."

Javier shook his head. He sipped the rum carefully. It looked as if he was thinking deep thoughts. He began questioning Vladimir: Did he ever smoke? When did he stop? How did he stop?

This apartment was really big enough for only one person with occasional romantic companionship. More than that was problematic. The thing with Terry had worked because she'd been down the hall in her own place most of the time.

Javier moved to sit on the windowsill, quizzing him with enthusiasm: Who were the important bands? Did Vladimir go dancing?

What did Diane look like? What did her predecessor look like? Did Vladimir have a type?

"A type?"

"A type. Are you always attracted to a certain kind of woman?"

"I don't think any of them have anything in common other than me."

Vladimir stood at the window, looking at the skateboarders smoking on the sidewalk next to the baseball park. These kids surely knew who the important bands were; he should send Javier down there to ask.

"Was Mom your first real girlfriend?"

"If you don't mind, I'd rather not discuss your mother."

Javier nodded, and continued: "Who are the neighbors? Is there anyone I should watch out for?"

"Javier. It's legal for you to be here. This is my apartment. I pay rent, I pay taxes. No one can tell me who I can or can't have staying here. This is the United States. You don't have to worry that you'll be denounced by the neighbors."

Javier nodded, smiling. "Where do you get food?"

"In stores and supermarkets. Without a ration card."

"Wow," Javier said, and began another question.

Vladimir interrupted: "You've had a big day, Javier. Why don't you get some rest? Tomorrow we can talk about what you'd like to do." He cut himself off before he added "while you're here."

Vladimir went into the bedroom. Javier followed him in.

"So how long have you been living in this apartment?"

Vladimir went to the bathroom and closed the door.

"Do you rent from the State?" Javier was standing right outside the door.

He had forgotten. Privacy was an Anglo concept.

"Javier?" he called through the door. "I'll be out in a few minutes."

"We have a lot of catching up to do," Vladimir said when he came out of the bathroom. "We won't be able to do it in one night. Let's get some rest, and we'll start this up again tomorrow."

"Will you take me to your office tomorrow?"

"Sure."

"Great! I want to meet your partner. Do you make models like Grandmother?"

"Yes. She taught me how. Go to sleep now."

Javier went into the living room and Vladimir shut the door behind him.

He probably needed help with the bed. Vladimir walked out. Javier was standing by the door looking guilty of something.

"If someone knocks on the door, what shall I do?"

"I'm not expecting anyone tonight."

"But what if they do come?"

"In the unlikely event that there is someone at the door, you look through this little hole to see who it is."

Javier looked at him. "And then what?"

Vladimir sighed. "Then come and get me."

He helped Javier make the couch into a bed, gave him a kiss on the forehead (his son wasn't taller than he was), and went back into the bedroom. He took off his shoes, sat down on the bed and opened up his divorce decree.

In her floral, adolescent handwriting, María had signed a document saying that the marriage was legally over.

"*¡Me cago en el corazón de la madre de FIDEL! ¡Ja Ja JA!*"

"Okay, Javier." Vladimir laughed. "Enough. Time to sleep."

"Freedom of speech!"

Vladimir took off his shirt. This piece of paper signed by María represented the time and inconvenience of standing on line; nowhere did it state that this bovine bulldozer had hijacked his life. Vladimir wanted her to sign a paper admitting that she'd gotten pregnant on purpose and that they'd been *much* too young to get married. He'd been only three years older than Javier was now when they'd met. The time he'd wasted.

It was quiet in the living room.

Perhaps too quiet.

Javier was standing by the window, looking down.

"Who are those people down there?"

"I have no idea."

"They're skateboarding, and they're good! Look at that!"

"Javier. Close the blinds and go to sleep."

"How?"

"How do you go to sleep?"

"No, how do I close the blinds?"

Vladimir showed him. Javier twisted the blinds open, and then smiled triumphantly when he succeeded in twisting them closed again. Then he opened them. Then he closed them. Then he opened them. Vladimir pulled Javier's head forward and kissed him again on the forehead. Before he could turn, Javier pulled him forward and kissed *him* on the forehead. Vladimir laughed, and walked back to the bedroom.

He sat back down on the bed and took off his socks.

He heard a sound between a laugh and a cheer.

"Dad! He made it over two trash cans!"

He had lost a wife and gained a son. What was he going to do with this kid? He sat back, waiting for the next interruption. He took off his pants. The house phone rang.

Javier flew into the room with a terrified expression. Vladimir put on a bathrobe and went to the intercom.

"Who is it?"

"It's Diane. May I come up?"

"Diane!" Javier said, looking relieved and excited.

It was almost nine-thirty. What was she doing? What did she want? She should have called. "Okay," he said, and pushed the buzzer.

He hadn't told her yet that Javier had arrived; the boy's presence would no doubt change whatever she had planned. In spite of himself, Vladimir was glad to have someone else there. He thought better of the bathrobe, and got dressed again. Javier hadn't undressed yet.

Diane arrived, looking giddy and hopeful, wearing a new outfit in wild colors. She took one look at Javier and burst into laughter.

"Wow!" she embraced him, kissing him on both cheeks. "No need to ask who you are!"

"I meant to tell you. My son is here. He arrived tonight. Javier, Diane."

"*Mucho gusto,*" Javier said, blushing as she hugged him.

"Look, it's the most gorgeous evening, and we have *A Hard Day's Night* playing, and tomorrow's Friday. Don't you just want to be *out there?*"

"I like this lady," Javier said in English.

"Come out, Vladimir. We can introduce your new roommate to the neighborhood, or go to the movies, I mean, *something.*"

"It's late, Diane."

"It's not late," she said, and then she and Javier were off and running, chatting and laughing. Diane corrected Javier's English tactfully; he offered her rum and poured her a glass. Altogether, they were behaving as if Vladimir were not there. Which was fine. He went to his computer, and tuned them out.

"So, Vladimir, shall we go?"

"I have work. You go," he said, and Javier jumped with excitement.

"Vladimir," she said, when Javier went to get ready. "You have a son!"

He'd have to tell her about the papers. "It's not that simple."

She looked a little drunk and annoyed. "Who said anything was simple?"

"Ready!" said Javier. He reeked of aftershave.

"You'll bring him back at a decent hour?"

"Right after the movie."

"Have a good time," he said, returning to cubaencuentro.com. He opened the blinds, although he wouldn't be able to see them if they were walking uptown to the theater.

But he did see them. They appeared by the skateboarders' jump and stood watching the stunts, chatting with one of the kids. They stayed there for a ridiculous amount of time. Then they started walking uptown.

He sat down on the sofa with an odd feeling, something he couldn't name. It wasn't irritation. It wasn't frustration. It wasn't about Diane, and it wasn't about Javier. It was something else. He studied the boy's backpack, which was overflowing with things from home: handwritten letters, guava paste.

It was astonishing: he had the urge to call María.

◆

IT WAS A FIVE-STAR June morning. Diane walked down Tenth Avenue, clutching her bag with the certified checks, ignoring truck exhaust and the aroma of fried grease. She thought about what hour she would have to leave the theater to be on time for the closing on the East Twenty-first Street apartment, how many new features she would need to book for the first season of Cinema II, whether she should buy new clothing for summer or just wait for the old stuff, which would come out of storage when she moved into the new place. She had a better class of problems as of today.

The series was "Fabulosity," and she'd scheduled her favorite British films from the sixties to coincide with freedom and summer vacation in the air. "Anyone who can remember the sixties was not in London at the time," Michael Caine had said of the period. "Everywhere you went there was someone who was going to do something great—if not in show business then in something else, and if not now, soon. The energy was like a giant express train of talent that had no stops or stations. . . . You met someone one day and the next day they were all over the papers for some reason; they had jumped from the train and landed safely."

Beneath a marquee announcing *Darling* (John Schlesinger, 1965), she saw Javier waiting for her with a dreamy expression on his face. His thick, dark curls were even more spectacular than his father's, and he seemed to be in the midst of important, creative thoughts. His face lit up when he saw her.

Coming out of the theater the previous night, he had said, "That is the bestest movie I ever see!" The air was sultry, the traffic had died down and she couldn't remember when she'd last felt so fine. She'd gone back to her rented room with kitchenette too tired and happy to kill the water bugs in the bathroom. There was something genuinely wonderful about Javier.

"My father says that you are one excellent teacher."

"Nice to hear! Is he around?"

"Yes, he is under construction. I love the *Hard Day Nights*. Thank you!"

She decided to avoid the construction for now, and brought Javier back to her office. He immediately pulled up a chair and sat astride it, facing her.

"Diane, what you do here?"

"What *do* I do here?"

"Yes, what *do* you do here?"

"I present classic films in a creative format." She gave him a current schedule. "I manage the theater, plan the film series. I'm overseeing this expansion that your dad is designing."

"Dad is a good architect?"

"Yes, he is a good architect," she said, smiling at his earnest expression. The phone rang, and a look of annoyance passed across his face, a look that reminded her so much of his father that she almost laughed. "I see you like jewelry," she said, when she hung up.

"This is from one girlfriend," he said, pointing to one of the rings. "This is from one mother. This is from one aunt. This is from Grandmother."

"Who's your girlfriend?"

His face darkened. "Not a good subject now."

"I see," she said.

He leaned forward. "I do not have a past in English. You help me?"

"I'll help you with English if you help me with Spanish."

"Good," he said, shaking her hand to seal the deal. "English first. I go to school," he said, as if making an opening move.

"I *went* to school."

"Yes, I went to school, and they teach me English."

"They taught me English."

"They taught me *bad* English. 'Tom is a boy.' 'Mary is a girl.' This is not real English."

"What's real English?"

" 'Don't fuck with me!' " he shouted, and she laughed. "What De Niro say, he is the real English. I want the *real* English. I want the *real* New York."

Vladimir arrived in her space, creating the conditions for panic in her stomach and sweat on her back.

"Hello," she said briskly, standing up.

"I understand you had a great time last night," he said.

"We did."

She smiled at Javier, who stood up and announced: "Diane shows me the real New York."

"That's great, because I have to go to the tile warehouse."

She stood there blinking. "Excuse us, will you, Javier?"

She pulled Vladimir out into the corridor.

"In almost two months, you haven't spoken to me about anything that isn't construction-related. Now I'm a tour guide on call?"

"He told me you two hit it off."

"We did."

"So what's the problem?"

Javier poked his head out and Diane was ashamed. She had hit it off with him; she would like nothing better than to show him the real New York. But she had a day full of plans, including an apartment closing.

"You have work, Diane," Javier said. "I understand. I will help you in the work."

"He wants to work," Vladimir said. "To be your intern. I thought we had discussed this."

"When . . . did we . . . discuss . . . *anything*?" Her voice rose an octave and some raw emotion surfaced in the stuffy corridor.

Vladimir inhaled, and looked away.

"I am here to work." Javier spoke to her directly, ignoring both her tone and his father's lack of interest. "It is the less I to do after you do to me the nice invitation. Then, after the work, you can to show me the Times Square?"

She exhaled. He was lively, interactive and spontaneous—everything his father was not. "Well, sure," she said, "but I don't think that's the real New York. That's the theater district and it's full of tourists."

Vladimir saluted her, as if it had been decided, nodded at Javier, and walked out. He didn't look like a man who had to deal with a problem in a tile warehouse. He looked far, far away as he wandered out. In fact, he looked a bit like Javier.

After introducing Javier around the theater, Diane sat down at her desk. Then she decided that specific tasks could wait till after she had a preliminary chat with him over lunch.

She led him down into the Houston Street station. Part of her wanted to take his hand to make sure he didn't wander off—he was very dreamy and fluid. On the train, he started reading the ads and questioning her.

"Is that beer? Do you drink beer, Diane?"

"Not often."

"More a drink for a man?"

"Depends on the man."

"What is that, Caribbean Star?"

"It's an ad for a cruise."

"What is that?"

"It's a vacation by boat. Sometimes it goes from one island to another."

"In a boat?"

"The boats are big. It was the way to go, before there were planes. There were some beautiful ships. I can show you online. Do you know about the Internet?"

"We have the Internet during a year, but now it is illegal."

"You *had* the Internet *for* a year?"

"We *had* the Internet *for* a year. Not now."

"Why?"

He stroked the imaginary beard the way his father did when referring to El Comandante.

When they surfaced in Times Square, someone was preaching with an amplifier on the sidewalk, and Javier came to a full stop in front of a morbidly obese man hollering about Jesus. She pulled him away.

"Freedom of speech," Javier said, as if it were threatened.

"Freedom not to listen," she said, and his eyes widened in amusement. "Here's the first lesson of the Real New York: Keep moving. You have better things to do."

They waded through the crowds. Javier was visibly jazzed by the people, the neon, the ads, the things for sale on the sidewalk.

"Who is she?" he pointed to a woman's image on the side of a building.

"I have no idea."

"Why is the face so big on the building?"

"That's an excellent question, Javier."

"And *who* is that?" He pointed to another enormous, shimmering ad.

"A woman with a marketable body."

"And she markets her body on the building? She is a prostitute?"

"Another excellent question, Javier. Basically, she sells the product."

"What's the product?"

"Soda. A soda she couldn't possibly be drinking, by the looks of her."

Diane found herself four feet ahead of him as he moved like a balloon on an airless day, pausing in front of every sidewalk dealer and store display. She feared that his head might explode from the excitement.

He made a full stop in front of a candied-nut vendor. "We will eat here?"

"We will not."

"I smell good."

"Well, yes, you do, Javier, but I think you mean to say '*It* smells good.' "

He hit his head with his hand. "Yes, IT smells good."

"Come," she said, turning him onto a side street and ushering him into the restaurant she'd had in mind. "This also smells good."

"¡*Volao!*" he said as they walked into the bright, open place. "¡*Cojones!*"

"Your father says that a lot."

"Who?" he said, and she felt a sudden, inexplicable happiness as they followed the hostess to a table for two in the back. He was taller than his father, and slimmer. He had Vladimir's curly black lashes and the heavy, directional eyebrows.

"What do you like to eat?"

"I have a big steak last night."

"So maybe you want something lighter today?"

"No, no: meat is good. Oh, Diane, I love the meat so much!"

When the waitress arrived, she ordered veal Milanese for him and a chef's salad for herself. She glanced up and found him watching her intently.

"Diane: you say me your life. I want to know everything."

"You *tell* me *about* your life, Javier."

"Okay. At school, I am not welcome. I do something very stupid, Diane."

"I heard there was a problem."

"I do more than one the stupid thing in this year, Diane. But the more stupid? I shave myself the head. Bad idea!"

She laughed, and he dove into the breadbasket with abandon.

"I know when I talk to you the first time that I like you, Diane."

"How?"

"I know. From talking to you," he said, eyes open wide. "Your voice. And then when you talk to my mother, I really know it."

"You heard about that?"

"My grandfather listen on the phone. He tell me."

"I see."

"You have no idea so much happy I am to be here and not there."

She smiled.

"My mother is very happy for this phone call. She wants to thank you."

"For what?"

"It is time. Even my grandfather say it is time. It is a good divorce."

His voice was younger than his father's and he had an unusual way of pronouncing the letter *s:* not a speech impediment, exactly, but an indirect approach. He focused in on her. "I want to thank you, for my mother. You do her questions and change her mind." That was something that his father hadn't actually said to her. Just the fact that he was talking to her was different.

"Well. It's probably easier to see things from a distance. Tell me about school."

A shadow passed over his face and traveled somewhere else. He smiled, displaying idiosyncratically charming teeth.

"A big mess. She is not worth."

"A female is part of the school problem?"

"She is my girlfriend in the winter. Yusleidis."

He began telling her a story, acting out the parts. He seemed very glad to confide in her. "You were expelled for trying to protect your girlfriend?"

He nodded. "If she thank me, if she look on me with respect, okay!"

"She didn't thank you?" He shook his head side to side. "Ungrateful, at the very least."

"Yusleidis is not a special person," he concluded. "Before, my girlfriend is Lady."

"Who was that?"

"A girl at a different school. Lady Gonzalez."

"Lady was her *name*?"

"This is the worse: in the Escuela al Campo, my girlfriend name is Milady."

"Lady, Milady and Yusleidis! You sure know how to pick them!"

He got serious. "Diane. These are stupid girls. Especially Milady."

"What's the school situation now?"

"They still want me in a *militar* school."

"Military school? Why?"

Disgust seeped into his features. "Because my grandfather is a son of a bitch, and my father is right to leave. I am not a *militar*."

"Soldier."

"Soldier. I am not! I want to go to university. But the *militar* school does not prepare us. They want us in the army, not the university."

"I want to help. Would you like to look into schools here?"

"I have to talk to my father about to stay."

She nodded, thinking about Vladimir floating around a tile

warehouse, playing online chess on his son's first night in New York. He didn't deserve Javier.

"I know that when *he* comes here for university, he stays in one dormitory. I don't want to be a problem."

"I don't think you should worry about that," she said, offended on Javier's behalf. "Your father has everyone walking on eggs, and it's not fair."

He gave her an inquiring glance. "He does not tell what happen with you."

"He won't tell me, either. He just leaves me hanging. And with everything else I have hanging, I can tell you that I am very, very . . . *frustrated*."

"We can have long talk of frustrated. You like I talk to him for you?"

She laughed. "Absolutely not! That would be the worst thing."

"Well, you think about. I am here to help."

He offered his hand. She took it. He held it in both of his hands, peering at her intently. This caught her off guard. She picked up her water glass.

One of these days, he would learn that all the Ladies, Miladies and Yusleidises of the world had no power over him, and he would leave a trail of bewildered women in his wake, just like his father. On the other hand, he was interactive, emotional, optimistic, enthusiastic—traits she didn't associate with Vladimir.

The waitress put the check down, and Diane took it. He looked away.

"I like the Times Square," he said, gesturing to the world outside the restaurant. "Busy busy busy."

"I don't know that it represents the Real New York. But I'll show you, not to worry. But not today. I have to get moving."

"I help you."

She smiled. "Maybe you'd like to see the movie."

"I *love* to see the movie." When was the last time anyone said that? He didn't even know what the movie was. "But I'm here to work. I watch after."

On the way out, he stopped in front of a concession stand.

"I want to see what they have here," he said, and scanned the shelves. "Diane, which is your cigarette?"

"I don't smoke. I like this one," she said, picking up an Almond Joy, "and this one," she said, picking up butterscotch Life Savers, "and these," she said, picking up a box of Tic Tacs. "And we'll also take this," she said, handing a map of Manhattan to the cashier.

He looked cowed and reverent as she paid. "Thank you, Diane."

"No cigarettes on my watch."

"You forbid me?"

"Yes: I forbid you," she said jokingly. She gave him the bag of candy, opened the Almond Joy and handed him half. "It's a stupid habit. Don't start."

"Too late," he said cheerfully, biting into the Almond Joy. "¡Volao! I really like this!" he said, stopping in the middle of the crosswalk to appreciate the candy. She ushered him out of traffic, past a million distractions while he looked here and there, and let himself be led, finally, reluctantly, into the subway.

"Who is that?" he asked of an ad.

She was exhausted. "I have no idea."

"Do you think he play baseball?"

It felt like he was trying to suck all the information out of her. She packed him off to see *Billy Liar* (John Schlesinger, 1963) and popped a new release into the DVD player growing bored with it almost immediately. Still: what a sweetheart, she said to herself. She could help him with the past tense. Interpret the culture. Take him to the movies. Help him figure out what his next step was. What a fun project. She tackled a mound of paperwork, and then popped in another DVD, a new French release that started as a thriller and took a sharp right turn and became pornography. Javier burst into her office and she quickly fumbled for the remote, ashamed to be caught watching it.

He was out of breath and flushed with excitement. "I cannot believe the idiot say no to this gorgeous girl in the train! I am so offensed by this movie!"

Her phone rang.

"Just calling to check in on you!" came Dorothy's imperious voice.

Javier was poking around her office, eager, animated and in urgent need of vital information. She made her excuses and hung up.

"Where is the food?" Javier asked.

"Are you hungry?"

"To buy the food. Where you go?"

"In your neighborhood, you have to walk a little bit. I can take you there, if you like."

"I do like." He smiled.

The phone rang again.

"Are you sitting down?" Paul Zazlow asked, and she sat, filled with a seeping dread. "The seller was in a car accident."

"What?"

"She's ready to take your money, but not ready to move out. The apartment is right near her physical therapy."

"No, NO, *NO!*"

She began laughing and crying and screaming at once.

"What?" Javier asked. "WHAT? *WHAT?*" He squatted into a ready position with his fists clenched. With a deep, breathy martial arts cry, he executed a fast kick, sending her Best Repertory Cinema Award flying off her desk into the pile of DVDs on the floor.

She fell onto the couch, heaving with uncontrollable laughter.

Javier was a lot more fun than Vladimir.

VLADIMIR STRAIGHTENED the bib and faced the interrogation light. The irony: he had volunteered for this pain, and they couldn't care less what he confessed. On his first visit to America, a dentist in Chicago had listed everything that had been done wrong, recommended a full overhaul and showed him what dental floss was. He shot out of the chair when she came at him with a needle.

"What do you mean, no injections? This is the anesthesia."

"In Cuba, we have it without the anesthesia."

"Because you're so macho?"

"Because the shot is old and doesn't work. So you have twice the pain."

She presented him with a box; he inspected the expiration date.

"How do I know that that's the box for this injection?"

"You don't. You have to trust me."

There would be several more visits with this woman. He looked at her diplomas on the wall. "If I don't trust you, then what am I doing here?"

"Exactly," she said, and leaned in with her weapon.

Now a different masked professional leaned over him with the mirror on a wand. Javier was in the waiting room, radiating anxiety. It was a big mistake to bring the kid to New York without a plan. Javier was hanging out with Diane every day, exacerbating an already awkward situation. He had to do something. He'd thought Diane had moved on; her spontaneous appearance at his apartment made him uneasy. He should have a talk with her. But it would be messy and awkward, especially with Javier hanging around the theater. On the other hand, when he brought Javier to the studio, Chris and Magnus chewed the fat with him all day, and nobody got any work done.

"So tell me about the field work for the Revolution," Magnus had asked Javier on the day Vladimir had introduced him at the studio. "Was the sugarcane harvest amazing?"

"Is he an idiot or just pretending?" Javier asked Vladimir in Spanish.

"Tell him," Vladimir said in English. "Explain to Magnus the concept of 'voluntary work.' He doesn't believe me."

"This work is very hot, very hard. All day. They don't give us enough food. And it is not voluntary: you must to go. Or big trouble."

Magnus blinked. He'd been alternating between rock band T-shirts and tight-fitting button-down shirts in colors like burgundy, pumpkin and avocado green. No Che of late.

"One day," Javier went on, "we are so hungry, my friend Néstor and I. We steal cans of milk, and drink in the fields. We see after we drink it that the date on the cans is the year we are born!" Javier collapsed in laughter.

"The milk had expired the year you were born?" Chris asked.

"I am so sick! We are so sick!"

"So the School in the Fields . . . ," Magnus said, trying to comprehend it.

"Is compulsory unpaid child labor," Vladimir finished for him.

Paul arrived, and Javier was presented all over again. Paul had his own questions for Javier, and it was a free-for-all. At some point Vladimir said, "I need to get some work done. Javier, would you like to help me?"

"You see—voluntary work!" Javier said to Magnus, and followed Vladimir to his desk. Vladimir would have to find him a class, preferably one that met all day, otherwise the kid would just drift from office to office, chatting and flirting and asking endless questions.

Now Vladimir squirmed and pushed back onto the headrest and tried to be calm as the dentist began poking with the pick. Although he was an old hand at First World dentistry by now, and everything seemed under control here, nothing—not the cleanliness, the fresh, unexpired anesthetic, or even the friendly practitioner—could undo the feeling of complete, abject terror in the blue chair.

Would Javier stay with him permanently?

The poking and prodding in awkward parts of his mouth made Vladimir think about the lack of fluoride and calcium, the fact that only children under seven were allowed milk on the ration card. Not that Cuban adults needed much milk—milk in coffee was an American phenomenon, clearly because there *was* milk in America. Coffee was another sore subject. The Cordón de la Habana, the line of trees that used to ring the Malecón, had been cut down in the early seventies to implement the Leader's brilliant idea of planting coffee trees. But coffee doesn't grow by the sea; every last tree died. Not a single tree now grew by the Malecón.

Vladimir held a hand up. The dentist paused with the pick. "I just want you to know . . . ," Vladimir said, removing the saliva-sucking hose. The dentist listened. "I really hate Castro."

The dentist nodded and went back to work.

Castro had also decided it would be efficient to interbreed dairy cattle and meat cattle; the experiment produced a new hybrid with bad milk and stringy meat. Vladimir held up his hand again.

"No: I *really, really* HATE him," he said, and spat blood into the running water.

When he walked out, he saw his son's face, stricken with worry. He was grateful that Javier was there to take him home: the light outside was so intense he couldn't even open his eyes to hail a cab.

He got into bed exhausted.

HE MUST have fallen asleep. He woke up drooling.

Javier offered him a glass of soda with a straw, and began chatting about how much he enjoyed visiting the studio, what fun people Vladimir worked with.

"Is Paul an architect, too?"

"No, Paul is there in his capacity as a friend of Chris."

"Are Chris and Paul friends from school?"

"Chris and Paul are best friends," Vladimir said. "They live together and love each other."

Javier's eyes widened. "You mean . . . ?"

He nodded. "I try not to judge. I work very well with Chris. We get along fine. Paul is a pain in the ass, but he's always around. Nothing I can do about it."

Javier took this in. Vladimir arranged his pillows to sit up in bed. "What about Magnus?"

"I think he's still available, if you're interested."

Javier cast a not-amused look at him.

The sun was going down and the sounds of a baseball game drifted in from the field. Javier went to look out the window.

Vladimir had missed the entire childhood of his son.

But how could he have done anything any differently? Who, in his position, with that impossible wife, in that impossible country, would have stuck around to see how much worse it could get? He'd made mistakes. He'd paid for them. He stood by his life.

VLADIMIR ARRIVED at the theater the following evening to begin his son's architectural education. Javier was waiting in Diane's office, and Diane followed them out with her bag. It appeared she was coming along. He would have to say something, and soon. He took them to the Chrysler Building, the Empire State Building, the Flatiron Building, a series of cast-iron warehouses in the West Twenties. Javier and Diane were chewing gum—were they listening to what he was saying?

"Enough for today. Dinner?" he asked, hoping Diane would say goodbye.

"Sure," she said, and recommended a place around the corner.

Since he had nothing else in mind, they went around the corner.

"So you eat at restaurants all the time," Javier said as they sat down at a place that was decorated like an old-time bar, with black-and-white photos and mounted fish on the walls and assorted picturesque junk on every surface.

"I don't cook," Vladimir said. Javier had been lobbying to get groceries.

"I love to cook," Diane said, swinging her new short hair. Vladimir still hadn't gotten used to it. "But I don't have a kitchen. I don't have a home."

"Still?"

She threw her hands up in a posture of rage and helplessness.

What was wrong with this woman? He'd been willing to believe she'd hit a run of bad luck, but this was ridiculous. She was clearly waiting for their situation to resume so that she didn't have to make any financial commitments. He wanted to be at home playing chess; he was playing three games simultaneously now at RedHotPawn.com.

"I was supposed to be a homeowner as of the other day. But the seller called half an hour before the closing to say that she'd been in a car accident, and she wanted a delay because her physical therapy is a block from the apartment."

"So you'll wait?"

"Two weeks, sure. Anything more than that, no."

He felt some pressure release in his side.

"It has a terrific little kitchen. Listen: It's painted HOT PINK!"

He recoiled. What had he ever seen in her?

Javier had eaten all the bread. *Take it easy,* Vladimir wanted to say, but the kid was so thin. Javier and Diane were making plans to go to a museum the following day. "Four o'clock okay with you, Dad?"

"Actually, some of us have to work," he said.

They both stared at him. In Spanish, Javier said, "Why are you so mean to her?"

"Mind your own business."

"She's terrific, Dad. I can't believe you treat her like this."

"Is that what she told you?"

"She didn't tell me anything. I have eyes."

Diane was alert; she could probably figure out what they were saying.

"Enough. I've opened up my life to you, and I'm glad to see you, Javier. But I'm warning you: Don't stir up trouble in my personal life."

Javier sat back.

"It's rude to speak in Spanish and not include Diane," Vladimir said in English.

"*Soy cubano,*" Javier said, in a fatuous radio-announcer's voice. "*¡Soy popular!*"

"Let's schedule that visit for a time when you can join us," Diane said.

"That's very nice of you," he said, thinking of how he might get out of it.

Javier drifted off to look at some photos in the bar. It was now or never.

"Look, I hadn't planned anything, because I was sure that his application would be denied, if not by the Americans, then by the Cubans. But I can find a class for him and he won't be a burden."

"Javier isn't a burden. He's a delight."

He forced himself to look at her. She smiled without cynicism and said, "When the apartment comes through, I really am going to cook for you two."

"What: a family dinner?"

Her face froze. "Why not? Family is what you make it."

"I have no idea what that means."

"Clearly. You know, Vladimir, I think the situation you moaned about all those years was really just fine by you. I think you don't want a family. Not just the one you were stuck with, but any family."

He shook his head. "I'm sorry, Diane."

"Were you even going to tell me about the divorce? I heard about it thirdhand."

"Javier brought the papers. It's official."

"So I was fun while you were unavailable, but now that you're a free man, you have better things to do with your time?"

Javier sat down eager to talk. "Those people have motorcycles!"

Diane was a study in disgust.

"Shall I go away again?"

"That's a good idea," Vladimir said.

In Javier's wake, they stared at each other across the table.

"Look, I'm tired and I'm angry and I've spent almost half my life fighting something and now it's over. I don't know what to do or what to think. Okay?"

"Are you saying you might be interested when you figure it out?"

"I can't tell you to wait until then. That wouldn't be fair to you."

"Oh, but stringing me along for almost three months making me wait for a single word of *anything* from you *IS* fair to me? Did you think I hadn't noticed?"

He sighed. Javier came back to the booth as his dessert was delivered.

"I can get a motorcycle license at the DMB," he said in a chatty way. "What's the DMB?"

"The DMV is the Department of Motor Vehicles, with a *V.* And you can't ride a motorcycle as long as you are under my roof."

"*Hasta mañana, socio.*" Diane rose, kissed Javier on both cheeks and walked out.

"She's not like Mom at all." Javier lifted his spoon and watched enchanted as the ice cream fell in a ribbon.

"Enough about both of them. And don't play with your food."

JULY

DIANE LOITERED across the street from the apartment with the hot-pink kitchen early on a dark, humid, claustrophobic morning. She didn't buy the seller's car-accident story, and needed to know whether to cut her losses. If the story was true, Tanya Morris, a middle-aged legal secretary, would emerge from the building on crutches and turn left for her daily physical therapy session.

Diane hadn't been up this early in a long time. Sometimes Javier would ask her questions, like, Does CVS belong to the State? Does the U.S. government pay your wage? There would be a free-ranging discussion, two hours would go by, and she wouldn't even notice. Javier was the highlight of her day.

Through a Paul Zazlow connection, she had found a beautiful, sleek, furnished one-bedroom month-to-month sublet in the West Village, and had moved out of the Commodore Club. She hadn't noticed until she moved into the sublet that the space was permeated by a faint smell of bleach. The second night, she turned on a light and found the phrase "R.I.P. Consuelo" scrawled in red marker on the back wall of a closet.

She called Paul. *"R.I.P. Consuelo?"*

"I didn't want to tell you," he said. There had been a murder in the apartment. Fairly recently. But it was a great location, an elegantly furnished place, and as good a temporary solution as she would find for the money—didn't she agree? As she undressed and got into bed, she thought of *The Tenant* (1976), perhaps Roman Polanski's most execrable movie, although the scene where Polanski—renting an apartment previously inhabited by a woman who threw herself out a window—pokes his finger into a hole in the wall next to the bed and pulls out a tooth had to be among the most magnificently creepy moments on film.

Diane checked her watch. Where was the wounded seller? She called the only physical therapy clinic in the neighborhood that she'd found listed in the phone book. "This is Tanya Morris," she said. "Could you look up what time I have my therapy appointment today?"

"Tanya Morris?" There was a moment of shuffling. "I don't have you in our system. Are you a new patient?"

Diane hung up. Everyone, but everyone, was wasting her time.

She stalked down the block, calling Paul. "This accident is bullshit! Could you line up a day of apartments for me tomorrow, please?"

There was a pause. "Actually, tomorrow I have the whole day booked."

"Are you getting rid of me, Paul?"

"Diane! How can you say that?"

"Why? I'm too much trouble? Not in a high enough bracket? What?"

"Diane, relax. What about Thursday?"

She stalked to Third Avenue. Nobody wanted anything from her. She bought a paper and sat at the coffee bar that should have been her local hangout by now. She combed the real estate section looking for owners selling without agents. She found an open house in the West Village the following night.

When she got to the theater, Javier was pacing the lobby with excitement.

He had discovered the Food Network.

He wanted to make dinner for her.

She sat down at her desk, which looked the way she felt: scattered, shabby, confused. "What will you make?"

"Applewood-smoked tilapia on a bed of frisée lettuce with pancetta and mango-corn salsa," he labored to read from a sheet of paper.

"Wow. Either that or an egg salad sandwich. Count me in!"

The new series was "Savoir Faire," classic comedies from France. The French made comedies that weren't funny. They made sex comedies about innocence, buddy comedies about men not bonding and family comedies that were inappropriate for children. And yet. As Truffaut said, "We always appreciate better what comes to us from afar, not only because of the attraction of the exotic but because the absence of everyday references reinforces the prestige of the work."

Dorothy Vail appeared, for no good reason, in a white-and-navy linen sailor suit with a crisply pleated skirt. Diane introduced her to Javier and asked him to bring sodas, just then noticing a pile of newspapers, magazines and DVDs scattered over the floor. Where had that come from?

"He's *delicious*!" Dorothy said when Javier walked out.

"Hey!"

"What? Such curls! You just want to run your hands through them."

"Dorothy"—she faced her directly—"what can I do to help?"

"I have an extra ticket to the ballet tomorrow night. Are you free?"

"Thanks so much, but I have an open house tomorrow night."

"What about the hot-pink kitchen?"

"Fell through. Beyond despair. Living in a crime scene now. If you hear of anything, in any price range, for rent, for sale or for sublet. Anywhere. Let me know."

Javier returned with three sodas and sat down on the sofa. He'd gotten into the habit of hanging out in Diane's office, and she hadn't dissuaded him. Minute by minute, she could see him absorbing information and acquiring new habits. He got something out of every encounter, every leaflet that was handed to him on the street, every ad on a passing bus. Right now he was eager to listen to Dorothy.

Smiling at the attention of this keen young man, Dorothy said to Diane, "There's somebody coming to the ballet that I'd love you to meet."

Diane laced her fingers on top of her desk. "No."

"Don't you want to know who he is?"

"I don't care who he is."

"But Diane. He's the son of Leona and Myron Gelbman. They've had the exclusive plumbing contract for all the Broadway theaters for many years."

"He's in plumbing? No wonder you want me to go out with him."

"A good-looking guy, a family business, *and* he happens to be Jewish."

"Since when are you such a yenta, Miss Vail?"

"I happen to know that *you* are Jewish, even if *I* am not. The Gelbmans aren't religious, but the son went to Israel after the divorce, and he is quite observant now."

"He's a born-again Jewish plumbing magnate?"

"And a serious tennis player, in the fifty-and-over league."

"I don't like this man for Diane," Javier announced.

Dorothy smiled. "You like your dad better?"

"Okay, everybody stop talking about me. I am here."

"Maybe not my dad. But this guy is not seem fun for Diane."

"Speak to my manager, Dorothy," she said, indicating Javier. "In the meantime, we have an urgent Rohmer screening. Would you like to join us?"

"Oh, no. I can't stand him. Talk talk talk."

"Yes!" Javier said, and engaged Dorothy in an impassioned chat about *Pauline at the Beach* (Eric Rohmer, 1982). Dorothy immediately invited him to lunch. He looked at Diane for permission.

"Of course," she said, making a do-what-you-like gesture. She felt annoyed. She liked the routine that had developed with Javier, where they had lunch, worked on cinema business and then watched the double feature at the end of the day. In fact, she'd watched more movies with Javier in the month since he'd arrived than she had in the previous six months. The previous evening, as they watched *Pauline at the Beach,* she'd been so comfortable she almost put her head on his shoulder.

After he and Dorothy had gone, she slipped another new release from France into the DVD player. Diane had learned many things from French films over the years: austerity is a virtue (Bresson); adultery is normal (Chabrol, Godard, Malle, Tacchella, Truffaut); incest is natural (Blier, Chabrol, Malle); talk is often better than action (Assayas, Desplechin, Leconte, Rohmer); audiences need not be entertained (Demy, Godard, Resnais, Rivette, Tavernier); there is nothing more stifling or dreary than a provincial French town (Bresson, Chabrol, Fontaine, Pialat); Paris really does set the standard for style (Assayas, Besson, Jeunet). Also: coming of age can be gut-wrenching (Breillat, Jaquot, Kurys, Malle, Truffaut, Varda), and youth are sexual beings (Andrieux, Blier, Chabrol, Malle, Truffaut, Varda).

She wondered where Dorothy would take Javier, and what they would talk about.

◆

"ENOUGH CHESS and architecture lectures. I want to go out."

Javier had doused himself with a pungent aftershave that came in a bottle Vladimir remembered from his own adolescence.

"So go out."

"I want to go out with you."

"I don't want to go out. So you can stay in with me, or go out yourself."

"You are so boring. Why did Mom wait for you all those years?"

An expression passed over Javier's face, making him look exactly like Pucho, and Vladimir almost choked. Resentment was to be expected; he'd been surprised that it hadn't surfaced. Without a doubt, there were hormones at work here; he hadn't provided a structure, a place where Javier could meet kids—girls—his own age. That didn't give Javier the right to speak to him that way.

"You wanted to come here. You're here. This is it. This is America. This is what I'm doing tonight. Do what you want to do, but don't insult me in my own home. It's ungrateful, and unnecessary."

Javier kicked his sneaker across the room.

Vladimir walked into the bedroom and closed the door. He'd moved his desk there to be able to work without disturbing Javier. He was now a prisoner in his own bedroom. The living room was overflowing with crap that Javier attracted—newspapers, magazines, gum wrappers, articles from the Internet, calendars from the cinema, museum floor plans, ticket stubs from concerts. Javier saved price tags. Javier was all over everything. When Vladimir opened the refrigerator, he found a dish of dense orange material. He took it out to examine it. It looked like a brick.

"What's this?"

"I tried to make a flan," Javier said. "I don't know what went wrong."

"Are you going to eat it?"

Javier shook his head, ashamed.

"Then throw it out."

"That's wasteful."

"So either make it correctly or don't cook."

Javier lowered his head, and Vladimir left the dish out on the counter.

"By the way, all this stuff"—he gestured toward the detritus floating around—"could you find a way to store it? It's making me crazy."

Javier made as if to hand him his demerit card. And then he turned his attention back to the TV.

Vladimir went to his computer. On cubaencuentro.com he read a piece by someone in Cuba who wrote, "How lucky we are to have the blackouts! We can see the beauty of the stars! We're not poisoned by bad TV!"

Vladimir exited the site in protest. You're welcome to your misery, he thought. Good thing you enjoy it, since you have so much of it. He went to RedHotPawn.com to catch up with his chess—he was now playing twelve games simultaneously. He made moves in four games where it was his turn; no one responded, so he'd just have to wait for his opponents to move.

ON SUNDAY MORNING, Vladimir reached for half-and-half for his coffee and saw the brick of flan back in the fridge. He put the dish out on the counter again. Javier had made it: he should either eat it or throw it out.

He searched online and found an intensive English immersion course that started in a week and met at the Fashion Institute of Technology. Javier could learn English, and pick up fashion students. The cost was almost fifteen hundred dollars. He thought, Javier doesn't deserve that class, and was instantly ashamed.

Of course Javier deserved the class.

In the meantime, Javier wasn't asking for the class. He seemed happy to follow Diane around like a puppy by day and watch double features at the theater every night. Everything was new and fascinating: Burger King and cable TV were revelations to him. The previous evening notwithstanding, Javier's needs were small, prosaic, incessant and kind of pathetic. His eyes lit up every time he saw an ice-cream shop. It was hard to turn him down.

There was a knock on the door.

"Dad, could I have some quarters for the arcade?"

"Come on, Javier." Since discovering the arcade, his son had turned into a gaming addict.

Javier sat on his bed, without being invited. "You know, I can't work here legally, but I'd like to earn money so I don't have to ask you for it."

"So you can throw it away at the arcade. Play," he said, setting up the chessboard, giving his son white.

"Oh, *come on,* Dad: let's go out! There's a farmers' market I heard about."

Vladimir didn't want anybody, including Javier, making demands on his time right now. If he wanted to stay inside with the blinds closed on a gorgeous summer's day, so be it. He worked hard enough, and this was his day off.

"The kids downstairs all have portable game players. So they don't have to go to the arcade; they can play anywhere they want," Javier said, and looked up at him with shining eyes. Periodically, Vladimir glimpsed what Javier must have been like as a child.

They began the opening moves.

"If you move there, I'll take you with my knight."

"What is MP3?" Javier asked.

"You could then take me here, but I'd take your bishop. It's up to you."

Javier made the move anyway.

"You know, if I were you, I'd feel lucky to have such a willing chess partner, someone who could really teach me strategy."

"What's MP3?"

"It's a digital technology."

Javier launched his queen into open space without backup.

"That's a bad move."

"Could I have digital technology?"

This brought up an issue he'd not addressed, that of an allowance.

"Okay, how's this? In addition to the walking-around money for food and transport, I will give you twenty dollars a week for whatever you want to do or buy. Including the arcade, and any technology you want to save up for."

He pulled a twenty-dollar bill out of his wallet; Javier stared at it.

"Twenty dollars in New York is not like twenty dollars in Havana," Vladimir warned.

Javier clapped him on the shoulders in a burst of enthusiasm. "Thank you! Let's play chess later, okay?" He bounded out of the apartment with the bill.

He wanted to do the right thing by Javier, but the idea of this hormonally charged adolescent staying on indefinitely made Vladimir short of breath. He collected his clothes for the dry cleaner. There it was again, Diane's green sweater. It was summer: she wouldn't need it. Why should he get involved with her dry cleaning? He took it out of the pile. But he couldn't hang it in his closet. So he put it back on the desk chair. He found the bad flan back in the fridge.

Anticipating his son's thunderous return was no more relaxing than being with him in the first place. Javier would probably lose some credits and have to work extra hard because of language issues if he finished high school here. But eventually he would graduate, go to college and live somewhere else.

How on earth would Vladimir pay college tuition?

◆

JAVIER SPENT HIS FIRST American money at the arcade and the convenience store: games, gum, juice and comics. Twenty dollars in twenty minutes. The end. He went back to his father's apartment feeling bewildered and burned.

"I just spent a Cuban professional's monthly wage in less than a half an hour," he announced.

Vladimir looked amused. "I told you. Come on," he said, setting up the chessboard again.

Enough chess! Javier hadn't known what to expect from his father, but he certainly hadn't counted on his being silent, impenetrable and humorless, constantly working or reading about Cuba on the Internet. And yes: it was thrilling to read cubaencuentro.com, but at some point, Javier wanted to talk. Vladimir had no talk.

"Why are you sad?" he asked his father.

"I'm not sad."

"You're not talking."

"Just because I'm not talking doesn't mean I'm sad."

"But Dad: you *never* talk."

"I really don't have much to say. It's all been said before."

"Not by me!" Javier said.

The person who liked to talk was Diane. He was always making links between ideas and learning wonderful new things from Diane.

There was so much stimulation around here, all of it foreign, interesting and thought-provoking. Since he'd arrived in America, he'd been so stimulated, he hadn't given a single thought to being combative in the unceasing struggle against Imperialism. It was restful not to have the constant Revolutionary soundtrack hectoring him, but he was exhausted trying to interpret the siren song of the Advertising that had replaced it.

Nothing was quite as he had expected in New York. The streets weren't paved in gold, but every little thing cost money, and it added up to a lot. Nobody drove anywhere, although there were cars everywhere, and they were *magnificent,* new, all of them—or at least less than ten years old. Hitching rides was pointless (no one would stop), dangerous and perhaps illegal. Taxis were everywhere and expensive. Everybody took public transportation, which was less crowded and more reliable than in Havana. People didn't speak to each other unless they knew each other, and even then there were unwritten rules about who could speak to whom. The woman who sold gum and newspapers, for example, pretended each time that she'd never seen him before, even though he was in her store every day.

The older kids who hung out in the baseball field wouldn't speak to him. Javier had had more success with the skateboarders; he went to the jump every morning before heading to the theater. The regulars—Tom, Blake, and Jamie—had each allowed him one chance on their boards, and Javier had fallen so spectacularly that it had been good for a laugh. Sometimes Blake's older sister Zoë showed up. Zoë had shoulder-length dark blond hair and great legs on display in olive green short-shorts. Other girls stopped by the jump, but they were less interesting. Zoë evaporated each time he saw her. All four of them teased him about his accent, but Diane had told him that they didn't speak "the Queen's English" either.

Something had to happen soon; Javier had almost touched Diane the previous evening when they watched *Stolen Kisses,* a French movie about a guy not much older than he was with a crush on his boss's wife. When the woman eventually comes to the guy's apartment to seduce him, Javier was acutely aware of Diane's smooth bare arm on the armrest, her elegant horselike neck, her thick black hair pulled back in clips. She was nothing like Yusleidis or anyone else he'd ever had a thing for; she smelled of oranges and radiated frustration and energy. Javier could talk to Diane for hours. Vladimir refused to discuss her. He was so lame, at home alone every night and weekend, in front of his computer. Vladimir had no idea what to do with Diane. He didn't deserve her.

ON MONDAY MORNING, Javier went to the convenience store.

"Hello, Fatima!" he said. He'd heard someone yelling her name the day before.

She looked at him with a wild expression. "How dare you address me this way! Abdul!"

A stocky man in a vest came out of the back of the store, chewing gum. Fatima said something to him rapidly in another language.

"Get out of here, now," the man said. "Never come back, understand?"

"But I come here every day!"

"We don't need your business."

"I'm only being friendly!"

"Go away." The man took the bottle of juice and the gum that Javier had been about to buy, and waved him off.

Maybe he had made a mistake in English. So much of the language remained beyond his grasp.

When he got to the theater, he went to the construction zone. He asked Joe, the contractor, if he could be of use. Joe told him again that he couldn't work, in case he got hurt.

"Why would I get hurt?"

"Nobody plans to get hurt, kid. It just happens. You're not covered on my plan, so I couldn't help you if you did get hurt. And you could sue me."

Javier turned to his father, who was squinting at the floor, measuring a set of steps. "What is he talking about?" he asked in Spanish.

"We'll talk about it later," Vladimir said, and handed him a note to give Diane. "Find out what she wants done with these steps."

A man wouldn't do that. A man would go into her office and ask her himself. A man wouldn't call her "she."

Javier found Diane writing a nasty letter to a distributor who had failed to deliver a movie. She read it to him and he clapped, and suggested a few more insulting rhetorical flourishes. He then told her about what Joe had just said.

"Joe's worried you'll sue him?" Diane explained the concept of litigation, telling him a story about a sixty-two-year-old man who had fallen in the lobby two years earlier on a rainy night and then sued the theater for two million dollars in damages.

"WHAT?"

"I'm not kidding. Fortunately, he was seen dancing at his niece's wedding right before the trial, so the case was thrown out of court."

America was a whole different universe. "How will I help you today?"

She smiled and asked him to change the printer cartridge, which he did.

"What else?"

She asked him to put mailing labels on the new calendars, which he did.

"What else?"

"Gosh, you're fast! Well, why don't you go have lunch?"

"Come with me."

"No, thank you, I have to get this done. If you don't mind, bring me a turkey sandwich when you come back," she said, and opened her wallet.

"I will pay for lunch." Vladimir had given him another twenty dollars for the week, after he had come back with empty pockets, promising to renounce the arcade.

"Absolutely not."

"Diane. You pay all the time for me."

"And you help me every day for nothing."

"And you sent to me my invitation, which I can never pay."

"And you do twice what my employees do, put together. And they do get paid."

This had become an issue. Storm had decided that Javier was a threat to her job, and routinely walked away while he was talking to her. Floyd ignored him, but not in an active way. Cindy, on the other hand, had been very friendly, and had recently invited him to dinner at her home. He'd accepted with excitement: it would be his first dinner in an American home. He didn't count Chinese takeout with his father in *his* home.

"Don't make a mountain out of a sandwich," Diane said, smiling. "I'm touched by the offer, but I can't accept it."

"By the way, this is from Vladimir," he said, and handed her the note.

She read it and went to give him her answer in person.

Diane was an honorable woman. He wanted to take her out to lunch and talk about *Claire's Knee,* which was boring and incomprehensible. This hypocritical Frenchman with his hands all over every female around the lake, talking to them about friendship, how he was getting married so he wasn't interested in women. The ugly, annoying teenager yapping constantly about love had reminded him of Milady; the passivity of her pretty stepsister, who did nothing to stop the older man's creepy caresses, had reminded him of Yusleidis.

When he came back with the sandwiches, he asked to join her for lunch, and they spread their sandwiches out on her coffee table and sat on the sofa.

"*Claire's Knee* is really annoying, and I want to tell you why."

"I saw most of Rohmer's movies when I was your age, and I was fascinated by them," Diane said. "But I've seen some recently and I have to agree with you. Talk is one thing. Annoying people talking incessantly and congratulating themselves is something else."

He told her about the Fatima incident, and she laughed very hard. "Was she wearing a head scarf?"

"How did you know?"

"She's probably a good Muslim woman, and that was her husband or father who told you to get lost. If you see a woman with a head covering, it's usually the case. Either Muslim or Orthodox Jewish—either way, they don't chat with men."

He told her that Cindy had invited him for dinner.

She raised an eyebrow and opened a soda can.

"What?" he demanded. "Say what you almost say."

"What you almost *said*," she corrected. "Nothing."

"You think I should not go?"

"No, of course not! Go, and have a good time."

"What do you mean?"

"You're a big boy, Javier. I don't want to know about it."

He snuck glances at Cindy all afternoon. She was so unbelievably not his type that it hadn't even occurred to him! Her age was unclear—she was older than Storm, younger than Diane. He wanted to get out of the dinner, but she cornered him at the concession stand after the second show.

"Diane agreed to let us off early, so it's a date!"

"Twenty-three," Cindy told him, as they sat side by side on the subway.

He was slightly appalled at the idea that people might think they were a couple. On the other hand, how often had he ever been in this situation? Never. He had always been the interested party.

Suddenly the train emerged into the open air and the car was flooded with light. They were above the ground on an elevated track in a different part of the city. He watched billboards and shop signs in a half-dozen languages flying by. He didn't know what he would do. He decided not to make a decision until the moment presented itself.

"I rarely have anyone over," she said as she opened her apartment door. "But you seemed like a good candidate for a home-cooked meal."

He was intrigued by a collection of plants on her windowsill. She showed him a fully grown plant that she had started from an avocado pit; all you needed, she said, was an avocado, a glass, water and toothpicks. She was making beans and rice. While things were cooking, she asked him questions about Cuba. He told her the story about the prison. She laughed when she was supposed to laugh, and was grave when he told her about the beating. He omitted the part where he performed aikido on his grandfather.

"Wow," she said when he was done.

"Are you a Muslim woman?"

She laughed very hard.

"I mean, the head thing," he pointed to her kerchief.

"Watch you don't trip." She pointed to the rug he was pacing over.

"It's okay. I will not sue you."

She laughed and the timer went off.

They gossiped about the Bedford Street Cinema. Cindy disliked Storm and Floyd, but she really resented Diane. "I shouldn't tell you this, but she's a terrible boss."

"Why?"

"She expects you to know everything. I'm not a mind reader. How am I supposed to know she wants the floor washed?"

"Isn't that a daily job?" Diane had told him that Cindy's attitude about washing the floor was one of her pet peeves. Then she'd explained what a pet peeve was.

"Yeah, but she acts like it's a cardinal sin if I haven't done it. I guess you have a different relationship with her. She doesn't invite *me* in for lunch in her office. To me, she's just a bitch."

"Oh," he said, deciding to warn Diane about Cindy in some vague way.

After dinner, he stood at the stove, scraping the pot for every last bean, licking the spoon. She came up behind him. "I really like you, Javier."

"I like you, too, Cindy," he said, trying not to panic.

She lifted a curtain and made a gesture leading the conversation into her bedroom. Here it was. He hesitated, holding on to the spoon.

"What's the matter?"

"I don't know." Here finally was a woman who wanted something, and what was happening? He wasn't interested in her, but so what? She was willing. How to get out of this gracefully?

"Well, the fact is, I like someone else."

She froze. "Who?"

"You don't know her."

"Okay, tell me all about her," she said, and lay down on the bed, patting a place next to her. This was strange. But he didn't want to insult her, so he sat next to her and leaned back, propped up against the pillow. He was still holding on to the spoon.

"Well, she's the sister of a guy I see on the skateboard jump. Zoë."

"Zoë what? You don't know? Have you asked her out? No? Why not?"

"I haven't got her phone number."

She rolled her eyes. "How old is she?"

"I don't know. Fifteen or sixteen."

Her face stiffened. "I am ready, willing and *here,* Javier. You are talking about a *teenager* whose last name you don't even know."

"But we work together."

"And?" She noticed the spoon, suddenly, and seized it from him and threw it into the kitchen. It clattered on the floor.

"Well, it is a delicate place, the cinema. It will be rare tomorrow if we"—he racked his brain for the polite verb—"eh, do this."

She laughed. "Rare?"

"What's the word?"

"Don't you think it would be rare tomorrow if we *don't* do this?" She guided his hand to her chest. It took him a moment to process the sentence and the physical sensations. She kissed him in an open manner that revolted him.

He pulled his head back and sat up on the bed. "It will be rare, one way or another. But I cannot do this, Cindy. I am so sorry."

"Fine." She rolled off the bed and stalked into the bathroom.

He was letting himself down. Néstor and Paco, too. He was letting down all Cuban men. But he just couldn't bring himself to move forward.

He heard her weeping. "But I like you, Cindy! No crying."

She came out. "You are *awful.*"

He kissed her cheek. "I want to thank you. Dinner is delicious."

"Dinner *was* delicious, and you are a tease."

"I don't understand, but okay, I am tease. You tell me how I go home?"

◆

DIANE WALKED UP CROOKED, carpeted stairs that seemed too narrow and steep. The open-house apartment was teeming with people inspecting the renovated kitchen with pass-through to dining area and an exposed brick wall.

In the bedroom, she saw Paul Zazlow checking out the closet space.

They looked at each other.

"You're not supposed to be here: you have a broker," he scolded her with a sly look after kissing her on both cheeks.

"You're not supposed to be here: you *are* a broker."

Voices were raised in the other room. They passed back into the foyer.

"You're an idiot if you don't use a broker," a squat woman with a red face was saying to a man in the open kitchen. She looked unstable, perhaps because she was wearing a thick black-and-white wool suit in July. Her chin-length jet-black hair had at least an inch of white roots showing.

"This is my property, and I can do whatever I want with it, including selling it myself." The owner was a stout, gray-headed man in his mid-fifties.

"You won't list it because you're too cheap to pay the fee," said the woman, making short choppy gestures that displaced a name tag on her lapel. It fell to the floor, and everyone looked at it.

"It's time for you to leave," said the owner.

"Okay, let's calm down," said Paul.

"Who the hell are you?" she demanded, bending down to pick up her name tag.

"I'm Paul Zazlow, a broker with Fiedler. You have no business here."

"Well, neither do you!"

"I am calling your office," the owner told the unstable woman.

"You *bastard*!" she screamed, throwing her weight against him and knocking him into the refrigerator.

"Don't!" Diane said, reaching out.

"Take your hands off me!" The problem broker shrieked, turned and swiped all at once. It happened so fast that Diane barely felt it, but blood began spurting out of her face. She felt a fog of nausea in the back of her throat, and slid down to the floor against the wall beneath the pass-through.

"Are you all right?" Paul asked, kneeling down beside her.

Blood was seeping between her fingers. "Dizzy."

Meanwhile, the owner had shoved the broker across the kitchen into shelves on the far wall, where she fell to the floor, taking glasses and dishes down with her. She lay among the shards with her legs exposed.

"You bastard!" the woman howled. "I'm bleeding!"

"Are you all right?" the owner asked Diane, handing her a paper towel.

"I just want a place to live," Diane said, holding the towel to her face.

Paul dialed 911. "We have a fight here, a real estate fight!" he said, giving the address of the apartment as he ran a paper towel under the tap. "A psychotic broker menaced the owner and she's just attacked an innocent client and everyone is bleeding."

"You'll pay for everything you broke here," the owner shouted.

"You brought this on yourself," the broker shouted back.

Paul dabbed at her face with wet paper towels and asked, "Did you disturb a coven of witches who put a hex on your head, Diane?"

"R.I.P. Consuelo," she said, trying to slow down her pulse by breathing consciously. When she closed her eyes, her head spun, so she kept them open.

A woman poked her head in, took in the broken dishes, the two women on the floor, the two men with a pile of bloody towels between them, and asked, "When did you buy the dishwasher?"

The broker stood up, shedding dishes, picking a shard of pottery out of her hand. She gathered her pocketbook and leather portfolio.

"You stay and wait for the police!" the owner shouted, but the broker had barreled her way into the open-house throng and out the door.

"What's the maintenance here?" someone else asked.

"Listed on the sheet," Paul called, dropping another bloody towel onto the pile.

"Where's the sheet? I didn't get a sheet."

"The sheet is in the foyer!" he shouted. "And this woman is bleeding!"

The owner knelt down on the floor and opened a first aid kit.

"I have that lunatic's card," he said, taking out an antiseptic to clean Diane's wound. "I'm calling her agency. This is insane. This is actionable."

"Oh, that stings," Diane said.

"What were *you* doing here?" the owner asked Paul.

"Same thing she was. I'm Paul, by the way. And your patient is Diane."

"Gregory."

"Sometimes," Paul said, "when an owner sees what's involved, the lunatics who show up at an open house, he's glad to let someone else take care of the sale."

"That assumes that the broker is saner or more savory than the apartment hunters," the owner said, fishing through the first aid kit. "Not always true."

"When did you buy the dishwasher?" the woman asked again.

"Last year," he called, applying an ointment to Diane's face.

A big, dark blue presence pushed into the kitchen: two cops presented themselves and asked who had called and what had happened. Another woman poked her head in as the owner began describing the situation.

"Is there a storage bin in the basement?" she asked.

◆

THE DAY WAS DARK and dank, with a greenish cast to the light over the baseball field. Vladimir dressed for work.

"What's this?" Javier held Diane's sweater.

"That's Diane's," Vladimir said.

Javier buried his face in the sweater. "Shall I give it to her today?"

That was the best solution, although it was bizarre that Javier wanted to wear the sweater around his shoulders, and on such a sticky day. They took the No. 1 train uptown. A conductor emerged from his cab and walked through the car. Vladimir sensed his son's anxiety. He tried to remember when his fear of subway personnel, postal carriers, ticket takers, bus drivers, policemen, doormen and neighbors had faded. He couldn't pinpoint a time, but he had lost much of that fear along the way.

"I want to have a job to earn money," Javier said, for the third time this week.

"You really can't, not legally."

"I need money. Twenty dollars is nothing here!"

Vladimir sighed. "What do you need?"

"I want to take Diane to dinner."

"Diane doesn't expect that."

"I don't care. I want to take her to dinner. And I want to take *you* to dinner."

"I appreciate that. But nobody expects you to pick up the check. It's inappropriate."

Javier slid down in his seat. He'd asked for permission to take over the grocery shopping for the household, and Vladimir had been delighted to say yes. Javier had insisted that they eat at home at least twice a week, and the previous evening he had made a pretty good although overcooked hamburger with a salad of special lettuces that he'd found at some market Diane had taken him to. Over dinner, he told Vladimir that for the next meal, he would smoke meat on the stove using only tinfoil, a wire hanger and an egg timer; he'd seen it on the Food Network.

"Perhaps that's a bit ambitious. What about pasta?"

Javier straddled a chair and fixed the big brown eyes on him: he loved pasta! He had seen a pasta-making machine the day before with Diane at Bed Bath & Behind—would Vladimir let him buy it? On the counter, as they washed up, Vladimir found the source of an odd smell that had been tormenting him over dinner. It was a bowl of coagulated milk wrapped in gauze.

"What is going on here?"

Javier was making yogurt.

"Did you know that they sell yogurt already made?"

"Just because I came from Cuba a month ago, you think I'm un-sophisticated? You think I'm a hick?"

"Only hicks have to make their own yogurt."

Javier corrected him with a pious tone: if you made it yourself, it was healthier and it tasted better. He wanted to make his own pasta; he wanted to make his own pizza; he wanted to make his own beer. Diane knew how to make bread, and she was going to show him how.

Vladimir could see his kitchen becoming cluttered with bulky, dust-collecting equipment from Bed Bath & *Behind*. He pointed to the bowl of milk. "Will this experiment go the way of the flan, is all I'm asking."

Javier stood up a little straighter and looked him in the eye. "It is an honest attempt."

"Okay, fine, but I don't want it hanging around for a week. Either eat it or throw it out, right away. What a bizarre smell."

AT HIS OFFICE BUILDING, Vladimir set Javier up in the café downstairs and gave him some money. Upstairs, he motioned to Chris that he needed to talk privately. Chris gave Magnus a pat on the back and joined Vladimir in the pantry.

"I have an awkward request," Vladimir began.

Chris looked at him directly. "Just say it."

"Can you take over the Bedford Street Cinema?"

"What do you mean, can I take over the Bedford Street Cinema?"

He took a deep breath. "I am afraid that it has gotten very awkward with Diane. I don't know how to put this."

"I speak to Diane all the time. She's fine. Don't worry about her."

"Javier is hanging out there. She spends more time with him than I do."

"You're a professional. She's a professional. You'll finish the job. Period."

So much for gay men being emotional and understanding about personal issues! Vladimir had never been handled with such efficiency. He went downstairs to talk to Javier over coffee. He presented him with the description of the English immersion class.

Javier read the printout, sipping his coffee. He looked very mature, Vladimir thought, and felt proud of his son, how he had turned out. A motorcycle idled at the red light in front of the café, shredding the air with unnecessary engine noise.

"That," said Javier, mesmerized by the motorcycle and no longer reading, "is so cool. I want one."

Some adult! "Not on my watch."

"Well, this is fine," Javier said in English. "But I have to say, my English is improving every day that I live here and work at the cinema. I don't know if a class is necessary, and it's very expensive."

"Don't worry about that."

"I'd rather use the money to buy that fermenting equipment."

"Not a chance. I think an English class this summer would be a good way of getting ahead in the language, which will be an issue if you decide to stay."

Javier looked at him with the big round wet brown eyes.

Vladimir switched back to Spanish. "Javier. I don't know what you plan to do. You may want to think about it for a while. Just know that I will do everything in my power to help you stay, if that's what you want. And if you want to go back, I'll understand that, too. The one thing you can't do is go back and forth. If you stay, that's it. And if you go back, there's no guarantee that you'll be able to get out again."

Javier nodded. "I will think about it."

"Good. You have until September third. If you do stay, and you go to school, things will be more normal. I mean, you'd meet people your own age, and your social life won't be so limited by your cranky old man."

Javier smirked.

"In the meantime," Vladimir continued, "don't you think you'd learn more English in a class?"

"Not necessarily. I learn so much from Diane. And not just English."

Javier really had been blossoming under Diane's attention.

VLADIMIR STOPPED BY Diane's office late that day. She had a bandage on her face, and it appeared that she had been crying. He pointed to the bandage. She closed her eyes and shook her head.

He cleared his throat. "Diane, thank you. You've been a big help with Javier."

"He's a big help to me, and a lot of fun."

"Good. You deserve fun." He was immediately annoyed with himself: such an American thing to say. "I think he's going to be doing an English immersion, so he won't be around so much. In your hair."

"He's not in my hair. I'd miss him, but whatever Javier wants to do is fine by me."

He walked out, disturbed. Of course Javier was fun! He didn't have a job, rent to pay, or even a date book to carry! He didn't have a business to run, or friends, or school, or anything else in his life to distract him: of course he paid attention to her!

◆

"DIANE, YOU HAVE done wonderful sing wiz zhe museum," Catherine Merveille said after they had ordered salads.

"The cinema, you mean?"

"Yes, zhe cinema. Zhe museum of cinema."

Catherine had called her up out of the blue to ask her to lunch. Diane was in no mood for surprises; she still had a big gauze patch on her cheek, and no apartment, and she wasn't inclined to chat. But why turn down a legendary film star? It wasn't polite to ask people right up front what their agenda was. So she waited, and studied Catherine's makeup.

"I want to talk to you about an organization I am involved wizh. Dario is also on zhe committee. In Chamonix. It is very close to my 'art because I spend winters there all through my shildhood. You have been in zhe area, of course."

The area was memorable for the day Diane had spent skiing, or, more precisely, the day she'd spent falling. This adventure had been in her early thirties; it seemed impossible now that she would do anything so reckless again.

"I 'ave a chalet on zhe mountain. We 'ave goats. So sharming. Zhe shildren love to ski," Catherine was saying. Diane was aware of people staring at her patch. She was possibly on the verge of tears. Some unknown thing was operating at a very deep level, keeping her life stalled, malfunctioning. The fact that an accomplished woman with long hair was talking at great length about her second home was no comfort.

"We make big, new, exciting event. I sink you are zhe one to run it."

"Run what?"

"Zhe Chamonix Film Festival," she said, as if they'd been discussing it all along.

"Well, thank you for thinking of me." It sounded stilted, canned. "I—things are very out of joint for me, as I don't have a place to live right now."

"So zhis is zhe perfect time to make a moof."

"I've had bad luck in the real estate business. Perhaps it is a sign."

"And I understand sings are finished in zhe personal business, so why not try a new place? Zhe pay is probably more zhan zhat slave driver give you here. And Heuropean men are so mush heasier for a woman like you."

Diane looked at the film star, so composed, so stylishly casual, and sitting so close that one could actually reach out and strike her.

"Sink about it," she said, putting a cool, jeweled hand on Diane's hand. "It's a good time for you to take sharge of your life."

The last time Diane had attended the film festival at Cannes, a world-famous Italian director became fixated on her hair. "I know you won't let me touch it, but let me dream," he whispered to the back of her head in an elevator. She was so creeped out by his hot breath in her hair that she shot out of the elevator like a greyhound when the doors opened.

"I make a film about your hair," he said the next time he saw her in front of the hotel, slipping his card into her hand as his wife, daughter and dog folded themselves into a limousine, casting evil looks her way. The farce continued when this nutcase scratched on her door in the middle of the night, begging for admission. She sent him away: she happened to be in bed with another ardent Italian at the time. (This was many years ago. Things like that happened to Diane back then.)

The next morning, she saw him in the elevator. He was accomplished and legendary; he was also on the verge of senility. Again he told her that he was intoxicated by her hair and announced that she forbid him to touch it.

Enough, she decided.

"You can touch it. Go ahead." She held out some hair for him to touch.

He looked crestfallen. He touched the hair softly, sadly, briefly, as if all he'd wanted was to be told no. The Italian she'd spent the night with the previous evening had been gorgeous, charming, and, yes: married. Come to think of it, European men were no picnic. But Catherine was right: there was nothing to keep her in New York. Everything had turned sour when she'd cut her hair.

Of course, things hadn't been going so well before that, either.

When she got to the theater, Javier was pacing the lobby in excitement.

"Diane! Look at it!" He held a summer calendar. "This is my mail! How this happen?"

"Remember how you stuck mailing labels on the new calendar? Well, one of them had your name and address on it."

"No, I mean, how it happen?"

"I put you on our mailing list."

"No, I mean, who brings it to me?"

"The mail carrier."

"How do you mail it?"

"You put a stamp on the envelope, then you put it in a mailbox or take it to the post office."

He waited.

She pulled a sheet of stamps out of her desk drawer to show him.

"I'll take you to the post office sometime. That may be a nice field trip."

The phone rang.

"Where are you living now, sweetie?" asked Estelle DeWinter.

"I just moved into a noisy sublet in a Yorkville tenement that is invaded by vile cabbage-y cooking smells every day. Near you, actually."

"Come for a walk tomorrow morning. We can talk about the benefit."

Another day, another random invitation. Not particularly what she wanted or needed, but who was she to turn down invitations?

She looked up: Javier was on her sofa, carefully examining the sheet of stamps. She'd never seen anyone touch anything with such reverence.

"DID I EVER TELL YOU about working in the second musical unit at MGM, Diane?" Estelle asked her as they strolled up the East River esplanade the following day. "One week it was medieval France. The next week, a Moroccan harem. But it was the same every time: if you were an extra, you were in the way."

Diane watched as a barge overflowing with garbage floated upriver.

"We made B pictures that sank without a trace. The leading lady was nobody at the box office. She knew her place in the commissary. But on the set, she was the *star*."

The wind was blowing the stench toward them. Diane tried to ignore it.

"I learned something very important at MGM. In my own life, I'm not an extra. Diane, you may not be Ann Miller, but you have power to take charge of your own life."

This was the second time in as many days that she'd heard this idea. What were these women talking about? Vladimir, obviously.

She had power over what, exactly? She got back to her noisy, humid, smelly tenement sublet and exchanged leggings for the no-longer-new turquoise swirl Capri pants. She was sick of them. She found a pair of wrinkled jeans to wear instead.

She had power over her dry cleaning.

AUGUST

VLADIMIR OPENED HIS E-MAIL and found a letter from his sister's e-mail address.

"Dear Javier," it began.

He read on.

"I am writing to you because I want to remember you on your birthday, and tell you that because of the evil, inconsiderate American regime, I cannot send you a present. Nadia and her husband ask after you. Your mother has been crying every day since you left! I have been awarded a Citation for Excellence for my work organizing the hotel staff for the July 26 protest in front of the American Special Interests Section.

"It is imperative now that you join the Communist Youth. You really should have done it last semester, as I arranged. You will acquire more responsibilities and demonstrate that you are combative for the Cause. This will go over well next year at El Cotorro. Assuming you work hard and behave yourself, you would move on to Cadet School the following year.

"You are eighteen. I would say that you are an adult, except for the thoughtless, impetuous behavior that you have not learned to control. Paco's father told me what you told Paco the day after your ridiculous episode at the police station. Forget about how you put my position in jeopardy when you talk shit like that. You have obviously been influenced by an undesirable element within the family, someone who already had a thick file for Individualism and Ideological Diversion when he was your age. In spite of all my efforts to educate him. My advice to you is to take notes and photos of the lack of humanity and selfish consumerism that corrodes the society in the US. My contact at the local Committee can arrange a slide-show talk for you at the monthly meeting when you come back, so that we can expose 'the American Dream' together.

"We miss you, and hope you are taking good notes for when you come home. Remember your daily pledge: Be like Che!

"Your loving grandfather, Pucho."

Vladimir shook his head, laughed once and printed out the letter for Javier, who was waking up slowly in the living room.

Every time he walked into the apartment lately, Vladimir cringed, wondering what science experiments he might find. An avocado pit pierced with toothpicks perched above a mayonnaise jar on the windowsill. Javier had started creating necklaces out of gum wrappers, and had made a workshop out of the dining room table. A red goldfish now orbited in a small glass globe on top of the toilet.

"Shouldn't we discuss having a new roommate before we invite him to live with us?"

"I won it at a fair!" Javier crowed.

Every day, Vladimir asked Javier to contain his junk, and every day the junk multiplied and spilled over into the common space.

But perhaps today was not the day to bring it up.

"Happy birthday," he said, and presented Javier with the electronic game that he'd found for him the night before. Javier ripped open the wrapping and immediately began playing the game with enthusiasm in bed. When Vladimir emerged from the shower fifteen minutes later, Javier was still at it.

"I hope you don't mind, I read this," he said, giving him Pucho's letter.

Javier ignored him and continued playing.

"Don't you want to read it?"

Javier put down the toy and scanned the letter. He scoffed at one point, laughed at another and threw the letter into the garbage when he was done.

The weather had turned sulfurous. Vladimir was already sweating as they went down in the elevator, and when they hit the street, which smelled of sewers and steam, he was reminded of Havana in August.

"I don't see how I can go back there," Javier said as they made their way up Hudson Street. "Not after seeing all the selfish consumerism and lack of humanity around here!"

"You've decided to stay."

"I don't want to be a burden to you."

"We'll figure something out. We have to start working on school for you now. Let me do some research."

They entered the sweltering subway.

"Thank you. He was like this with you?"

"Always. He's a cockroach, Javier."

Javier cackled. "He is, isn't he?"

"He's an opportunist, a sadist, and a son of a bitch."

Javier laughed long and hard. "Listen," he continued in a chatty mode, "the last time he started his business on me, I flipped him over onto the floor in front of Mom, Nadia, Hanoi, and Mercedes. He was flat out on the dining room tiles!"

"Where did you learn how to do that?"

"I started karate when I was eleven. You knew that."

He should have known that.

"This last year, I was working on aikido. I hadn't tried anything on him until that day. But it was just too much. I should have done it years ago."

"Maybe you'll teach me."

"Sure! Let's go to the park!"

"Javier, it's a heat wave. Another time."

Javier sagged slightly. And went back to the electronic game.

There really wasn't enough time for all the bonding he should be doing with his son. But if Javier stayed, they would have more time. It was hotter on the street than it had been in the station. The Chelsea Piers sports complex had teen programs—basketball, rock climbing, and so on—that Vladimir kept meaning to check out. But now he would have to investigate schools immediately. It was August 1.

◆

DIANE SHOWERED in the corroded Yorkville tenement bathroom, worried about generations of unchecked bacteria infecting her feet. Perhaps Bedford Street was a dead end; perhaps New York was old hat. But Chamonix couldn't possibly be the answer: she had turned down Catherine's job. The following day, she'd received another job offer from a former colleague, this one in Rome. Perhaps the wall-to-wall lack in her life—home, furniture, clothing, man—was liberating. A temporary situation in Rome was no worse than a temporary situation in New York. Why had she turned the offer down? Wasn't everything a temporary situation?

Diane emerged from the bathroom just as the front door opened.

A balding man in his late fifties dressed for the beach and holding an overweight spaniel on a leash stood gawking at her.

"What are you doing here?" she asked, pulling the towel higher.

He closed the door. He wasn't leaving. "I could ask you the same thing." He walked to the kitchen as if he owned the place. "This is my apartment."

"You could have rung the bell."

"I didn't think you'd be here."

"That's no excuse. You owe me the courtesy of ringing the doorbell."

She picked up the phone and called Paul. "Paul? There's a man in the Yorkville sublet harassing me. He came in with the key."

"You're still there? Today is the first."

"The first what?"

"August first. Your contract ended yesterday."

"Ah, shit."

She hung up, sick again of her circumstances. "I'm very sorry. Could you give me ten minutes?"

He exited with an impatient look. She closed the door behind him and fastened the chain lock. She dressed and packed, cursing the dingy halls, rickety stairs, narrow corridors, panic-inducing elevators, lousy wiring, repulsive smells, grimy corners, aging fixtures, deaf neighbors and unpleasant surprises that subletting entailed. With all her worldly goods in a ripped shopping bag, she stood on Second Avenue in shimmering heat, trying to stay cool and hail a cab. Even bad hotels were two hundred dollars a night in Manhattan.

In the cab, she called her parents.

"Come home," said her father.

She almost cried. "That won't solve anything."

"Maybe not, but it doesn't smell here, and the price is right."

"Thank you."

"You don't need to sign a contract, or be out by a certain date."

"Tomorrow night," Diane said, wondering why she didn't just say yes.

The series "Savoir Faire" had segued, seamlessly, into "Endless Summer," a selection of films about childhood. She was cheered that the first person she saw at the theater was Javier; she deflated slightly when he handed her a green wool sweater that seemed to be covered in fine gray hair.

"So that's where it was."

She sat down at her desk, unsure of what she should do. Javier watched her. What would happen if she just left for the day, right now? What would happen if she didn't repackage everything anew each year? What difference would it make if she showed *Amarcord* (Federico Fellini, 1973) in a Fellini festival or a childhood festival, or if she showed the same childhood festival every year? What if she just showed the Miramax catalog? Would anyone even notice?

The phone rang: Dorothy. Estelle had broken a hip at LaGuardia.

"Oh my goodness. How?"

"I don't know. Doing handsprings on the baggage carousel? She's at her apartment. She's not doing well."

"I'm so sorry to hear that. How's Herb?"

"Like a child in his mother's sickroom. I'm going over there in half an hour to cheer her up."

The idea of Dorothy cheering anyone up was a bit of a joke.

"I'll meet you there."

Javier asked to tag along.

"Wait: Isn't it your birthday?"

He smiled and ducked his head.

"Don't you want to do something fun?"

"It's fun to be with you."

How she yearned to run her fingers through his hair. "What are the birthday plans?"

"I don't know what my father is planning."

Knowing Vladimir, nothing. "Let's go ask him."

She found Vladimir measuring something in the dark.

"I was wondering how you intend to celebrate Javier's birthday."

"I hadn't made specific plans, but I thought we'd go for steak, if that suits you," he said, glancing at Javier.

"Yes!" Javier shouted.

"Could you go on the early side so he can be back for the nine-thirty show?"

"Yes, we can do that." He thought a moment. "Would you like to come?"

Javier nodded. "Yes, Diane must come."

"I'll come to dinner, if you come to the movie. We're showing one of my favorites, the one that made me want to devote my life to film."

"What is it?"

"*Small Change.*"

"About money?"

"About children, and growing up, and crushes, and senseless cruelty."

"Ah. I think I might be working."

"He either wants to do it or no," Javier said. "You can't make him do nothing."

"*Any*thing," she said.

"*Any*thing."

Vladimir looked at Javier and then turned to her. "Shall I pick you two up at seven?"

As THEY WALKED east on Eighty-sixth Street, Javier grilled her about the two-party system, the popularity of rap and the history of the slogan "Just do it," while she pondered what to get him for his birthday, and when she would have the time to buy it. They passed three shoe stores in a row. She looked at his feet and had her answer.

"What's The Velvet Cove?" he asked as they passed an adult toy store.

"That's a good question."

He came to a complete stop. "You always say that and then you never answer."

"Not so. I answer all your questions."

He stood still on the sweltering pavement. "I am not a child, Diane."

She turned around. "The Velvet Cove is an adult toy store."

His face lit up. "Let's go in!"

"You are an adult, but that's not something you do with me."

He turned on an electronic game and played as they walked. She bought flowers and cookies at a bodega and had them wrapped. He offered to carry them and she gave him the packages. At East End Avenue, a man and a woman with a soccer ball cut in front of them and ran into the park. She sensed his excitement.

"You want to hang out in the park?"

He gave her a sheepish look.

"Javier, it's a sickbed visit. I have to do it, but you don't. Go ahead. I'll come find you when I'm done."

He unloaded the cookies and the flowers and trotted off into the park.

Herb answered the door dressed like a twelve-year-old boy on the tennis circuit, in a navy nylon tracksuit and sneakers, with a visor; everything had white racing stripes. He greeted her and led her down a hall into a highly air-conditioned bedroom decorated in shades of peach and pale yellow.

"I hate these old-lady problems," Estelle snarled in greeting. "I feel totally useless."

Diane kissed her cheek and gave her the cookies and the flowers, which looked tatty in the careful opulence of the room. Dorothy was sitting in an armchair near the bed; Diane kissed her, too, and sat down by the window.

"My trainer is coming tomorrow," Estelle said.

Dorothy gasped. "Is that wise?"

"For the arms!"

"What can you do with your arms?"

"Plenty. Weights, resistance, stretching." She played a piano on the blanket in front of her. "Plenty to do with the arms and the hands."

"So, fine, you're in great shape," Dorothy said.

"Let me tell you about dancing to Tito Puente at the Palladium," Estelle said. "*Then* I was in great shape. I was seventeen at the time."

"You were not," Dorothy said.

"I was seventeen," Estelle maintained. "And I had dropped out of high school to be in the chorus of *Paint Your Wagon* on Broadway the year before."

"She was twenty-seven if she was a day," Dorothy told Diane.

Diane let the talk flow over her and glanced down at the park. Javier was standing by the edge of a large field, watching the couple with the soccer ball kick the thing back and forth. She saw him enter the field, walk around the side, and sit down on the grass halfway between the man and the woman to watch. Diane sensed a ripple of wordless communication between the couple as Javier followed the ball back and forth with his eyes. *He's not a creep! He just wants to play with you!* After a few minutes, the young woman made a hand gesture; the two players met in the center of the field, kissed, spoke briefly, picked up the ball, and walked off. Laughing.

All he wanted was to be asked to play! She felt like his mother.

Javier could go in any direction. You could see it on him, the malleability, the curiosity, as well as the stubborn layer beneath, the part that would not be led. Any encounter he had now could be the decisive one for him.

Herb tottered back into the room, dressed now in a pressed powder blue polo shirt tucked into neat little khaki pants with perfect creases. He had powder blue socks to match. He looked like a clean turtle on his way to school.

"I'm going to play cards at the club," he announced. "Nice to see you, ladies."

"Bye, darling! Don't forget your pills!" Estelle called with a bright face. She slumped visibly when he was gone. "He can't find the dry cleaner," she whispered. "He can't make coffee."

"He can't make coffee?"

"She's too young to understand," Estelle said to Dorothy.

"Men of a certain age don't have the aptitude," Dorothy explained.

"Did he make coffee when he was younger?"

"Of course not. It's a good thing this happened here. We can get everything delivered. If we were in Westchester, now, forget about it. Where are you living, Diane?"

"Nowhere."

"I have a great idea, Diane," Dorothy shouted. "Stay with *me!*"

"Dorothy, you know I don't leave until after the late show."

"I'm up all night! We can watch *The Late Show* together! I wouldn't be doing you a favor—you'd be doing *me* a favor!" Trying not to cringe, Diane turned the invitation down with a lie about another sublet. After a half an hour of meandering chat about the gala, she emerged into piercing sunlight and massive heat that lay thick over the pavement.

Javier was standing in front of the building, kicking things into the gutter.

"They took their ball and left!"

"Oh, Javier"—she laughed and gave him a hug—"I saw."

"I just want to play! Why do they leave?"

"I'll play with you," she promised him.

"Yes, but when? When you will play with me, Diane?"

She put her arm around his waist and walked with him. He fell into step with her nicely, and put his arm around her shoulder.

"How would you like some snazzy new shoes for your birthday?"

"Shoes? I like shoes."

They strode west together as if they were a couple. Eventually, the wall of heat they were walking into slowed them down. They separated. He was taller than his father, she noticed.

THE BIRTHDAY DINNER was in an overpriced, overloud steak house in Midtown packed with large groups of shouting men in shirtsleeves. How could this possibly be fun for Javier? What was going through Vladimir's mind? He was a complete cipher to her since he'd begun his retreat. It occurred to her now that the process of withdrawal had started with the phone call to María—possibly sooner. Perhaps Vladimir hadn't been running away from her from the start, but he certainly hadn't been running toward her.

Small Change (François Truffaut, 1976) always drew a respectable crowd, so she had Floyd save seats in the back ahead of time. As Truffaut once said, "All films about children are period films, because they send us back to short pants, school days, and the blackboard, summer vacations, our beginnings." As always, she was swept away by the sweetness of the childhood crushes and the direct portrayal of the antisocial behavior of the abused boy whose sad story is discovered in a medical exam at school. The French habit of presenting the full range of human emotions beat the American habit of whitewashing and tear-jerking every time.

Both Javier and Vladimir were rooted in their seats at the end of the film. As the crowd filtered out, they sat in silence, not looking at each other. She was reminded that she'd never had access to anything important to Vladimir. He turned to Javier and embraced him suddenly. This lasted longer than she would have expected. They broke apart, both of them wiping their eyes and laughing with embarrassment. They stood up, patting each other on the shoulders.

Well, that was something.

And then they left. She watched them push open the glass doors, two slim, dark, curly-headed men in khaki pants walking away from her.

The ticket holders trickled in for the late show. Storm worked through the line at the concession stand. Cindy closed the ticket booth and left for the evening. Diane stood in the empty lobby, feeling completely deserted.

She walked east on abandoned streets: anyone with a watering hole to go to had gone to it. This moment—leaving the theater, no one to share the film with and nothing to look forward to—made drug addiction look reasonable. Rachel had offered to let her stay again. Diane decided she'd rather take an iffy room in an unknown hotel than be weird, pathetic Aunt Diane again.

She checked into the busy bed-and-breakfast she used to pass daily in her old neighborhood. Her room was next to a pack of soused Australians screaming fight songs. At midnight, she took the coffin-style elevator downstairs to demand that the night clerk tell the Aussie horde to shut up. The clerk dialed, and asked them— rather too politely, she thought—to keep their voices down. She took the coffin back upstairs. As she feared, the maneuver backfired: they were riled up and spiteful now. She hesitated in front of their door; the fumes of alcohol and all-male yelling intimidated her, in spite of her rage. She packed her shopping bag and checked out, ripping up the credit card bill instead of signing it.

She took a taxi to the theater, let herself in with her key and opened her office door. When she turned on the lights, she saw a dark gray thing on the sofa move suddenly and then tear across the room.

It was a cat. It was the fattest cat she'd ever seen.

"You!" she shouted, and the animal curled into a ball and hissed at her. She dropped her shopping bag on the floor. The cat sprang to the top of the filing cabinet.

More tasks she lacked the skills for: three-dimensional fighting, animal management.

"Get out of here!"

The cat wasn't moving. It looked like this might be a very long night.

"I'm too tired for this. I'm sleeping here. I won't bother you, don't you bother me," she told the cat, and sat down on the couch, which had a gaping wound on one side, with the innards spilling out in wedges of yellow sponge. She was getting settled, if not comfortable, when the cat sprang to the floor, scattering all the DVDs from the top of the cabinet in every direction. The cat hesitated by the door, then came straight at her, scratching her face and hand.

Diane screamed and stood up. The cat bounded out of the room.

She ran to slam the door. With her heart knocking in her throat, she cleaned her face and hands with an antibacterial wipe, returned to the torn couch, and laid her head on the green sweater. At the very least, one daily mystery had been solved.

◆

BACK AT THE APARTMENT, Vladimir turned on the computer and discovered that Fidel Castro—infuriating, infallible and heretofore immortal—had provisionally delegated his duties to his brother, Raúl, while he was undergoing intestinal surgery.

Vladimir sat back on his chair, processing this astounding bit of news.

"Javier, this is a historic moment," he said quietly, surprised that he could be surprised that an elderly man in frail health who kept a crazy schedule could have medical issues. In spite of the rumor of Parkinson's disease, the rumor that he slept only four hours a night and the rumor that he was constantly moved from residence to residence by the secret police, Vladimir was still surprised. He honestly believed that the dictator would outlive everyone.

Javier read the information and sat back on his haunches. "Do you know I haven't thought about him once since I've been here, unless someone else brought him up?"

"He could be dead."

"You think?"

"Remember when he fell, and he had the knee surgery without anesthesia, because he was 'taking care of the important business of the State' during the operation? He didn't delegate then, why should he now?"

The phone rang: it was Bebo.

"Brother, I'm sorry to call so late, but we have an agreement!"

They talked until one-thirty, and Vladimir was up till four a.m. monitoring the situation on the Internet. It was all speculation.

At eight o'clock, Vladimir dragged himself out of bed to take a shower. A death now would be a Pyrrhic victory: he wanted the despot on trial, he wanted the psychotic dictator to apologize and repent. He began to shave. By the time he was done, he was sweating again. He took a second shower in cold water. Death was too easy for him! He'd be a martyr, a hero. When Vladimir left the apartment, he was hit with a blast of heat so dense and overwhelming that he had to go back inside the lobby to cool off.

He needed to finish the construction documents for a new office renovation and file them by the end of the day. He was meeting Chris and Magnus for lunch at twelve-thirty to discuss the new project, and the Department of Buildings closed at five; he would have to hustle. At the studio, he made a pot of espresso. Periodically, he checked on the status of the dictator's health, but there was no news. The temperature had hit 101 degrees before noon.

He was in a full-body sweat when he got to the café Chris had chosen; an employee at the counter greeted him. He nodded at her and stood in front of the air conditioner, and rotated so that the cold air hit him in various places. After a few minutes of this, he decided he really should sit down, although he wasn't hungry. This space was so poorly designed and put together that even a paint job couldn't help it. He was nauseated and still sweating. He drank two glasses of water straight down and put the remaining ice on his face, his neck.

Chris arrived. "You heard the news?"

He was too tired to speak, or even nod.

"Hey, partner, you don't look so good!"

"I can't speak," he said, and he felt his knees give way beneath him.

◆

IN A BLUE AIR-CONDITIONED cubicle at the back of the Emergency Room, Chris sat in the corner while Vladimir was given a thorough questioning by a nurse in green surgical scrubs. The nurse, who had a classic Irish face, perked up when Vladimir responded, "Married. No, wait: divorced."

"Are you married or are you divorced?"

"Finally. Yes, divorced."

She exchanged a look with a nurse dressed in bubblegum pink surgical scrubs who was bustling around.

"And you are . . . ?" the green nurse asked Chris.

"I'm his partner."

"*Business* partner," Vladimir specified. He looked pale, sweaty and weak.

Vladimir began shivering, and the pink nurse nipped out and returned with a sheet to drape over him. "Okay? Want a blanket?"

"This is fine," Vladimir said.

He really did look dreadful. The moment when the blood drained from his face and he dropped to the floor had been one of the most frightening things Chris had ever seen. It was lucky that he'd opened his eyes a minute later, and that the ambulance came right away and the traffic wasn't too bad and the hospital had air-conditioning.

There was another long wait and then a round of tests (blood, urine, blood pressure, electrocardiogram). Vladimir was in no mood to talk, and Chris was glad he had brought the newspaper. To calm down after the scary drama, he was reading about strokes, deaths, fights, power outages and other assorted ills of the heat wave.

Diane and Javier arrived, out of breath and sweating. Javier took his father's hand in a very sweet way. Diane waved hello to Vladimir and he nodded to her without energy.

She came over to the corner where Chris was sitting and greeted him warmly. Of course, he'd had nightly updates about Diane's absurd real estate saga from Paul, but he hadn't seen her in quite a while, or spoken with her in at least a month. She looked tired, disheveled and harassed. Vladimir hadn't mentioned her again, so Chris had assumed that they were both behaving like professionals.

"He didn't sleep last night," Javier told Chris in an aside. "He was up all night monitoring the Developments."

"What developments?" a sleek, dark-haired woman in a white coat asked as she entered the room with authority.

"The situation in Cuba," Javier said gravely.

"Ah, Cuban!" the doctor said with interest, and checked Vladimir's pulse. "What do you think will happen to the Revolution if Castro isn't around?"

"Stop calling that a revolution," Vladimir said as the doctor placed her stethoscope in her ears. "Who did he pass the reins to?"

"His brother?"

"Exactly. So it's a monarchy after all."

"Oh, ho, ho!" the doctor said. "Hold your breath."

Vladimir held his breath, looking at Javier, who was playing an electronic game.

"Okay, release," said the doctor.

"You're ruining your eyes and learning nothing from that," Vladimir said.

"I'm improving my eye-hand coordination and my mental reflexes," Javier said.

"He makes a point!" the doctor said, and ordered an intravenous drip for Vladimir.

"And you gave it to me," Javier said.

"I didn't think you were going to become addicted to it."

The pink nurse organized the equipment and attached the tube to Vladimir's left hand. Javier grimaced as if he himself had been pricked.

"So listen," the doctor said, sitting down on the bed. "The heat is terrible, but what else is going on? Are you under stress?"

"The usual amount. I was up all last night."

"Have you been drinking a lot of coffee?"

"Yes, I had a lot of coffee this morning. Four or five cups."

"Caffeine can dehydrate you. Even if you're drinking water."

Paul arrived. "What happened? Your hero is admitted to Havana General, and you have a sympathetic response?"

Vladimir grinned and said softly, "I think he's dead."

Paul looked at Vladimir as if he had performed an astounding magic trick.

"He's dead already, and they're buying time? That's good! I hadn't even thought about that."

"Already dead, or they're using this as a test run, to see what happens when he does die. Who comes up out of the woodwork."

The doctor was reading Vladimir's chart.

"Interesting theory," Paul said. "What do you think about Raúl?"

"Murderous bastard. But he can't hold it together."

The green nurse paused in her ministrations, and the doctor looked up from the clipboard. "You think there'll be an uprising?" the doctor asked.

"Things will change without an uprising. It's too hot down there to be brave."

"It's too hot up here to be anything," the green nurse said, as she finished taking his temperature.

"If he is dead, or goes eventually, are all the Cubans here going to go back?" Paul asked.

"Of course not. More likely, you'll see people down there coming here. After almost half a century, they want to live their lives. What's left of their lives."

"I saw in the paper," Paul continued, "the Cuban people are praying for Castro's speedy recovery."

"They're praying for the man who criminalized religion," Vladimir said, raising his voice. "What does that tell you about the Cuban people?"

"Do you think that everyone who had the gumption to protest has already left?" Paul asked, and Vladimir sat bolt upright and nearly knocked over the IV.

"Let's not upset Vladimir," Chris said, ostensibly to the room at large. "I think he's had enough stress on his system for one day."

Vladimir lay back with an impatient expression on his drained face. "It is impossible to explain fear to Americans. You can't even imagine a life without cable TV, so how could you imagine a crowd pelting your home with rocks and chanting slogans against you twenty-four hours a day while the police supervise?"

Javier looked up from his toy. "There was an act of repudiation in our block last year," he said. "We had to throw rotten tomatoes at their house and play music all night into their windows so they can't sleep."

"You had to?" Paul asked; he was too far away for Chris to lean on him to stop talking.

"My grandfather organizes this. I had to be there. I left when he wasn't looking. Afterwards, he find me and hits me for going away."

Paul looked like he might ask another follow-up question; Chris cast a look of dire warning at him.

The doctor said, "You really do need to avoid stress of any kind. Perhaps your friends can wait for you outside?"

Chris escorted Paul out to the hall as the pink nurse walked back into the room. Paul pulled his cellphone off his belt and began to make calls. Javier and Diane stayed in the cubicle.

"Did you know you can lose a gallon of water in an hour?" the pink nurse said, placing a pitcher of water and a styrofoam cup on the rolling table in front of Vladimir. "So you have your work cut out for you. Drink."

Chris, watching from the hall, was suddenly aware of Diane. She didn't appear annoyed, impatient, jealous, wistful, or any of the obvious things one expected from a recent ex. She looked on with calm interest as Vladimir was taken care of by the female medical professionals who surrounded him. Chris was once again amazed at Vladimir's ability to rivet attention, to spark the imagination and inspire fond wishes from even those who found him problematic.

"Who will you play chess against if he dies?" Diane asked.

Vladimir inclined his head, as if considering the question, but didn't answer.

Javier poured a cup of water for Vladimir. "Did you really fall on the floor in the restaurant?" he asked.

"Passed out cold!" Vladimir said with relish. "I think we cleared the place out. And let me tell you, if I were that restaurant, I would be thrilled to have me pass out there. I bet they all got to go home for lunch."

◆

BEFORE AND AFTER the English class, most of the students still chatted in Russian, Chinese, Hebrew or Spanish. What was the point, Javier wondered. Each time the woman who usually sat next to him, a Guatemalan, spoke to him in Spanish, he responded in English. She rolled her eyes and made the effort in English, only to revert, a sentence or two later, to Spanish. Everyone was older than he was by at least ten years, and there were no female students of interest to him. Still, it was better than the English classes he'd had at school: *Tom is a boy. Mary is a girl.* He decided to focus on learning slang and idiomatic expressions.

Since the heat wave, the skateboarders had moved indoors to the arcade for much of the day. Javier spent almost three hours one day hanging out with them, hoping to see Zoë, and perhaps ask her to a movie. When she arrived at the jump, she was vague and difficult to engage in talk; she looked beyond his head while speaking to him, and perked up when a wiry twenty-something guy with frizzy red hair and enormous gold medallions walked by. She followed the guy around the fence to the bleachers by the baseball field. A different crowd—tougher, older white kids dressed like rappers—hung out over there, even in the heat, apparently.

A week after the trip to the Emergency Room, with things largely back to normal although still unbelievably hot, even for one raised on a tropical island, Javier went to a deliciously air-conditioned palace of provisions, the Gourmet Garage, where he browsed in a happy trance among foods that were forbidden, un-known or impossible to find in Cuba. He loved this place; he loved that it was indoors, fully stocked with fancy foods and climate con-trolled. He loved that there was good, if old, music playing on the stereo. Unfortunately, the store was also shockingly expensive; he bought the vegetables, meat and dessert here, and went to a super-market closer to home for more ordinary supplies.

On the way home, he paused at the skateboard jump to practice some new slang he'd learned from Magnus and Paul. An enormous white Hummer with tinted windows sidled up to the curb, impos-sible to ignore. Diane had been derisive about a car like this when they saw one at the botanical gardens. But Javier found the car fas-cinating.

One of the windows rolled down.

"Javier," someone called from inside the car.

He turned around, breathless. It was Zoë. She knew his name.

"Come here," she beckoned, and opened a door.

He got into the backseat next to her, with his grocery bags. He smelled overpowering incense in the car. This was the first time he'd been inside a new American car, not counting taxis. There were five people in the parked car, and a bottle of clear liquid was being passed around. The redheaded guy with the big jewelry looked back from the front passenger seat.

"This the guy?" he asked.

"This is Javier," Zoë said, but didn't introduce any of the others.

"He would do," said a fat guy with a shaved head, handing him the bottle. Javier recognized the vodka label from a commercial on TV, but he declined to drink. *What* would he do?

"What's all this about?" Javier asked Zoë, passing her the bottle.

"Don't be stupid," she said, knocking it back.

"Why should we trust him?" asked the driver, who didn't look much younger than Vladimir. There was an enormous amount of gold jewelry in the car, Javier noticed. Was this the selfish con-sumerism and lack of humanity that corroded the American soci-ety? He looked around at this collection of cool people, and thought suddenly of what he might have been doing in Havana on a Friday evening at six. In the midst of this peculiar moment, being in two places at once in his mind, Javier heard tires screech and brakes squeal. There was a massive, loud jolt and shake as the Hummer was hit by a car.

The driver was out of the car in an instant. "What the fuck?"

"Whoah, whoah, whoah!" said the medallion man.

There were shouts and the slamming of car doors; the car rocked back and forth as people crawled over Javier and his groceries to jump out. Nothing good could come of this. Javier stepped out of the enormous car and fell, not expecting so much distance to the curb. He pulled himself up and grabbed his grocery bags as the two drivers argued in the middle of the street; the Hummer driver yanked the other guy's hair and in short order it was a full-fledged fight. Javier began backing up as the woman in the blue car that had hit the Hummer began shrieking.

"Get the gun!" shouted the medallion man.

A sudden crowd of spectators had emerged around this event, including Zoë, who stood there in her short-shorts as if watching something on TV.

A siren split the air. The last thing Javier needed was Vladimir picking him up at the police station. He began walking downtown, against the traffic, with deliberate slowness, as if he had nothing to do with this. And, in fact, he didn't have anything to do with this. Three blocks later, he crossed the street, walked a block east, and turned around to go back home. This was the end of passing the time at the skateboard jump. This was also the end of Zoë.

"What's all that racket outside?" Vladimir called from his computer.

"I have no idea," Javier said, which was true.

He put the food away and took a shower. What had they wanted him to do, and would he have done it if the out-of-control car hadn't changed everyone's plans for the evening? He debated whether to tell Diane about what had happened, or almost happened. He decided to focus on learning to conjugate verbs in the imperative, conditional and future tenses.

◆

DIANE HAD CHECKED INTO a fiercely stylish hotel in the Meatpack-ing District that Chris had renovated before his partnership with Vladimir. Everything was softly lit from below; underage models swung their naked midriffs down every hallway, well-tanned athletes opened doors and young gorgeous men smiled at the front desk. Her passages in and out would have had the atmosphere of a music video, except that she had checked in with two ripped shopping bags and was often sporting the same outfit and sweating. She was wearing a necklace made of gum wrappers that Javier had given her. They probably thought she looked insane or homeless or both. She supposed she was.

She'd been offered another job, this one in Hollywood, with a major film archive, through a Ronnie Lipsky connection. If all New York stories were about real estate, then all Hollywood stories were about popularity. It seemed to be about real estate (Meg Ryan lived here), but it was really about one's position on the food chain (I'm friends with Meg Ryan). *Gladiator* (Ridley Scott, 2000) may have been the most honest statement Big Hollywood ever made about it-self, Ancient Rome reimagined as a popularity contest. All the per-sonality disorders were collective in Los Angeles and she had never felt at home there. She also didn't trust Ronnie Lipsky. She turned the offer down.

Now that Javier had started an English class, Diane saw him at night and on the weekends. They went to films and museums, con-certs and parks, kitchen supply stores and farmers' markets. He was equally excited about video games and nice restaurants, the people on the subway and the audience at City Center. He wanted to talk about baseball, capitalism, the Patriot Act, bathing suits, reality TV, the Supreme Court and electric guitars. No sooner did she answer one question than he asked another. She never knew that she knew so much. He wore his blue birthday sneakers every day.

I'm dating a seventeen-year-old, she thought.

Eighteen, she corrected herself. And she was just showing him the town. Javier struck up conversations, with anyone, about anything, with no embarrassment about his English, which was improving daily. He was pure interest and energy, applied in seven different directions, a communicator. With Javier, she felt like she was in the presence of a blooming plant.

What had she been like at eighteen? As far as she could remember, she'd been bored and anxious, unwilling to throw herself into anything, because everything seemed futile. In a recent biography, Diane had read that George Soros had been on fire as a young man in London. "I felt things and absorbed ideas intensely, but I was unable to make an impact," he'd said in an interview. "Later on, when I was much more able to make an impact, I would feel things much less intensely." For some reason she remembered this now. Why was Javier bothering with her, when he could charm any female between the ages of thirteen and thirty? Perhaps he was too young to know how compelling he was. Vladimir was no longer a factor in their plans; she didn't know what he was doing, and she didn't care.

Toward the end of the month, after two weeks of toxic humidity and incessant rain, an apartment came through: a studio on a tree-lined street in the West Village. A rental! A one-year lease! It was clean, and odor-free. The noise came from the music school next door, people practicing the piano, some of them quite good. She was cautious, but elated. As she signed a contract, she said to the super, "What will it take to make sure that all parties honor this contract?"

"We honor all our contracts. You'll want to decorate, right?"

"No."

"Paint?"

"No. I mean, maybe later. I just want to move in as soon as possible."

"How does tomorrow sound? The place is just sitting empty anyhow."

She kissed his cheek. She ran out onto Grove Street reckless and joyful. She passed a pile of garbage that actually smelled kind of sexy.

She ran to the theater. She called her parents and left a message;

she called her sister and left a message. Who else could she call? Javier was her best friend now, but she didn't want to talk to Vladimir, or leave a message on his machine. Fortunately, Javier arrived in person to see another serious French comedy of awkward adolescence, *Peppermint Soda* (Diane Kurys, 1977), just as she was arranging for her furniture to be moved out of storage. He offered to help her set up in her new place.

"You can come after your class?"

"Diane finds an apartment? Are you kidding? I skip my class!"

"Don't skip class. Come afterwards."

"I will make you dinner in your new apartment!"

"That may be a little ambitious for the first night."

SHE SPENT the following day waiting in the unfamiliar space, which was too small. The truck with her furniture was three hours late. The place was filthy. Not all the piano students were so accomplished. It was probably too late to take up a new instrument. She supposed that a year of not playing had eroded much of her ability on the guitar. She left a note on the door, ran out to buy supplies, returned and began to clean. The bathroom was crusty. Some stains could not be removed. She wanted to be renewed and excited, but she was hot, bored and distracted. She couldn't wait to get out of the apartment.

The French made adult comedies about children. For example, in *Beau-Père* (Bertrand Blier, 1982), the attractively sorrowful character played by Patrick Dewaere is seduced by his fourteen-year-old stepdaughter after her mother is killed in a car accident. When their affair winds down due to stresses (jealousy, high school), the melancholic Dewaere begins to sniff around a woman for whom his stepdaughter babysits (Nathalie Baye). The final shot rests on the eyes of her five-year-old child watching fascinated as the woman finds affection in the arms of this gloomy oddball, and the viewer is left to imagine the story repeating itself.

If this were an American movie, the Special Victims Unit would be on to him. Or he would have to undergo a morally uplifting catharsis in the last reel, just as every tragedy out of Hollywood had to have a happy ending, and every movie had to have lovable characters. Diane resented the manipulation: present the situation, and she would decide whether to laugh or cry, and when to laugh or cry. French films at least gave you the freedom of your own opinion. You rarely loved the characters in a French movie. (Did the French? Could her position on this be merely cultural ignorance?)

The furniture arrived finally: mismatched, stained and broken. It depressed her. Before she could even get to the guitar, she cut her palm on a piece of glass pulling something out of a box. She was able to pick out a large shard, but she couldn't be sure she'd removed all the slivers. There were fine invisible flakes of glass in her skin that might never come out.

She was weeping by the time Javier bounded in, sweating and in high spirits.

"I love the music!" he said, his arms full of bodega flowers. "Diane! What happen?"

She sobbed with her bleeding palm held aloft.

"You have the, the, the little hospital in a box?" he asked.

"A first aid kit."

"Don't laugh at me, I am not in my first language."

"I'm not laughing at you. I don't know if I have one, or where it is if I do."

"Stay here." He ran out the door.

He was back in minutes with a tall woman and a first aid kit.

"I hear you had an accident," the woman said briskly, like a no-nonsense British wartime nurse from Central Casting.

"Forgive me for not getting up," Diane apologized. "This is really no way to make an impression on a neighbor."

"First things first," the neighbor said, snapping on a pair of latex gloves. "What happened? A piece of broken glass, yes? Let's clean it and have a look. So you're the new tenant. I was wondering when we'd meet. Lucky me, I get you on opening night. Now, how does that feel? Do you think there's any more in there? Perhaps your son would like to hold this, while I open the gauze."

"Not my son."

"Interesting. How's that?" she asked, referring to the wrapped hand.

AFTER THE WOMAN LEFT, Diane gave Javier a Chinese take-out menu and lay on the sofa with her eyes closed. Normally, she started him off with a push, told him what to say. Now she let him fend for himself.

"I like to eat dinner, you will bring it to me?" he began, and quizzed the Chinese restaurant about the menu. "*Ants on tree? Really? There are bugs in the food? No? There are trees in the food?*"

Javier was flirting on the phone; this could take quite some time.

She shifted to roll onto her back, with difficulty. She was about to open a second screen for new features, something she'd been longing to do for ten years. She finally had her own apartment, which would be fine once she fixed it up. Why did she feel exhausted, defeated, uninspired? In the ten months since her eviction, she'd programmed fifteen film series and sent four catalogs to the printer. She'd stayed with four different sets of friends and family, and in four different sublet situations and three, maybe four, hotels. She'd been walking with Estelle and to the theater with Dorothy. She'd been book shopping with Daniel and had eaten in delicatessens with Lipsky. She'd been to museums with her sister, the park with her niece and nephew and concerts with her parents. She'd seen apartments with Paul, and she'd gone to restaurants and fabric showrooms with Vladimir. But the only one she ever went to the movies with was Javier.

He sat down on the floor next to the couch. Here he was, in her apartment, the younger, sweeter, more accessible, hormonally driven and energetic version of Vladimir. The same springy, curly lashes on eyes that were bigger, darker and always looking directly at her. Such a gorgeous kid. She couldn't help feeling as if she were around the young Vladimir, before bitterness and frustration took over his life. Before he turned into the married bachelor from hell.

She shook her head.

"Diane, why you fall apart now? You have a great apartment!"
She laughed.

"All summer you are running: apartment here, apartment there, bad apartment, apartment take away. Be happy! You have an address now."

She leaned over to him and kissed him on the mouth. Just like that.

"Diane," he said, kissing back. He tasted of Juicy Fruit; he smelled faintly of the spicy aftershave she had come to enjoy in his presence.

"Come here." She pulled him up onto the couch. He tried to hold her hand. She pulled it away, giving him the hand without the bandage. He took the hand as if it were a live bird. He licked her mouth with a quiet intensity, and pushed her back until he was lying on top of her. Why had she not spent the entire summer like this, on any couch, with this charming person? The neighbor with the first-aid kit floated back into frame in her mind.

"No," he said, as she pulled away. "Come back."

They were very involved.

A buzzer sounded, and they both jumped.

She gave him cash to pay for dinner, and he put the bag on the kitchen counter, which was crowded with chipped mugs and mismatched cutlery that surely belonged to someone else. He looked at her with sweet longing, and began kissing her forehead, her arms, her left hand. She let him lead her into the bedroom alcove. She was glad that the first box she'd opened had sheets, and she'd had the good sense to put them on the bed right away. She was glad that she didn't know anyone in the building yet (nurse neighbor notwithstanding). She was glad that she was finally getting to put at least one hand into his beautiful hair. Sounds of the city filtered through the window, the ever-present rumble of millions of people going places, doing things. There was nowhere else she would rather be. I have no idea what I'm doing, she thought, as the teenage son of her ex-boyfriend pulled off the turquoise pants, and she let him. Moreover, she thought, I don't care.

—

A SERIES OF inappropriate images surfaced afterwards: Vladimir in moments of passion, Vladimir in moments of anger, Vladimir talking on the phone to María about Javier, exploding, "*Cojones!*"

Couldn't she have a moment of happiness? She scattered thoughts of him away. She remembered the ex-boyfriend who lulled himself to sleep by rubbing his feet together. The ex-boyfriend who got short of breath after eating dried apricots. The ex-boyfriend who got leg cramps in the middle of the night. Who were these people? These glimpses of intimate situations that had gone nowhere didn't improve her mood.

Javier was on his back, swollen with sleep, arm flung above his head, legs entwined in hers. What did she know of love? She knew about intrigue and infatuation; she knew about letdown, resentment, hostility and disgust. What she knew about was *waiting* for love. This felt right. This was the first time she had ever spent nearly three full months getting to know anyone before touching him. He was a teenager. And Vladimir was his father.

How unbelievably inconvenient.

LABOR DAY WEEKEND

◆

THEY WERE LYING together on her bed; an orange glow and the sound of the nighttime traffic came in through the open window. Javier had never been in this situation with a woman. Yusleidis was like a cartoon compared to Diane. Even the ridiculous episode on the roof with Milady was irrelevant. All he wanted was to dig in and stay with Diane, mingling their limbs until they fell asleep again. But Diane was pushing him out of bed. He put his head on her stomach and wrapped his arms around her and squeezed—he wasn't moving.

"If you don't go home tonight, we have no options," she told him.

"That is not home. Home is where you are."

She kissed him in a conclusive way, and as she sat up he noticed the articulations of her neck, her clavicle, her collarbone.

"Go home, and don't say anything, for God's sake."

"Why not? I am ready to shout the love for you on the Seventh Avenue South! In the Times Square! I want everyone to know."

"Javier. Listen to me. If you do, anyone could accuse me of taking advantage of you."

"That's bullshit. I consented. Come here, Diane. I consent again."

"Consent or no consent, it's awkward. Because I'm older."

She was resisting him as he tried to put his arms around her. She was being dry and precise and unavailable.

"So what? You know that age has no meaning. You of all people."

"It has nothing to do with what I know or don't know."

She was trying to get him to leave. This was terrible.

"Diane, I don't care how old you are. You are my country now. Come here."

She got out of the bed, and he got up to follow her. He tripped over something on the floor and landed directly on his kneecap. He sat on the bed, in tremendous pain, holding his vibrating knee. She was in her bathroom, unreachable. He wanted to help her settle in. He wanted to live with her in her new apartment. He wanted to go to the supermarket and the cinema with her, and do normal everyday things. She came back and sat down next to him on the bed.

"Javier, if you want to see me again, go home now and say nothing," she whispered, her hand on his rounded back. "Otherwise, we have no options. Do you understand?"

JAVIER DRESSED AND LEFT, in spite of his better judgment. He'd discovered something critical, and he didn't want anything to upset that. He didn't take his game out. He walked down Seventh Avenue South, awake, alive. Everything was bright, outlined, intriguing and new.

Vladimir was on the sofa, writing in a checkbook.

Javier's mood soured. He put his key in the bowl by the door.

"You're home late," Vladimir said.

And what are you going to do about it?

"What did you do?"

Javier wanted to tell him about every last caress, and then tell him to go fuck himself. He wanted to say, *You know nothing about life, you know nothing about Diane, you are a blind, selfish fool.*

Instead, he took off his shoes. "We saw a beautiful French movie."

That shut him up. His father didn't even like movies! How can you be alive and not like movies? Javier contemplated taking a shower, but it would be sad to wash the smell of Diane off his body. He stayed in the bathroom, looking at himself and thinking about her for the longest time. He was ready to do whatever she told him.

◆

DIANE WOKE UP feeling as if she'd just driven a car into a preexisting train wreck. Information began passing through her head.

"OH MY GOD!" she said out loud, and tripped over a box of long-lost junk as she staggered into her new bathroom. She resented every last piece of chipped pottery, beaten-up furniture and all the pointless equipment—humidifiers, dehumidifiers, hair driers, rags. Why hadn't she thrown all this crap out? One-room living only worked if you were monastic about it.

She felt better once she was in the shower; she felt better than she had in years. She connected with Javier on every possible level. She had never been more in tune with a person: this had to count for something.

Still. What a mess this was going to be.

No shampoo: she hadn't set up the bathroom yet, and she didn't want to get out and hunt for it—it could be anywhere. She wanted to stay in warm water all day.

You couldn't just have a normal boyfriend, said a voice in her head that sounded like Connie Kurasik on helium. *Like David Blicksman on Norwood Avenue: he had such a crush on you and you ignored him. And that nice fellow from the film archive, who followed you out to California. He was so interested in you, and you paid absolutely no attention. And what about that older man, the psychiatrist you met at the cooking class in France? That could have gone somewhere.* This interlude was noteworthy in that all the men mentioned had been happily married to other women for fifteen or twenty years by now. There hadn't been a "normal boyfriend" in well over a decade.

She had to get out of the shower sometime.

In *Lovely and Amazing* (Nicole Holofcener, 2002), a self-involved and professionally frustrated married woman in her late thirties (Catherine Keener) takes a job at a one-hour photo shop and begins a distracted affair with her seventeen-year-old co-worker (Jake Gyllenhaal) out of boredom and despair. Her interest in him becomes more active, and she's caught completely off guard when his mother arranges for her to be arrested for statutory rape.

The moving-day disarray was out of control; the remains of the previous evening's Chinese takeout were scattered over the tops of several boxes. Diane sat on the couch in a towel. She had to organize. She had to unpack. She had to do something with this chaos. But first she had to call Vladimir.

She realized she had misdialed his number and she stabbed the button to end the call as a cranky male voice answered, "Hello? Who is that? Hello!"

She kept pressing the button, and he kept saying "Hello?"

She hung up. When she picked up the phone again, the same man's irritated voice was saying, "Who is this? How dare you?"

"I'm terribly sorry, I dialed a wrong number," she said, and hung up again. She waited a moment, and picked up the phone.

The wrong number was still on the line. "You didn't even have the courtesy to apologize."

"I just apologized."

"Afterwards. When you had to," he said with venom. "You didn't take responsibility initially. You just hung up."

"Look, I'm sorry; I have an important phone call to make."

"And it's okay to disturb me on a Saturday?"

"What kind of disturbance? Your phone rang. If that's too disturbing, maybe you shouldn't have a phone." She hung up.

She waited a moment. What time was it? She didn't have a clock. Somewhere among her effects were a watch and a cellphone that had the time. She couldn't be bothered to look. She needed to reach Vladimir.

The phone rang. She picked it up, and heard someone hanging up.

Twenty seconds later, the phone rang again.

It could be Javier. She answered it.

"So, how does that feel to you?" the wrong number said.

"What a miserable, pathetic life you must have to hold someone hostage like this. I'm calling the phone company to report you for harassment."

"I could do the same thing."

"You DO that. Now hang up the phone."

She hung up, and rose in frustration.

Well, why call Vladimir in the first place? Was she seeking his approval? She didn't trust Javier not to tell him; perhaps she wanted her version to reach him first. What version? Your son makes you look like a rigid, embittered old man? She dressed rapidly and ran out of the new building with one thing on her mind: to see Javier.

In the final scene of the seriously underrated *Spanking the Monkey* (David O. Russell, 1994), the hero walks away from home in the rain the morning after spending a night in bed with his mother. Shocking, of course, but a perfectly logical extension of all that had come before in the film, which laid out in harrowing detail the particular dysfunction of a middle-class family in Connecticut (with the miserable mother immobilized in a leg cast, attention-starved and drinking; the intransigent father traveling on sales calls; the premed student forced to stay at home and help his mother instead of taking a coveted internship); and the potent mix of gin, frustration, pity and desire that led to the incestuous climax. The next day, Jeremy Davies, who plays the son, is seen hitchhiking on a highway, drenched and shocked. He looks like he's been scalded.

This was how Diane felt. Scalded. Terrified.

And happy, truly happy.

She may have been involved with Javier's father, but she wasn't his mother, after all.

◆

IT APPEARED that the madman was still alive after all. Step by step, they had orchestrated proof: the photo of the dictator in bed in an Adidas warm-up jacket, with an obviously dyed beard, reading a

copy of *Granma* on his eightieth birthday, with his eightieth birthday as the headline; the photo of Hugo Chávez visiting his aging
professor, the two of them wearing the same tomato-red button-
down shirt; the photos of the concerned but quiet Cuban people
gathered on the street to hear official notices. The fact that all the
reports about the dictator in Havana had the byline "Mexico City"
or "Santo Domingo" was not discussed.

That day he had the studio to himself: Chris and Paul were in
Atlanta for their first weekend in the house and Magnus had gone
home to Maryland to shock his bourgeois family. Vladimir dearly
hoped that Magnus's parents had tattoos of their own when Magnus
arrived in a sleeveless T-shirt to show off his snake. Vladimir took
advantage of the quiet to spend the day sorting through piles of papers and old drawings and straightening out the bookshelves.

He made a pot of decaffeinated coffee. The images of the tract-
able people of Cuba anxiously awaiting news of the health of their
Great Leader disturbed him. Perhaps all the independent, confron-
tational, stubborn people with minds of their own *had* left by now,
as Paul had suggested. Perhaps the Revolution *had* created the New
Man after all—fearful, compliant, nonconfrontational, opinion-free.
Perhaps Little Brother could run an island populated by these new
people, even without the charisma of Big Brother. He poured himself a cup of the decaf.

This was nonsense. Yes, there were New Men in Cuba, as well
as people who pretended to be New Men. But there were plenty of
others who would jump at the chance to be free once the machine
guns were pointed in a different direction. People were waiting to
see what happened: running out into the eye of the storm was stupid and self-destructive. There would be change in Cuba.

He hadn't been able to get through by phone since the an-
nouncement on August 1, but he'd received a cryptic e-mail from
his mother about some kind of medical aid from the people of
Madrid to the people of Havana. Back when he lived on the island,
he'd understood this kind of coded message; now he had no idea
what it meant. On the other hand, he'd also received another e-mail

from her announcing, "We still haven't heard any news about whether Javier's grandmother can come to visit him, but we are crossing our fingers."

The censors would *never* be able to break *that* code.

Javier wasn't picking up the phone at home, and wasn't at the theater when he tried to reach him there. Vladimir hesitated a moment, then tried Diane on her cellphone. He didn't leave a message.

AT FIVE O'CLOCK, Vladimir entered his apartment and was hit by a warm smell of fermentation, as if he had walked into a brewery.

He put his keys down. "I am not even going to ask," he said.

"I'm making bread," Javier said, hovering over a glass bowl of brown paste.

"I called you before, but I guess you were out. We're going to Bebo's for dinner tonight."

"Is Diane coming?"

"You see Diane every day. I think you could give her the night off."

"No," Javier said, turning on the TV and staring straight ahead.

"Excuse me?"

"If Diane isn't coming, then I don't want to go."

Vladimir took the remote control. "You know, it's over between me and Diane," he said, turning off the TV. "You're not getting us back together."

Javier said, "Ha," and turned on his portable toy.

"You know, you can play chess on that thing."

He nodded. "Right. I'm going out."

It was probably a good thing that he didn't have to include Javier in every outing. Dinner at Bebo's would be a boring obligation for Javier.

"You know how to get where you're going?"

He nodded.

"You need money?"

Javier pulled a MetroCard and some cash from his pocket.

"When are you coming back?"

"I may stay with Diane tonight."

"Where is she staying now?"

"A new place."

A thought crossed his mind, and he dismissed it. "Okay, have a good time."

"In fact, I think I might move in there," Javier said, walking out the front door.

Vladimir sat a moment, staring unfocused at the screen.

He poked his head out into the hall, where Javier waited in front of the elevator.

"You heard me," Javier said, and stepped into the elevator.

The doors closed.

Things had been going much too smoothly. He hadn't really had anything like a personal discussion with Javier. He probably shouldn't have discouraged him from hanging out with the skateboarders and the kids in the neighborhood. Almost anything could have happened while he was playing chess on the Internet; he had twenty-three games going on at once now. He stared at his RedHotPawn personal page, where his wins, losses, draws and numerical ratings were displayed in color. A new assessment came to him unbidden: bad person. He tried to remember a time when he didn't have the feeling that he'd let everyone down.

◆

PREVIOUSLY, when she was alone, understimulated and left to her own devices, Diane had felt as if the great big wide world was passing her by. Now, in the midst of everything, Diane felt as if the great big wide world had run her over.

The moment she reached the theater she realized she should have stayed home. She accomplished nothing that afternoon: her head was a scramble of desire, censure and rationalization. All she wanted was to get Javier back into her apartment. Javier had no problem with her proportions. In fact, he told her that a big ass was a great thing for a woman to have. However, like Vladimir, he wouldn't let her touch *his* rear end. Was this a Cuban thing? You often heard about macho Latin behavior; she hadn't experienced classic machismo with either of the Hurtados. But if she'd learned anything from Vladimir, it was that "Cuban" and "Latin" were rarely synonymous.

She was changing the display on the bulletin board in the lobby, thinking that he had held her hand in the same way he'd held the sheet of stamps, when Javier burst through the door. She ducked her head and made herself busy with the thumbtacks; she was in high school and had spotted a crush in the hall. He came up behind her and put his arms around her waist and put his mouth on the back of her neck.

So much for keeping a low profile. Diane broke away and whispered at him to follow her. He followed her down the empty corridor. She was almost positive that Cindy had seen them. Diane closed her office door with care.

"Look, you can't do that," she said, as Javier came at her and kissed her with an open mouth. "Javier, stop. We have to be very careful."

He pulled away. "You're not sorry?"

"Of course I'm not." She put her head on his chest. "But it's touchy."

"Touchy-touchy," he said, touching her rear end.

"Javier. It's awkward. How can I make you understand?"

He laughed. "Diane. I come from a place where everything is illegal, except this. You can't expect me to be scared. I want to live with you."

She sank into the chaotic sofa. "Oh, what a mess this is going to be. What a big mess."

"I'm ready."

He began kissing and touching her face in a very sweet and ardent way.

This was wrong. This was fun. This was the point of life. What possibly was more important? Diane let her mind drift. They were smooching on the couch like this for some time when Cindy arrived.

"You're sick, you know that?" Cindy shouted. "Storm, get in here!"

So much for waiting for the other shoe to drop.

Storm arrived in a hurry, taking in the scene. "What's the problem?"

Cindy pointed at Diane and Javier on the couch. "Look at this: Is she fifty years old, or what?"

"Okay, let's calm down," Diane said. She felt short of breath.

"I don't want to work for you anymore," Cindy said. "You are disgusting."

Javier said, "Cindy, that's enough."

"And you! You're a liar!" She made a nasty face at him.

Diane was so tired.

"This is my resignation. I've been meaning to do this for a long time, Diane," Cindy announced. She threw her keys on the floor and slammed the door behind her.

Storm waited. "Well, that was exciting. But the show must go on. Shall I take over the ticket booth?"

Diane nodded. "I'll work concessions, and we can switch after the second show."

She turned to her boyfriend, who was, yes, a teenager. She almost did the math again, but stopped herself.

"I will do anything you tell me," he said, with questions on his face.

"Why don't you take tickets?"

"And we'll go home later? Okay! I'll do a quick errand, and be right back."

She smiled as he trotted out. A positive note, lost in the midst of the mess: She had a home to go home to! She sat at her desk, thinking abstract thoughts about what she would say to Vladimir, her parents, her sister, her friend Claire, for example—Claire, whom she had known for twenty-seven years, which was nine years more than Javier was alive. Math, such a pointless subject. There was nothing to say.

She looked up to find Vladimir standing in front of her, his head in a sweat.

"I want to know what exactly is going on between you and Javier."

"Vladimir." She swiveled a little in her desk chair.

"Well?" Vladimir was planted there, he wasn't moving.

"There's no easy way to tell you this. Javier and I have become involved. Romantically."

"How is this possible?"

"Where have you been? We've spent all day, every day together, for almost three months. And I've loved every minute of it."

"I enrolled him in that class to get him away from you."

"Because I was such a horrible influence, taking him to movies and museums and concerts? Explaining democracy, private property, advertising and the post office—everything that you didn't do with him? You didn't even get him a map, Vladimir."

He stared at her blankly.

"Meanwhile, you made it perfectly clear that you and I were finished, that you wanted nothing from me. So what do you care?"

"You did this to get back at me?"

"This isn't about you. This is about Javier, who is . . . interactive! Let me tell you what a refreshing change that is."

"And the fact that he's a minor doesn't bother you?"

"He's eighteen."

"Hardly an appropriate choice for you, Diane."

"Here finally is someone who wants something from me. He and I laugh all day long. So he's eighteen. That's not my fault."

He clenched his teeth as if she had angered him. "How will it end, Diane?"

"Who cares? Javier is like fresh air! What's wrong with that? I *DO NOT CARE* what happens in the end. I am only concerned with today, tomorrow, and next week. If things work out for next month, next year, then, terrific."

He said with a nasty edge, "And then you'll get married?"

"Since when do all involvements lead to marriage? When you and I got involved, there was no possibility of marriage, and that was just fine with you. If it was fine with you, why shouldn't it be fine with me? I know it's weird and awkward that he's your son, but I can't help that. Get over it."

"It will end in tragedy."

"Everything ends in tragedy. At least it will have been worth it. Some people don't even give you pleasure to begin with."

"Thank you, Diane. That's very nice."

"Fuck off, Vladimir."

He raised his finger to her. "You'd better pay attention. He may not be a minor, but he is my son, and in my care. And I'm not satisfied with this explanation."

She felt her lips twist into what must have been a nasty expression.

The father continued lecturing piously. "You forget I know a little about you, Diane. You're desperate, lonely and getting old."

What a horrid man. What a petty, nasty person. Why had she given him chance after chance? She must have been desperate, lonely and getting old.

"As far as I'm concerned," Vladimir went on, "the place for him is on the next plane back to Havana."

"So you'll make an irrevocable decision about his life, ignoring what he wants, just the way your father did for you, when you were his age."

He became so overcome with rage that he clenched his teeth. "I was twenty-one when my father did that! Twenty-one years old! He had no business forcing me into marriage. But Javier is seventeen."

"He's eighteen."

"At this age, every month counts, Diane."

"And you know this because you've spent so many months with him, watching him grow."

"I've not been a good father. I'm the first one to say this. But he's with me now and you require my permission to see him. I think this is wrong."

He continued to outline how he knew it was wrong: She was too old. She was taking advantage of Javier. Just a few weeks ago, he was a minor.

"He's happy, and you just can't stand it, can you?"

"Happy? Such a stupid American argument. Of course he's happy! He got laid last night. You're taking advantage of him, and he doesn't even understand."

"How am I taking advantage of him? I love him."

"You're homeless and bored—personally, professionally and sexually. As far as I'm concerned, he's not mature enough to make his own decisions." Javier arrived in the doorway with a bag of oranges just as Vladimir announced, "He belongs on the next plane to Havana."

"What gives you the right to talk about me like that?" Javier demanded.

Vladimir turned around. "You be quiet. You are in way over your head."

Javier started to argue, but Vladimir was on a roll. He repeated everything he'd told her for Javier's benefit, shouting down his objections. She knew this mode: Vladimir would now bombard them with legalities and nitpick over the usage of words. He'd harangue them for hours, going back to the beginning each time someone interrupted, repeating his diatribes until he beat them into the ground, winning the argument just by being willing to go on arguing forever.

"Goddamn you, Vladimir!" she said. "You are just like Fidel Castro!"

Vladimir stared at her with a wild, searing look of rage. He leaned forward and slapped her face, hard. She fell back into her desk chair, winded, stinging, with a dirty metallic taste in her mouth.

◆

BEFORE VLADIMIR HAD a chance to say anything more, Javier picked him up in the air; it was done so deftly and rapidly that Vladimir wasn't even sure how it had happened. Javier then threw him down, and there were loud crashes and sharp pain as he hit hard objects, probably the desk and the coffee table, on the way to the floor. Vladimir lay in shock. He was flat on his back on the carpet, surrounded by broken DVD boxes, on the spot where Diane's computer wires, pinned down by electrical tape, crossed the floor. Back when they were involved and he took her mess personally, Vladimir had offered to streamline both her wiring and her paperwork. She had turned him down. She hadn't deserved the offer, and he was glad he hadn't wasted his time.

His head was still ringing from the impact. Javier was kneeling over him, staring at him intently. Vladimir held his hand up, hoping his son would help him to a sitting position. Instead, Javier put his knee on his chest, pinning him to the floor in an unnecessary display of dominance. So this was what he was dealing with.

He tried to resist this aggression.

"Don't move," Javier said, like a kung fu thug.

"I can't breathe," Vladimir said.

"You have no authority over me," Javier answered in Spanish, releasing some of the pressure on Vladimir's chest. "I make my own decisions. Considering that you don't want me in your life and never have, this sudden fatherly concern is pretty surprising."

Vladimir coughed, and Javier leaned back a little more. The carpet was filthy; Vladimir was almost positive that this office had never been vacuumed. Diane, her face white, sat a few feet away, watching the two of them with a shocked expression. He was not sorry he hit her. He'd never hit a woman in his life. Well, María: once, in response, if not exactly in self-defense.

"You want me out of your life so badly you can't wait!" Javier was laughing as he said it, still speaking in Spanish.

"That's not true," Vladimir said wearily.

"So what's the difference if you put me on the next plane to Havana or if I move uptown and never see you again?" Javier leaned back on his haunches, waiting for an answer. Vladimir sat up, and felt the blood drain from his head. He was dizzy and nauseated. He was acutely aware of the bones in his skull and every nerve in his back that had hit the desk, the coffee table, the wires and the floor.

"You made it clear that you have no interest in Diane," Javier said. "For this, you're an idiot, but I benefit, so I thank you for being so stupid. So what's the problem, 'Dad'?"

A good question. Was his problem with Javier, or with Diane? Or with the combination? He had no idea why he was so bothered, or even if he was bothered at all. What did it matter, really, if Diane was taking Javier to the movies or to bed? Did it affect him in any way?

"And: HOW DARE YOU HIT DIANE?" Javier demanded in English. He grabbed Vladimir's shirt as if to rip it off, but then let go in disgust and fell back on the sofa with his arms folded. "You're worse than Castro! You're just like your father."

SEPTEMBER

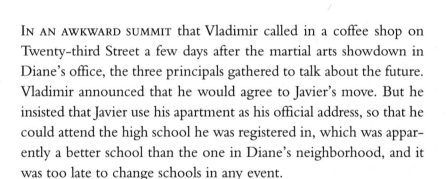

In an awkward summit that Vladimir called in a coffee shop on Twenty-third Street a few days after the martial arts showdown in Diane's office, the three principals gathered to talk about the future. Vladimir announced that he would agree to Javier's move. But he insisted that Javier use his apartment as his official address, so that he could attend the high school he was registered in, which was apparently a better school than the one in Diane's neighborhood, and it was too late to change schools in any event.

"I also want you to know that if you ever want to come back, for any reason, at any time, my door is always open to you," he said. "No questions asked."

Diane was not prepared to be moved at this meeting. "Oh, Vladimir. You're a decent man. That's what a good father would say to his son."

Vladimir stared at her with some malice.

So did Javier.

Vladimir asked for a few moments to speak to Javier alone, and Diane went next door to the magazine shop and browsed. In a not-so-recent French film with relevant content, *Le Petit Amour / Kung Fu Master* (Agnès Varda, 1987), Jane Birkin plays a forty-year-old divorcée who becomes obsessed with a fifteen-year-old schoolmate of one of her daughters. The schoolmate is truly on the cusp of adolescence, not a boy and not a man, obsessed with a kung fu video game. He receives her attentions with gauche indifference. When she takes him on vacation with her daughters to her parents' home in England, her mother approves of the crush (it's a French movie), and sends her off to a family house on a nearly deserted island with just the younger daughter and the young man. The *folie* ends in much embarrassment for the older woman, of course.

Javier came to find her, and the meeting ended on a cordial note: Vladimir wished them both well on the avenue as buses passed by, belching black smoke. There were no kisses or handshakes. He hadn't apologized for slapping her; she hadn't apologized for falling into bed with his son. Vladimir turned to walk west to his office. She and Javier stopped at an office supply store on the corner: he had orientation at school the following day.

As he selected binders, Javier told her that in their private talk, Vladimir had said, "Listen to me, because I'll only tell you this once. You have your entire future ahead of you. Don't be stupid. You'll have only yourself to blame if Diane gets pregnant." Javier was standing still, holding three binders in his hands, looking at her intently. She was having a hard time deciphering his expression.

"Well, that must have been awkward for you," she said finally.

"He must think I'm an idiot. He thinks you want to trap me."

"He just wants you to keep your options open. Don't worry: so do I."

Javier now looked as if he might cry. "I will never be more to him than the mistake that screw up his life."

"I'm not so sure about that."

Was it too much to hope for that Javier and Vladimir would get to know and appreciate each other as adults? How could she make that happen? Of course, if they did, it wouldn't be because of something that she initiated.

When they approached the counter, Vladimir was on line buying rolls of paper, and he smiled as if they had caught him doing something shameful. He insisted on paying for the school supplies, and as he handed over his credit card, Diane wondered what kind of life he might have had if he'd heeded his own advice nineteen years earlier. They said another awkward goodbye outside. In spite of everything that had transpired, she felt bad for Vladimir.

Diane had never quite bought the premise of the love triangle in *Jules and Jim* (François Truffaut, 1961), even if Jeanne Moreau was compelling enough to explain everyone's fascination with her. Few films ever bothered to explore the third leg of the triangle, the relationship between the two men. That film had a terrible ending. But love triangles always ended terribly. Never mind, she decided. It was precisely in those things that had no future that one found freedom, joy, inspiration and everything else worth getting nostalgic about later on. And if it had taken her forty years to figure this out, so be it.

DIANE ACCOMPANIED JAVIER on his first day of school. The teenagers on the train and the street displayed loud, obnoxious juvenile pack behavior. By contrast, Javier seemed like a sober anthropologist looking on and taking notes. He was mature, in spite of the omnipresent electronic toy. Often he ended grown-up discussions by saying, "Okay, Diane, I need to go shoot things now." As they approached the enormous redbrick building that was already hopping with activity, Diane again lectured him on why public displays of affection were forbidden. Javier responded to this by squeezing her ass goodbye in front of all of Seventh Avenue South.

At the end of *Le Petit Amour / Kung Fu Master,* Julien, the adolescent, is hanging out in the courtyard of a new school, telling a group of boys about his older lover: "She was just a housewife with big feet and no tits. . . . She was nuts about me, so I played along. She wasn't much of a lay—no spring chicken and a bit of a drag. But I did my duty." The final sound of the film is a school bell, ringing to announce the end of classes.

Javier could go in a lot of different directions, Diane reflected. The people he met, the things he chose to get involved with now, all of this would be critical for his development. And no, she wasn't his mother, but she had a great deal of responsibility toward him and impact on him, more than she'd had toward a run-of-the-mill adult boyfriend—his father, for example.

Diane walked away from the school, feeling the shrug taking over her entire body, her shoulders up to her ears and her head falling at an odd angle. Her life had turned into an implausible French movie. The only time she was relieved of this bizarre position was when she was with Javier, and everything made perfect sense.

Diane had programmed a week of "Backstage Dramas," a prescient theme given the chaos that characterized the period just before the grand opening gala. The new marquee wasn't up yet. The lobby was covered in drop cloths and abandoned equipment. Diane had a vision of 250 people drinking cocktails and falling onto table saws. When she telephoned the contractor, his assistant told her that Joe Franco was out of town.

This was horrendous. "Oh really? Doing what?"

"Buying real estate in Florida."

"WHAT? Nothing has been done in a month! Where's the crew?"

"They're on another job."

"What *other job*? This is the job, and the job is not done!"

She called the architects, and fortunately got Chris.

"Let me talk to Vladimir about this," he said.

"You're passing the buck?"

"No, I'm figuring out the fastest way to solve this. Joe is slightly afraid of Vladimir and he doesn't listen to me. Believe me, I'd call him if I thought it would do any good."

As she was making arrangements with a pest-control service to deal with the cat, and whatever was making the cat so fat, once the cat was gone, Vladimir called.

"I just heard from Chris," he said. "I'll meet you there in half an hour."

He came in with a sour expression, but brightened once he looked around.

"It's just the seats and the equipment. This can be done in a couple of days."

"Really? And the marquee?"

"That's separate. Let me call them. But it will be done. I promise you."

Her boyfriend's father, her former boyfriend, was being a professional.

She thanked him, aware that her face was flushed red. He walked out of the construction zone. She'd become a trite example in a women's magazine ("Diane—not her real name—") of what can happen when an office romance goes wrong.

THE FOLLOWING DAY, Bobby Wald tripped on a drill box and landed on his kneecap; Diane raced him to St. Vincent's in a cab. As she waited for him to be treated, she received a call from the special-events-equipment rental company: they didn't have a permit to unload in front of the theater the day of the opening.

"Well, get one!" she shouted.

A cleaning crew, the regular staff, two newly hired employees and three of the contractor's men had methodically transformed the scattered construction site into the new and improved Bedford Street Cinema Twin, with new seats in both theaters. The popcorn machine broke down the first day, but was fixed by the weekend. The enlarged lobby with a newly configured ticket holders' line was a much better arrangement.

Dorothy came to inspect the renovation on the first day of business and arrived in Diane's office after a screening of *Stage Door* (Gregory La Cava, 1937).

"What a dump!" Dorothy said, looking around. Diane still hadn't had time to completely organize what the cat had torn apart. "Your architect must hate you!"

"Indeed," she said.

There followed a discussion of what people were wearing to the gala. Dorothy announced that she would be wearing red; she'd heard that Estelle, who still wasn't dancing, or even walking, would wear yellow. She waited. Diane didn't have a dress or a clue.

"You've been too busy cavorting naked to worry about clothing," Dorothy said.

"Excuse me?"

"Don't play dumb. I have my sources. Get it while you can, Diane."

Diane inhaled, looking down at her hands folded on the desk.

"But when you come to your senses, remember Estelle's nephew. He's giving up his dental practice and retiring: he'll have lots of time to go to the movies."

Diane could go in a lot of different directions, too.

◆

"YOU NEED A DRINK," Chris said as he and Paul pushed Vladimir to the back of the restaurant. "You need to talk."

Vladimir seemed angrier than usual. "Why?"

"Because it's shocking," Paul said, as if shocked.

"This is not a topic of conversation for you," Vladimir said.

"You're wrong," Paul said with relish. "It's a major topic of conversation for me."

Vladimir cast a nasty look at him.

Drinks arrived. There was silence for a moment, as Paul looked around the restaurant and Vladimir sipped his drink, staring into the middle distance. In the last few weeks, Vladimir's hygiene had taken some kind of nosedive. He was unshaven, unwashed and he looked as if he hadn't slept in a good long time.

"Is it spite, do you think?" he asked Chris.

"Absolutely not," Chris said.

Vladimir looked up. "No?"

"No. I think Diane is cut up about it."

"Have you spoken to her about it?"

"No, but I can tell," Chris said.

In fact, the one who had spoken to him, at length, was Javier. He'd called Chris the previous night, asking if he could come over to talk. This came in the midst of a mind-numbing argument that had lasted most of Labor Day weekend, the first weekend at the renovated house. The fight had begun when Paul said something nasty about someone passing by. Chris told Paul that if he couldn't stop speaking ill of people, then he wasn't welcome on the porch.

"Oh, come on. Did you see that ass? As big as a motel room."

Paul was systematically setting out to destroy any ties Chris had made, or might make, in the neighborhood. Or so it appeared.

"Making comments like that is rude and inconsiderate. It says more about you and your bad character than it does about the person passing."

"I'd forgotten I was sitting with your mother."

"I mean it, Paul. Next time, you're not invited."

"Promise?"

It went on like this all weekend, and during the flight back to LaGuardia and the cab ride to the apartment. It was still going on at dinner on Monday night, which was when Javier called, asking to talk; Chris invited him over with some relief. It had to be something important. On the other hand, at eighteen, what wasn't important?

"Excellent," Paul had said, tossing aside a magazine. "Anything has to be more interesting than being scolded by Letitia Baldridge."

Javier arrived almost immediately, radiating energy and joy. There followed a long, meandering chat at the kitchen table about life, love, Cuban military school, teenagers versus real women and the karate maneuver Javier had used on his father at the cinema.

"Vladimir flat on his back on Diane's coffee table! I'm so sorry I missed that," Paul said. "Show me how you do it."

"Don't tell him I tell you," Javier warned.

"Paul would never use a confidence against someone," Chris said, looking directly at Paul. "Paul doesn't gossip. Does he?"

Paul ignored this. "Promise you'll teach me. Not now: I'm swimming in beer."

"I promise to teach you, but you have to promise never to use it."

"Never use it? What's the point, then?"

Javier began explaining the principle behind martial arts, but cut himself off.

"Oh, fuck karate! Let's talk about Diane!" he said, and fell into an extended swoon. Diane, she knew so much. Her hilarious stories, her way of looking at people. Her light blue eyes and straight black lashes. The way she corrected his English without making him feel stupid. He could talk to her about anything. The girls in Cuba— these young ladies had some of the funniest names Chris had ever heard—were nothing compared to Diane. They were *dogs* compared to Diane. "She says her hair was so long before. Did you see it?"

"It was hard not to see it, down to there," Paul said, pointing at the floor. "I don't think you missed anything."

"So, what do you think you'll do, Javier? You think you'll stay?"

"Oh yes, I will stay."

Paul made a toast. "To Javier, who will stay!"

They touched bottles.

"And to Diane," Javier insisted.

They toasted Diane.

"And a toast to your father," Chris said. "My great partner, a man of many talents, who is learning much more from you than I bet he ever thought he would."

Javier had exited, fueled on optimism, beer and teenage hormones, on his way back to his Real Woman. Chris wished he felt about Paul the way Javier felt about Diane. Had he ever felt that way about Paul? Was such a thing possible at this late date?

As if aware of the trend of his thoughts, Paul asked, "Do you remember being that young and in love?"

Perhaps such a thing was inappropriate for this stage of life. "Every day, I feel that young and in love."

Paul burst out laughing. "Bullshit."

"I didn't even think about it, but do you think it was okay to give him beer?"

"If he's old enough to handle Diane Kurasik, he's old enough for beer."

"You have a point." Chris cleared the table.

"Vladimir gives him rum. I know this from Diane."

"Thank God she has an apartment now."

"Can you imagine?" Paul said, washing the beer bottles out in the sink.

"Diane and Javier is a very different picture than Diane and Vladimir."

"Indeed. This is getting more complicated than a Mexican soap opera."

"I'm glad for her," Chris said, opening the recycling bin.

"And I thought she was ready to marry the next shlub Dorothy Vail pulled out of her handkerchief drawer," Paul said as he was leaving to take the recycling out to the incinerator room. "You never know what people will do."

THE RESTAURANT was getting loud.

"I saw this coming from a mile away," Chris told Vladimir.

"Really?" Vladimir said, running his hand across his unshaven face.

"It's not a terrible thing," Chris said. "An awkward situation, sure. But I don't think either of them is treating this lightly. And Javier is clearly happy and learning. This is an appropriate stage for him, if an unusual choice."

"You think she loves him?"

"Of course she does," Paul insisted. "And it's not hard to see why."

Vladimir flashed him a look, and Paul raised an unrepentant shoulder.

"It can only end in tragedy," Vladimir said, leaning back.

"Probably, but so what?" Chris said.

"That's what Diane says." Vladimir socked back his drink. "Why do I always order rum? I don't even like rum." He called the waiter over. "Give me something else. A beer. Please."

They looked at him.

"My life has always been a mess. This is just another chapter of an old, messy story. Let's leave it at that."

WHEN VLADIMIR LEFT, the specter of their ongoing disagreement washed back into the space he'd just vacated.

Paul raised an eyebrow, waiting for Chris to begin.

Chris didn't want to renew hostilities. The argument had soured what had actually been a very big victory for him, on Saturday afternoon, when Nick and Kelly arrived with the kids.

"Here's your uncle Chris!" his brother shouted. "And this must be Paul."

"Nice to meet you, Paul," said Kelly, bright and peppery and enthusiastic. As always, she was well made-up and nicely dressed— the perfect corporate wife. "Kids, let's meet Paul."

The kids stood at attention to shake hands.

"What do we call you?" asked Brittany, now eight, petite and blond like her mother.

"Paul," said Paul.

"Just Paul?" she said suspiciously.

"You don't like Paul? You can call me Uncle Paul, or Mr. Zazlow. You pick."

"Mr. Zazlow!" shouted Neil, the five-year-old, punching Paul in the knee.

"Neil, apologize to Uncle Paul," said Kelly.

The child opened his mouth to show some food he was keeping for display purposes.

"He's a monster," she said. "Hey, kids, let's check out this gorgeous house! Maybe Uncle Paul would like to give us a tour?"

"And I thought this was a day off. Silly me," Paul said, and took them inside.

"How's life?" Chris asked his brother. "What's new?"

"Life is great," Nick said, sitting on the porch steps. "You're the news around here."

Chris sat down next to his brother. This might have been their first time meeting Paul, but Nick and Kelly always asked after him. Chris had spoken to them about moving in with his friend Paul, Paul switching agencies, Paul's aunt's funeral, etc. But the specific role Paul played in his life was never, not once, discussed. Well, Chris hadn't brought it up. Kelly was too polite to ask directly, and Nick Wiley would probably rather submit to corporal punishment than discuss such a thing.

"I hear this is an up-and-coming neighborhood," Nick said, alluding perhaps to the gay real estate vanguard that cleaned up shady city neighborhoods and made them chic and safe for white professionals. "You were smart to buy here."

"We like it. Or, anyway, I like it."

"Paul doesn't?"

"Paul doesn't understand the South."

Nick nodded slowly. Paul was Jewish, too—Chris often forgot about this in New York. He had really tested the outer limits, hadn't he?

"And he hates to fly," Chris went on. "I mean, *hates* it."

He heard shrieking and laughing, and supposed Paul was entertaining the children and Kelly. They began chatting about people: who'd gotten married, who'd gotten sick, who'd died, who'd moved away. Kelly returned to the porch and sprawled in a natural way on the love seat. Crayons and paper appeared, and the children sat down at the table and began to draw. Paul arrived with a tray and poured iced tea into glasses.

"So I hear you hate to fly, Paul," Nick said.

"The idea that I have to go through the whole ordeal again on Monday makes me physically ill. I don't even want to think about it."

"I took a class this year to get over the fear of flying," Nick said.

"I didn't know that," Chris said. "You're afraid to fly?"

"Ever since that terrible winter—when was that? Five years ago?" Kelly said. "When he had to fly every week to Miami. It got so bad that year, we had to drive to Chicago."

"What did you do in the class?" Paul asked.

"Mainly relaxation exercises. Guided visual imagery and things to distract us from catastrophic thinking and nausea. Ultimately, we took a plane to Charlotte, for the day."

Paul closed his eyes and leaned back on the love seat with two fingers over each eye. "You took a completely unnecessary flight?"

"Two completely unnecessary flights. There, and back."

"*Vey iz mir.*"

"To get over it."

"And did you?"

"Not really!"

Chris looked around: a relaxed Saturday afternoon on a swept porch with iced tea and family beneath a swiftly turning ceiling fan. Perhaps the whole Atlanta project hadn't been about escaping the noise of New York, or even the potential of big public works. Perhaps it had just been about getting Paul, Nick, Kelly and the kids in one space.

CHRIS FINISHED his gin and tonic and looked at his partner of three years. On further reflection, Paul's behavior had been no different on the porch than it would have been in a lobby or an elevator, the equivalent locale where neighbors crossed paths in New York. If Chris didn't approve of Paul, what was he doing with him, in either location?

In his favor, Paul was confident, unpretentious and unedited. Paul would say absolutely anything to anybody—not always a positive thing, but hilarious on occasion. Paul was never embarrassed, nor was he different around different people; Chris appreciated this. Paul was always ready to take on tasks around the house and even in the office; he was a font of Manhattan business information in general, and an expert in real estate law and arcane local history. Paul was categorically gorgeous, and not as vain about it as he might have been. He was a news junkie, a snappy dresser and, like clockwork, he sneezed three times after every meal.

Still: Paul could be nasty, judgmental and loud. Paul brushed his teeth and shaved in the shower while listening to news radio. He was rarely as amusing as he thought he was. He routinely imitated

Chris's facial expressions and verbal tics, which was annoying. Still, Chris liked having him around.

If Paul promised to control the constant stream of critical commentary, Chris was prepared to have him back on the porch. The problem that day had been Chris's own lack of preparation. If he'd put a newspaper on the porch—even a local real estate circular—Paul wouldn't have lifted his head all afternoon. Who said he had to choose between a man and a house?

◆

THE DAY OF THE GALA, Storm's face burst into bright salmon-colored welts, an allergic reaction to whatever she'd eaten for lunch. Cindy's replacement, Angela, took her to the Emergency Room at St. Vincent's in a cab. Floyd cut his thumb opening a carton of soda and Diane bandaged it using the new first-aid kit, begging him to be careful. The cat was back: one of the new chairs was ripped. Her heart stopped for a moment when Floyd arrived to announce that he couldn't locate the print of one of the films, *The Bad Sleep Well* (Akira Kurosawa, 1960). Everything stopped for twenty minutes while they tore apart the office and projection room until they found it. From a wheelchair, Bobby Wald supervised the final installations, including the handicapped-access ramp, which he would be using for the near future. Lipsky's ex-wife turned up wanting a ticket to the party, demanding fifteen minutes of diplomacy.

A series of sirens shrieked through the air at about two o'clock.

A kitchen fire across the street had spread to the first floor of a brownstone, and the street was closed to traffic. Diane tried to call the equipment rental company to alert them. There was no dial tone.

"Floyd, could I use your cellphone?"

"It never works in here. Go around the corner—it usually works there." ·

Diane took a walk. Seventh Avenue South was also blocked off by squad cars. In fact, the entire intersection was closed to traffic. Ambulances, fire department vehicles, squad cars, phone company trucks and assorted personnel had converged on Barrow Street in a scene reminiscent of *Dog Day Afternoon* (Sidney Lumet, 1975).

"It's a hostage situation," said a woman standing nearby.

"What? How many hostages?"

"He doesn't have people," said a man in a jumpsuit who held a walkie-talkie. "The guy has taken equipment hostage. He's shut down service for eight square blocks."

"Two silos of phone equipment in the basement?" she asked, and was ushered center stage.

"I think this is Sid Bernstein," Diane told a man who seemed to be in charge. "He's been trying to get rid of that equipment for forty years, so this is not a surprise."

He held out a bullhorn for her to take.

"Can't we just call him?"

He looked at her as if she were a stupid child. "He's shut down everybody's phone service, including his own. You know his cell-phone number?"

"I doubt he has a cellphone."

He gestured to the bullhorn. "So you're on."

"Hey, Sid, it's Diane Kurasik."

There was a crashing as if some garbage cans had been displaced. He stood in the narrow space between the building and the side-walk, almost completely concealed by a thick gray wall. All she could see was the top of his head down to his eyes, and the kitchen knife in his clenched fist.

"They want full access to these monsters? Tell them to take them away! Then they can have access anytime!"

She turned to the phone company representative. "Will you do that?"

"Apparently the wiring is antiquated and complicated," said the representative from the phone company. "It's easier not to move them."

"Clearly. But I can't believe you wouldn't just move them into his basement."

"He lives in the basement."

"A different part of the basement."

"I can't negotiate with a maniac with a knife."

"Sid, you have to give up the knife," she called. "You lose the moral high ground when you threaten people with knives."

"Without the knife, nobody listens."

"Okay, we're listening now. Drop the knife on the other side of the wall."

Nothing happened.

Sidney Lumet said that if a film is cut at the same tempo throughout, it feels hours longer than it really is. "It is the change in tempo we feel, not the tempo itself," he wrote in *Making Movies.*

"Will you come to the gala tonight?" Diane called.

"Depends on how my afternoon goes."

"When can we use the phones, already?" a loud, annoyed female voice in the crowd piped up. "My sister's in the hospital, and I can't get through. Stop chatting and knock that guy's door down!"

"Do I have to take hostages to get on the Bedford Street Board?" Sid called.

"Not such a great idea, Sid. But you know I always take your suggestions."

"You didn't play *North by Northwest.*"

"It's an inferior film."

"YOU'RE WRONG, DIANE!"

"Where's the SWAT team?" called the woman with the sick sister, in a voice strong enough to blister paint off the side of a boat.

"I'll let them in on two conditions," Sid called. "They remove these things by the end of the day, and you do a complete Cary Grant retrospective."

"Cary Grant!" The cop threw his hands up in disgust. "What the hell is this guy playing with? People have lives, businesses to run."

She could schedule Cary Grant right after the Errol Morris festival in the spring. "Sid!" she called. "Drop the knife on the other side of the wall, and you'll get your retrospective! Give the phone company access and they'll start moving the silos!"

"I also want an apology."

"Oh, come *on!*" said the aggrieved woman.

As Cary Grant well knew, the distance between the movies and real life was often a torment. One day when he was ten, Archibald Alexander Leach came home from school to find his mother gone; his father told him she was away "having a rest." In fact, his father had committed the woman to an insane asylum, and he never provided his son with further information. Archie ran away from home at thirteen to join an acrobatic troop on the English vaudeville circuit. He didn't see his mother for twenty years, by which time he'd become the international screen sensation Cary Grant, a handsome, debonair star living in terror that his public mask would slip.

Uncomfortable with people socially, a thorn in the side of most directors, nitpicky about sets, costumes, and scripts, Cary Grant felt unappreciated by the studio and angry that he was never nominated for an Oscar. He spent evenings morosely leafing through his scrapbooks, brooding about all the movies he should have made. He married five times, and reportedly beat at least two of his wives, sometimes inviting the servants to watch. He usually ate dinner— both with and without company—in bed, in front of the TV, in black tie. He named his terrier Archibald Leach. In the early 1960s, plagued by insomnia and depression, he relived childhood traumas by means of weekly injections of LSD under psychiatric supervision. "Everybody wants to be Cary Grant," he once said. "Even I want to be Cary Grant."

WHEN DIANE RETURNED to the theater, the caterers were setting up a bar in the lobby and there was still no dial tone. She spent the rest of the afternoon making and receiving phone calls on Floyd's cellphone from the café around the corner, running back to the theater to see what had been done. At five fifty-five, she closed the door of the projection booth, wiped her face and armpits with antibacterial towels, slipped into a green party dress from her sister's collection, checked her growing, but still too short, hair in the sliding glass window, and returned to the scene, hoping to close the door on a day that had been one long continuous interruption.

But no: Storm reported an overflowing toilet in the ladies' room. The photographer Diane had hired to commemorate the evening tripped over the red carpet, landing on his wrist; Angela took him to the Emergency Room at St. Vincent's in a cab.

Javier arrived, wearing one of his father's suits and the birthday sneakers.

Diane gave him a camera she kept in the office, and asked him to take photos as people walked down the red carpet.

"Like paparazzi," he said with enthusiasm, trying to kiss her.

"No kissing or touching tonight," she commanded, and as he was about to object she said, "No arguments."

By six o'clock, a small crowd had gathered on either side of the red carpet to see who showed up. Dorothy arrived, a vision in red chiffon.

Javier snapped photos and shouted, "Dorothy! Miss Dorothy Vail, big star at MGM! Is it true about you and Leonardo DiCaprio?"

Miss Vail lit up on cue, and floated down the red carpet in a lingering fashion, waving to her fans. "Every word! It's all true!"

Estelle arrived in a wheelchair; she was wearing a red sailor suit and matching hat. Herb stood at her side looking immaculate and nautical in a blue blazer and white pants.

"Estelle! Estelle DeWinter!" Javier cried out. "Give us a smile!"

Dorothy immediately pulled Diane aside: Estelle was wearing red.

"Yes, she looks beautiful. And so do you."

"She *said* she would be wearing yellow!" said Dorothy.

Lipsky had eaten half the chopped liver by the time the guests began to filter into the lobby. The klieg light lending a starstruck atmosphere to Bedford Street sparked and popped at six-fifteen, leaving a wisp of sulfurous smoke in the air and no light. Vladimir, Chris and Paul arrived together dressed in slick black suits. At least two hundred and fifty people showed up, including four major film directors, three famous movie stars, and ten lesser-known working actors, along with the mayor, Diane's parents, Rachel and Dennis, Lara and her husband and Claire, out for a rare night without husband or kids. During cocktails, Diane was in the midst of a circle made up of Gary and Mary Masters, who were the lone couple in black tie, Jan Mattias, and the cultural affairs commissioner of the City of New York, when Javier arrived and presented himself. Immediately, he was asked what kind of accent he had.

"There are no young Cubans," Mary said accusingly. "So you must be a defector."

"Yes, I am defecting, and this woman is my new country," Javier announced, squeezing Diane's waist and kissing her cheek. Gary and Mary Masters nodded with frozen smiles on their faces, then wandered off to stare in disapproval from a distance. Thereafter the night was a blur. Obliquely, Diane saw Lara wagging her finger at Vladimir, Javier chatting animatedly with Rachel, Gene introducing himself to Vladimir, and Connie and Dorothy deep in conversation, pointing at her. All of it was out of her control. More than half the crowd went to see the new French feature, and a healthy number chose the Kurosawa retrospective.

And everyone had a wonderful time.

SHE BOBBED on the ragged edge of consciousness after the party. She was sitting with Javier on the ravaged couch in her office with shoes off and feet up on the broken coffee table when Vladimir arrived.

They looked up at him expectantly.

"It was a great night, Diane," Vladimir said.

"It's a beautiful theater, Vladimir."

"Thank you."

"It is, Dad."

"You better take Diane home," he told Javier. "She looks done out."

"Done out?" Javier asked.

"Done in?" Vladimir asked.

"She is dead," Diane agreed.

Vladimir sank into the sofa on the other side of her. He looked tired, too. "Perhaps you'll let me clean up this space for you now that the main work is done."

"I can't handle more construction."

"Not construction. Carpet, paint. Shelves for your things. This couch is a horror show."

"You have no idea," she said, falling sideways onto Javier's lap. Vladimir made a noise of objection as she put her feet up on his lap. Perhaps Javier cast a conspiratorial look at his father, but she couldn't really be sure—she immediately dropped into sleep.

◆

THE CONVERSATION shifted into Spanish.

"I'm taking drawing," Javier said.

"Good," Vladimir said. "You can never draw too much."

"Diane and I may go to a museum this weekend. Maybe you'd like to come."

"I wouldn't want to intrude."

"She wants things to be normal."

"Normal is probably not possible."

"Nevertheless. She wants things to be as normal as possible."

Vladimir thought about this. Diane's feet were heavy on his thighs. She was an inconvenient woman, a selfish woman, a slob, perhaps a slut. But she meant well. "I'll check my schedule."

"Diane wants us to spend time together. I mean, you and me. Separate from her. Without, eh, trouble."

"That would be nice."

The film had been refreshing, a great escape. He was as proud of the theater as he'd ever been with a project; he wasn't fond of the movies as a rule, but if ever he had to see a film, this was the place to do it. He could see himself coming here, with or without Javier.

Paul and Chris stood at the threshold, taking in the sight of the two of them on the couch with Diane lying across their laps.

"Not another French movie," said Paul.

OCTOBER

Sometimes the movies can disappoint you. Diane thought of all the many old, obscure and/or foreign films to which she'd dragged people and for which she had not been forgiven. *Rocco and His Brothers,* for example, a 1960 Visconti effort that started out well enough and then turned into preposterous schmaltz; or the five-hour documentary about the Sinai Campaign shot in the desert in real time; or the Belgian film about people addicted to removing upholstery buttons from strangers' furniture with their knees. Diane spent her life in the dark, so she was willing to take chances. But some people only saw one movie a year, so it had to be *the* movie that everyone was talking about.

As part of her "How to End a Picture" series, she had scheduled *Get Out Your Handkerchiefs* (Bertrand Blier, 1978), in which a husband (Gérard Depardieu) at his wits' end with his wife's depression approaches a total stranger in a restaurant (Patrick Dewaere) to beg him to be her lover and cheer her up. Reluctantly, the stranger lets himself be dragged into their lives, but he can't help the wife (Carole Laure), either; she knits and cleans and cries. The men become friends; they agree that the wife would be happier if she had a child, but she doesn't conceive with either one of them. When the three become counselors at a summer camp, the wife finally finds personal and erotic satisfaction with a thirteen-year-old camper. When she becomes pregnant by him, she moves in to care for him and his aging father, as their maid, in a classic French maid's outfit: a French ending, if ever there was one. Sometimes, movies made no sense, but the French ones, anyhow, were so light and casually elegant that it didn't exactly matter—they were like mini French vacations, after which you went back to your heavy, unfashionable life with its moral accountability and undistinguished food.

Rachel had found out about Javier from Bobby Wald, her new best friend. She had alerted Connie by saying, "Hey, I think Diane may finally get to go to the prom!"

"Darling, do what you want," Diane's mother told her on the phone. "But remember that you don't always do what's good for you."

Well, what did she expect her mother to say?

Her father picked up on the other extension. "Are you happy?"

"Very."

"Well, finally! I'm so glad for you."

"I did think it was strange that you never introduced us to the father," Connie said. "So he must not have been very important. You know, before I married your dad, I dated his best friend, who was also his cousin. And look how well that turned out!"

It was one of their courtship stories, how Connie had dropped something under the table during a double date, and Gene had leaned down to pick it up. They'd had a little tête-à-tête under the table, and she'd given him her phone number. Over the years, there had been disagreement over what she dropped. Gene said it was a glove. Connie insisted it was a handkerchief. "I would never have dropped a white glove on the floor," she always said.

"Let's meet this guy," Diane's father said. "If you like him, I bet we'll like him. He's how old?"

Diane agreed in theory to this meeting, but continued to avoid scheduling it.

Sometimes a movie can survive a terrible ending because the rest of it hangs together so beautifully. Take *Woman of the Year* (George Stevens, 1942), with an ending tacked on by the studio in spite of furious protest from screenwriters Ring Lardner, Jr. and Michael Kanin. The film is remembered in spite of the vindictive ending, which puts Katharine Hepburn "in her place" in the kitchen, thereby undercutting the spirit and premise of the strong-willed-career-woman picture.

Endings were not on Diane's mind, however.

ON A CHILLY NIGHT in early October, Diane brought Javier to an old-fashioned deli to introduce him to cream soda, pickles and hot pastrami on rye. He took a sip of soda through a straw, and his face opened wide in appreciation.

"Diane! This is amazing!"

As they ate their sandwiches, he taught her a whole series of Spanish curses that fanned out from the basic formation "I shit on your mother."

"I shit in the heart of your mother," she repeated in Spanish, and Javier dissolved into laughter. Apparently, she spoke Spanish with a German accent. She continued repeating what he told her in Spanish: "I shit in the heart of your mother the whore." "I shit in the heart of your mother the epileptic." She practiced diligently, amused by the waiters, who lingered by their table to laugh at her. It was nice that Javier believed that she could learn Spanish.

Sometimes, when they were walking down the street, people passing did a double take, scanning her face, Javier's face, making calculations and, no doubt, passing judgment. Had she supposed this would be easy? Had she supposed that their togetherness wouldn't provoke commentary? And would Javier one day look at her and think her old and unattractive?

Javier pushed aside his plate and took out his electronic game.

He grinned at her; he was completely present. He really, truly seemed besotted with her. She didn't feel old around him; she felt young around him. How she aged would be something else entirely.

When a new song came on the radio, Javier asked, "Who are they?"

"They are Donna Summer," she responded.

One day, when he already knew all there was to know about delis and disco, he would find someone else with something new to teach him. In the meantime, they walked west on Twelfth Street with their arms wrapped around each other beneath a large, yellow moon, and he explained the difference between *ser* and *estar.* The evening was cool and promising, and she had that back-to-school feeling.

VLADIMIR SAT in a sterile, fluorescent-lit room in the Greater New York Federal Building on Hudson Street, waiting to be fingerprinted for his citizenship application. He'd received an unexpected phone call that morning from his mother, from Madrid. She'd managed to get out of Cuba using an invitation letter from the Preservation Society of Spain. As astonishing as it was that the Ministry of the Interior hadn't compared notes with the Ministry of Culture to deny her an Exit Visa, especially during this time of lockdown, it was even more astonishing that she hadn't told anyone that she was leaving. If Alicia Padrón could keep a secret, then anything was possible.

The strength of the despot was waning; another operation couldn't be far away. Most likely, it would kill him. The dictator had weighed so heavily upon Vladimir, for so many years; even if the monster was never brought to justice, the mere idea of putting Castro in the past tense was an appealing one.

"So why have there been no protests?" Paul had asked the previous evening, as Vladimir was closing his computer down for the night. Sometimes he felt like he was lecturing Paul, but Paul had more questions than a talk show host. Paul should thank his lucky stars that Vladimir had the patience to sit and educate him. Not that he appeared to be learning anything.

"When a feudal lord falls, people wait to see if he dies or survives," Vladimir said. "Whoever comes after him—Raúl, Alarcón, whoever—won't have the power or charisma to distract everyone from the hunger, the repression, the bankrupt economy and all the vast failures of the Revolution."

"When will it happen?"

"Once the new regime shows its weakness, then you can expect a change."

Chris and Paul had been a great help to him in the previous month. They had taken him out to lunch, dinner and a photography show; one weekday, they had distracted him with tennis matches in Flushing Meadows. Chris was very attentive to his shifts in mood. Occasionally, Vladimir would remember what had occurred just recently, and find himself pulling his hair and growling. At these moments, Chris would come by to give him a mint, a steady hand on the shoulder and a sympathetic nod. There was really nothing else to be done. He had found a new site, uChess.com, where you could play in real time. When he had a bad moment, he would sign up for a five-minute game, which went by so fast it was almost like aerobic exercise—much more satisfying than these games that went on for weeks.

"What do you think Raúl will do?" Paul asked.

"When Raúl was placed provisionally in power, instead of trying to endear himself to the public, what did he do?"

Vladimir waited: his pupil had no response.

"He sent out the troops and the police, he called in the Army reservists. So we can expect that this is what he'll do once Castro dies. If he tightens the grip further, then there may be a revolt. Or he may take power and start making concessions. I think we can hope for a velvet revolution."

"Too hot," Paul said. "A *linen* revolution, perhaps."

Paul was the only one who wanted to talk about Cuba lately. All Vladimir's Cuban friends checked the news constantly; they were sick of the waiting and had nothing to say to one another until it happened. And all Javier wanted to talk about was America.

Magnus had stopped asking questions about the Revolution. He had moved on to Zen, and was now talking about sitting meditation all day long.

"Magnus, I have an idea," Vladimir had told him the previous day. "Why don't you practice your quiet contemplation while you're in the studio, and talk about it when you go home?"

Even Chris laughed at that one. I'd be grateful to have a partner like me, Vladimir thought.

AN OFFICIAL mispronounced his name. Vladimir rose and walked into a back office. Everything was digital now: he put his fingers on a glass, one by one, and watched as the computer ran through millions of fingerprints in a database to see if he was wanted anywhere. He held his breath with each finger and both palms. He wasn't wanted. The processing usually took between ten months and a year; they told him he would receive something in the mail. When he became an American, perhaps another layer of worry and anger would dissolve. When he became an American, he could petition to bring his mother to America as a permanent legal resident. And his son as well—it might be faster than having Javier himself apply for legal residency. As he left the building, looking forward to that day, Vladimir did a double take—he thought he saw the island of Cuba on a passing T-shirt. At the very least, he was imprinted. Perhaps Diane was right: he was obsessed.

Three blocks away, he entered a juice bar and ordered a mango-banana-strawberry shake for the third day in a row. Nobody needed to know about this expensive new ritual. A woman on line in front of him, with straight blond hair falling on bare shoulders, began talking to him. She was on Rollerblades—young, but not a teenager. For God's sake! He wouldn't even think about it.

Her shake arrived, and she lingered, chatting. She asked about his accent. He decided not to hold it against her: she was attractive. Before he'd even paid for his shake, she asked about his marital status.

"Well, my wife will not give me a divorce," he said, without thinking.

He felt his face flush, his mouth go dry. He almost took it back.

But she was brimming over with questions: "How long have you been married? Do you live with her?"

He thought a moment. "No, she lives in Cuba."

"In *Cuba*? Do you ever see her?"

"Not in twelve years. Thirteen now."

"Wow," she said, eyes wide, a complication junkie ready for anything.

He took a sip of the shake, wondering if he should tell her the real story. The liquid was thick, intense and delicious; he was right, he did deserve a shake a day. Why not? As addictions went, it was pretty harmless, and since he was taking advantage of the fresh weather to walk to work, it livened up the journey. This juice girl was very nice, but probably not a serious person. If he was wrong about that, he could deal with it later.

He pulled out a chair for her and sat down next to it.

"And what about you?"

◆

THE TREES WERE CHANGING, turning colors, dropping leaves everywhere. It was arresting, disconcerting. School was unimaginably exciting. For his political science class, Javier had written an essay, packed with personal examples, about the definition of a dictatorship. The professor had corrected his spelling and grammar, but had given him an A, and asked him to read it aloud to the class. Afterwards, many of the kids had looked at him with something like respect, and one, Nurbu, a Tibetan American also learning English, had engaged him in conversation. Soon they were eating lunch together in the cafeteria. Diane encouraged him to bring Nurbu to the movies, but begged him not to tell Nurbu about their living situation, for obvious reasons.

The third week of school, Javier received a letter from Paco, sent from Paco's father's e-mail address; it accused him of being a coward and antisocial scum in the service of Imperialism for staying in

America. He read on with increasing detachment, doubtful that Paco had taken the time to crank out such an elaborate denunciation. Somebody else had written it; perhaps Paco's father.

Pucho had written Javier a nasty letter of his own.

Never mind: one day after school, instead of going straight to his books, he turned on the TV and discovered the sex channel. People were doing it right there at four in the afternoon on TV! He turned it off quickly, embarrassed. He turned the set back on, with the sound down very low, so none of the neighbors could hear. It was a torment: he didn't know which he wanted to watch more—the sex channel or the food channel.

He was a long way from Cuba.

Vladimir was obsessed with the news. Javier figured that if Fidel Castro died, he'd hear about it one way or the other; being the first to know wouldn't make that much of a difference. Whenever Cuba came up with his father—which was constantly—Javier changed the subject to something he had learned that day, in or out of school. He'd conducted two more experiments with yeast, but the bread had come out chewy and tasteless the first time, and hard and dry the next. He would persist until he got it right.

Diane had a guitar, and she was encouraging him to play; it was possible that he might even get guitar lessons. In front of their apartment building, steam was emerging through a dirty white duct behind some barriers in a scene of municipal repair. When he asked Diane if the city was so charged with energy that the authorities had to break the crust in some places to let steam escape as a precautionary measure, she closed her eyes and gave him a wordless smile that felt like a standing ovation.

On the way to their nightly date at the cinema, Javier saw mounds of yellow leaves beneath a massive yellow-leafed tree. The sky was a bright salmon glow behind the branches and buildings as evening fell over the city. A piano student played scales in the brick building next door. White steam from the center of the earth escaped in a steady plume through the duct. A push of wind scattered yellow leaves across the pavement and the new cars cruised by slowly, almost as if on parade. He was on his way to see a classic samurai movie with a woman who taught him amazing, unexpected new things every day. There was something heartbreakingly beautiful about this scene, even if it was getting cold. He slipped into the theater just as the lights went down. She hooked her arm in his as they waited for the drama to unfold in the dark.

ACKNOWLEDGMENTS

My husband, Alexis Romay, plays many roles in my life: ideal reader, motivation coach, muse, copyeditor and all-around go-to guy. For this book, he gave me invaluable background material, fact checking and proofreading on demand. I thank him for his patience, positivity, generosity and sense of humor. He is as fine a partner as any writer could ever wish for.

I'm indebted to Oxana Alvarez, Elizabeth Cerejido, Veronica Cervera, Eida Del Risco, Enrique Del Risco, Nestor Díaz de Villegas, Carlos Galvizu, Orlando Justo, Alexis Romay, Victoria Romay, Jaquelyn Verdecia and Maria Werlau, who kindly shared their stories of Cuba and exile. I am grateful to architects Stella Betts and David Leven of LevenBetts Studio, NYC, for sharing an inside look into a working studio and an architect's education. I thank Alix Biel for a vital idea that led to many others. I thank Alexis Romay, Barbara Block, James Block and Sally Higginson for reading early drafts with diplomacy. I thank Peter Block, Emanuelle Block and Sally Higginson for encouragement in general.

I'm very lucky to have Nancy Miller as an editor: her good judgment and high standards have made me a better writer. I am grateful to my agent, Gail Hochman, for her loyalty, enthusiasm and bright ideas. I'd also like to thank Brian McLendon and Patricia Park of Ballantine Books, and Marianne Merola and Joanna Brownstein of Brandt and Hochman.

I had a good forty-seven years to write this book and have it be fresh and evergreen. As luck would have it, while I was congratulating myself for finishing the third draft, a health crisis caused Fidel Castro to cede control of Cuba to his brother—an event that would change my characters, an event that was not possible to ignore. I scrambled to include this episode and its fallout, knowing that this would fix all aspects of my "timeless" story to a specific period. Wherever possible, I tried to respect history. When a date was incompatible with the needs of the novel, I chose fiction over fact, and hope the reader can forgive me.

I discovered compelling details on the history, hearsay and divine trash of the cinema in a variety of sources, including: *Three Phases of Eve,* by Eve Arden; *The Movie of the Week,* by Peter Bogdanovich; *Lucille, the Life of Lucille Ball,* by Kathleen Brady; *The Memory of All That,* Betsy Blair; *What's It All About?* by Michael Caine; *Mommie Dearest,* by Christina Crawford; *Bette: The Life of Bette Davis,* by Charles Higham; *The Directors: Take Three,* by Robert J. Emery; *Fellini on Fellini,* by Federico Fellini; *An Empire of Their Own,* by Neal Gabler; *Life: The Movie,* by Neal Gabler; *Goldwyn, a Biography,* by A. Scott Berg; *Haunted Idol, the Story of the Real Cary Grant,* by Geoffrey Wansell; *Judy,* by Gerold Frank; *Me,* by Katharine Hepburn; *Hitchcock,* by François Truffaut; *5001 Nights at the Movies,* by Pauline Kael; *A Kind of Autobiography,* by Akira Kurosawa; *I'd Hate Myself in the Morning,* by Ring Lardner, Jr.; *Screwball: The Life of Carole Lombard,* by Larry Swindell; *American Movie Critics: An Anthology from the Silents Until Now,* edited by Phillip Lopate; *Making Movies,* by Sidney Lumet; *You'll Never Eat Lunch in This Town Again,* by Julia Phillips; *Intimate Strangers* and *The Men Who Made the Movies,* by Richard Schickel; *All the Way: A Biography of Frank Sinatra,* by Michael Freedland; *Screwball: Hollywood's Madcap Romantic Comedies,* by Ed Sikov; *Elizabeth Taylor: The Last Star,* by Kitty Kelly; *François Truffaut,* by Annette Insdorf; *The Films of My Life,* by François Truffaut; and *Conversations with Wilder,* by Cameron Crowe. Among the many films consulted, but not named in the text, I'd like to single out *American Masters: Sam Goldwyn* (Peter Jones, 2005).

I found many sources helpful in my research on Cuba, Cubans and exile, especially *Before Night Falls,* by Reinaldo Arenas, translated by Dolores Koch; *View of Dawn in the Tropics,* by Guillermo Cabrera Infante, translated by Suzanne Jill Levine; *Cuba on My Mind,* by Roman de la Campa; *A Girl Like Che,* by Teresa de la Caridad Doval; *The Cuba Reader,* Aviva Chomsky, Barry Carr and Pamela Maria Smorkaloff, editors; *North of Hell,* by Miguel Correa Mujica, translated by Alexis Romay; *Waiting for Snow in Havana,* by Carlos Eire; *Waiting for Fidel,* by Chris Hunt; *Havana and the Night,* Pico Iyer; *Journey into the Heart of Cuba,* by Carlos Alberto Montaner; *Selected Writings of José Martí,* edited and translated by Esther Allen; *Finding Mañana,* by Mirta Ojito; *Life on the Hyphen,* by Gustavo Perez Firmat; *Flight to Freedom,* by Ana Veciana-Suarez; *Bridge in Darkness,* by Carlos Victoria, translated by David Landau. Other books I found useful were *SOROS,* by Michael Friedman, and *The Private Life of Rome,* by Paul Veyne.

There are many great movies about contemporary Cuba, notably *Improper Conduct* (Néstor Almendros, 1984); *Hacerse el Sueco* (Daniel Díaz Torres, 2001); *Strawberry and Chocolate* (Tomás Gutiérrez Alea, 1994); *Guantanamera* (Tomás Gutiérrez Alea, 1995); *Bitter Sugar* (Leon Ichaso, 1996); *Calle 54* (Fernando Trueba, 2000); *The Buena Vista Social Club* (Wim Wenders, 1999); and *Havana Blues* (Benito Zambrano, 2005).

Long-lost movies can be unearthed at Facets Multi-Media in Chicago, which has the old, obscure and foreign on tap in its wonderful Videotheque. I have found enlightenment in the dark in many places, but I'd like to mention just two, Film Forum and the Walter Reade Theater—both very special cinemas, both in New York City.

ABOUT THE AUTHOR

VALERIE BLOCK is the author of the novels *Was it Something I Said?* and *None of Your Business.* She lives and works near New York City.

She can be reached at her website,
www.valerieblock.com

ABOUT THE TYPE

This book was set in Bembo, a typeface based on an old-style Roman face that was used for Cardinal Bembo's tract *De Aetna* in 1495. Bembo was cut by Francisco Griffo in the early sixteenth century. The Lanston Monotype Machine Company of Philadelphia brought the well-proportioned letterforms of Bembo to the United States in the 1930s.